MANITOU BLOOD

Graham Masterton

This first world edition published in Great Britain 2005 by
SEVERN HOUSE PUBLISHERS LTD of
9–15 High Street, Sutton, Surrey SM1 1DF.
This first world edition published in the USA 2005 by
SEVERN HOUSE PUBLISHERS INC of
595 Madison Avenue, New York, N.Y. 10022.

British Library Cataloguing in Publication Data

Masterton, Graham
  Manitou blood
  1.   Horror tales
  I.   Title
  823.9'14 [F]

    ISBN-10 : 0-7278-6291-X (cased)
               0-7278-9153-7 (paper)

Typeset by Palimpsest Book Production Ltd.,
Polmont, Stirlingshire, Scotland.
Printed and bound in Great Britain by
MPG Books Ltd., Bodmin, Cornwall.

....

PLEASE RETURN TO THE ABOVE LIBRARY OR ANY OTHER ABERDEEN CITY LIBRARY, ON OR BEFORE THE DUE DATE. TO RENEW, PLEASE QUOTE THE DUE DATE AND THE BARCODE NUMBER.

Aberdeen City Council
Library & Information Services

Recent Titles by Graham Masterton available from Severn House

The Jim Rook Series

ROOK

THE TERROR

TOOTH AND CLAW

SNOWMAN

SWIMMER

DARKROOM

Anthologies

FACES OF FEAR

FEELINGS OF FEAR

FORTNIGHT OF FEAR

FLIGHTS OF FEAR

Novels

DOORKEEPERS

GENIUS

HIDDEN WORLD

HOLY TERROR

MANITOU BLOOD

1

BLOODWORK

It was only a few minutes after eleven in the morning, but already the sun was beating on the sidewalks as hard as a blacksmith's hammer.

As he crossed Herald Square, in his flappy brown linen suit and his green *Matrix*-style sunglasses, Dr. Winter saw a small crowd gathered outside Macy's. At first he thought they must be looking at a new window display, but then he realized that a mime artist was performing in front of the store.

Frank Winter had an irrational aversion to mimes, or jugglers, or clowns, or any other kind of street performers. Behind their painted-on grins, he had always suspected that they were sly, and spiteful, and out to cause mischief. But this mime caught his attention. She was a girl, to begin with—a very thin, small-boned girl, in a one-piece suit made of tight silver fabric. Her short-cropped hair was stiff with silver paint, and her face was painted silver, too.

Frank stopped for a moment, and watched her. Her suit was so tight that she could almost have been naked. She was small-breasted, with very prominent nipples, and her buttocks were as tight as a boy's. Underneath her Tin Man makeup she had a thin, sculptured face that was almost beautiful, in a starved, waiflike way, and pale, blue staring eyes.

But it wasn't only her appearance that held him there: It was her extraordinary performance. She swayed from side to side, giving the impression that she was defying gravity. Then she began to mime that she was climbing, and somehow she made it appear as if she was actually making her way up a ladder. At the top of the ladder she teetered, and nearly lost her balance. Two small children who were watching her stepped instinctively back, as if she was really going to fall on them from twenty feet up.

Frank pressed his hand to the back of his head, because the sun was beating on his neck. It was well over 93 degrees, with 85 percent humidity. Nobody could walk around the city without gum sticking to the soles of his shoes, and the crowd around him was mostly dressed in T-shirts and shorts and sandals, and were furiously fanning themselves with newspapers and tour guides. It had been sweltering like this for over a week now, since the second day of August, and the weathermen were predicting the longest heat wave in New York City since the summer of 1926.

Up on top of her imaginary ladder, however, the girl began to clutch herself, and shiver, as if she were freezing. She stood on the sidewalk quaking and even though the sun was beating on the back of his neck, Frank could almost feel a chill, too, as if somebody had opened up a refrigerator door, right behind him. He turned to the man standing next to him and said, "She's something, isn't she?"

The man looked Italian, or maybe Greek. He was bearded, with a flattened nose like an osprey's beak, and bulging brown eyes, and he was wearing a strange dangling earring, like a miniature dreamcatcher, all feathers and beads and fishhooks. He raised his eyebrows and smiled but didn't reply.

Frank wasn't sure if the man had understood him. "I mean the way she's shivering like that . . . she's actually making *me* feel cold."

"Well," said the man, still smiling. "She is one of the pale ones, that's why."

"The pale ones?" said Frank. He shook his head to show that he didn't understand.

"I would gladly explain it to you, sir, but you would probably not believe me."

"You could try me. I'm a doctor and you know us doctors. We're ready to believe anything."

The girl began to climb down her imaginary ladder, until she reached the ground. Then she sat on her red-and-yellow rug on the sidewalk and twisted her arms and legs together so that she tied herself into human knot. If he hadn't seen it for himself, Frank would have said that it was anatomically impossible. Her face was looking at him from between her legs, emotionless, remote, but strangely threatening, as if she were warning him to keep his distance.

She rolled around the sidewalk in a ball, and then, in one fluid movement, she disentangled her arms and legs and stood up, her arms spread wide. The small crowd applauded, and two ConEd workers gave her a piercing whistle.

Gradually, dropping nickels and dimes into her silver-painted basket, the crowd dispersed, but the girl stayed where she was, leaning against Macy's window with both hands, breathing deeply, staring at herself. The Greek-looking man stayed, too.

Frank took off his sunglasses. He could see himself reflected in the store window behind her—a tall, broad-shouldered man with brushed-back hedgehog hair that was graying at the sides. "That was quite some performance," he told her. "I'm a doctor, and believe me—I've never seen *anybody* who can tie themselves up like quite like that."

The girl lifted herself away from the window and turned around. She looked Frank up and down as if she already knew who he was, but she didn't speak. Frank wondered if she might be such a good mime because she was genuinely mute. He glanced again at the Greek-looking man, but the Greek-looking man didn't seem to be interested in contributing anything to the conversation, either.

"Well, great show," Frank told her, uncomfortably. "I have to be getting on."

He took out a dollar bill and he was leaning forward to drop it in her basket when the girl suddenly raised her hand to her throat and made a gagging noise. She took a stiff-legged step toward him, and then another. At first he assumed that she was acting, but her eyes were wide and she kept opening and closing her mouth, as if she couldn't breathe.

Without warning, she vomited blood. A bright-red clattering cascade that splattered the sidewalk in front of her and splashed all over Frank's shoes. She tilted back, and then sank to her knees. Frank knelt down beside her and put his arm around her.

"What's wrong? Are you sick with something? Have you been to see your doctor?"

The girl shook her head. She looked terrified.

Frank shouted, "Call 911!" but there was no reply. "I said, *call*—*!*" he began, but when he turned around the Greek-looking man was hurrying away, like the White Rabbit. "Listen," he told the girl, reaching into his shirt pocket for his cellphone. "I'm going to call for an ambulance, get you into the emergency room right now."

The girl nodded. She started to say something but then she vomited even more blood, so that Frank's sleeve was soaked. A few passers-by had stopped to watch them, but most people were staying well away—even crossing over the street. Frank didn't entirely blame them. He and the girl were plastered in so much blood that it looked as if they had been fighting each other with box cutters.

All he could do was kneel down beside her and hold her close against his chest while she sicked up more and more blood. She was shaking wildly, and now she felt genuinely cold.

It seemed to take an hour for the ambulance to arrive, although it was probably less than ten minutes. The sun beat down on the blood that was spattered on the sidewalk, so that it steamed. Frank heard sirens, and banging doors, and the rattle of a gurney, and then he was being helped up onto his feet.

A woman paramedic was staring very closely into his face. "Where are you injured, sir? You want to show me where you're injured?"

Dr. Gathering said, "The *good* news, Frank, is that she's HIV-negative."

Frank was standing by the window of his twenty-seventh-floor office at the Sisters of Jerusalem, looking down at West Thirty-sixth Street below. The traffic was sparkling in the sunshine, and the crowds far below him were dressed in bright reds and yellows and greens, like a scattered assortment of jelly beans.

"What's the bad news?"

George Gathering opened the plastic folder that he was carrying and took out three sheets of test results. "I'd call it *bewildering*, rather than bad. She must have vomited more than two liters of blood, not counting the blood she brought up before we got into her emergency. By rights, she should be dead."

"I thought it might have been a perforated ulcer."

"Well, that was *my* first guess, too. But we haven't found any serious erosion of the stomach lining, although I think it's worth doing another X-ray. We haven't found any varices in the esophagus, either. Her liver's healthy, and she has no portal hypertension.

"So where was all that blood coming from?"

"We're not sure yet. But you know how ulcers can hide themselves out of plain sight."

"Still—this is very unusual, wouldn't you say? Usually, if a patient's bringing up *that* much blood—well, it's almost impossible to stop it."

"Like I say, I want to try another X-ray. But she has some other unusual symptoms, too."

"Oh, yes? Like what?"

"Her digestive chemistry is seriously out of whack for a young woman of her age. Her stomach lining is secreting less intrinsic factor than an eighty-year-old's. Which means of course that she isn't absorbing vitamin B12."

"So she's anemic?"

"Yes, she is. Not only that—or maybe *because* of that— she's hypersensitive to sunlight. We cleaned all that silver paint off her, but when we tried to put her in a bed by the window she literally screamed. We had to move her into a room of her own with all the blinds pulled down."

"What's her history?"

"She says that her name is Susan Fireman. She's twenty-three years old and she's a third-year fashion student at The Beekman College of Art and Design. She shares a loft on East Twenty-sixth Street with two other girls and one of their boyfriends. The mime thing is just a hobby, apparently.

"Her medical records are still held by her family doctor in New Rochelle . . . that's where her parents live. We're trying to contact him now. Apart from the usual childhood diseases, though, she says that the only problems she's ever had are painful periods and an allergy to steamers."

"Have you contacted her parents?"

"Not yet. She specifically requested us not to. She says that her dad has a serious heart condition and she doesn't want to worry them."

"I see. Has she been out of the country lately?"

George sorted through his notes. "The last vacation she took was to Mexico, last October, eleven days in Cancun."

"Have any of her friends or acquaintances shown any signs of sickness?"

"Not so far as she's aware. But there's one other symptom. She's been having a persistent nightmare."

"A *nightmare?* Nightmares don't make you vomit blood."

"Of course not. But for some reason she seemed to think it was important. She's been having it night after night, for more than a month. Always the same one."

"Go on."

"She thinks that she's deep inside a ship, somewhere in the middle of the ocean. But she's shut up inside a box, and it's totally dark, and she can't get out."

"That's it?"

George closed his folder. "That's it. But she says that it's so realistic that she doesn't like to go to sleep any more."

"Yes," said Frank. He thought about the time that his father had taken him to the circus, when he was five, and a clown had come right up to him and screamed in his face. "I used to have a nightmare like that."

Frank had given his assistant Marjorie the day off today, so that she could visit her elderly mother in Paramus. He put on his Armani half-glasses to check his e-mail, most of which was spam from pharmaceutical companies. Then he sorted quickly through his letters, tossing aside the circulars and tearing open the envelopes that looked as if they might contain checks. He called Pediatrics to check when he was due for his afternoon clinic (3:45, on the sixteenth floor.) Then he bought himself a large double-strength espresso from the vending machine and went down to the eleventh floor to visit Susan Fireman.

"I've been praying on my knees for this heat to let up," said Sister Dominica, in the elevator. "I had to use the subway this morning, and I do believe that the Lord was giving me a preview of the Other Place, in case I was ever tempted to misbehave."

Sister Dominica must have weighed over 225 pounds and her face was pale and knobbly like an Idaho potato. She might have been *tempted* to misbehave, thought Frank, as the elevator doors opened yet again, and more people crowded in, but where was she going to find somebody to misbehave *with?*

He walked along the shiny corridor to Room 1566. The door was ajar, but it looked as if Susan Fireman were sleeping, so he stepped quietly inside without knocking. The blinds were all drawn down over the windows, but a faint, moth-shaped twist of sunlight quivered on the wall, illuminating a picture of Jesus, standing by the sea of Galilee. The air-conditioning had been turned to Nome, Alaska, and Frank couldn't stop himself from shivering, just like Susan Fireman had shivered at the top of her imaginary ladder.

Frank went up to her bedside and looked down at her. She was breathing steadily, with an oxygen tube in her nostrils. Her face was so white that her skin was almost translucent, like a death mask molded out of candle wax, but she seemed to be peaceful. The nurses had combed most of the silver paint out of her short dark-brown hair, but it was still dry and tangled and out of condition.

He balanced his cup of coffee on the bright red crash cart next to her bed and checked her monitor. Her blood pressure was low and her pulse was a little too quick, but there was no arrhythmia. He was tapping the touch-sensitive screen to check on her CO_2 and her FiO_2 when he became aware that her eyes were open, and that she was watching him.

"Oh . . . you're awake," he smiled. "How are you feeling?"

"Sick," she whispered.

"You *can* talk, then?"

She nodded. "Yes . . . but only when I have to."

"Is there a reason for that?"

"Not really. But if you stay silent, you can never tell lies, can you? And nobody can ever misquote you."

He finished checking her vitals. "I don't think I'd last very long in *my* line of work, if I had to mime everything."

"Oh . . . you'd be surprised," she said. She circled her head around and around, with her eyes crossed. "Dizzy spells," she explained.

"Okay," Frank conceded. "I guess it's just as well that you're so good. There's no way I would have stopped to watch you, otherwise."

"You don't like mimes?"

"Unh-hunh. All that smelling pretend daisies and leaning up against pretend walls—that doesn't do anything for me, I'm afraid."

"I see. You're one of those people who refuse to believe that things exist unless you can actually see them."

"When it comes to walls, yes."

"How about ladders?"

"Okay . . . for a split second, yes, you did make me believe that you *were* climbing a ladder."

She gave him a faint, sloping smile. "I could have climbed higher, but I lost my nerve."

"Sure," he said. He leaned over her and shone his flashlight into her eyes, one after the other.

"You took care of me," she told him.

"Hold still. Of course I took care of you. It's my job. You were lucky that the finest gastroenterologist in the entire Western hemisphere happened to be watching you when you started to bring up all that blood."

"Do you have any idea what's wrong with me?" she asked him.

"Not yet. You have very low blood pressure, which is

causing us some serious concern. Your CBC shows that you also have pernicious anemia, which is probably caused by an inability to absorb sufficient quantities of vitamin B12. But neither of those conditions would directly cause you to hemorrhage, and so far we haven't been able to detect any lesions in your digestive tract or any vesicles in your esophagus."

"I'm not sure I know what any of that means."

"It means, simply, that we haven't yet discovered what's wrong with you."

She didn't answer him directly, but turned her face away, so that she was staring at the picture of Jesus. "He looks sad, don't you think?"

"Have you been feeling at all sick lately?" Frank asked her.

"No, not exactly. I've been feeling . . . *different.*"

"Are you on any medication? Antianxiety agents? Antidepressants? How about diuretics?"

"I take ginger and yarrow, for menstrual cramps."

"Okay . . . how about alcohol? How much do you drink, on average?"

"A glass of red wine, sometimes. But not very often. I get drunk very easily, and I don't like losing control."

"Street drugs?"

"Never. Well, once, but that was over a year ago."

"Tell me about your diet. Are you a vegetarian?"

She nodded, although she still kept her face turned away.

"Sometimes strict vegetarians suffer from vitamin B12 deficiency," Frank told her. "It's pretty easily sorted, though, with tablets or injections."

He scribbled a few notes, and then he said, "Dr. Gathering tells me you're very sensitive to sunlight. How long have you suffered from that?"

"I don't know . . . three or four days. Maybe longer. I can't really remember."

"Is it just your eyes, or is your skin sensitive, too? Do you get a rash or anything like that?"

Susan Fireman shook her head. "I can't go out without my makeup, even if the sun's not shining."

"What happens if you don't wear makeup?"

"It *hurts*. It feels like I'm standing an inch too close to a furnace."

Frank made a note to talk to Dr. Xavier, the skin specialist. Then he said, "You've been having recurrent nightmares, too, I understand?"

Susan Fireman pulled a dismissive face, as if she didn't want to talk about it.

"A recurrent nightmare can sometimes be a symptom of an underlying medical problem. It's your body sending a warning to your brain that something might be seriously wrong."

"I don't know . . . this feels more like a *memory* than a nightmare."

"You keep dreaming that you're on board a ship, is that it? And you're shut up inside a box, in the dark."

"Not just shut up. The lid's screwed down tight. And there are more boxes stacked on top of my box, so that I couldn't possibly get out, even if it *wasn't*."

"I see. So how do you know you're on board a ship?"

"Because I can feel it moving. It pitches up and down, and then it rolls. And I can hear timbers creaking, and the sound of the ocean. Sometimes I hear somebody shouting, in a very singsong way, and that frightens me more than anything else."

"Do you know who it is?"

Susan Fireman turned back and looked at him. "It's a boy, by the sound of it. He shouts out something like *tatal nostru*, over and over again. There's a whole lot more but when I wake up I can never remember it."

"Tattle nostrew? Do you have any idea what language that is?"

"None. But it frightens me, because the boy sounds so frightened."

Frank said, "We're going to have do some more tests. Some allergy tests, and some eye tests, and at least one more X-ray, to see if we can find an ulcer. I think we need to contact your parents, don't you, and let them know what's going on?"

"My dad's real sick. I don't want him upset."

"Well, maybe we could talk to your mother first, and let *her* decide how to tell him."

Susan Fireman thought for a moment, and then she said, "No . . . leave it for now. Please. I'll tell her myself."

"Is there anyone else you want us to talk to? How about the people you share with?"

"No—don't tell them."

"Don't you think they're going to be worried, when you don't come home?"

"*Please . . .*"

Frank tucked his notebook back in his pocket. "Okay, you're the boss. I'll come back later and see how you're getting along."

He was walking back through his office door when his beeper went off. It was Dr. Gathering, and it said urgent. He pressed his phone button and said, "George? What's happening?"

"Willy's sent me up the final results of Susan Fireman's bloodwork. She's anemic, no question about it, but there's something else, too. Willy says that she has some enzyme in her bloodstream that he can't identify. He might have to send it off to Rochester."

"Well, I've just been down to talk to her, and there's definitely something unique about her."

"That's not all, Frank. Willy also tested a sample of the blood that she vomited."

"Yes?"

"It's not hers. In fact, it's two different blood types altogether. She's type AB, but the blood that she vomited was a mixture of type A and type O."

"*What?*"

"I'm afraid so, Frank. That blood didn't get into her stomach from internal bleeding. She *drank* it."

2

BLOOD THIRST

While Frank and George sat on the low-slung leather couch and watched him, Dr. Pellman skimmed through the results of the blood tests, tapping his ballpoint pen furiously against his teeth. Eventually he threw himself back in his chair and said, "*Christ.*"

"We thought you ought to see it ASAP," said George.

"Well, you're damn right about that. We need to call the police, and we need to call them now." He leaned across his desk and flipped his intercom switch. "*Janice?*"

"Yes, sir?"

"Get me Captain Meznick at Midtown South, and make it snappy."

He read the blood tests again, more slowly. "We're sure about this? There's no room for any mistake?" He was a small man with a high white pompadour and compressed, Hobbit-like features. His staff called him The Death Troll, but they respected him. He was fierce and quick-tempered and a formidable stickler for detail.

"No mistake, sir," George told him. "Willy repeated his

tests twice, just to make sure. It's human blood, and there's no question that it isn't hers. Unless she stole it from a blood bank, or she's been keeping it refrigerated, there have to be at least two people out there who have lost a serious amount of blood. Almost certainly, a fatal amount."

The intercom buzzed. "*Lieutenant Roberts on the phone, sir. Captain Meznick is away in Philadelphia, at a law-enforcement convention.*"

"Okay, that's okay." Dr. Pellman picked up his phone. "Lieutenant Roberts? This is Harold Pellman, senior VP and medical director at the Sisters of Jerusalem. I won't beat around the bush: We have a young woman here who appears to have been drinking blood."

Frank could only guess what Lieutenant Roberts' reaction was on the other end of the phone, but Dr. Pellman had to repeat himself twice. "Drinking *blood*, lieutenant. Human blood, and other people's blood, not her own. And unless they've been given an emergency transfusion, whoever she drank it from is probably dead."

He spelled out Susan Fireman's address and personal details, and then he hung up the phone. "That's it, gentlemen. There's nothing else we can do."

Frank stayed in his seat. "With all due respect, sir, I think I should try to talk to Ms. Fireman before the police get here. We really need to find out *why* she ingested all that blood, and who she got it from."

"Bad idea," said Dr. Pellman. "You're not a detective, Frank, and I don't want anybody on this hospital's medical staff laying themselves open to accusations of compromising a police investigation. You remember what happened with the Koslowski kid. Nightmare."

"Yes, sir," said Frank. "But Ms. Fireman is still our patient, isn't she, no matter what she's done? We're morally bound to pursue our diagnostic procedure until we find out what's wrong with her."

"Frank—for Christ's sake, we *know* what's wrong with

her. She's been binging on other people's circulatory systems, and it's almost a certainty that she's killed them in the process."

"I realize that, sir. But for all we know, drinking human blood may be a key symptom of her condition. If we don't investigate it—well, I personally think that we'd be failing in our duty as physicians."

George said, very quietly, "I'm afraid I have to agree with that. Supposing her condition can be transmitted? If one of our staff catches it, or one of our other patients goes down with it—I mean, the legal consequences don't bear thinking about."

"So that's it," said Dr. Pellman. "We're damned if we do, and doubly damned if we don't."

Frank said, "All I need to do is ask her some very straightforward questions. Like, whose blood did you drink? Where did you get it from, and how, and why did you drink it?"

"And what do you think the cops will ask her? Exactly the same things."

"But once the police get here, she's far less likely to respond to any questions about her condition, in case she incriminates herself—and if she gets herself a lawyer, forget it, we won't have a hope in hell of finding out what's wrong with her. She has a highly unusual combination of physical symptoms—her anemia, her sensitivity to light—and she obviously has severe psychological problems, too."

Dr. Pellman tossed down his pen. "Okay. But don't ask her anything other than medical questions; and if she refuses to answer, don't push her. And don't instigate any new diagnostic procedures until you've cleared them with me."

They were just about to leave his office when Frank's beeper buzzed again.

"Okay if I use your phone, sir?" he asked Dr. Pellman. Dr. Pellman gave him a wave of his hand and Frank picked it up.

"Dean Garrett here, Frank, in the emergency room. We've just had a young man brought in here, vomiting blood. His symptoms are very similar to that girl you brought in this morning."

"I'll be right down." Frank cradled the phone and then he looked at Dr. Pellman with a serious expression. "Sounds like we've got ourselves another one."

Frank and George went down together to the ER. As they arrived, seven victims of a gang fight were being brought through the doors by paramedics, all shouting and swearing and covered in blood.

Dr. Garrett grabbed one of the gang members by the lapels of his sleeveless leather vest. "What's your name, *bobo?*" he demanded. Dean Garrett was thin and unshaven and he had a drooping moustache, like Wyatt Earp, but he was so wired and wild-eyed that the boy couldn't help stumbling to attention.

"Julius," the boy blurted out. "What's it to you?" He had one eye closed by a big purple bruise and a deep diagonal cut across his lips.

"What gang do you belong to, Julius?"

"The Blue Moros."

"The Blue Morons? That's appropriate. And those other *bobos?* Which gang do they belong to?"

"The X-Skulls."

"Okay, Julius, my name is Doctor Dean and I belong to the Screaming Medics, and this emergency room is my turf from which you will not escape alive if you so much as break wind out of tune. Look at you—you think this is tough, what you *gilapollas* have done to each other? Superficial scratches, that's all. I've been trained to take a man's entire insides out without him even knowing that I've done it, take them out in *handfuls* and heap them on the nightstand next to his bed, and if you don't behave yourself I promise I will do it to you."

Julius opened his bruised and bloodied lips, but said nothing, and when Dean Garrett let go of his vest, he sul-

lenly beckoned the members of his own gang over to the
far end of the emergency room, well away from their rivals.

"Kids," said Dean. "That's all they are, kids—and you
have to treat them like kids."

George said, "I don't know how you cope with it, Dean.
Most of my patients are dear old ladies with purple hair,
and *they* run me ragged."

"It's simple," said Dean. "You have to be ten times more
scary than they are, that's all."

"You are, believe me," Frank told him. "What's a *gilapolla?*"

"A *gilapolla?* Roughly translated, a dickhead."

Dean led them down to the last triage cubicle, farthest
away from the doors. He dragged back the curtain and
there lay a skinny young man of about nineteen or twenty,
shaking and shivering, his T-shirt thick with glistening
blood. The young man's hair was sticking up, and his eyes
were flickering wildly from side to side. A big black emergency nurse was adjusting his saline drip, while a spotty
blonde one was standing beside him with a stainless steel
basin.

Almost as soon as they came into the cubicle, the
young man sat up with a spastic jerk, and vomited blood
into the basin. He retched, with strings of blood swinging
from his chin, and then he dropped back onto the bed,
still shivering.

The nurse was about to take the basin away, but Frank
said, "Don't throw that away. Take that to Dr. Loman for
analysis. We need a blood sample out of his veins, but we
also need a sample of the blood that he's just vomited."

"You think he might have been poisoned?" asked Dean.

"It's possible. But if he's anything like the young lady
we're looking after upstairs, we need to check what type it
is. The blood that *she* was vomiting wasn't her own."

"You mean—Jesus."

"Frankly, Dean, I don't know what I mean."

Frank approached the bed and leaned over it. The young man's eyes were wide open but his pupils were still darting around and he was muttering and twitching and occasionally he arched his back, as if he were being electrocuted.

"Listen to me, son," said Frank, loudly. "Listen to me—do you know where you are?"

The young man clutched at the sheets, obviously making an effort to control himself. "I'm ah—I'm *gah*—"

"Listen to me, try to concentrate. My name is Dr. Winter and you've been admitted to the Sisters of Jerusalem. Can you tell me your name?"

"I'm ah—I'm ah—"

"Where was he picked up?" asked Frank.

"Port Authority. He was standing in line for a bus ticket when he collapsed."

"Any ID?"

"Nothing. The paramedics said they couldn't find a wallet. Either he didn't have one, which seems unlikely, since he was waiting to buy a bus ticket; or else somebody lifted it while he was lying on the ground puking his guts up."

"It's a happy world," said Frank.

"Okay," said Dean. "We'll run the usual tests and let you know the results *pronto*. But I just thought you ought to see him."

"Sure."

They heard shouting, and whooping, and clattering. The Blue Moros had started taunting the X-Skulls from opposite ends of the emergency room, and one of the X-Skulls had picked up a chair and was brandishing it in the air, as if he intended to throw it. Dean said, "Excuse me for a moment. I have some heads to crack."

George checked his watch. "I have to go, too, Frank. Lunch with my tax lawyer."

"Okay," said Frank. "Let's talk later."

Frank stayed beside the young man's bed for a little while longer. His face was even whiter than Susan Fireman's, and he seemed to be much more distressed. At least Susan Fireman had been reasonably coherent. It was difficult to tell if this young man even knew where he was, or what had happened to him.

"I—can't find—can't find—*gah*—" he gagged.

"You can't find what?" Frank asked him. "Your wallet? Is it your wallet you're worried about?"

"I can't find—where I have to *go*—"

"You were standing in line for a bus ticket. Do you know where you were intending to travel?"

"Got to—*ucchh*—"

Frank took hold of his hand. "Listen, the best thing you can do is get some rest. We're running some lab tests, and once we've done that we'll have a clearer picture of what's wrong with you."

"*Tatal—tatal nostru—*"

"What did you say?"

Frank looked up at the big black nurse, but all she could do was shrug. "Sounded like something to do with his nose," she said. "Maybe he's having difficulty breathing."

"*Tatal nostru*," the young man repeated. His heart rate was jiggling excitedly up and down, while his blood pressure had started to sink like the *Titanic*. He spluttered, and then he coughed up more blood, and snatched at Frank's sleeve. "*Tatal nostru!*"

Frank turned to the nurse and said, "Epinephrine, and quick." Then he turned back to the young man. "Listen— can you hear me? Try not to get too stressed. Your whole system's had a serious shock, and you really need to stay calm."

"*Tatal nostru—carele este in ceruri—*" the young man panted.

"Don't try to talk," Frank told him. "Breathe deeply and evenly, that's right, and relax."

The young man stared at Frank wide-eyed. Bubbles of

blood were frothing at the corners of his mouth, and his chest was heaving up and down as if he had been running a marathon. "—*sfinteasca-se numele tau—vie imparatia ta-faca-se voia ta—*"

"Please, don't try to talk," Frank repeated. "You need to keep as quiet and as steady as you can."

The nurse came back with a bottle of epinephrine and a hypodermic. Frank lifted up the young man's blood-crusted arm, wiped it with an antiseptic tissue, found a vein, and injected it.

"*Painea noastra—cea de toate dane-o astazi—*"

Frank waited. One minute passed, then two. At first he thought he might have made a mistake, and that the young man wasn't suffering from an anaphylactic seizure after all. But gradually the young man's heart began to beat more steadily, and his blood pressure began to climb, and he stopped panting for air.

All the same, his lips kept moving, as if he *had* to finish his recitation, no matter what.

"*—si nu ne duce pre noi in ispita—ci ne scapa de cel rau—*"

After a while, though, he stopped talking and his eyes closed. Frank peeled back his right eyelid with his thumb, and although his pupil was still darting wildly from side to side, he was clearly unconscious. Frank said to the nurse, "I need you to keep a real close watch on him, okay? It's possible that he may suffer another allergic episode when this wears off."

Dean came back, looking harassed. "Sorry to leave you like that, Frank. How's he doing?"

"Anaphylaxis. He had a severe allergic reaction to something he's ingested or something he's touched."

"He's okay now?"

"I gave him two milligrams of epinephrine."

Dean bent over the young man, frowning. "These symptoms . . . I don't know. They don't seem relate to each other in any logical way at all. There's something weird going on here."

"You think? That isn't the half of it. He was talking in some foreign language."

"Really? Which one?"

"Nothing that I've ever heard before. Middle-European maybe, but it wasn't Russian. I can recognize Russian, and it didn't have enough *zees* in it to be Polish."

"Well, people say some pretty wacky things when they're sick."

"Not as wacky as this."

"What do you mean?"

"The first few words he came out with—they were exactly the same words that the girl upstairs has been hearing in her nightmares."

"You're shitting me."

"No . . . she says she has a recurring nightmare in which she's trapped inside a box, on a ship. She can't get out, but she can hear this boy's voice saying 'tattle nostrew,' over and over, like he's really frightened."

" 'Tattle nostrew'?"

"Something like that . . . that's about as close as I can pronounce it."

"And this guy said 'tattle nostrew' too? Maybe they know each other. It might explain why they're both suffering from the same condition. Something they've eaten, maybe."

"I don't know," said Frank, looking down at the young man in his blood-soaked T-shirt. "For some reason, I have a very bad feeling about this."

He went to the washbasin to wash his hands. Before he squirted out the medical cleanser, though, he lifted his fingers to his nose and sniffed them, and then sniffed them again.

"What's wrong?" asked Dean.

Frank held out his fingertips so that Dean could smell them, too.

"That so much reminds me of something," said Dean.

"Don't tell me."

"If you don't know that this is, you haven't been on vacation for a very long while. It smells like pina colada. It's sunblock."

When Frank went back to room 1566, Susan Fireman seemed to be sleeping, but when he carried a chair over to her bedside she opened her eyes.

"Dr. Winter . . ." she said, dreamily. "I thought you might be back."

"So you have a good idea what I'm going to ask you?"

She nodded.

"Okay then . . . subject to further tests, it appears that you're not suffering from any internal bleeding. No ulcers, no varices. The blood that you were vomiting came from somebody else." Pause. "In fact, it came from *two* somebody elses."

He waited for a moment, and then, when she didn't answer, he said, "Do you think you can maybe explain that?"

"I don't know why," she whispered.

"You don't know why *what?*"

"I don't know why I did it. It was like . . . I wasn't even me."

Frank said, "You *drank* all of that blood, didn't you? It wasn't yours at all."

"I don't know why. I can't understand it."

"Whose blood was it, Susan? What did you do to them?"

"It was so *confusing* . . . I could see myself doing it but it was like I was watching somebody else."

"Whose blood was it, Susan?"

She closed her eyes and didn't answer. Frank waited for a long moment and then he said, "Susan—I need to know who that blood came from."

"Why?" she said, without opening her eyes. "What difference does it make?"

"It makes a difference because anybody who lost that much blood is most likely dead."

"That's what those people are *for*, isn't it?"

"I don't understand."

"That's what those people are born for . . . to give us their blood."

Frank said, "Open your eyes."

"Why?"

"I want you to look at me when you're talking to me. Or are you scared to?"

"I'm not scared of anything."

"I think you are. I think you're scared of yourself. I think you're scared of what you did."

"I drank blood, all right? I needed to."

"*Why* did you need to?"

She suddenly opened her eyes, and exploded in fury. "*I was burning! I was burning all over! I was on fire and that was the only way to stop it!*"

"So you had to drink blood, to stop the burning?"

"You don't understand! My whole body was on fire! I would have died without it!"

"So whose blood was it, Susan?"

"Don't you get it, *I would have died!*"

She stared at him fiercely, but her ferocity didn't last for very long. He sat back and said nothing, and she began to relax. After a few moments she closed her eyes again and lay on her pillow utterly still, as if she were sleeping, or dead. Frank waited. He was tempted to ask her again whose blood it was, but he had the feeling that she was going to tell him, if he gave her enough time.

Eventually, she spoke, in a very flat, detached voice. "Look at me," she said. "I'm opening my bedroom door."

She paused for a moment, licking her lips, as if they were dry.

"Where are you now?" Frank asked her.

"I'm in the corridor. The sunlight's falling across the corridor *this* way—" indicating a diagonal slant. "It's falling right on the poster of Jim Morrison with gardenias in his hair. I can smell coffee . . . and I can hear Prissy in the kitchen singing *Man on the Moon. 'Do you believe . . . they put a man on the moon? Do you believe . . . there's nothing up their sleeve?'* "

Another pause. After a while, Frank asked, "Now what are you doing?"

"I'm walking into the kitchen and Prissy turns around to me and smiles. That's the last time she smiles at me. That's the very last time. *Tatal nostru. Carele esti in ceruri.*"

"What does that mean, Susan?"

"I feel like I'm burning. There's so much *sunlight*. The whole kitchen is filled with sunlight and it *burns*! It's like I've had acid poured all over me. I'm burning all over, even my feet. Oh God, I'm going to die. I start screaming at Prissy but Prissy doesn't understand what's wrong with me. She starts screaming too. We're both screaming but *she's* screaming because she's frightened while *I'm* screaming because I'm on fire."

Susan's hand scrabbled sideways, touching Frank's arm. "I pick up the knife . . . *the knife* . . . there's a big knife lying on the counter and I pick it up. I don't hesitate. I can't hesitate, I'm on fire. I cut her like this, across her throat. There's blood spraying everywhere, all over the kitchen. All up the blinds and over the draining board. Blood, blessed blood.

"Prissy falls to the floor with her arms waving and her legs kicking. I kneel down beside her and I cover her wound with my mouth. I drink and I drink but I scarcely have to swallow because her blood is pumping right down my throat, and it's warm and delicious and it eases my burning. I drink so much that I almost drown, and Prissy's blood is running out of my nose."

Susan lay quietly for another minute, as if she were reliving the relief that her friend's blood had given her.

"Is Prissy dead?" asked Frank.

Susan nodded. "She looks very pale, doesn't she? But that was what she was born for. From the day she came out of her mother's womb, that was her destiny. To feed me, and to stop me from burning alive."

"Now what do you do?"

"I'm standing up . . . my bathrobe, it's so heavy, it's warm and it's soaked in blood. I need to go back to my room and change. But look—the door's opening—the door's opening and it's Michael. He stands there staring at me and he can't believe what he's looking at. What's happened? What's all this blood? Prissy! What's happened to Prissy?

"He doesn't understand that it's me, and that *I* did it. He kneels down beside Prissy and while he's holding her head I pick up the knife again and—" she didn't finish her sentence, but mimed the way that she had cut Michael's throat, right down to the little wrist flick that she had given the knife so that the blood would fly off the tip.

She clutched the side of her neck. "Michael topples over sideways, on top of Prissy. He's trying to push me away but he's too busy trying to stop the blood from spurting out of his neck. Spurt! Spurt! It's everywhere, all over the floor, all over my face, all over my legs. I pull off my wet bloody bathrobe so that I'm naked, and I'm smearing his blood around and around, all over me."

Frank sat and watched as she caressed her breasts and her stomach and her thighs. "Blood, all over me, sticky and warm . . . and it eases my burning so much . . . blood everywhere, blood between my legs, I can massage myself with fresh blood and it feels *wonderful* . . ."

She let out a long quiver of satisfaction. Then she said, "I bend over Michael and he's staring at me. I smile at him and I whisper, 'thank you, Michael, you're an angel.' I press my mouth against that gaping slit in his neck and I swallow his blood, gulp, gulp, gulp, even though I know that I'm being a glutton. Look at me! I've got blood pouring out of the sides of my mouth and dripping off my chin.

"But now I've sicked some up. I can't drink any more. I'm standing up now . . . I'm walking along the corridor leaving bright red footprints. I sick up some more. Splatter, onto the floor. Then I go into the bathroom and look at myself in the mirror. Blood woman! *Blood woman!* Scarlet face, scarlet arms and legs, scarlet body. But I'm not burning any more. I'm calm now, and my skin feels so much cooler. And I feel so . . . what's the word? Serene."

She opened her eyes, and smiled at him. "That's what I feel. *Serene.*"

Somebody cleared his throat. Frank turned around and saw a tall black man in a black linen suit, waiting in the doorway. There was another man with him, a sallow-skinned white man in a short-sleeved shirt with jazzy red patterns on it and a blood-colored necktie.

"Dr. Winter? I'm Lieutenant Hayward Roberts and this is Detective Paul Mancini."

Frank pushed back his chair and stood up, and almost lost his balance.

"Are you okay?" Lieutenant Roberts asked him.

"No," said Dr. Winter. "I think I need a very stiff drink."

3

BLOOD ROOT

I looked up from the cards with the most serious frown that I could manage. It was pretty hard to be serious when the sixty-seven-year-old woman sitting opposite me was wearing a bright pink straw hat covered in china cherries and a multilayered pink organza dress that looked as if she were all dressed up for a children's birthday party. And pink knee-high socks. And two-toned cheerleaders' shoes, custom-made, also in pink.

"You have a weekend of very heavy financial losses ahead of you," I told her. "By Monday, you're going to be $17,480 poorer, with nothing to show for it."

Mrs. Teitelbaum gnawed at her lip. She didn't say anything, but I could tell by the hunted look in her eyes and the way she was clutching the strap of her purse how anxious she was. Mrs. Teitelbaum's money was dearer to her heart than her grandchildren. If there was any legal way that she could have married her deposit account at Chemical Bank, she would have done it, and she would have taken it on a honeymoon to Jamaica, too.

"Tomorrow—let's see—tomorrow you're going to drop your purse."

"You're sure? That's terrible!"

"Oh, it's worse than that. Your purse is going to be picked up."

"Picked up? Surely that's good?"

"Not if the person who picks it up is a manic depressive who uses your credit card to buy 300 challah loaves from Eli Zabar's."

"No!"

"That's not all, by a long shot. Friday, your late husband's portrait is going to fall off the wall and break one of Widdly's hind legs, which costs you more than $800 in veterinary bills."

"I can't bear it!"

"It gets worse, believe me. Saturday, a distant relative is going to call and ask you to make bail for a trumped-up charge of insurance fraud—which, out of the goodness of your heart, you do, especially since he offers you his Mercedes as security. Unfortunately, he disappears and you never hear from him again, and it turns out that his Mercedes has already been repossessed.

"Sunday, while you're out having lunch with your friend, Moira, Mr. Polanski upstairs leaves the water running in his bathroom. Your apartment is flooded and all of your Persian rugs are ruined. While you're clearing up the mess, somebody sneaks into your bedroom and steals your best pearls."

Mrs. Teitelbaum leaned forward and peered through her gold-rimmed spectacles. "This is what it says in my cards? For real?"

"There, look," I told her. "The smiling fool, with armfuls of bread. The man in prison, with his horse-and-carriage being taken away. The rainstorm, with the drowning woman underneath. And the beach-comber, stealing pearls from the oysters. It's all there, Mrs. Teitelbaum, as clear as the nose on your face."

Mrs. Teitelbaum prodded her nose as if it were somehow to blame for what was going to happen to her. "So how do you know seventeen thousand and what's it, so exact?"

"Mrs. Teitelbaum, that's what you *pay* me for. My psychic numeracy. I count the number of cards and multiply them by the number of times you've come here to ask my advice, plus Mr. Teitelbaum's age when he passed away, which was seventy-six, and the twelve tribes of Israel, that's twelve. Then I deduct your age and the last two digits of your cell-phone number and that's the exact figure."

"Seventeen thousand and what?"

"Seventeen thousand four hundred and eighty."

"So what can I do?"

"I don't think there's anything you *can* do. Fate is fate. Destiny is destiny. The cards don't make the future, they only warn you what to expect."

I pushed back my chair and stood up, accidentally step-ping on the hem of my dark green robe and tearing the stitches. "At least none of this will come as a shock, will it? I mean, you'll be well prepared for it."

Mrs. Teitelbaum's cherries rattled. "But, I don't want to lose all this money! This is the reason why I come to see you, Mr. Erskine! I come here to find out what is going to happen to me, so that it won't!"

I went to the window and parted the dusty brown velvet drapes with two fingers. Down below, on Seventeenth Street, a young Hispanic woman was leaning over her stroller, wiping ice cream from her toddler's mouth. She had masses of black curly hair, and she was wearing a tight yellow top with an embroidered sun on the front of it, from which her enormous breasts seemed desperate to escape by any route possible; and the smallest pair of white cotton shorts. I think God was punishing me for not keeping up my Spanish lessons. I could just imagine her reaction if I went down to the street and tried the only Spanish come-on line that I knew, "*Le importa si me siento aqui?*"—"Do you mind if I sit here?"

I came to terms with reality and let the drapes fall back. "There *is* something you can do, Mrs. Teitelbaum. If you really want to change your weekend, you could try a little something from the Magic Pantry."

"The Magic Pantry?"

"I don't often recommend that my clients should resort to spells, Mrs. Teitelbaum. I'm not saying that they don't work. Oh boy—*what!*—there's no denying that they *work!* But they're not cheap, and they can have unpredictable side effects."

"I certainly don't want to lose seventeen thousand dollars, Mr. Erskine, whatever the side effects."

I went to the glass-fronted cabinet at the far end of the room and made a performance of producing a key on the end of a very long chain. I unlocked the doors, which actually wasn't too difficult because the lock had been missing when I bought it. Then I reached inside and brought out a green glass jar with a tarnished brass lid. I opened it, and let Mrs. Teitelbaum smell it.

"Herby," she decided. "What is it?"

"Spikenard. If you put a few leaves in a bag, and keep the bag under your pillow, all of your possessions will remain safe, at least for as long as the spikenard stays fresh."

"Well, that sounds ideal."

"It does, doesn't it? But there is a very dramatic side effect, I'm afraid."

"What's that?"

"Spikenard will also make you irresistible to younger men. If you sleep on a bag of spikenard every night . . . well, the chances are that you'll soon find yourself a vigorous young lover at least half your age. He'll have a very big—well, let's not get too descriptive about it, but you won't be disappointed."

Mrs. Teitelbaum's left eyelid started to twitch. "This really works?"

"Of course. Spikenard is one of the most powerful herbs in the Magic Pantry. Definitely not to be sneezed at."

"Well, if it really will protect my money, maybe I'll take some. How much is it?"

"Two-fifty for three leaves, I'm afraid."

"If it saves me seventeen thousand, that's nothing. As for the side effect . . . well, I guess I can live with the side effect."

I picked out three leaves, but then I hesitated. "I just thought of a problem."

"Problem? What problem?"

"Well, spikenard will keep your money safe, and you'll get your young stud. But when you've grown tired of him, you won't be able to get rid of him—ever."

"Never?"

"No—not so long as you're sleeping with spikenard under your pillow. If you want him to go, you'll have to throw away the spikenard, but that means that you'll lose your money, too. It's a question of losing it later, rather than sooner."

Mrs. Teitelbaum poked her nose into the jar and took a deep, appreciative sniff. For a few seconds, I could see that she was very close to deciding that $17,480 wasn't too high a price to pay for several weeks of bedroom gymnastics with a younger man. But in the end, she couldn't bring herself to two-time her bank account. She handed back the jar and said, "Oh, well. What else do you have?"

I went back to the hutch, rummaged around, and produced another green jar. "Here, try this," I suggested. "Blood root. *Sanguina canadensis.* It's a member of the poppy family. The Native Americans used blood root to stain their bodies before they went out scalping people, and they still use it today, as a dye."

Mrs. Teitelbaum sniffed at this jar, too, and wrinkled up her nose. "Musty," she decided.

"Ah, yes, but heap plenty powerful. If you keep blood

root in your purse, Mrs Teitelbaum, you will never lose your money, ever. You can use it to protect your home, too—simply by nailing a small piece of it under your windowsill. I promise you, if you take blood root home with you tonight, your weekend will be totally different. No lost purse, no falling picture, no flooded carpets, no stolen pearls. Everything that came up in the cards will be canceled."

"*Canceled*? You're sure?"

"They don't call me the Incredible Erskine, Herbal Visionary, for nothing. I see, I interpret, I fix. I can heal the future before it happens."

"So, for the blood root, how much?"

I sucked in my breath. "It's pretty hard to get hold of, these days, Mrs. T. Most *sanguina canadensii* have been wiped out by genetically modified sarsaparilla. But I guess I could let you have a couple of inches for six-fifty."

Mrs. Teitelbaum opened her purse, took out a money clip that looked like a raccoon trap, and tugged out a ten dollar bill. "Can you break this for me?"

I didn't allow myself to waver. When it comes to extracting money out of wealthy old women, wavering is fatal. Wealthy old woman have gotten wealthy by being totally unscrupulous—by marrying bald, rich, old bastards for lucre, not for love—by tactical divorcing and equally tactical remarrying—and they will screw you for the price of a day-old newspaper if you show the slightest hesitation. They're vampires, and the only way to get the better of them is to hammer a stake through their checkbooks.

"Actually . . . it's six *hundred* and fifty," I told her. Then I let out my famous high-pitched laugh, as if she had just played an incredibly funny practical joke on me. You knew all along that it was $650, you wicked, wicked woman! You were pulling my leg, weren't you? What a rib-tickler you are!

She tugged out six $100 bills, one at a time, and then five tens. This was where not wavering came into it. What was she going to say? That she had really expected me to sell her a whole two inches of rare Apache blood root for $6.50? I mean, how stupid would *that* have made her look?

I took her money with that special sleight-of-hand they teach you at magician's school, so that the mark is barely aware that it's gone. Money—*fwwp!*—no money. Then I leaned forward and said, very confidentially, "You promise you won't tell anyone how much I charged you, will you?"

She looked up at me, not quite understanding what I meant.

"That's a *very* special price," I explained. "I wouldn't sell blood root to anybody else for that kind of money."

I let out another scream of laughter, and this time Mrs. Teitelbaum laughed, too.

As I opened the door of my apartment, however, she hesitated. "Mr. Erskine—" she said.

I thought for a split second that she was going to say, "Give me back my six hundred and fifty dollars, you double-dealing two-bit chiseler." But instead she whispered, "That *other* herb, the first one you offered me—?"

"The spikenard?"

"That's it, the spikenard. I was wondering . . . so long as the blood root can guarantee to keep my money safe . . ."

"Oh . . . you were wondering if the spikenard could keep it *doubly* safe."

"Well, yes. Kind of extra security, if you know what I mean."

"In spite of *the side effect*."

"Mr. Erskine, I haven't had a side effect since Mr. Teitelbaum passed over."

"I don't know, Mrs. Teitelbaum. You're sure you can handle it? Some of my ladies have complained of getting *very* tired."

"I'm in the best of health, Mr. Erskine. I eat only fish. Well, sometimes a little chicken; and maybe a cream strudel now and again. But I do Pilates, and I walk ten thousand paces a day, every day, and always in a different direction."

"Well . . . okay. So long as you don't hold me liable for any—you know—*overexertion*."

"Mr. *Erskine!*" Mrs. Teitelbaum protested, all flushed and coquettish. And she hadn't even *bought* any spikenard yet, let alone found herself an eager young lover with a very large resumé.

I opened up the cabinet, took out the green glass jar, and gave her three leaves of spikenard. "Under your pillow, Mrs. Teitelbaum, in a pure white linen bag. That'll do the trick."

She tugged three hundred dollar bills from her money clip and held them out to me. But just as I was reaching forward to *fwwp* them out of her fingers, she snatched hold of my wrist, and held it tight. "There's just one more thing."

What? I thought. *She's wearing a wire and I'm under arrest.*

"You didn't give me my mystic motto," she said, reprovingly.

"Oh! Oh, yes! Your mystic motto! How could I forget?"

Shit, I thought. I used to own a rare nineteenth-century copy of *Bultitude's Compendium of Astrological Admonitions*, but I must have dropped it in the street when I had to move out of our apartment on East Eighty-sixth Street. I'll bet some wino found it, and even now he's terrified of sitting cross-legged under a medlar tree on the eighth of August, or seeing two gray cats through the rungs of a ladder. But the real nuisance is that, these days, I have to invent my own mystic mottoes.

"Ahhmmm . . . 'If you stand under a lemon tree for long enough, the falling blossom will turn you into a bride.'"

"Mr. Erskine." I swear to God there were tears in Mrs. Teitelbaum's eyes. I gently eased the hundred dollar bills from between her fingers, one, two, three, smiling all the time.

"Good-bye," I said, ushering her toward the door. "Next week, same time?"

"There's just one more thing," she told me.

"Ye-e-es?" I asked, sweeter than ever.

"Fifty dollars change."

But that was another day's consultations over. I went to the window and dragged back the drapes, in the faint hope that the bosomy young Hispanic woman with the stroller was still out there, but of course she wasn't. Anyhow, think about it, she was probably hopelessly devoted to the father of her child, who was built like The Rock and worked as a bodyguard for some famous Cuban *guaracha* band, and who would rip the arms off any man who came within breathing distance of her, especially a forty-three-year-old mystic in a green cape made out of a stretch-nylon couch cover and a golden skullcap that was actually a Mickey Mouse hat with the ears unstapled.

"Harry . . ." she would pant, her glistening lips only two-and-a-half inches from mine, so that I could smell the extra-hot salsa on her breath, "I want you so bad . . . but I have promised my impossibly bulging breasts and my endless legs to Raimondo."

And I would say, with infinite tenderness, *"No tiene usted algo más barato?"*

I went through to my tiny kitchen, opened the icebox and took out a bottle of Guinness. It's an acquired taste, Guinness: like burnt toast, only beer. But it's good for a man living on his own, because it's food and drink in the same bottle, and you never have any dishes to wash. I took a long swallow, burped, and then I went back into the living area to tidy up my fortune-telling cards.

How are the mystic fallen, I thought. Up until thirteen months ago I had been living with Karen and Lucy in faded grandeur up on East Eighty-sixth Street, now here I was in this dingy little two-room apartment over Khaled's Pakistani Provisions, in a rundown district that I liked to call Upper Greenwich Village.

I hadn't even unpacked properly yet, although I had managed to buy nine mismatched bookshelves and stock the walls with all my tatty old volumes of magic and fortune-telling and demonic arts. I had covered my table with a crimson candlewick bedspread, and set out my crystal ball and my phrenological bust, and I regularly burned sandalwood incense to cover the smell of dry rot and Indian cooking from downstairs. What can you say? Life's a bitch and then you smell of fenugreek.

I don't really know how or why our marriage came apart. I guess it was mostly my fault. I'm never truly fulfilled unless I'm desperate. Like the painter Edouard Munch of *The Scream* fame once said, "Without anxiety, I would have been a ship without a rudder." There was nobody else involved, even that smug tangerine-tanned bastard Rodney Elwick III who kept inviting himself around for large glasses of chilled sauvignon whenever he felt like it, and laughing with Karen in the kitchen while I was playing drafts with Lucy.

"Something funny?" I used to say, appearing in the kitchen door, and they both used to look at me as if I had a booger hanging out of my nostril. I was an outsider. I wasn't even *new* money. I was no money at all, of any age. All the money was Karen's.

But Rodney Elwick III wasn't totally to blame. I was jealous, yes, but I have to admit that I was also bored, and discontented, and kicking my heels. I felt that my life was being wastefully torn away, day by day, like the blank pages from somebody else's diary. I had discovered the terrible truth that happiness isn't everything. To know that we're alive, we need challenges, and we need problems, and most of all we need *worry*.

So here I was, the Incredible Erskine, Herbal Visionary, with all the worry that anybody could wish for, and absolutely no money, but alive.

A blonde woman in a turquoise blouse appeared in the entrance to the antiques store on the opposite side of the street, and stood there, smoking. She had dark roots in her hair, and her stomach bulged over her denim mini skirt, but she had a hair-raisingly pretty face, like an angel out of a Florentine painting. I wondered what would happen if I went across and introduced myself.

"I've been watching you, my dear, and I think you're beautiful, in a strange, trashy way."

No, that wouldn't work. And I was still trying to work out something more seductive to say to her when my doorbell rang. My doorbell made a wonderful glissando noise like a xylophone and it had cost me only $7.88 in Wolfowitz Discount Electrics on Second Avenue.

I opened the door. A young man of about twenty-five was standing outside in the corridor, blinking. He had messy blond hair and he was dressed in a white T-shirt with *Molten Iris* printed on it in red, and jeans. He was snub-nosed, very pale, with pale green eyes, and blond eyebrows, and he had a 9 kt gold crucifix dangling in his left ear. I could tell by the yellow on his fingers that he smoked, but he was only wearing one ring, and that was a heavy silver skull. You notice details like these, when you're a fortune-teller.

One of the most interesting details about him, though, was that he was here at all. Young men don't consult clairvoyants, not as a rule. Ninety percent of my clientele was female, and the few men who did come had either been diagnosed with a terminal illness and wanted to know how long they had left, or were interested to know in advance which horse was going to win at Aqueduct.

"Can I help you?" I asked him.

He frowned at the folded-up paper napkin that he was holding in his hand. "Are you—uh—the Incredible Erskine?"

"Incredible as it might seem, yes."

"My sister said maybe I should come talk to you."

"Your sister?"

"Marilyn Busch. I'm Ted Busch."

"Do I *know* your sister?"

"I don't think so, but she's friends with a girl who's the niece of a friend of yours. She said I should talk to this friend of yours, but this friend of yours said she didn't do psychic stuff no more but *you* did so maybe I should come see you."

"What's that in Earth-speak?"

"I keep getting this nightmare, okay? So my sister's friend said I should talk to her Aunt Amelia."

"Aunt Amelia? I don't know any Aunt Amelias. I don't know any Aunt Anythings. I mean, look at me. Do I look like a nephew?"

"Amelia Crusoe? She's called Amelia Carlsson now, but that's the name my sister told me to tell you."

Amelia Crusoe. Oh, God.

I used to love Amelia Crusoe. I *still* loved Amelia Crusoe. Apart from having a husky voice and vulnerable, pre-Raphaelite looks, Amelia was a *real* psychic, a real medium who could talk to dead people as easily as you and I can talk to people on the bus. She had always talked about giving up the séance business, and she had, more than once, but I always knew that she could no more give up talking to the dead than I could give up worry. She *needed* it, to remind herself that she was still alive.

I said, "You'd better come in. You want a Guinness? It's Irish. You drink enough of it, you pee green."

"I'm cool, thanks."

"Sit down," I told him, dragging out a bentwood chair. "What did you say your name was? Fred?"

"Ted—Ted Busch. That's Busch like in Anheuser, not Bush like in George Dubya."

"Okay, Ted," I said, adjusting my golden skullcap. "I think the best thing I can do is read your fortune in the cards, and see if this nightmare of yours is going to have a deleterious effect on your life, or whether it's just a harmless nocturnal terror."

Ted nodded. "I understand."

I was glad about that, because I didn't. "I'll have to charge you a fee," I told him. "My rates are very reasonable, I'm not one of these Upper West Side celebrity mystics with a self-help book on *The New York Times* best-seller lists and a gold Lexus in the garage. But peering into the unknown, it's a very complicated business, and it takes years of dedication to perfect it, so I have to ask my clients for the nominal sum of fifty-five dollars, inclusive of tax."

Ted opened up his left hand and there was a $100 bill, neatly folded. "Amelia said that I'd have to pay you, but she didn't know how much."

Terrific, I thought. *I should have asked for a hundred.* But I took the money and gave Ted $45 change, including five dollars in nickels and dimes, which I shook out of my jelly jar.

"So tell me about this nightmare," I asked him, as I reopened the deck of fortune-telling cards and started to lay them out.

"Uh . . . don't I have to tap the deck or nothing?"

"Where do you think we are? Reno? No, you don't have to tap the deck. They know you already, these cards. Look at this top one—a young man with messy hair climbing up a flight of stairs—they even predicted that you were coming to see me."

"Hey." Ted looked impressed.

"This is the *Jeu Noir*," I told him. "The Black Game—the most accurate fortune-telling cards you can buy, if you can ever find them. They're banned, in most countries, and do you know why? People were using them to predict the date of their own death, and then killing people they didn't like on the day before they were due to die anyhow, so they wouldn't get executed for it."

"Really?"

"Sure. Look at these cards—exquisite, aren't they? Look at the detail. Do you know who designed them? French prisoners of war, in England, in Napoleonic times. The artists weren't allowed to have pens, so they cut all the flesh off the tips of their fingers, and drew the designs with their own sharpened bones, dipped in a mixture of boot-polish and rats' blood."

Ted peered across the table with what he obviously thought was a knowledgeable frown. I doubt if he had heard of Napoleon Solo, let alone Napoleon Bonaparte. He sniffed and said, "I have the same nightmare just about every night. I feel like I've been sleeping, okay, and then I suddenly wake up."

"But in reality you're still asleep?"

"That's right. It's pitch dark, and when I try to sit up, I can't. I'm trapped inside this wooden box, like a coffin."

"Carry on." I kept on laying out the *Jeu Noir* cards, in rows of seven, six, five, three and four.

"I'm pounding on the lid with my fists, but it's fastened real tight and I can't budge it, and in some way I know that there's another box on top of me, with somebody in it, and another box on top of that, with somebody in that, too."

I glanced up at him. He was clutching himself like he had the stomachache and there were clear beads of perspiration on his upper lip. It was a sweltering day, granted, but my rattly old air-conditioner didn't work too bad.

"So . . . you're feeling very claustrophobic?" I asked him.

"I'm *suffocating*, man! I'm banging and I'm banging but I know that nobody's going to answer me and nobody's going to let me out."

"Is that it? You bang on the lid and nobody lets you out and then what?"

Ted said, "This box I'm in . . . I think it's on a ship. It's going up and down like a fairground ride, and after a while I start to feel like I'm going to barf. I can hear the ocean, and the wind, and clanking noises. I can hear somebody calling out, in this really high voice. Maybe it's a girl but it sounds more like a very young boy."

I put down the second-to-last card. "Can you catch what he's saying?"

"Not really. It doesn't make any sense. I'll tell you what it reminds me of, though. The super's kids, when my family lived on Twenty-fourth Street. The Popescus, that was their name. I hear this voice, and it sounds just like one of them."

"So you hear the voice calling . . . and that's when you wake up?"

"Jesus, I wish! Nothing else happens, but I still don't wake up. Sometimes the nightmare seems to go on and on for *hours*, with the ship heaving up and down, and the kid calling out, and I can't do nothing at all but lie there, and I'm gasping for air."

I looked at him narrowly. "Is there anything happening in your life right now to make you feel trapped? Are you stuck in a job you don't like? Maybe you've just gotten engaged?"

"Not at all, man. Everything was totally cool before I started having these nightmares. I got myself a new job at the beginning of last month, at Lasky's Camera Store, and a new place to live, and I'm gigging in the evenings at the Gothicka club. I don't have a care in the world, man, apart from these nightmares."

"All right, then," I told him. "I've laid out the twenty-eight Predictor Cards so that we can see what your immediate future is going to be. The last card we don't turn over till the very end."

"You can really read these things?"

"You think I'd have the nerve to charge you fifty-five bucks if I couldn't?"

"Okay," said Ted, dubiously.

I pointed to the first card, The Sweet Heart. "This is a good start! You're going to meet a new girl this weekend. She's sitting on the bed, see, and she's smiling flirtatiously, and that definitely means romance, even if it's only a one-night stand."

"Yeah? Then who's *that*—looking in the window?"

I jerked up my head in alarm, but we were three stories up and of course there was nobody. "Jesus," I told him. "You scared me."

"I meant there in the card," said Ted, pointing at it. "The girl's sitting on the bed but there's somebody, like, *spying* on her."

"Really?" He was right. I had never noticed it before but right in the corner of the card there was a window, and a parchment-colored face was peering into it. A mask, rather than a face, with a slit for a mouth and two slitty eyes. Talk about Leatherface, in *The Texas Chainsaw Massacre.*

"That face—that's your *conscience*," I improvised. "When you take the girl to bed, your conscience is going to be watching you and saying, excuse me, Ted, are you doing the honorable thing here? Or are you merely playing with this young woman's affections? See here, beside the bed, there's a chessboard with all the pieces knocked over . . . that's a symbol of the fickle game of love."

"That conscience dude . . . he's pretty scary looking."

"Well, your conscience is *supposed* to be scary. He's supposed to make you think twice."

"Man, if I saw *that* dude staring into my bedroom window, I wouldn't have to think twice. I'd crap my pants and run for the door, in that order."

"Let's take the next card then. This is you, talking to all of your friends. It may not look exactly like you. I mean you don't have red hair and bright green pantyhose. But it *represents* you. You're smiling, you're relaxed. That's good news."

Ted picked up the card and scrutinized it for nearly half

a minute. He was obviously determined to get his fifty-five bucks' worth.

"So who's this?" he wanted to know, turning the card around so that I could look at it, too.

"Who's who?"

"This dude way off in the distance, all dressed in black, with the tall black hat, and his face all wrapped up in a scarf."

"Oh, him! He's not . . . specially significant. We should go on to the third card."

"No, hold up, man. Here's all these people laughing and joking, okay? But this guy right at the back, he's looking toward this guy dressed in black, and he's definitely scared. He's not laughing and joking like the rest of them, is he? He's got his mouth wide open like he's definitely scared."

I took the card reluctantly and examined it myself. "Well, I guess you're right. He does look a little concerned."

"So why is he concerned?"

"You don't really want to know that."

"I do, actually. Like, if this is my future, and somebody's looking scared, I really want to know why."

"All right," I said. "This black figure appears on only seven cards in the *Jeu Noir*, at various distances from the main protagonists. Sometimes he's far away, sometimes he's practically breathing down their necks. But what his appearance actually *means*—that's open to very wide interpretation."

"But who *is* he? That's all I'm asking."

"He's, um, Imminent Death."

4

BLOOD ON
SEVENTEENTH STREET

"Imminent Death?" Ted blinked. "What does *that* mean?"

"Like I say, it's open to very wide interpretation. But basically it means that you're going to die. More or less imminently."

"You're putting me on."

I lifted both hands to show him that I was helpless. "What can I tell you? You wanted to know exactly what the cards predicted, and that's what the cards predict."

"Do they say *how?*"

I scanned the twenty-seven cards that I had already turned up. "Without going into too much detail, you've already met the person who's going to kill you. See here? That's you in the blindfold, talking to her. She's a woman, and you even know what her name is, although you don't know her *real* name, and never will. That's the significance of the blindfold."

"Jesus. Do they say who she is?"

"Not specifically, but she comes from very far away. Have you met any foreign women lately?"

Ted nodded. "I met a girl at a party in SoHo last weekend. She spoke pretty good English—but, yes, *she* was foreign. Russian, maybe."

"Russian?"

"Maybe. Russian-*type*, anyhow."

"Well, maybe the cards are referring to her. They also tell me that you've been given a gift that you won't be able to get rid of, even if you want to. See this card here? The Gift. A young man's holding a birdcage with a bright red parrot in it. He likes the parrot, he's smiling—but if you look closer you can see that the bottom of the birdcage is actually fastened with bolts that go right through the palms of his hands. He can never put it down. Quite literally, he's screwed."

Ted said, "She gave me a medallion. Look." He reached into his T-shirt and pulled out a heavy pewter amulet, about the same size as an Oreo. He held it out so that I could inspect it.

The medallion had a man's face embossed on it, with a border of snakes and stars. The man's eyes were closed, and he looked almost laughably grim. On the back, an inscription was engraved in italics, but it was written in some language that I couldn't understand. *De strigoaica, de strigoi, si de case cu moroi.*

"This Russian-type girl . . . did she tell you what these words meant?"

Ted shook his head. "She said it would bring me good luck, that's all."

"In that case, let's hope that *she* was right and the cards are wrong."

Ted didn't look convinced. "You said they were the most accurate fortune-telling cards that money could buy."

"That's true. I did say that. But they can be unnecessarily pessimistic. Like, they may say Imminent Death but how imminent is imminent? If you're a Galapagos turtle, imminent could mean sometime early next century."

I turned Ted's medallion over again, and it was then that I felt a crawling sensation up the back of my neck, like ants running into my hair. *The man's eyes had opened, and he was staring straight at me, and smiling.*

I flung the medallion away from me as if I had suddenly found a spider on it. Ted said, *"What?"*

"Muscular spasm, sorry. My fingers just—*jerk*, now and again. Ruined my career in netsuke-carving."

Maybe I should have told him that the man's face on his lucky medallion had appeared to open his eyes, but it could have been a trick of the light, couldn't it, or maybe the medallion had been made in such a way that it was supposed to do that. But Ted already looked so anxious that I thought it better if I said nothing. I may make a living out of telling fortunes, but I can assure you that finding out what the future has in store for us does nobody any good. Especially since we can't do a damn thing about it, not even with blood root.

"Let's turn over the last card, shall we?" I suggested. "This is what we call the Decider Card . . . the card that finally tells you what's going to happen to you."

"Supposing this Decider Card says Imminent Death, too?"

"No problem. We can always tell your fortune again, with a different deck of cards. Maybe the Tarot, or the gypsy cards. Or we could even try the crystal ball. You have to understand, Ted—the future . . . the future is only *a matter of opinion.*"

Ted kept his eyes shut while I turned over the last card. I was hoping to God that it wasn't The Serpent, which means certain death before the next moon rises, but it was almost as bad. It was The Water Woman . . . a picture of a woman floating just below the surface of a river, with un-dulating green weed, instead of hair. I had never turned this card up before, but I knew what it signified. Death by drowning, or some other unpleasant demise that involved water.

Ted opened his eyes and frowned at it. "The Water Woman? Is that bad?"

"It's not *bad*—but I have to be frank, it's not especially good either. Don't let it worry you, though. The cards are *warning* you, rather than telling you. They're saying, *be careful, Ted!*"

"Be careful of what?"

"Just be careful. Don't go swimming, don't accept gifts from damp-looking women, and look both ways before you step in front of a fish truck. That's the message they're giving you about Imminent Death. You're not going to die tomorrow so long as you keep your wits about you."

I started gathering up the cards.

"Is that it?" said Ted. "What about my nightmare?"

"Oh . . . your nightmare."

"That's why I came to see you, man. To see if you could stop the nightmare."

"Of course. But quite frankly I don't think your nightmare is anything for you to worry about. You're suffering from stress is all."

"Stress?"

"Sure. You may think that everything in your life is hunky-dory, but you've taken on a whole lot of new responsibili-ties, haven't you? So you're subconsciously beginning to feel that things are getting on top of you. Hence, the box you're trapped in, and all of the boxes piled on top of you. I can let you have some snakeweed for that . . . put snake-weed powder under your pillow and you'll never dream about yourself again, guaranteed."

Ted said, "Amelia said that you could maybe call on your spirit guide, to tell me what was wrong."

* * *

I stopped picking up cards. "My spirit guide?"

"She said you had a Native American spirit guide. Some medicine man you once used to know, who got killed."

"Amelia told you about that?"

"Sure. She said that you had a real talent, when it came to telling fortunes, but you hardly ever used it."

"Oh, really? Did I just read your cards for you, or did I imagine it?"

"Yes, you did. But Amelia said if you got in touch with your spirit guide, you could actually *show* me what was going to happen to me."

"She said that, too?" I thought for a moment. Then I dug into the pocket of my jeans and took out his $100 bill. "Ted, do you know what I'm going to do? I'm going to give you a full refund, no questions asked."

"But I don't want a refund, man! I want to find out what my nightmare is all about! Amelia said you could do it, man! I can't sleep! I haven't slept in over a week! It's driving me out of my skull!"

"Why do you think Amelia didn't want to help you? It's unpredictable. It's *dangerous*. Sure, I contact my spirit guide. Sure I can show you what your nightmare is all about. I can also stick a .45 up my ass and pull the trigger, but that doesn't mean it's a good idea to do it."

Ted lowered his head and stared at the table. He sat like that for so long I was beginning to think that he had fallen asleep.

"Listen," I said, "I haven't done that kind of thing in a very long time. You should try the snakeweed. I can let you have a teaspoonful for forty-five dollars, that's a genuine bargain."

Still he kept his head down.

"Contacting dead people . . . it's a very risky business. Amelia will tell you how risky it is, and she was doing it for years. Why do you think she doesn't do it now?"

I stood up, and went to the window. The blonde woman with the roots was still there. *"I couldn't help noticing you. . . ."* I could say to her. *"The way that the cigarette smoke leaks out of your mouth and disappears up that cute retroussé nose . . ."* No, that wouldn't work, either.

Ted said, "I don't know what else to do, man. I went to my doctor but he said the same as you. Stress, and put me on Ativan. I took them but they only made the nightmare worse. Shit, man, I'm too scared even to turn out the lights."

"I can't help you, Ted. I'm sorry."

He looked up, and I was shocked to see that his face was smothered in tears. "You have to, man. There's nobody else. *Please.*"

The blonde woman looked up and saw me staring at her. I smiled, and winked, but she turned her back on me and went inside her store. Oh, well. She was probably a transvestite, anyhow.

I didn't know what to do. I hate disturbing the dead, and if Amelia hadn't sent him, I would have told Ted to forget it.

"I'm really not sure, Ted," I said. "I guess I could *ask* my spirit guide if he can help you. But I can't give you any guarantees, and if it looks too risky—"

"Please, man. You don't know what this means."

I hesitated. I really didn't like this at all. I had made contact with the so-called spirit world only three or four times in the past, but each time it had been a catastrophe, and I had been lucky to escape with my life. You think dead people are docile? You think they all go off to Rapture, and spend their time dancing in meadows and playing the ukulele like a bunch of hippies? Ha! Dead people are bitter and twisted and vindictive and they *hate* the living like you wouldn't believe. Put it this way: If *you* were dead, how would *you* feel about all those smug bastards who were still alive, especially if they kept getting in touch with you and saying *Hello? Hello? Is anyone there? What's it like being dead? Where did you hide the US Steel stock certificates?*

"Just hold on a moment," I told Ted. I pulled out the bottom drawer of my cabinet and took out my address book. I found Amelia's number and punched it out on my cell phone. It rang and rang but all I got was her answering message.

"I'm not here right now but I really want to know why you called me."

Amelia. That same husky voice. I cleared my throat, and then I said, "Amelia . . . it's Harry. I have young Ted with me. Ted Busch like in Anheuser. I'm going to do what I can to help him, but I'd like to know what *you* think about this nightmare he's been having." I looked at Ted, who was biting his thumbnail, and then I said, "Call me back, can you? Love, Harry."

I snapped the phone shut. "Okay, then, Teddy boy. Let's see if I can get you some assistance from the world beyond."

I tugged the drapes together so that the room was dark, except for a few sharp chinks of light that shone around the edges. I took three church candles from the kitchen drawer, and lit them. Then I took off the black bead bracelet that I always wore, the bracelet that Singing Rock had given me, and dropped it around the candles so that it encircled them.

"You see this?" I said to Ted. "This bracelet is made out of polished stones from the Okabojo riverbed in South Dakota. The guy who gave it to me said that when he died, his soul would be divided into twenty-one parts, and that each of these beads would contain one of those parts. The things he had seen, the things he had said, the things he had tasted, the things he had touched, and so on. This bracelet is like a recording of who he was."

Ted said, "I'll try anything, man, I really will."

"Okay, then." I reached across the table and held both of Ted's hands. "I want you to close your eyes and think of your nightmare. I want you to imagine it as clearly as you can. The box. The weight on top of you. The ship tilting up and down."

Ted nodded. I waited for a while but he kept on nodding. "Close your eyes, then," I told him. "I'd like to get started sometime this week, if I can."

"Oh, sure. Sorry." Ted closed his eyes and at the same time gripped my hands even tighter.

I sat there for a while, watching his face. It's extraordinary, how much people reveal of their thoughts, when they have their eyes closed. Even more, when they're asleep. Myself, I tried to think of Singing Rock, the very last time that I had seen him, turning toward me, just about to say something. He hadn't looked much like a Cheyenne medicine man. Short, stocky, with a broad, good-humored face, and glasses. You would have thought he was an Eastern European mattress salesman rather than one of the most powerful workers of Native American magic since Hastiin Klah.

"Singing Rock," I said, "I need to talk to you."

A car honked its horn in the street outside and somebody started shouting. "*You stupid? What are you, stupid, or what?*"

"Singing Rock, I have a troubled young man here, and I need your guidance to help him."

The candle flames flickered, and dipped, but I didn't feel that there was any presence here, apart from me and Ted, holding hands. I couldn't hear anything, either, apart from the commotion down in the street, and the endless *takka-takka-takka* of my air conditioner.

"Singing Rock, this young man has been having terrible nightmares, and he needs to understand what they mean, and how he can stop them."

I thought: This is hopeless. Ted and I are going to sit here, with our hands becoming increasingly sweaty, and nothing is going to happen. Singing Rock had probably been dead for far too long for me to be able to call him back; or else he simply didn't feel like helping an insomniac paleface. We had been friends, Singing Rock and I, but he had never been a lover of white men, as a race. His great-great-grandmother had been killed by the U.S. Cavalry at Whitestone Hill, in Dakota Territory, along with five more of his family, only babies at the time, and over two hundred other men, women and children of the Yanktonai and Hunkpatina Sioux. Singing Rock used to talk about it with such rage you would have gotten the impression that it had happened only a few days before, instead of in 1863. Time isn't always the Great Healer, believe me, especially when it comes to Great Injustices.

"Singing Rock, I'm asking you a favor here. I need you to open some doors for me, and show me the way through."

Ted opened one of his eyes. "Do you really think this is going to work?" he asked me, dubiously.

"Not if you keep peeking it isn't. Keep thinking about your nightmare, okay?"

He closed his eye again, and squeezed his face in concentration.

"Singing Rock," I intoned. "I think that something seriously bad could be happening here, and I really need your help."

I waited, and waited, and I really began to believe that Singing Rock was going to ignore me. Why should he help me, after all? If I hadn't meddled in Native American magic, he would probably still be alive today.

But just as I was about to twist my hands free from Ted's sweaty grip, I heard something, and it wasn't the traffic, or the air-conditioning unit, or the *binky-bonky* drums of the world music store across the street. It was a very high-pitched keening sound, like metal scraping on metal—so high that it was almost inaudible to the human ear, although it probably would have set the dogs howling.

"*Singing Rock?*" I peered slowly around the room. Nothing appeared to have changed, but there was no doubt about it, there was somebody else here. The balance of the room felt as if it had shifted. Things appeared to have moved, even though they hadn't. The books looked as if they had rearranged themselves, and the photograph of Karen and Lucy that hung on the wall in the corner had infinitesimally tilted.

"Singing Rock, are you here?"

The keening sound grew louder—so loud that it began to set my teeth on edge. Now I could hear another sound, too. A soft, insistent chanting, and the tapping of sticks. I thought I could smell smoke, too, and hear the wind rustling through slippery grass.

Singing Rock was here, or not very far away, anyhow. I was sure of it.

"Ted—" I told him. "I think my spirit guide has arrived."

"What do you want me to do, man?"

"Think of your nightmare, as clearly as you can. See it in your mind's eye. Show him how claustrophobic you feel, trapped inside that box. Show him how the ocean's going up and down. Let him hear that young boy's voice."

"I can see it, man. I can feel it. I can hear it."

The tapping of sticks became quicker, and more staccato. I could definitely hear somebody chanting now. I didn't know what dialect it was, but it was definitely Native American, and I would have taken a guess that it was Sioux.

"Singing Rock, this young man is deeply troubled by his dream. He needs you to show him what it means, and who could be causing it, and why."

Singing Rock didn't answer, but the black bead bracelet started to shake, as if it were a rattlesnake's tail.

"Show him how he can rid himself of this dream, and sleep peacefully again."

The bracelet shook even more violently, and the candles began to splutter and to burn more fiercely.

"What's happening?" said Ted.

"Keep your eyes closed! Concentrate on your nightmare! He's here now! Show him what's been scaring you!"

"Oh, Jesus, man! This is worse than when I'm asleep!"

"*Concentrate!* He needs to see your nightmare as clearly as you do!"

Ted gritted his teeth, and perspiration was dripping from the end of his nose. The bracelet continued to rattle, and the candle flames burned so furiously now that they were crackling and spitting out sparks. I felt as if the whole room was rushing through time and space, completely out of my control. It was like being on a fairground ride when you're nauseated and desperate to get off but it just goes on and on and on.

"*Singing Rock!*"

At that moment, out of the corner of my eye, I saw a blurred figure disappear into my bedroom door. It was tall, and it was dark, and strangely *stretched out*, but it disappeared so quickly and jerkily that I couldn't see who it was. What really scared me, though, was that the door was closed, and that the figure hadn't opened it. *It had vanished straight through the brown-stained wood.*

I wrenched my hands away from Ted's, and awkwardly stood up, so that my chair fell back onto the floor with a sharp bang.

Ted opened his eyes and blinked, "What?"

"I think he's here," I told him. Even I was excited. I circled around the table, straining my ears.

"You think *who's* here?"

"Whoever's been causing your nightmare. Singing Rock has managed to bring him here, so that you can see him for yourself."

"I don't get it."

"It's simple. Nightmares are always caused by spirit activity, of one kind or another. When you have a bad dream, that's always caused by a dead person, disturbing your sleep. Most of the time they don't do it deliberately, but sometimes they really want to scare the shit out of you."

I paused, still listening. Then I said, "The only way you can find out which spirit is giving you nightmares is by asking a spirit guide to show you who it is."

"And that's who's here?"

"You got it."

Ted looked warily from side to side. "So where is he? I don't see nobody."

"He's in there," I said, and pointed toward the bedroom.

"In *there?* How the hell did he get in there?"

The bracelet gave a sharp, impatient rattle. It had probably cost Singing Rock an exhausting amount of spiritual energy to find out who was responsible for Ted's nightmares, and to bring him here. It had probably been highly dangerous, too. A spirit who could create the illusion of a suffocating box, and a fully laden ship at sea, was obviously not to be messed with.

"Follow me," I said, and beckoned Ted across to the bedroom door. I pressed my ear against one of the panels, and listened. At first the room seemed to be silent, but then I heard the softest of whispers, hundreds of whispers, *thousands*, like a whole cathedral filled with fervently whispering nuns.

"*Tatal nostru carele esti in ceruri, sfinteasca-se numele tau—*"

I reached for the old brown plastic doorknob. There was only one way to find out what this spirit looked like, and that was to face it. But I can tell you that my heart was thumping so hard against my ribs that it hurt.

"*Vie imparatia ta, faca-se voia ta—*"

"No!" said Ted, hysterically, in a just-broken voice like a teenager.

"Ted—he's here—but Singing Rock can't keep him here for very long."

"I don't want to see him!" He was almost screaming. "Please, man, I can feel how evil he is! *I don't want to see him!*"

On the table, the beads gave another brisk rattle.

"This is your only chance, Ted! If you don't face up to him now, you could go on having this same nightmare for the rest of your life! Ted! Listen to me! *Ted!*"

But Ted was backing away from me, with both of his hands raised, shaking his head violently from side to side. "I can't do it, dude! I can't face him! I can feel how evil he is! I never felt anything so bad!"

"Ted, you *must!* You don't have any choice!"

I didn't want to open that bedroom door any more than Ted. It sounded as if the whisperers were growing ever more numerous—as if there were *millions* of ghostly spirits crowding against the other side of the paneling, praying hungrily for their release. And there was a *smell*, too—a really sickening smell, like cheap chicken meat with the first shadow of olive-green decay showing through the skin; and drains clogged with dripping gray hair; and lumpy milk.

All the same, I knew that we had to confront this spirit that Singing Rock had brought to show me. If we didn't, I might never be able to call on him again. A Sioux would give you everything he possessed, if you asked him, or even if you didn't. But he would never forgive ingratitude.

"I'm opening the door, Ted!" I told him. "You have to see this, no matter what!"

Ted dropped onto his knees. "I can't, man! *Please!*"

I heard a furious pattering against the other side of the door, like a shower of locusts. On the table, however, the bracelet gave a single desultory shake, and then lay silent; and the candles began to dip and gutter, as if they were starved of air. I knew that if I didn't look in the bedroom now, I would never know who was giving Ted his nightmares, or why, and that he would probably end up gibbering mad, or suicidal, or both.

So I opened the door.

5

CITY OF BLOOD

"Can we talk to her?" asked Lieutenant Roberts, nodding toward Susan Fireman's bed. His voice was extremely deep and resonant, as if he were hiding a double bass inside his suit, and Frank detected a Southern accent, South Carolina or Georgia.

"Not yet," said Frank. "I don't think you'd get a whole lot of sense out of her, in any case."

"She spoke to *you*, though?"

A pale and pimply young nun was hovering close by, trying hard to look as if she wasn't listening. Frank said, "I think you gentlemen had better come up to my office. You sent somebody around to her apartment, I presume?"

"Oh, you bet," said Lieutenant Roberts. "They'll contact me, just as soon as they've checked it out."

They went up to the twenty-seventh floor in silence. There was nobody else in the elevator except for a diminutive Korean nurse in huge white sneakers who kept yawning, which made Detective Mancini start yawning, too. Frank ushered them inside his office and closed the door.

"You want to sit down?" he asked them.

"Not especially," said Lieutenant Roberts. He was tall and grave, more like a preacher than a detective. He was not only wearing a black linen suit but a black silk shirt with a black silk necktie, and very shiny black patent shoes.

Frank said, "Ms. Fireman was partly delirious, so I can't vouch for the veracity of what she told me."

"You're not on the witness stand, doc. Just tell me what she said."

"She shares her apartment with a young woman called Prissy and a young man called Michael. She told me . . . well, she said that she cut their throats with a kitchen knife, and then drank their blood directly from their severed arteries."

There was a very long silence—so long that Frank began to wonder if Lieutenant Roberts had heard what he had just said. But at last Lieutenant Roberts took out a very white handkerchief, unfolded it, and blew his nose—and, to his credit, didn't inspect it. "Is there any reason for you to suspect that she might be making it up?"

"As I say, I can't be one hundred percent sure. But the blood that she vomited was human, and it wasn't hers, and the amount she vomited is consistent with what she's been telling me."

"There's no chance that either of her victims might have survived?"

"Very unlikely. The average person has about five-point-five liters of blood, and if they lose more than twenty percent of it. . . ."

Detective Mancini's cell phone warbled like a homing pigeon. "Ryker?" he said. "Okay—just a minute, I can't hear you, you're breaking up." He turned to Lieutenant Roberts and said, "It's Ryker—I'll have to take it outside." He left the office and went out into the corridor, closing the door behind him, although Frank could still hear him shouting to make himself heard.

"You're in there? You're in there now? What do you mean nobody's answering? They're supposed to be dead, you moron!"

Lieutenant Roberts was silent for a moment, as if he were thinking about something completely different. Then he said, "What is actually wrong with Ms. Fireman?"

Frank shrugged. "Physically—several things. She's anemic. Her blood pressure is way down and she's also hypersensitive to light. That's why the blinds in her room are all pulled down."

"So she's suffering from *what*, exactly? Does it have a name?"

"Quite frankly, we don't know. We're carrying out further tests, but until we get the results we're pretty much guessing. She's carrying some kind of unusual enzyme in her blood, but we haven't yet identified it."

"Is there any known disease that makes people want to drink human blood?"

"No. But having said that, there might be some delusional psychoses which lead the sufferer to believe that they need to."

"So Ms. Fireman is a nut job?"

" 'Nut job' isn't a term we generally use here at the Sisters of Jerusalem, Lieutenant. For one thing, it's not clinically specific. There are scores of different types of nut jobs, from bipolar depressives to full-blown sociopaths. And as I say, we haven't yet completed all of our tests."

"Did she tell you *why* she drank the blood?"

"She said that the sunlight in her apartment made her feel as if she was burning, and she had to drink her friends' blood to save herself from being cremated alive. It's possible that the burning sensation was a genuine physical symptom, but her response to it was psychotic. It happens.

I once had a patient with stomach cancer who seriously believed that he was being eaten from the inside out by alien insects, and tried to swallow Raid to kill them. When people suffer unbearable pain . . . well, it can seriously distort their perception of reality."

"Okay, accepted," said Lieutenant Roberts. "But what I'm trying to ask you is, do you consider that she's mentally competent? Do you think she can tell the difference between right and wrong?"

The phone buzzed. Frank said, "Excuse me for a moment," and picked up the receiver. He listened, and nodded, and then he slowly put the receiver down again, and kept his hand pressed on top of it, as if he were trying to make sure that it didn't ring again.

"We have a problem, Lieutenant."

"A new problem, or the same problem got worse?"

"I don't know. Maybe both. About an hour ago, a young man was brought into the emergency room, vomiting blood like Ms. Fireman. He showed some signs of being sensitive to light, too—his skin was all covered in sun block. We analyzed the contents of his stomach and I've just been given the preliminary results."

"And?"

"Over three liters of blood, none of it his."

"Jesus."

"That's not all. Dr. Garrett has just had another one brought in. A middle-aged male, also vomiting blood, his face and his hands covered in thick foundation cream."

"Another one? Maybe it's some kind of blood-drinking cult."

"There's no way of telling *what* it is, not yet. It could be a virus, incubated by the heat and the high humidity. Or maybe it's not a physical sickness at all. Maybe it's some kind of mass hysteria."

"You think it could be catching?"

"There's no way of telling, not yet. We're carrying out all the regulation disease-control protocols, in case it is."

Detective Mancini shouted, "*Okay, Ryker, for sure! I'll talk to you later!*" He pushed his way back in through the door, catching his foot on the wastepaper basket.

"Well?" asked Lieutenant Roberts.

"Right on the button, Lieutenant. They found them in the kitchen. Two dead, a man and a woman, both in their twenties, both with their throats cut, both bled out." He checked his notebook and sniffed. "Mr. Michael Harris and . . . Ms. Priscilla Trueman."

"Oh, God," said Frank. In spite of her confession, in spite of all the medical evidence, it still came as a shock to him that Susan Fireman's story was true. He felt as if the lights had suddenly gone up in the middle of a horror movie, and he had found himself spattered in real, warm blood.

"Well," said Lieutenant Roberts, "it looks like we have ourselves a double homicide, and that's just for starters." He checked his large Rotary watch. "Since Ms. Fireman isn't in a fit state to be interviewed, I think we'll go take a look at her handiwork for ourselves, and come back later, if that's convenient with you. I'll also need to interview those other two patients of yours, down in emergency—ask them whose blood *they've* been drinking."

"Of course," said Frank. "However you want to do it." He felt suddenly very cold and watery, and he dragged out his tan leather chair and sat down. "I'll call you, shall I, if Susan Fireman shows any signs of coming round?"

Lieutenant Roberts stopped, unbalanced, and frowned at him. "Are you okay, doc? You're looking kind of queasy."

"I'm fine. Just a little shocked, I guess."

"Well, that's understandable. You take it easy, we can see ourselves down to the emergency room."

"Wait, Lieutenant—before you go—"

"Yes, doc? What is it?"

"I don't know, maybe this isn't important. But Susan Fireman was talking in some foreign language. Nothing that I've ever heard before . . . eastern European, by the sound of it. But the young man they brought in, *he* was talking the same language."

"Really?"

" '*Tattle nostrew*,' something like that. But there was a whole lot more of it."

Lieutenant Roberts raised both eyebrows. "*Tattle nostrew?* Doesn't mean anything to me. Still—" he said, tugging out his notebook and jotting it down. "*Tattle nostrew.* I'm glad you remembered it. You never know."

"Dr. Garrett and I thought that maybe there might be some kind of connection between them. You know—maybe they're terrorists or something."

"Well, sure. It's worth bearing in mind. They could be al Qa'eda, trying to spread this disease deliberately, like anthrax. On the other hand, like you say, maybe it isn't a disease at all, and maybe they simply belong to the same Esperanto club. Maybe it's the heat, and everybody's gone bananas and developed a raging thirst for Rhesus negative, instead of Coke. Until we find out what the hell's going on, we don't know what the hell's going on."

The phone buzzed again. This time, Frank flicked the intercom button so that Lieutenant Roberts could hear it, too. "Frank, it's Dean Garrett again. Ambulance Battalion Eight has just called in to say they're bringing us three more people barfing up blood. And they warn us that we might have to expect more. Apparently NYU Downtown has reported five similar cases; St. Luke's has three and Lenox Hill has two."

Frank said, "Christ—this is turning into an epidemic."

"Either that, or a massacre," said Lieutenant Roberts. "Or *both*. Let's think about it—if all of these folks have been drinking human blood, how many throats have they cut to get it?"

Detective Mancini's phone warbled again. "It's a message from Inspector Conroy, Lieutenant. He wants us back at the precinct, urgent."

"Okay, doc," said Lieutenant Roberts. "It looks like we'll have to love you and leave you."

Frank said, "Sure. You still want me to call you about Susan Fireman?"

"Oh, yes. I got this very voodoo premonition. I think that you and me, we're going to be sorely in need of each other's help in the next few days."

Frank drank a glass of water and then he went back down to see Susan. Her skin looked even more luminous than it had before, and when he approached her bed she could smile only very weakly.

"Who were those men?" she asked him.

"The police. They sent some detectives to your apartment. They found your friends."

"I see."

Frank cleared his throat. "They'll want to talk to you when you're well enough."

"What time is it? I've been asleep."

"Two-thirty-five. Why don't you try to sleep some more? The best thing you can do is rest."

Susan shook her head. "I can't . . . I keep having that dream."

Frank stood beside her bed for a while, saying nothing.

"I'm in trouble, aren't I?" asked Susan.

"If it was you who killed Prissy and Michael, then yes."

"It won't matter. They can't convict dead people, can they?"

"What do you mean? You're not going to die."

"I'm not going to live, either."

Frank looked at her for a few moments longer, and then he said, "I have to go. There's a hell of a crisis going on downstairs."

"You don't hate me, do you, for killing Prissy and Michael?"

"It's not my job to hate my patients, no matter what they've done."

"I'm glad about that. The funny thing is, I don't hate myself, either. At least they died doing something useful, didn't they, which is more than most people can say?"

"Susan," said Frank, "have you ever heard of *the pale ones?*"

Susan shook her head. "No," she said, "no, I never have."

"You're sure about that? A man who was watching you this morning . . . he said that you were one of the pale ones. He said he couldn't explain it to me, because I wouldn't understand what he meant."

"I never heard of them, never. I promise you, I never heard of them." Susan's voice was suddenly different— rambling and blurred, as if she were concussed, or talking in her sleep. "I promise you . . . I really promise you." She kept on shaking her head, but as she did so, her eyes kept rolling up.

"*Susan*—" said Frank. He glanced up at her monitor, but her heartbeat was steady and her blood pressure was constant, even if it was still very low. Her eyes were closed now and she was breathing soft and steady.

He waited a little longer and then he left the room and walked along the corridor toward the elevators. He had almost reached them when he had the unnerving sensation that Susan had climbed out of bed and was following close behind him, in her white hospital gown. He stopped and turned around, but the only person in the corridor apart from him was a cleaner, mopping the floor and singing *Lazy River.*

He pushed the button for *down*. As he waited for the elevator to arrive, he kept glancing back toward Room 1566. A nurse went in, and then came out again. He felt distinctly unnerved. He was sure that Susan had been only inches behind his back.

"*You're not going to die,*" he had assured her. But what had *she* said, in reply?

"*I'm not going to live, either.*"

What the hell did she mean by that? Either you live, or you die. You can't do both.

The elevator pinged and the doors opened up. A man was standing inside, his head wrapped up in white bandages, so that his eyes and his mouth were nothing but slits, like a mummy. Maybe you *can* do both. Frank took a deep breath and stepped inside.

When he stepped out of the elevator on the ground floor the emergency department was already in chaos. He found Dean helping a young woman in a lime-green summer dress who was vomiting blood all over the gurney and all over the floor.

"Oh God," she kept mumbling. "Oh God, oh God." Then her throat constricted and another gush of blood came up. Dean was doing his best to catch it all in a pressed-cardboard kidney-bowl, but there were pints of it. He was unshaven and sweaty and his hair stuck up like Stan Laurel's.

"You look like shit," Frank told him.

"You're about the tenth person to tell me that," said Dean.

"Are they going to give you some more help?"

"Oh, sure, they're bringing them in from all over. Kieran Kelly's come down from intensive care; and Bill Medovic's coming back from White Plains; and I'm supposed to be getting five more technicians and seven more nurses. But if it carries on like this I'm going to be swamped."

"Have you heard from The Death Troll?"

"Not yet. But Kieran said that if the casualty numbers go over fifty, he's going to declare an Emergency Code Red."

The young woman sat up and retched, but this time she brought up only a few spatters of blood. When Dean had wiped her mouth, Frank leaned over and said, "Miss—my name's Dr. Winter. Can you tell me *your* name?"

"Kathleen . . . Kathleen Williams. Oh God, I'm burning all over."

"You feel like your skin's on fire?"

"I'm *burning!* Help me!"

"We're going to do everything we can for you, Kathleen, I promise you. But I need to know whose blood you've been drinking."

"What?" she said, staring at him in horror.

"*Frank*—" Dean protested. "You can't ask her a question like that!"

"You drank somebody's blood, Kathleen," Frank persisted. "You have to tell me whose blood it was."

"I didn't drink anybody's blood. I'm *sick*, that's all."

"Listen," said Frank, "I know what you did. Do you hear me? *I know what you did.* This isn't your own blood, is it?"

"Leave me alone! I'm hurting! I can't bear it! I'm hurting so bad!"

"You'll be hurting even more if we refuse to give you treatment."

"You can't do that! I'm burning up! Doctor! Help me! I'm burning up!"

"Frank, for God's sake!" hissed Dean, looking around to make sure that there weren't any witnesses. "We could be sued from here to next Hanukkah."

But Frank stayed where he was, and when a nurse came to push the gurney away he said, "*No.* Wait. Kathleen has something she wants to tell us."

The young woman opened her mouth, and closed it again, and then she moaned and said, "All right. I *did* drink their blood."

"Whose blood? Come on, Kathleen. You have to tell me."

The young woman's eyes suddenly overflowed with tears, and her mouth was pulled turned downward by grief. "My children. My two little children. I couldn't stop myself."

"Holy mother of hamsters," said Dean, pushing his fingers through his mussed-up hair.

"What did you do?" Frank pressed her.

"I can't tell you! It wasn't me! I would never hurt them, ever!"

"Tell me what you did, Kathleen. It's the only way we can help you."

"I was—I was burning up all morning. I couldn't stand it. I felt like my skin was shriveling up, it was so hot! I kept thinking about their little hearts beating, and all that blood in their bodies. I kept thinking that it would cool me down."

Dean covered his face with both hands, but Frank persisted. "How did it happen, Kathleen? Come on—if you don't tell me, you'll have to tell the police."

"Oh God, I was making their lunch. Cutting sandwiches for them. But all the time I felt like I was on fire. I pulled all the blinds down, to keep the sunshine out, but I was still burning. Then Marty came into the kitchen and asked me why it was so dark. I looked at him and I knew what I had to do. I couldn't stop myself."

"How old is Marty?"

"Eleven . . . and Melissa, she's nine. When I was finished with Marty, I went through to my bedroom. She was sitting in front of my dressing-table mirror, playing with my lipstick. She saw me in the mirror and she thought I was angry with her but I wasn't angry with her. I was still burning up and I needed her blood."

"So you cut her throat?"

The young woman swallowed, and nodded. "I'm going to go to hell for this, aren't I?"

"Hell?" said Frank. Then, under his breath, "You'll be lucky if they let you in."

Dean led Frank out into the corridor.

"They're murderers, aren't they? All of these people."

Frank said, "Yes. It looks like it."

"God almighty. We've got more than thirty of them now, and they're still coming in."

"We can't judge them, Dean. That's for the courts to decide, not us."

"That's if they survive. Some of the early ones are in a pretty bad way."

"Let me take a look."

Dean led him across to the pediatric crisis ward, which he had set aside for hemorrhage cases only. A large red-lettered notice warned QUARANTINE AREA KEEP OUT.

"Just a precaution," Dean told him. "There's no evidence at all that this is contagious, or infectious, or that it's caused by any kind of toxin."

Inside the ward, all the blinds had been drawn down tight, so that the physician assistants and emergency nurses were working in twilight, like pale green ghosts. Frank walked up and down the aisle, stopping to examine each patient in turn. Some of them lay silent and white-faced, as if they were sleeping, or already dead; but some of the newer admissions were crying and screaming and retching and begging for mercy. The stench of partially digested blood was so thick and fetid that Frank could taste it in his mouth.

All the time the sirens kept whooping, as more people were brought in from the sweltering city outside, and the plastic doors kept flapping open, and gurneys rattled along the corridors, and paramedics shouted for assistance.

Frank and Dean went back into the emergency room and tugged off their masks. "Anything new from Willy?"

asked Frank. The vinyl-tiled floor was sticky with blood, so that the soles of his shoes made a scrunching sound.

"He's been testing for everything you can think of, from sarin to ricin to mustard gas. He's testing for anthrax, cholera, chicken flu, three kinds of plague and you name it. Nothing so far, but he hasn't given up, and he's still screening samples from every patient we bring in."

"How about the enzyme?"

"Nothing conclusive, not yet, but it's a metallozyme, apparently, with a silver component. He has some idea that it might be related to the aging process, but he'll have to do some more work on it."

As he reached the doors, Dr. Pellman came in, accompanied by his deputy medical director, Ingrid Kurtz, both of them looking grim-faced.

"The mayor's declared a state of emergency," said Dr. Pellman. "Up until fifteen minutes ago, there were three hundred seventy reported cases of people vomiting blood, citywide, and so far the police have found ninety-three exsanguinated bodies."

"God," said Frank. "This is beginning to sound like *Dawn of the Dead.*"

Dr. Pellman said, "You can forget about the legal niceties, Dr. Winter. We urgently need to find out what's wrong with these people. We need to know what they have in common . . . what they've eaten, where they've been, who they've had any kind of contact with. We need to pinpoint where each of them lived, and where they were when they started to show signs of sickness. The CDC is sending us two senior advisers, and I've also been talking to Medcom. You call in as many of your own staff as you need. All leave is canceled until we've got this situation under control."

"Yes, sir."

"And, Dr. Garrett—"

"Yes, sir?"

"As soon as you can, take a couple of hours off. Take a shower and get yourself something to eat. You look like shit."

As Frank returned to the eleventh floor, he could see that the scale of the panic was rising by the minute. Every time the elevator doors opened, more and more people pushed their way in. Crowds of non-critical patients were being moved in wheelchairs to the convalescent wards, anxiously clutching their belongings on their knees, while technicians and nurses hurried along the corridors, and telephones warbled urgently at every nurses' station. In the space of only a few minutes, the hospital had turned into a noisy, crowded, chillingly air-conditioned Babel.

He was only halfway along the corridor to room 1566 when his beeper went. He took it out of his pocket and looked at it, and then broke into a run. He arrived in the doorway at the same time one of the emergency technicians was coming out, and they almost collided.

"What's happened?" he demanded.

"She's asystolic. No warning."

Frank peered past the technician into the darkened room. Three nurses were gathered around the bed, and Susan Fireman's nightgown had been dragged up to expose her sparrow-like chest. One of the nurses was already holding up the bright yellow defibrillator paddles, and shouting *"Clear!"* But for some reason Frank knew for certain that Susan Fireman's soul had already left her body.

He stepped into the room. He felt as if he were walking in slow motion, while the crash team was rushing around the bed in a speeded-up frenzy of activity. They shocked her, and shocked her, and shocked her again. But her face remained deathly white, and her skinny wrists flopped like a doll's, and she showed no signs at all that they might be able to save her.

He waited in the shadows with his hand pressed over his mouth. There was nothing else he could do. In the end, the emergency nurse backed away from the bed and returned the paddles to the crash cart. "Sorry, folks. We've lost her."

Frank stepped forward and stood at the end of the bed. "Sorry, Dr. Winter," said the nurse. "We did everything we could."

"Her heart just stopped," said another nurse, popping his fingers. "One second all her stats were looking pretty steady. The next second, snap, flatline."

Frank looked down at Susan Fireman and he was surprised to feel so upset. Usually, when his patients died, he felt nothing more than professional regret that he hadn't been able to give them longer to live. But only a few hours ago, Susan Fireman had been contorting herself outside Macy's, and climbing a ladder that wasn't there, and he hadn't had the chance to ask her what she was doing, and what she was trying to say, and he realized now that he had really wanted to know.

In spite of her waxy pallor, however, Susan Fireman looked completely composed, and he could almost have sworn that she was smiling to herself.

"Do we know how to get in touch with her family?" asked one of the nurses.

"Yes," said Frank. "You'd better go. You'll be needed in the emergency room, all of you."

The nurses packed away their equipment and unfastened her drips and at last he was left alone with her. He studied her face under the lamplight and thought, *I wonder what really happened to you, Susan Fireman?* It occurred to him that he was probably going to find out, within the next few hours, if more and more people died of the same condition. But whatever had taken her, she had been a strikingly attractive young girl, and this was a very sordid ending to a very short life.

"When you were climbing that ladder," he asked her,

"where were you going? Where did you think that was going to take you to?"

Without warning, *she opened her eyes.* Those pale, ice-blue eyes, and stared at him.

6

BLOOD LUST

"What's *in* there?" screamed Ted Busch. "For Christ's sake, dude, what is it?"

I cautiously pushed open my bedroom door. Inside, it was very gloomy, because I hadn't had time to fix up any proper drapes, and the window was covered with a droopy purple bedspread, fastened with cup-hooks. But there was nothing and nobody there. No whispering hordes, no locusts, no dark stretched-out figures. Only my lonely unmade bed with the crimson quilt and the stained black satin sheets, and the paint-spattered kitchen chair that served as my bedside table. Only the tattered poster of a magic design by J.F.C. Fuller, a friend of Aleister Crowley's, the master of the black arts—all planets and wavy lines and naked women with their hair on fire. And most of my clothes, of course: crumpled, dirty, and heaped on top of my suitcase.

However, I was sure that I could *smell* something. Usually my bedroom smelled of stale Indian spices and damp plaster, with a strong note of Eternity aftershave. But I could detect something else—a very sharp, burned aroma, like a recently lit match—and the smell of *disturbed air*. I sniffed, and sniffed again. There was a curious feeling that somebody had been here, and had only just left.

I peered around the door. There was nothing there, either, except for my shiny new golf clubs and my stiff unworn Burberry trench coat—souvenirs, both of them, of my evaporated life with Karen. I may have lost my dignity, but by God I had kept my putters.

"Anything?" asked Ted, keeping his distance.

"Nothing," I told him. "Whoever it was—*whatever* it was—it came and then it went."

"I'm sorry, dude," said Ted. "I was too scared, honest. I could feel how evil it was. I could *feel* it. It was like when I was a kid, and there was my He-Man bathrobe hanging on the back of my bedroom door, and I just *knew* that it was alive, and as soon as my mom went downstairs it was going to jump on me."

"No, Ted," I said, trying to be patient. "It wasn't like that. Your He-Man robe wasn't alive and it didn't jump on you, did it? Your *fear* of your robe—that was real enough, I'll grant you. Me—I used to be scared of the wood grain in my closet door. It looked like a wolf, and I couldn't look at it, in case it tore my throat out, but of course it never did."

Ted said, "The thing that was here—what the hell was it?"

"The thing that was here *was* alive. We missed seeing it, that's all."

"I could feel so much *evil*," said Ted. "I could feel my skin creeping. And I could *smell* it, you know. It smelled like *bleaugghh*."

I lifted off my gilded skullcap and ran my hand through my hair. I was seriously worried. Whatever that dark stretched-out figure had been, it appeared to have deeply malevolent intentions, at least as far as Ted was concerned. That meant that I was faced with a very uncomfortable choice. Either I could sell Ted a handful of herbs from the

Magic Pantry and send him on his way (which, I have to admit, was my immediate inclination); or else I could try to find out what this thing actually was, and why it was giving him nightmares, and whether I could send it back to whatever cobwebby corner of the spirit world it had come from.

So far, however, in my short but rackety life, my experience of things with deeply malevolent intentions was that they resented being interfered with. Any attempt to get rid of them usually resulted in mayhem, and mass destruction, and finding yourself face-to-face with manifestations that forever afterward would have you screaming in your sleep.

I compromised. I went to the closet, unscrewed a yellow glass jar, and took out a bunch of of dried mugwort. "Look, Ted," I said, "you can have this for nothing."

Ted inspected the mugwort suspiciously. "What do I do? Smoke it?"

"I wouldn't if I were you. Tie it to the head of your bed, and it should protect you from bad dreams."

"It's a weed."

"Yes, but it's not any old weed. It's mugwort, which the Celts used to call witch-weed. Unlike any other plant, it leans to the north when it grows, which means that it's magnetic, and that it's highly responsive to supernatural messages. You never know . . . it might tell you why this— *thing*—keeps disturbing your sleep."

"Is that it?" Ted asked me. He looked seriously disappointed.

I put my arm around his shoulders. "I don't know what else I can do, Ted. I tried my darndest, but it was really up to you. I found out what was giving you nightmares, but if you didn't want to face it, what could I do?"

"Maybe we should ask your spirit guide to give us an action replay."

"I'm sorry, Ted, he won't."

"I'll be much more hyped up for it this time, I promise you." He took a deep breath that whistled in his nostril, and then another, and stood up ramrod-straight. But I shook my head, and continued to shake my head, and he gradually sagged.

"Ted," I told him, "Singing Rock is a Sioux medicine man and *very* proud. The Sioux get extremely huffy if you take them for granted, and Singing Rock gets huffier than most. Conjuring up that thing for us, that probably took him more effort than you and I can even imagine. But what did we do? We didn't even have the *cojones* to take a peek at it. You seriously think he's going to give us a repeat performance?"

I could almost hear Singing Rock saying, in that dry, sarcastic voice of his, "*You white men! What great warriors you are! If I killed a bear with my own hands, and laid it bleeding at your feet, you would scamper away screaming like frightened children!*"

Ted said, "Okay. I understand." He wiped his nose with the back of his hand. "Maybe we could have another shot tomorrow?"

"I don't think so, Ted. This wasn't like chickening out of a dental appointment."

"Would you at least *think* about it? I mean, I'll try this weed on my bed tonight, but if I have another nightmare—"

I could hear an ambulance siren whooping, two or three blocks away, and then another one, much closer, and then another. For a moment, I was reminded of September eleventh, and all the sirens that had whooped that morning, and that terrible gut-sinking feeling that the whole world had collapsed beneath our feet.

"Okay," I agreed. "I'll think about it. Sorry I couldn't help you any more." I showed Ted to the door. When he reached the landing he turned and looked back at me like a stray puppy, but when he saw that I wasn't going to change my mind he slowly trudged downstairs, one step at a time, and I could tell that he was trying to make me feel guilty with every step.

When I heard him slam the street door I went back into

the living room and tugged back the drapes, so that the sun could flood in. I took off my robe and hung it on the hat stand. Then I retrieved my can of Guinness, and eased myself back into the old green-velour armchair that I had rescued from the alley behind the Algonquin. It was well past its prime, even for an armchair. Its back was broken and its stuffing was bulging out. But who knows, Alexander Woollcott might have sat in it, and Alexander Woollcott was one of my heroes. "There is some cooperation between wild creatures," he once remarked. "The stork and the wolf work the same neighborhood."

I found the remote control under the cushion and switched on the television. I flicked from channel to channel, looking for the baseball, but almost every station was showing pictures of New York hospitals, and ambulances, and doctors. The running captions were reading "VAMPIRE" EPIDEMIC HITS MANHATTAN . . . SCORES SEIZED BY THIRST FOR BLOOD . . . OVER 100 DEAD . . . MAYOR BRANDISI DECLARES STATE OF EMERGENCY.

So that's why the sirens were whooping. I turned up the volume and I could hardly believe what I was hearing. A senior official from the Centers for Disease Control appeared on screen, a balding man who looked like the medical hologram from *Star Trek: Voyager*. He was saying, ". . . insatiable thirst for fresh human blood, which has led them to kill acquaintances, friends and even their own children. Once they have satisfied their thirst, however, they seem to be overtaken in a few hours by violent nausea and cardiac arrest. Seventeen of those afflicted have so far died, and I'm afraid that we're expecting many more."

A black woman reporter pushed a microphone into his face. "Sir—do you think you're getting any nearer to isolating the cause of this outbreak?"

The official shook his jowls. "All I can tell you at this time is that it bears absolutely no resemblance to any known disease, and in fact it may not even *be* a disease, in the generally accepted sense of the word. We have CDC and Medcom specialists working flat out to identify it, with the assistance of senior pathologists at every major hospital in New York."

"So what can the public do to protect themselves?"

"Our advice is for people to continue about their business as normal, but to watch closely for any signs in yourself or others of a burning sensation of the skin, or of hypersensitivity to sunlight, or of strong or unusual thirst."

I swallowed Guinness, and burped. In spite of the sirens outside, I was starting to think, *this has to be a put-on, surely?* An updated spoof like *The War of the Worlds.* Like, *vampires?* Oh, right.

But then the CDC official glanced down at his notes and said, "I am also told that a reliable early indicator of the so-called 'vampire' condition is nightmares. These frightening dreams usually start three or four days before the crisis, and are associated with a feeling of claustrophobia, or being shut in a box, as well as a strong sensation of motion sickness, as if the sufferer were on board a ship."

I slowly sat up. I heard another ambulance, speeding up Sixth Avenue; and then another; and another. A handheld news camera showed a young woman on her knees on the sidewalk outside FAO Schwarz, vomiting blood. Then they showed a man being rushed through the doors of the Sisters of Jerusalem hospital, his clothes smothered in scarlet, like the victim of a bomb blast.

Jesus, I thought. *Nightmares.* That was exactly what Ted had been suffering from—and the same kind of nightmares, too. Shut up in a casket, on an oceangoing ship. Then I thought: What if this *was* an infectious disease? Ted had been standing only two feet away from me, and I had been *breathing the same air.* I had shaken hands with him, and the chances were that microscopic droplets of saliva had sprayed out of his mouth when he had talked to me.

I hurried through to my bathroom, soaked my facecloth

in scalding water, then squeezed it out and pressed it over my face. I shouted out *ahh!* when I did it, because it was so goddamned hot, but if there were any viruses on my skin, this would fix them. If *I* couldn't bear it, neither could they.

After a few moments, however, I thought: Just a minute, if my séance with Singing Rock had shown us anything at all, it had shown us that Ted's nightmares hadn't been caused by a virus at all, but by some malevolent spiritual presence. A presence that I had actually seen for myself, tall and dark and stretched-out, and sliding through my bedroom door. I peeled off the facecloth and stared at myself in the mottled mirror that hung over my basin. I looked hot. I looked very hot.

What the hell was I supposed to do now? Call Ted, and warn him that he was just about to turn into a bloodthirsty vampire? Call the CDC, and tell them that all of their experts were wasting their valuable time, because the "vampire" epidemic wasn't caused by a virus, but by some kind of spiritual manifestation?

I could imagine myself trying to explain it. "Like, I contacted this dead Sioux medicine man I used to know, and asked him to lure this malevolent spirit into my bedroom, which he did. Unfortunately my client was too chickenshit to open the door, so I never really got to see what the being looked like, not properly. So I gave my client some mugwort and sent him home."

Bellevue? My feet wouldn't touch the ground.

I sat for almost an hour in front of the TV, watching as the epidemic grew steadily worse. Each successive newsflash showed more and more people regurgitating blood and more and more bodybags being wheeled away on coroners' gurneys, and with every passing minute I felt increasingly guilty and frustrated. By 3:39 P.M. the death toll had risen to 119 so-called vampires and 147 homicide victims.

I called Karen, to make sure that she and Lucy were

okay. All I got was her answering service, and she didn't respond to her cellphone number, so I called Herman, the doorman. "Mrs. Erskine left about an hour ago," he told me. "She took Lucy to visit her grandmother in Albany." Karen's mother wasn't answering, either, but I left a message that when Karen and Lucy reached Albany, they should stay there until this epidemic was over. That would be one less problem for me to fret about.

I was desperate to tell somebody in authority about Ted's nightmares and Singing Rock and the tall stretched-out figure that had walked through my bedroom door, but I knew exactly what would happen if I tried. At best, they would dismiss me as a publicity-seeking charlatan. They had only to look up my court record. In October of 1978 I was convicted of dishonestly acquiring a five-year-old Chevy Malibu by persuading an elderly lady from Englewood Cliffs that I could only communicate with her recently dead husband through his car stereo. Not only was this a lie, the car turned out to be a total lemon, so that didn't say much for my psychic abilities, either.

That's it, I thought. I need a psychic to speak on my behalf—a *believable* psychic. Somebody respectable, somebody with *gravitas*—somebody who's going to be taken seriously.

I knew two psychics like that: Leon Borderman, from the New York Institute of Psychic Research, who claimed to have regular conversations with Benjamin Franklin—although I doubted if he would even deign to talk to me, the patronizing old gasbag. Then of course there was Amelia Carlsson, née Crusoe—but I was pretty sure that Amelia had probably had enough of me for one lifetime. I'm not saying that she didn't *like* me any more, but I always seemed to turn up on her doorstep with a motley entourage of Grief, and Complications, and all kinds of Shadowy Terrors from God Alone Knew Where, even when I didn't intend to.

Not long after, however, the TV news showed a re-spectable middle-aged woman on her hands and knees, vomiting blood all over the floor of Bloomingdale's shoe department. That's when I thought *wotthehell wotthehell* I have to try this even if Amelia won't talk to me. I picked up the phone and punched out Amelia's number.

As it rang, I rehearsed what I was going to say. *Amelia, don't put the phone down, it's Harry. Amelia, I desperately need your help. New York needs your help. Amelia, I don't know how to tell you this, but—*

The phone rang and rang, and I was beginning to think that I would have to leave another message. But then a man with a Scandinavian-sounding accent picked up and said, crossly, "Bertil Carlsson."

"Oh, hi! You must be *Mister* Carlsson."

"That's correct. Bertil Carlsson. Who's calling?"

"This is Harry Erskine." No answer. "Harry . . . Erskine?"

Still no answer. I was just about to repeat myself, when Bertil Carlsson said, "Well?"

"Ah—I used to be a friend of your wife, Mr. Carlsson. I'm *still* a friend of your wife, I hope. We didn't have a falling-out or anything, it's just that we haven't touched base in quite a while. Quite a few years, as a matter of fact. Well, two, anyhow, maybe three."

"I know who you are, Mr. Erskine. My wife has men-tioned your name."

"Oh, right! Glowingly, I hope."

"Glowingly? No."

"Right, well she wouldn't, I don't suppose. Not that there was anything—I mean the last time we saw each other, it was all quite amicable."

"What do you want, Mr. Erskine?"

"Have you been watching the news? This epidemic thing?"

"Yes, we're watching it now. Or trying to."

"So Amelia's there, with you?"

Another long pause. Then, "I don't think I want you to talk to her, Mr. Erskine. Perhaps she may not have told me about everything that you and she were involved in, but I would rather that she didn't get involved with you again." He pronounced it "inwolwed," which made me wonder how he would say "Volvo."

"Listen, Mr. Carlsson, I can understand how you feel. I really can. If I were you, I wouldn't my wife to be inwolwed with me, either. But you've seen this epidemic on the news. I really think I know what's causing it, and I think I could save a great many people's lives."

"Well, Mr. Erskine, I'm certainly not stopping you."

"I know. Of course you're not. But my problem is that I have to find somebody in authority who's prepared to believe me, and for one reason or another people in authority tend not to believe me."

"I can't for the life of me think why."

"Mr. Carlsson, I wouldn't have dreamed of calling Amelia if I'd been able to think of any other way. But you've seen how many people are dropping dead, and you've seen how many people have been murdered. I mean, we're talking *hundreds*, and where's it going to stop? I mean— supposing *you* catch it? Supposing Amelia catches it?"

"Mr. Erskine—"

"Please, Mr. Carlsson, call me Harry. And please don't think that I would let anything happen to Amelia, ever. You're the luckiest man on the planet, being married to her. But I need to talk to her, at the very least, even if she tells me to take a running jump."

At that moment, an extension phone was picked up.

"Harry?"

I felt as if a punching bag had swung back and hit me square in the chest. "*Amelia.*"

"What's happening, Harry?"

For a moment, I couldn't speak. My throat tightened up, and I couldn't do anything but open and close my mouth like a recently caught codfish. Amelia and I had never been lovers, except in my dreams, but somehow I had always felt that our destinies were tangled together. I had made the wrong choice, all those years ago, like I always make the wrong choice, and it was almost unbearable, talking to the person I could have shared my life with, if I had only been humbler, and kinder, and less of a smart-ass, and seen her for what she really was.

"I didn't really *want* to call you," I garbled. "No—that came out wrong. I didn't want to involve you in anything, that's what I meant. I should have called you years ago, shouldn't I? But—you know—there was always a reason not to."

"I saw your ad in the *Village Voice*," she said. "That's how I knew you were still alive. Are you and Karen still together?"

"Not exactly, no. I think it was a case of I say potatoes and you say *pommes dauphinoise*."

"That's a pity. I always thought you and Karen were so good together."

"Karen was always good with me. I guess I was always better on my own."

"I'm sorry, all the same. By the way, I got your message. That young kid came round to see you, didn't he? The one with the nightmares?"

"Ted Busch like in Anheuser. Oh, yes, young Ted came to see me. That's the whole reason I'm calling you."

"Harry, don't even ask. I don't do that stuff anymore."

"I know. Ted told me. The thing is, though—" and I got this in quick, before she could stop me "—I read his fortune with the *Jeu Noir*, right, and his Predictor Card was The Water Woman."

"Harry! I don't want to know that! I really don't!"

"But The Water Woman, Amelia" I persisted. "That's a pretty goddamned scary prediction, wouldn't you say?"

Amelia hesitated, and then she had to admit, "Yes. It's a pretty goddamned scary prediction."

"It's worse than that, though. Ted persuaded me to call up Singing Rock."

"I'm sorry, was that a problem? That was my idea. I thought maybe Singing Rock could help you to discover what was wrong."

At that moment, I heard the other phone being cradled, very discreetly. Bertil Carlsson obviously didn't want to listen anymore. It's bad enough, hearing another man chatting to your wife, without hearing him chatting about things that you know nothing about. I sympathized, I really did, but I had to talk to Amelia. There was no other way.

"I asked Singing Rock to open up the doors, and to show me what was causing Ted's nightmares."

"And did he?"

"Oh, yes. I saw it with my own eyes, and it was frightening, believe me. It was tall and it was dark and it was *stretched out*, you know, like somebody's shadow when the sun gets low. It went right through my bedroom door without opening it, but the problem was that Ted was too scared to see what it was. By the time I opened the bedroom door, it was gone. Vanished. *Disparu*."

"I'm sorry, Harry, but I don't see how I can help you."

"Amelia—did Ted tell you what *kind* of nightmares he's been having?"

"No, he didn't. Only that he was having them night after night, and he was frightened to go to sleep."

"You've been watching the news, right? Did you hear the guy from the CDC, talking about this epidemic? Before they get this terrible thirst for drinking human blood, people start having nightmares. They keep dreaming that they're shut up in a coffin, or a box, and that they're being tossed around in a ship. They *all* dream it, all of them! And Ted was dreaming it, too—that exact same scenario. Coffin, ship, the very same thing. So what does *that* tell you?"

Amelia hesitated for a moment, and then she said, "People *can* have similar nightmares, Harry, especially if they're suffering from a common illness. I was reading about people with leprosy . . . they often have nightmares that their flesh is melting, like butter. And people with a high fever can see cockroaches crawling all over them."

"Okay, sure . . . I'm sure that's true, so far as it goes. But we're talking about hundreds of people here, aren't we? And what Singing Rock summoned up, that wasn't a virus, or any kind of disease. That was a *thing*. A person, or a presence, I don't know how the hell I'd describe it."

"So what you're trying to say is, this *thing* is responsible for everybody else's nightmares, too—and this whole epidemic?"

"You got it. This isn't a disease, this is a war. This is some kind of malevolent spirit, taking over people's minds, and then their bodies. And who the hell knows where it's going to stop? Today, New York City. Tomorrow, New York State. The day after, the whole eastern seaboard."

"Harry, for God's sake! You're letting your imagination run away with you! I'm sure that isn't going to happen. Whatever it was that Singing Rock summoned up, that was probably one of Ted's phobias, nothing more. Some bogeyman from his childhood, who's suddenly surfaced out of his subconscious. That can happen when people suffer from stress."

"Amelia, you're beginning to sound like Karen's shrink. Bogeymen from your childhood don't give you the identical nightmare to three hundred other people. Bogeymen from your childhood don't make you want to cut your children's throats and drink their blood, straight out of their carotid arteries."

Amelia said, "Maybe they do and maybe they don't. But, like I say, I don't *do* this stuff any more."

"Because of you, or because of Bertie?"

"*Bertil*. Because of both of us. And because—and because—every time I hold a séance, it opens up coffins that ought to stay closed."

"Amelia . . . I honestly truly believe that this epidemic is being caused by some malevolent spirit—that same spirit that walked through my bedroom door."

"Harry, have you heard yourself? You sound like somebody in a Marvel comic."

"But I can *feel* it! I can feel it in the air! It's like an electric storm coming! You remember what it was like, just before Misquamacus came out . . . it was like dogs barking and cats creeping under the couch and your hair standing up on end! And this is the same!"

The other phone was picked up again. "Mr. Erskine, I don't want to be rude to you, but I would like you to cut this conversation short. You are causing my wife some distress."

"Mr. Carlsson . . . Bertie . . . please, I wouldn't upset Amelia for the world. But I have to see her. I have to discuss this with her. We could be talking about the end of human civilization as we know it."

I could hear Bertil Carlsson take a very deep breath. "Mr. Erskine, everything that my wife ever said about you is true. You are completely and absolutely doolally."

7

BLOOD LINE

Even though he knew she was dead, it was hard for Frank to believe that Susan Fireman wasn't staring at him, and that she wasn't about to speak to him. He felt as if his skin were shrinking, and it took all of his strength not to turn around and hurry out of the room.

He slowly approached the bed and bent forward to examine her—so closely that he could have felt her breath on his face, if she were still alive. But, no, she wasn't breathing, and although her eyes were wide open, they were focused on nothing at all.

All the same, she still had that small, secretive smile, as if it amused her that she was dead, and found it funny that she had unnerved him so much.

"Susan?" he said, and he shook her shoulder just to make sure.

At that moment Dr. Gathering came in, carrying an untidy sheaf of medical records. "Erm . . . she can't hear you, Frank."

"No, George, I know."

"Sister Perpetua told me she'd shuffled off the mortal coil. I thought you'd be here."

"Yes," said Frank. He tried to sound efficient, and practical, even though his heart was still hammering. "We're going to need a full postmortem, and we're going to need it pronto. Especially the bloods."

George dropped some of his papers onto the floor and bent down to pick them up. "It's Dante's Inferno down in the ER."

"I was down there. It looks as if it's going to get worse."

"The Death Troll has a theory that this could be a Western variant of dengue hemorrhagic fever."

"Oh, does he? Well—I suppose he has to find some way of justifying that all-expenses-paid trip to Bangkok."

George peered over at Susan Fireman. "To be fair, this does seem to exhibit several similarities to DHF. It starts with a minor respiratory infection, doesn't it, and that could account for the nightmares. Then there's a period of extreme sensitivity to bright light, followed by total collapse, and a catastrophic drop in blood pressure."

"Sure. But so far as I'm aware, people who get DHF don't feel an unquenchable thirst for other people's blood, and they don't go cutting their children's throats to get it."

"True—but The Death Troll was careful to say '*variant*.' "

"Well, he would. He's a politician, not a doctor."

Frank turned back to Susan Fireman. He felt reluctant to leave her, because he knew that he would never see her again—not in one piece, anyhow. The pathologists would cut open her breastbone with surgical shears, and rummage through her organs; and then they would open up the top of her skull with an oscillating autopsy saw, and lift out her brain.

George said, "The reason I came up here, the Death Troll says that you should take the rest of the day off and get some rest. He'd like you back here at 2 A.M., to help out the night shift."

"I'm fine, George. I'd rather stay here."

"Frank—you won't be any good to anybody if you're to-tally bushed, you know that. Go home, relax. We'll call you if there's a crisis."

"This isn't a crisis?"

"Not yet. This is only your ordinary, everyday, garden-variety disaster."

Frank reluctantly left the Sisters of Jerusalem and walked home. Midtown, the streets were still screaming with sirens, and medical helicopters were clattering overhead and people were hurrying in every direction as if the end of the world was coming.

It started to rain, and the rain was so warm that it felt like blood. He suddenly realized how tired he was, and how unsettled. There was nothing worse than having to deal with patients who couldn't be saved, no matter how hard he tried to keep them alive. He found himself praying that he wouldn't come across somebody throwing up blood in a doorway, because he would have to stop and take him back to the emergency room. George had been right: He badly needed to rest, and to think, and to get himself ready for a very arduous night.

He heard a woman screaming, somewhere on the next block, and a man shouting, "*Get away from me! Get away from me!*" Then he heard breaking glass, and two loud bangs that could have been gunfire. He had seen disaster movies in which the social fabric had torn apart, almost immediately, but he had never believed that it would really happen, not until now.

Sixth and Fifth avenues were both blocked off by police barricades, so it took him nearly twenty minutes to reach the tree-lined street in Murray Hill where he lived, and by the time he got there his pants were chafing with sweat and his shirt was clinging to his back. It was almost 5:00 now, 91 degrees, with 87 percent humidity. The afternoon had turned a dull bronze color, as if it were going to thunder.

He climbed the white stone steps to his front door. Halfway up, he caught sight of a middle-aged man kneeling by the mailbox on the corner of the street. He stopped, and took off his sunglasses so that he could see better. The man's face was crudely smeared with bright blue paint, so that it looked like an African tribal mask, and his T-shirt had ridden up under his arms so that his big white belly hung down. He was gripping one leg of the mailbox with both hands, as if he were terrified that he was going to fly off the face of the earth. As Frank watched him, his belly convulsed, and convulsed again, and a fountain of dark ruby vomit gushed out of his mouth and splattered onto the sidewalk. Frank took out his cell phone and punched out 911, but it beeped and beeped and nobody answered. He hesitated. He was a doctor. It was his moral duty to go to the man's assistance. But he knew there was absolutely nothing he could do to help him, and the man had probably murdered two or three people to drink so much blood. The man slowly turned his head toward him, and he looked utterly desolate. Frank hesitated a moment longer, but then he put his sunglasses back on, climbed up the last three steps, and opened up his front door. He went through and closed it behind him. Click.

The apartment building was stuffy and hushed and dimly lit. It was like living in an Edward Hopper painting. There were dusty silk lilies in a tall green vase beside the umbrella stand, and a tall rectangular mirror in which one only seemed to be able to see half of oneself, or the back of somebody disappearing through a doorway. Somewhere up at the top of the building, someone was vacuum-cleaning; and as he climbed up to his second-story apartment, Frank heard sad, reflective piano music, Debussy maybe, or Satie.

As he was about to unlock his apartment door, his key raised, he thought about the blue-faced man in the street.

He was tempted to go back. After all, if the man was suffering from the same condition that had killed Susan Fireman, he hadn't *wanted* to murder anybody: He had been driven to do it by his raging thirst for human blood. But the same could be said of crackheads who murdered innocent people to feed their addiction, or drunk drivers who knocked down schoolchildren. Frank had told Susan Fireman that he didn't judge his patients, but he had been lying. He had nothing but contempt for people who injured themselves or others through willful stupidity, or lack of self-control. Once he had sat all night by the bedside of a twenty-seven-year-old woman who had been so drunk that she had swallowed concentrated drain-cleaner, and he had never been able to find it in his heart to forgive her for what she had done to herself.

He hadn't forgiven Susan Fireman either, for murdering her friends instead of trying to get medical help. All the same, he regretted that she was dead. For some reason, he felt that she had the answer to something that he needed to understand.

His apartment was high-ceilinged and austere, with dark brown carpets and cream-colored walls and a few abstract paintings in varying shades of brown and cream. The furniture was Italian, mahogany-colored leather, very square and very expensive. In one corner there was a Bang & Olufsen CD player. In the opposite corner stood a 1920s-style cabinet which contained bottles of liquor and Jazz Age cocktail glasses.

Frank was thirty-seven in January and he was still married, although he and Christina had already talked about divorce. The starkness of this apartment was in direct contrast to their house in Darien, Connecticut, which was crammed with antique colonial furniture and embroidered cushions and china dogs. Frank had felt that

Christina was cluttering up his head with so many knick-knacks and frills that there wasn't any space left for serious thinking. One day he had gone to the Sisters of Jerusalem and stayed late in gastro-entorology and never returned home. Even today, seven months later, he couldn't really explain why, not to anybody else. He spent long evenings alone, reading; or listening to music; or staring at the wall and doing nothing at all.

Maybe, like many doctors, he had secretly begun to wonder what he was doing, saving lives that were nothing but a waste of everybody's time, including the people who were living them. He stripped off his chilly, sweat-soaked clothes and climbed into his black glass shower-cubicle with the volcanic stone base. As he soaped himself, he could see half of his face in the circular shaving mirror next to the black marble basin, as if he were being spied on from a parallel existence. He toweled himself with a dark brown towel and rubbed his chest with Dolce & Gabbana body lotion.

Afterward, with a fresh towel wrapped around his waist, he went into the stainless-steel kitchen and took a bottle of Perrier water out of the icebox. He would have preferred a Heineken, but he was going to need all of his concentration when he went back to the Sisters of Jerusalem in the early hours of the morning. He supposed he ought to eat something, even if it was only a cheese sandwich, but he didn't feel hungry. He kept thinking about Susan Fireman, staring at him with those china-blue eyes, and the blue-faced man vomiting blood in the street outside.

He lay back on his king-size bed. In the corner of his bedroom was the only antique in the whole apartment: an oval cheval-mirror that was reputed to have belonged to Ulysses S. Grant, and which Grant had taken with him on his campaign in Chattanooga. Frank didn't particularly like it, but it was worth more than a quarter of a million dollars, and he didn't want Christina to get her hands on it.

He switched on the wall-mounted plasma-screen television. Almost every channel was still running minute-by-minute news of the "vampire epidemic." Cases had been reported as far uptown as 125th Street, and Mayor Brandisi had ordered police checkpoints set up on all bridges and tunnels, although he had to admit that he didn't really know what they were supposed to be looking for, apart from people who appeared to be sick, or who had covered themselves with sunblock.

So far, more than two hundred victims had been found with their throats cut, and the mayor estimated that there could be "twice—maybe three times—more."

Frank switched off the television and lay back on his dark brown sheets. His apartment was soundproofed, but he could still hear sirens echoing and the dull thumping of helicopters. He wondered what it would be like if he woke up to find that he was the only person in Manhattan left alive. He imagined himself wandering from street to echoing street, past abandoned taxis and windblown newspapers.

He fell asleep. When he was an intern he had trained himself to sleep whenever he had the chance, and he could sleep deeply and dreamlessly and wake up exactly when he knew that he would be called for, to the second.

Outside his bedroom window, the howling of sirens went on, like wolves. Daylight disappeared early, without any sunset, and by 9:00 it was dark. He carried on sleeping, lying on his back, motionless, except for the slightly curled fingers of his left hand, which occasionally twitched.

A few minutes after 11:30, there was a creaking noise at his window. It didn't penetrate his sleep, even when it was followed by a sharp click, and then the sticky sound of rubber seals being parted as his window was opened. A warm surge of air swelled into the room, smelling of gasoline fumes, and hot concrete, and steam.

He thought he felt somebody stroke his forehead, and play with his hair. He snorted, and irritably shook his head. He didn't want to wake up yet and he didn't want to dream. He never allowed himself to dream. In dreams people told you critically important things that you couldn't understand, and you formed attachments to people who didn't exist.

"*Frank*," said a soft voice.

He snorted again, but still refused to wake up.

"Frank, it's me."

He turned over, tugging at the sheet.

"Frank, it's no use pretending. I know you can hear me."

He licked his lips, which felt very dry. Then he gradually opened his eyes. Someone was sitting on the bed, right next to him. A woman, wearing something pale. The light from the hallway was shining behind her head, so that he couldn't clearly see her face. He lifted one arm to shield his eyes and said, "Christina?"

"I thought you were going to sleep forever."

"What the hell are you doing here?" He tried to sit up, but the woman pressed a cold hand flat against his chest, and pushed him firmly back down again.

"Christina—there's a full-scale medical emergency, you shouldn't have come to the city."

"But I'm not Christina, whoever Christina is."

Frank reached across and switched on his square bedside lamp. "Oh, God," he said, when he saw who the woman was. "Oh, God, it can't be."

Susan Fireman reached out and took hold of his hand. Her eyes still seemed unfocused, and her face was still pallid, but she was smiling at him, and there was no doubt that she was alive.

"I thought you were dead," said Frank, in a voice that sounded like somebody else's. "You died, didn't you? Your heart stopped."

"I thought you would have known about death, being a doctor."

"What are you talking about?"

"Death is for people who were born to die. Not for people like me."

Frank took hold of her wrist, lifted her arm away and sat up straight. Susan Fireman continued to smile at him, her expression so beatific that it almost looked as if she were mad, or an angel, or a nun who had experienced a divine revelation.

"*Frank*," she admonished him. "You mustn't take death so *literally*."

"I'm dreaming," he said. He slapped himself, hard, across the face. "Shit. I'm not dreaming. Maybe I'm dreaming that I'm dreaming."

Susan Fireman touched his cheek with her fingertips, and they were very cold. "I know that you liked me. I know that you found me attractive. I saw how sad you were when you thought that I was dead."

"For Christ's sake, you *are* dead!" Frank rolled across the bed, away from her, and stood up. "I was there when you died. They tried to resuscitate you but they couldn't. I'm dreaming this; or hallucinating. Maybe I've contracted your infection. Maybe this is one of those nightmares."

"Frank, I thought that you *liked* me."

"Like you? How can I like you? You're dead, and it's absolutely impossible that you're here. Logically, medically, it's impossible."

Susan Fireman stood up, too, and walked around the bed. She moved with an extraordinary jerking motion, as if she were in a film, and some of the frames were missing. She raised both arms as if she wanted him to embrace her. "I'm here, Frank, and that's the only logic that means anything."

"How did you get in?" he said, and almost as he said it, he caught sight of the bedroom window, tilted ajar.

"I can get in anywhere. The pale ones always can."

Frank still thought that he was dreaming. Susan Fireman had denied any knowledge of the pale ones, hadn't she?

"I'm going to wake up," he told her. "On the count of three, I'm going to wake up, and you, my dear, will no longer be here. One, two, *three!*"

"We could be so good together, Frank. *You* could be a pale one, too."

He closed his eyes tight, waited, and then opened them again. But Susan Fireman was still standing in front of him.

"If I can't make you disappear, I want you to go. However you managed to get in here, I want you to leave the same way."

"But Frank . . . don't you want to know what happened to me? Don't you want to find out why all of these people seem to be sick?"

"What are you talking about?"

"This epidemic—all of these people killing their friends and their loved ones and drinking their blood."

"You know why they're doing it?"

"Of course . . . it happened to *me*, didn't it?"

"Why didn't you say something before, when you were in the hospital?"

She reached her hand out again, but Frank stepped back and said, "Just don't touch me, okay?"

"Frank, don't be angry with me. If I had understood what was happening to me when I was in the hospital, I would have told you, I promise you. But I didn't, not then. I needed to pass through . . . to see it from the other side."

"So you can tell me now? This is crazy. I must be suffering from overwork."

She smiled at him slyly. "First things first," she told him. She crossed her arms and lifted off her nightdress, so that she was naked. Her breasts were tiny, but her nipples were hard and knurled. She had a gold piercing-ring shining between her hairless lips.

Frank said nothing, but watched her, warily, keeping his hands by his sides, and breathing very deeply. He had been caught before by a frustrated female patient who had accused him of molesting her, and it had led to months of legal argument and thousands of dollars of expense. He didn't want anything like that to happen again.

Susan Fireman sat down on the bed. "Come here," she said.

Frank shook his head. "No way. One, I don't believe that this is really happening. You're some kind of hallucination, and I don't even know why I'm talking to you. Two, if this *is* happening, and you *are* real, I don't want to have anything to do with you."

"Frank, this isn't a dream. You're awake."

"How can I be? Even if you didn't die, you couldn't have left the hospital and climbed in through my window. There's a sheer drop out there—seventy-five feet at least."

"Any wall can be climbed, Frank, if you have the ability to climb it."

She waited for a moment and then she stood up again. He backed away from her until he reached the bedroom wall, and he couldn't back away any further. She came up so close to him that he could feel how cold she was. It was almost as if she was draining the warmth right out of the surrounding air. "You're desperate to find out what happened to me, aren't you? And you *want* me, too. You know you do."

She reached down and took hold of his penis through his thin blue-striped cotton shorts. Although her fingers were so cold, he felt aroused, and he began to stiffen. She slowly rubbed him, up and down, digging her thumbnail into the ridge of his glans.

"You see?" she challenged him. "I was right on both counts. I'm real, and you want me."

Frank had never felt anything like this, ever. He was so frightened that he was shaking, but his fear seemed to excite him more than he had ever thought possible. What was happening to him was the stuff of insanity. Susan Fireman was dead, and so she couldn't have climbed into his window, and she couldn't be talking to him, and rubbing his penis. The madness of it made his erection stiffen harder and harder, until it hurt, and he didn't know whether to wrench himself away, or shout out for help, or allow Susan Fireman to go on rubbing him. He couldn't think straight. It seemed as if the only way to escape from this nightmare was to live through it, until he woke up.

Very softly, Susan Fireman said, "I didn't know it myself, not until now, but there have always been *other people*."

Frank couldn't speak. The coldness of her hand had made his penis feel numb, and the coldness was beginning to penetrate deep between his legs, as if somebody was pushing an icicle into his bowels.

"*Other people*, do you understand what I'm telling you? Different people, who live different lives. In darkness, and shadows, and closed boxes."

With one hand, she tugged down his shorts, and they dropped onto the floor, around his ankles. She gripped his bare erection even harder, and each downstroke was so powerful that he felt as if she were trying to rip his skin off.

"They've always been with us," she whispered. "They've always been hiding, and waiting. And now they're free!"

Still gripping his penis, she dragged him toward the bed. He felt totally helpless, as if he had to do whatever she told him to do. She lay back on the bed, and opened her legs wide. Even inside her, her flesh was pale, although it was shining with juice. "Come on, Frank," she urged him. "You know how much you want me."

He half-stumbled onto the bed. "Here," she coaxed him, and she pulled him nearer, and then she guided him into her. Inside, she felt chilly and slippery, like wet filleted fish. But even though the sensation of penetrating to her was so unpleasant, he couldn't find the strength or the focus to pull himself out of her. She gripped his buttocks and began to urge him rhythmically forward, smiling at him all the time. He couldn't believe how strong she was, for a girl so slight. She pulled him more and more forcefully, her nails digging into his skin. "You're *mine* now, Frank," she panted. "My protégé. One to another, like Chinese whispers, that's how it goes. It's a secret message."

"Guh-*god*," he stammered.

Triumphantly, gasping, she pulled him into her: pull—*pull*—pull—*pull*, and with every pull she arched her back, so that he could feel her bony pelvis tilting up to dig into his hips.

He began to shudder. He felt as if his testicles had frozen solid, into eggs of ice, and that they were gradually being crushed, with greater and greater force. The cold between his legs was almost unbearable, but at the same time he felt an overwhelming urge to climax, and he began to push forward—until she no longer needed to pull him, because he was forcing his penis into her as if he were trying to split her in half.

He grunted, and stammered, and snorted, and then he ejaculated. He felt as if thick jets of freezing slush were pumping out of him—one, two, three. When he had stopped quaking he knelt between Susan Fireman's legs with his head bowed, while Susan Fireman stroked his shoulders with her cold, trailing fingertips, and his back, and his hips, and cupped his shrunken scrotum in the palm of her hand.

Frank eventually fell sideways, and lay there, shivering, like a dog dragged out of a river. Susan Fireman turned to him so that their faces were only three or four inches apart, almost too close for Frank to focus.

"A secret message," she breathed.

"What secret message? I don't understand."

She kissed him, twice. "They brought it all the way from the home country, don't you see, hidden in their blood."

"Who did?" he croaked. "Who are you talking about?"

"*Strigoi*, they call themselves. The people who never die."

"*Strigoi?*"

"That's right. And now they've brought their message here, and we can help them to spread it. Me, and you, and anybody else we choose. It isn't a written message. Not a message that anybody can whisper." She sat up, and looked down at him. "In a few hours, my darling Frank, you will pass through, too, and understand everything."

He tried to lift his head, but she pushed him back down.

"There's one more thing," she said. "We have to make sure."

She climbed on top of him, with those thin, chilly limbs, and straddled him. Then she maneuvered herself upward until her shins were pressed hard against his shoulders and she was kneeling over his face. He looked up and he could see the pale bloodless waves of her lips, and her gold piercing-ring. She was brimming with semen, and two pearly drops were sliding down her thigh.

"What are you doing?" he said. He was beginning to wonder if this wasn't a nightmare after all, and that Susan Fireman, even if she was dead, was really here.

She looked down at him. Her eyes looked dreamy, but she was no longer smiling.

"We have to make *sure*, Frank," she repeated.

He tried to struggle himself up, but as he did so, a drop of cold semen fell onto his lips. He tried to spit it away, but Susan Fireman stuck out her finger and poked it into his mouth.

"There," she said, smiling again, and climbed off him.

He spat again, and sat up, and furiously wiped his mouth on one of the pillows. "What the hell did you do that for?"

She laughed, and pirouetted away from him, across the bedroom. She *flickered*, as she danced, like an old hand-cranked movie.

* * *

Frank hobbled into the bathroom, feeling as if he had been fighting in an alley, and lost. He switched on the light and stared at himself in the mirror and he had never seen himself looking so haggard. He twisted around so that he could see his buttocks, and they were criss-crossed with bloody lacerations. How could he be dreaming, when he felt so sore? His penis was reddened and his scrotum was smeared with blood where Susan Fireman had scratched him. How could he be dreaming, when he could twist the faucet and splash his face with warm water?

He pressed his face into a towel. *I can feel this, and I can't wake up. I'm going to have to accept that it's real. As crazy as it is, as scary as it is, it's* real.

He dropped the towel onto the counter and went back into the bedroom. "Okay," he said, "supposing this *isn't* a nightmare—why don't you tell me what the hell is going on?"

But there was no answer. Susan Fireman wasn't there.

"Susan?" he demanded. He stalked through to the living room but there was no sign of her. Not only that, the security chain was still fastened, so she couldn't have slipped out through the front door. He switched on the fluorescent light in the kitchen but that was empty, too. The only sound was the humming of the icebox.

He returned to the bedroom. "Susan? This is ridiculous!"

He opened the closet. She wasn't hiding in there. There was only an inch clearance under the bed, so she couldn't be hiding *there*, either.

He searched his apartment again. He even looked in the dirty clothes hamper. She was gone, and there was absolutely no trace that she had been here, except for the rumpled-up bed. He looked up at the window, but it was five feet up from the floor, and it was only open three or four inches. Even if she had managed to climb *in* that way, he very much doubted that she could have climbed out. There was nothing around that she could have stood on to reach it.

"I'm losing my mind," he told himself. He stared back at himself from the mirror in the hallway, and his reflection didn't even try to deny it.

8

BLOOD BATH

After Bertil hung up on me, I sat in my Alexander Woollcott chair for a while, drinking and thinking. Even though I had turned down the volume, the TV news channels were still filled with flickering images of people plastered in blood, and the numbers of dead and murdered were clocking up higher and higher, like the score on a pinball machine, with no sign of them slowing down.

If I couldn't persuade Amelia to talk to the city authorities, I had to try to talk to them myself, didn't I?—even though I knew how skeptical they would be. I couldn't just sit here in this tatty old chair drinking Guinness and watch all of these people die. But what if the authorities simply refused to believe me, which they probably wouldn't?

Maybe I should make another attempt to contact Singing Rock. He probably wouldn't agree to bring the malevolent thing back to my bedroom, so that I could see it for myself, but maybe he could tell me something about it, and why it was spreading this blood-drinking epidemic. Even a name would help: I could look it up on the Internet. You'd be surprised what malevolent things you can find on the Internet. I once looked up Misquamacus, the Algonquin wonder-worker who had killed Singing Rock and had almost killed me and Karen, too, and I found an actual picture of him, on some obscure Web site devoted to Keiller Webb, a nineteenth-century frontier photographer.

There he was, Misquamacus, standing in the background of a daguerrotype taken at Pyramid Lake in 1865. He was a wearing a tall black stovepipe hat and he was glaring at me, as if he had *known* when this picture was taken that I would be looking at it one day, in a hundred and forty years' time. He was stony-faced, his cheeks scarred with magical stigmata, and his deep-set glittering eyes looked like cockroaches nestling under a window ledge.

There hadn't been very much text to accompany the picture, except a brief excerpt from *Native American Magic*, by Roland Hunsiger and Merriam West. "Misquamacus was said to have possessed the power to appear in several different places simultaneously, sometimes thousands of miles apart. He was also credited with the ability to travel through time by swallowing blazing oil and being reborn in the body of any unsuspecting woman who happened to be in the locality of his self-immolation—either in the future, or in the past, whichever he chose.

"Misquamacus and his followers fought several notably bloody battles against the earliest Dutch settlers in New Amsterdam, and the wooden palisades for which Wall Street was named were specifically built to keep out his marauding warriors. Although Misquamacus' tribe was scattered in the spring of 1655, he made a solemn oath that one day he would drive out every last colonist. It is seriously thought by many Native American elders that the catastrophic collapse of several buildings in Manhattan in the 1990s was a last attempt by Misquamacus to destroy the white 'invaders' and drive them from American soil. They even believe that he might have succeeded, had not his destruction of high-tension power cables led to a massive discharge of electrical energy, which vaporized his *manitou* (spirit), and dispersed it amongst the four elements. He is now condemned to perpetual imprisonment in the earth, the fire, the wind and the rain."

The name *Misquamacus* still gave me a rusty taste in my mouth, even after all these years. He had first come into my life when he had chosen Karen as the host for his first reincarnation. Once he was reborn out of Karen's body, he had tried to summon the Great Old Ones, the Indian gods of total destruction, the ones who lived in the Empty Time (before time as we know it had actually begun.) He had almost succeeded, but Singing Rock had helped me to stop him.

Misquamacus had tried to be reincarnated again, and again, and Singing Rock had been killed as we struggled to send him back to the Happy Hunting Ground once and for all. Misquamacus was an incredibly powerful wonderworker, no doubt about it, but in the end it was no contest. His magic might have been pretty damn devastating in the days of rain dances and war parties, but he didn't stand a chance against twenty-first-century technology. Who's going to be bothered to blow magic powders into the wind to find herds of buffalo, when there's a Wal-mart only ten minutes down the road, with pre-packed USDA-grade steak? Who needs to go to a sweat lodge in search of visions, when they can buy ecstasy, and DVD players with cinemaquality sound? The Indians were simply left behind, standing with their pipes and their feathers and their beads beside the highway, while the rest of the world went careening onward, into the future. Even Singing Rock used to say: *It's no use crying about Native American magic, my friend, it's one of those things we don't need anymore, like cotton diapers and typewriters.*

I picked up the bracelet that Singing Rock had given me, and slipped it back on. Its black stones looked very dull now, for some reason, as if all the life had gone out of them. I clasped my right hand around it, and closed my eyes.

"Singing Rock . . . I really need your help right now. I admit that we didn't have the guts to look when you first tried to show us what was causing Ted's nightmares . . . we were cadmium yellow, I admit it. But that doesn't mean that I don't deeply appreciate what you did for us, and that I don't admire your bravery. Singing Rock . . . I'm begging you now. I'll make any sacrifice you want me to. Anything. People are dying out there, hundreds of people, and it seems to me that this *thing* that's been causing Ted's nightmares . . . well, it could be responsible for killing these people, too."

I waited, listening for some kind of response—a tap on the window, or a whisper, or a scratch on the wall. All the time the day gradually grew darker, and the sirens went on whooping and wailing. I heard screaming, and a catastrophic crash of glass, like a storefront window being smashed, and shots. Helicopters were beating over Central Park like distant tom-toms.

"Singing Rock, please. I know that I must have appeared ungrateful for what you did for me, but believe me I thought it was very, *very* amazing. If you can't conjure up that actual thing a second time, or if you don't feel in the mood, at least just give me a clue. Tell me what that thing is, or what it's called. Tell me where it comes from, or what it wants."

I heard people running along Seventeenth Street, scores of them. I stood up and went to the window just in time to see them crossing Sixth Avenue. There must have been over two hundred of them, men mostly, but some women, but I had no idea why they were running. They weren't crying, or shouting—only running. It was one of the scariest things that I had ever witnessed. They turned northward and they were gone, although I could still hear the clattering sound of their feet, for almost fifteen seconds afterward.

"That's it, Harry," I said, out loud. "Doomsday scenario."

I turned back into my gloomy room, and jumped with shock. Singing Rock was standing in the darkest corner. I could see the light reflected from his glasses, and his greased-back hair, and the black suit that he had been buried in. He wasn't entirely substantial: I could still see the bookcase behind him, and even the titles of the books.

"Hallo, Harry," he said. His voice had a crumply quality, like tissue paper, or the wind blowing into a sports-reporter's microphone.

"Singing Rock. I was beginning to think that you weren't speaking to me."

"There are some friends and some enemies on whom we can never turn our backs."

"So I'm which? Enemy, or friend?"

"You have to ask me?"

"No, of course not. I'm sorry. If I wasn't your friend, you wouldn't have drummed up that thing for me, whatever it was."

"If that's what you wish to believe."

I circled cautiously around the table, but the closer I got to Singing Rock, the dimmer he became, until I could barely make him out at all, only his lips moving. I stepped back, and he became clearer. He would have been nearly seventy-five now, if he had lived, but he hadn't changed. I guess that's the only positive thing you can say about death: It doesn't age you.

"How are you doing?" I asked him.

"I am dead, Harry Erskine. I exist only in the great world of blackness beneath your feet. That's how I am 'doing'."

"But you know what this thing is, don't you? You know why all of these people are having nightmares and drinking blood? I mean, they're *killing* each other out there, Singing Rock, they're cutting each other's throats. Women, children, anybody. It's a massacre."

"Yes, I am aware of that. I can see those innocents who have been murdered. Their spirits are falling into the blackness below like the snow falls in winter."

"You can't show me that thing again? That presence, whatever it was? I saw it out of the corner of my eye . . . it was kind of dark, and *stretchy*. And I heard it whispering, too."

Singing Rock shook his head. "I would show you, Harry Erskine, if I could. I don't blame you for your lack of courage. It is a creature of the darkest dark, from a very ancient heritage of which I know nothing. I caught it by surprise, and led it here with an old Lakota spell, but it soon broke free, and it will not be surprised a second time."

"Do you have any idea what it is, or where it comes from?"

"I can tell you its name only by suggestion. If I were to speak it, or to write it, I would instantly attract its attention, and it would come after you faster than a ravenous bear in the forests from which it first emerged. Let me warn you, Harry Erskine: This spirit is greedy and cruel and it will stop at nothing to spread its kind as far and as fast as it can."

"Okay, then, if you can only tell me its name by suggestion—suggest away."

"Not now. But you will know the name when I give it to you."

"Singing Rock, this is *urgent!* Mothers are drinking their babies' blood, even as we speak!"

But Singing Rock firmly said, "*No.* Don't you understand? You are special. By chance, you are the only one who has guessed that the plague has been caused by a spirit, and not by a virus. If *you* were to be killed, who else would guess? Your white doctors have long ago lost touch with the spirit world, and with the powers of nature. If they cannot see their enemy wriggling under their microscopes, they refuse to believe that he exists."

"So how do I convince them?"

"I cannot say. You are a white man and you know better than I do how to talk to other white men."

"For God's sake, you used to be a realtor. You can convince anybody of anything."

Singing Rock turned to me, and I thought that he looked weary and sad, as if he were tired of being dead. "I will tell you the name, Harry Erskine. What you do with that knowledge is up to you."

I tried to give him an encouraging smile, but it wasn't easy. He began to fade, and after a few moments he had vanished altogether, and the only evidence that he had visited me was the faint aroma of lavender hair oil.

But at least he had agreed to help me. I didn't know *how* he was going to give me the name of the malevolent thing, but I knew that he would keep his promise.

It occurred to me, though, that he still hadn't told me if I was his friend or his enemy. Maybe he regarded me as a little of both.

I took a shower, standing in the tub with the shower fixture rattling and shaking and letting out explosive sneezes of hot water. Without drying, I wrapped myself up in the thick navy-blue toweling robe that Karen had given me, with my monogram embroidered on the pocket, and I sat by the open window perspiring and drinking Guinness and listening to the terrible sounds of the night.

Sirens were echoing from every direction, and every now and then I heard masses of people running. Thick brown smoke was rising from the garment district and helicopters were circling around Times Square with crisscrossing floodlights.

Even though I knew that Singing Rock wouldn't let me

down, I was becoming increasingly worried and edgy, and I kept getting out of my chair and pacing around the room. I had switched the television off. By 9:15 it was reported that 347 people had died from the "vampire plague" and 511 had been found with their throats cut. More people had been murdered in New York City in a single day than were usually murdered in a year.

Mayor Brandisi had admitted that it might take "days, weeks, or even longer" to isolate the cause of the epidemic. Manhattan was now completely sealed off, with roadblocks at every bridge and every tunnel entrance. From Washington, D.C., the president had promised that the federal government would give New York City "every conceivable assistance." He also swore that if the epidemic were found to have been caused by terrorists, retribution would be "swift and terrible."

I was tired, and hot, and I was debating with myself whether I ought to go to bed, when I heard a scrabbling noise at my door. I leaned into my cramped little hallway and listened. There was another scrabble, and I called out, "Who's there? Is there anybody there?"

There was no reply, but I was sure that there was somebody out there. I tried to peer through the spyhole, but some joker had stuck something over it—chewing-gum, probably. I waited for a short while, and then I said, "Who is it?"

Still no response. It could have been Mrs. Zolbrod's dog, the one that looked like Harpo Marx's wig. Or maybe it was a rat. But for some reason I was certain that it was a person. I could feel his tension, even through two inches of door. I could almost hear him sweating.

I pressed my ear against the door, and held my breath. It was then that he hammered loudly on the door with his fist, and almost deafened me.

"*Jesus!*" I shouted, and opened the door.

I didn't recognize him at first, because his face was streaked with something thick and black and greasy, and so were his arms. But when he coughed and said, "Help me, dude. I really need some serious help," I realized it was Ted Busch. He looked even more disheveled than he had before. His *Molten Iris* T-shirt had a dark sweat-stain down the front of it, and his hair was sticking up as if he had been electrocuted.

"You'd better come in," I told him. I didn't really *want* him to come in, but what else could I do? Supposing something gruesome happened to him because I had turned him away?

He stumbled into the living room, and collapsed into my Alexander Woollcott chair.

"I'm burning up, dude," he told me.

"How about a glass of water?"

"No, no, not water. I can't touch water. Water's going to make it worse."

"What's wrong with you? You're sweating buckets. And what's all that black on your face? Jesus, Ted, you look like Al Jolson."

"I'm burning up, dude. It's like my skin's on fire."

"You need to go to a hospital, you really do. I can't help you here."

"I tried . . . I went to the Sisters of Jerusalem, but you can't get anywhere near. The whole place was like hundreds of people, all crying and screaming. The doors were shut and they had cops on the doors to stop people getting in."

"Ted, I'm a fortune-teller, not a doctor. There's nothing I can do for you, except give you a drink."

Ted stared at me, his eyes so wide that he looked as if he were mad. "You don't get it, do you? My skin's on fire. After I left you I tried to walk home but the sun was burning me and all I could find was motor oil to cover my face and my arms but I'm burning even worse. You have to help me, dude, or else I'm going to die."

I didn't know what to say to him. It was obvious from the way that he was trembling and clutching himself that he was in agony, but what can you do for somebody who's been infected by spiritual malevolence? Calamine lotion might be good for poison ivy rash, but it doesn't have much effect on cruel and ferocious things from beyond.

"I can run you a cold bath," I suggested. "And how about a couple of Anacin? That might help to bring your temperature down."

He twitched and sniffed and kept on shuddering like a junkie.

I picked up the phone. "I could try calling a doctor but I don't think there's any point. If you can't even get into a hospital—"

Unexpectedly, he let out a high, coyote-like howl, and the hairs on the back of my neck stood up. "*I'm burning!*" he screamed. He held up his hands to show me, as if they were actually on fire. "*Look at me, I'm burning!*"

"Listen!" I shouted back at him. "You have to calm down! You might feel like you're burning, but you're not! It's all in your mind, or your autonomic nervous system, or wherever! Just sit tight and sweat it out, that's all you can do!"

"But my skin's on fire! I'm *shriveling*, dude! I'm getting cremated!"

I decided to run him a cold bath. It might not work, but I couldn't think of anything else to do, apart from hitting him over the head, very hard, with my heaviest skillet. I'm good at saving the world, but I don't have a whole lot of patience when it comes to individuals.

I went through to the bathroom and turned on the big old cold-water faucet. The bath was vast, and it had a strange blood-colored stain down one side, as if a young bride had recently been murdered in it. I had been trying to bleach the stain out with Clorox, but it only seemed to make it look more bloodlike. The water was brown, and not particularly cold, but it would have to do.

I was leaning over the bath, checking that the plug was in properly, when somebody wrapped his arm around my neck. I saw something flash in the corner of my eye, and I instinctively ducked my head down, just as a craft knife slashed across my face, cutting my left cheek almost down to the bone.

Blood sprayed everywhere. It spattered up the side of the bath and blossomed in the water like roses. I twisted myself around, grunting and struggling, and I felt the craft knife cut cold across my knuckles.

I was never any good at fighting, but I was shit-scared and I was angry, and I lashed out with everything I had, like a demented windmill. Ted fell backward, jarring his shoulder against the edge of the door, and then I seized his sweaty T-shirt and hurled him against the towel rack, and then against the basin, and then I heaved him over the side of the bath so that he splashed into the water. He still had the craft knife but I grabbed hold of his wrist and bent it so far back that he dropped it.

I managed to hold him down on the bottom of the bath even though he was screaming and kicking and trying to bite me. I picked up the full half-gallon bottle of Clorox from under the back of the bath and hit him with it, *boff, boff*, again and again. He was stunned for a moment, but then he gripped the sides of the bath with both hands and tried to pull himself out. I hit him again, and he fell backward. Then I unscrewed the cap from the Clorox and emptied it into his face.

I will never be able to forget that shriek of agony as long as I live. He jumped blindly out of the bath—nobody could have stopped him—not me on my own—not even me and six other men. He collided with the door again, and then he staggered across the living room, scattering my *Jeu Noir* cards, knocking over my framed photograph of Karen and me and little Lucy, breaking the blue-glass vase that I had won in Atlantic City. He managed to open the front door and crash his way out of it, hitting the door on the other side of the corridor so hard that he split one of the panels. A muffled voice from inside shouted, "*Hey!*"

I was already feeling a surge of guilt, because I knew that I could have blinded him. I shouted, "Ted! Come back!" and went after him. But by the time I got to the door he was already lurching toward the top of the stairs.

"*Ted!*" I yelled at him.

He turned, and raised his head. His face was red and blistered, and smoke was actually rising from his hair. Both eyes were closed, and his lips were puffed up like two giant maggots. He opened his mouth and said, "*Tatal—tatal nostru—*"

"Ted, for Christ's sake, get back here, and let me splash some water on you!"

I don't know if the bleach had poured into his ears and deafened him, or if he simply didn't want to hear me, but he turned back toward the stairs and it was then that he lost his footing and disappeared, like a magic trick. One moment he was standing there, the next moment he was gone.

"*Ted—!*"

I could hear him tumbling down the stairs and I was sure that I could even hear his bones cracking, although it was probably the banisters. By the time I reached him he was lying on the dirty green linoleum on the landing, his neck twisted one way and his body twisted the other. One leg was crooked back, in a position that even a contortionist couldn't have managed.

I came slowly down the stairs and hunkered down next to him. His eyes were open but the pupils were sightless and milky white. I know that he had tried to cut my throat, but I still felt overwhelmingly guilty. It wasn't *his* fault that he had been infected by a malevolent spirit.

I stood up. The left side of my face was sticky, and blood was running from my knuckles.

"Singing Rock!" I shouted. "If you're going to give me a sign, then you'd better get your ass in gear, because I'm running out of time here! You hear me? Singing Rock?"

Laticia from the room opposite called out, "Harry? Harry, is that you? What the hell is going on down there?"

There was no point in asking her to call 911. "It's okay," I called back. "Somebody fell, that's all."

I stood up, nursing my dripping hand. It was then that I caught sight of a label that had been stuck onto the apartment door right next to me, Mrs. St. John's. She had been handwritten in large red letters, St. John, but most of it had been ripped off, so that all that remained was "St."

Don't ask me how I knew that this was the first part of Singing Rock's message. There are times when you just *know* things—like one of your friends is in trouble, or somebody's died, or the weather's going to change for the worse.

"Okay, Singing Rock," I told him. "An 's' and a 't'. But you'd better give me the rest of it real damn quick."

Laticia was standing at the top of the stairs with her hair piled high and decked out with purple ribbons. She was wearing a purple satin robe and she was smoking a small cigar.

"Harry?" she said, hoarsely.

"It's the end of the world, Laticia," I told her. "Next time you get down on your knees, you'd better start praying, too."

9

BLOOD AND THUNDER

Frank Winter opened one eye but all he could see was blackness.

I've been sleeping, he thought. *But I don't remember going to bed. The last thing I remember is—*

He tried to sit up, but his head hit something solid. He tried to move his arms, but they were pinned tightly to his sides. He struggled to turn himself around, but there wasn't enough room.

He felt a dark wave of pure panic. He was shut up in a narrow box, with no light, and no air, and with the lid fastened down. Oh my God, he thought. I'm in a coffin. Somebody must have found me sleeping and thought that I was dead. Oh God, don't tell me that they've buried me already.

"*Help!*" he shouted. "*Help! Somebody get me out of here!*"

There was no answer. He managed to wrestle his right arm free, and hammer on the lid with his fist. "*Help! Help me! There's been a mistake!*"

Still no answer. He started to hyperventilate, his chest rising up and down as if he had been running upstairs. But then he told himself: Calm down, Frank. This isn't going to help. You're going to use up all of the air that's left to you, and all you're going to do is distress yourself. Keep calm. Think. Try to think what happened to you.

The trouble was, his memories seemed to be all broken up. He could distinctly remember that he had been hiding in a very dark place, very high up. Somewhere in the rafters of a barn, maybe. He had heard men shouting, and dogs barking, and he had seen torches dancing behind the trees. He had crept back farther into the darkness, but he couldn't recall what had happened after that.

"*Help!*" he called out, beating on the lid of his coffin. "I'm not dead! You have to get me out of here!"

It was then that his coffin suddenly lurched sideways, and knocked against something else wooden. Another coffin, maybe. Frank listened, wide-eyed in the blackness, trying to hear what was happening outside. His coffin lurched again, and then he felt a dipping motion, almost as if he were floating.

"*You have to get me out of here!*" he screamed. "*I can't breathe! For God's sake get me out of here before I suffocate!*"

He managed to twist his left arm free, too, and set up a furious, crippled banging on his coffin lid. But nobody answered, and the dipping motion became more pronounced, until he felt his coffin rising, and then hesitating, and then falling.

He heard a deep creaking noise, and then a windy rumble, which could have been sails. He realized that his coffin was on a ship, and that the ship was maneuvering out to sea. He thought he could hear seagulls crying, or it could have been the desperate screams of other people, trapped in other coffins, just like he was.

He was about to scream again, but then he thought: *relax*. Nobody's going to let you out. All you can do is lie here, and wait, and conserve your energy. They might have shut you up in a coffin, but they haven't killed you, and they're taking you someplace, for whatever reason they have in mind.

He felt the ship turning into the wind, and for a long time his right shoulder was pressed painfully hard against the side of his coffin. But then it righted itself, and began to sail reasonably steadily, although it wasn't long before the end-less rising and falling made him feel nauseated. He tried to remember the last time that he had eaten, and what it was, but he couldn't.

It was then that he heard somebody clambering on the coffins all around him.

"*Help!*" he shouted. "*Help, I'm still alive!*"

The clambering noise stopped, but he was sure that the person was still close by. He waited, holding his breath. "Help," he whispered. "Please, for God's sake, get me out of here."

A long time went past. Then he heard a high, trembling voice say, "*Tatal nostru carele esti in ceruri . . . sfinteasca-se numele tau . . .*"

Tatal nostru! It hit him so hard that he felt as if somebody had punched him in the stomach. *Tatal nostru!* The same words that Susan Fireman had been chanting, and the young man in the emergency room, too!

"*Let me out here!*" he screamed, hammering even more furiously with his fists. "*Let me out of here! Let me out of here!*"

"Sshh," said a woman's voice, very soft, and very soothing. "Ssh, Frank—you've been having a nightmare, that's all."

He struck out wildly with his right arm, but instead of hit-ting the side of his coffin, he knocked his nightstand, and his digital alarm-clock tumbled onto the floor.

"What? What's happened?" he croaked, and opened his

eyes. It was still night, but streetlight was shining in through the half-open window. It must have been raining outside, because shadowy drops of water were crawling across the ceiling like amoeba. He could hear the *whip-whip-whoop* of ambulance sirens, and people shouting.

He sat up. Susan Fireman was sitting on the end of his bed wearing one of his white shirts, her hands in her lap. He stared at her. He couldn't remember if she was still alive, or if she was supposed to be dead. Her eyes glistened so pale that she looked as if she had been blinded.

"Frank? It's only me. You were having a nightmare."

"What time is it?" he asked her. She didn't answer so he had to lean over the side of the bed to see the red numbers of his digital clock on the floor. 11:57. Three minutes to midnight.

"Are you all right?" Susan Fireman asked him.

He eased himself into a sitting position and massaged the back of his neck. He felt as if he really had been shut up in a coffin, bruised and scraped all over.

"I thought you'd gone," he told her.

"Of course not. I'm going to stay here to take care of you, Frank."

"Is this a nightmare, too?"

"What do you mean?"

"You—everything—the epidemic. This feels like a nightmare inside of another nightmare."

Susan Fireman held out her hand to him, palm upward, as if she were offering him the answer to everything. "All life is a nightmare, Frank. The only difference is that some of us never wake up."

Frank sat for a moment with his head bowed. Maybe this wasn't real. Maybe it was still last night, and he hadn't yet woken up and walked to the hospital through Herald Square. Maybe there was no silver-painted mime and no regurgitated blood. Maybe there was no citywide massacre.

Maybe *tatal nostru* were just words that he had picked up unconsciously from a passing patient, or the radio playing in a taxi.

He looked at Susan Fireman for a moment. *You look as though you're sitting on the end of my bed but maybe you're not.* Without saying anything to her, he stood up and walked through to the kitchen, and switched on the lights. The kitchen was modern and stark, with black granite worktops and a stainless-steel oven by Smeg. The only decoration was a tall, triangular glass vase, containing a single arum lily, blood-red.

He went to the fridge and took out a bottle of Perrier water. As he reached up to one of the shiny black cupboards to find himself a glass, he became aware of Susan Fireman's reflection. She was standing on the opposite side of the counter, her arms by her sides.

Without turning around, he said, "Listen, Susan, I don't know if you're alive or if you're dead, or if I'm dreaming, but I'd really prefer it if you left me alone."

"I can't do that, Frank."

Frank poured himself a glass of fizzy water and then he turned around to face her. "This is *my* nightmare. That means that you have to do whatever I tell you, doesn't it?"

"But this isn't your nightmare. This is *everybody's* nightmare."

"What do you mean?"

"You'll find out, when you pass over, too."

"I don't have any intention of 'passing over.' "

Susan Fireman came up very close to him, and lifted her hand to touch his cheek. He swatted her away as if she were an irritating blowfly.

"Oh, *Frank*," she chided him. "You don't have any choice. None of us has any choice."

"I need to go back to sleep," he said. He was talking to himself, not to her. "I need to go back to sleep, and wake up for real. This is still Monday night and none of this has happened."

"You can deny it all you like," she said. "But the sooner you accept it, the better. There's a dark cloud moving over us, Frank, like a great black bird's wing, and it's moving very fast. It won't be long now, and the daylight people will be gone forever."

"Bullshit," Frank told her. "None of this has happened." He lifted his glass but for some reason the thought of drinking water made his mouth feel greasy. He emptied the Perrier down the sink, put the glass back in the cupboard, and walked back to his bedroom, leaving Susan Fireman standing in the kitchen. He lay down on his wrinkled sheets and closed his eyes. If he could only sleep, then Susan Fireman would vanish and everything would go back to normal.

Five minutes went past, but he was still wide awake. It was obvious that things were different, and that something had gone badly wrong. After midnight, Manhattan always echoed with car horns, and firetrucks bellowing, but it was never as noisy as this. Tonight, the screaming of sirens never stopped—siren upon siren, like the hallelujah chorus from hell. He could hear barking noises, too, like people trying to break doors down with axes; and the terrible crackle of glass breaking; and a deep, intermittent rumbling.

He opened his eyes. It was 12:11 in the morning. Susan Fireman was still there—standing in the doorway, watching him.

George Gathering had asked him to report back to the Sisters of Jerusalem at 2:00 A.M. *Well,* he thought, *even if this is a nightmare, I can't get to sleep in it, so I might as well take a shower and get dressed and go back to the hospital.*

He sat up again.

"No luck?" asked Susan Fireman.

"This isn't a nightmare, is it?" said Frank. "Even if I *do* get to sleep, I'm not going to wake up and find that I never met you."

"No, Frank, you're not."

He stepped out of his front door into the sticky, noisy night. It couldn't have rained very hard, because the sidewalks were drying out already, but the humidity was almost tropical.

There were no taxis anywhere in sight, so he started to walk. He had left Susan Fireman in his apartment, standing in the hallway, still smiling at him. He had asked her not to be there when he got back, but she had simply said, "Time will tell, Frank. Time will tell."

The blue-painted man who had been clinging to the mailbox had gone, but the rain hadn't been heavy enough to wash away the pool of blood that he had left on the sidewalk. There were bloody handprints, too, leading across the street, so it looked as if the man had crawled away on his hands and knees, and not so long ago, either.

Frank wondered for a moment if he ought to follow the handprints, to see where they led. Maybe he could save the blue-painted man, after all. But then he decided that he would be better employed at the Sisters of Jerusalem, taking care of as many people as possible, instead of tracking down one man, just because he had a conscience.

He walked south on Second Avenue, which looked comparatively quiet. There was almost nobody around, even though the sidewalks were strewn with broken bricks and and sparkling glass. Everywhere, there were abandoned shopping carts, some of them still filled with looted televisions and bottles of liquor and designer jeans. Human greed never ceased to amaze him. It was the end of the world, so people went out and stole televisions.

He was just about to cross Thirty-ninth Street when he heard somebody call, "*Help me!*"

He turned around and saw a girl of about fifteen years

old, crouched in a drugstore doorway. Her blond hair was matted with blood, so that it looked pink, and her white T-shirt was caked with blood, too.

"Help me!" she repeated. Her voice was a high, breathy scream. "Sir—please help me! I'm burning up! I'm *burning!*"

Frank approached her. "I'm sorry. There's nothing I can do to help you here. Do you think you can make it to the Sisters of Jerusalem? Do you know where that is? I'll see what I can do for you there."

"I can't! I can't move! My skin's burning!"

He hunkered down next to her. She was snub-nosed and boyish-looking, and he would have guessed that she had Chinese blood in her. She was shaking wildly, and her little eyes were darting from side to side as if she felt that she was being hunted.

"You'll have to come to the ER," Frank told her. "I can't treat you here in the street."

She reached up and clung to the sleeve of his linen coat. "You *can* help me, I know you can. Please, come closer, and I'll show you."

Frank tried to pull himself away. "I'm sorry. But there are hundreds of other people who need my help just as badly. I'll help you walk to the hospital, but—"

Without warning, the girl pulled at Frank's sleeve and dragged herself onto her knees. "*Aaaaahhhhhhhh!*" she screamed at him. She swung back her right arm and Frank saw glass flashing. He raised his left elbow to protect himself, but she cut right through his sleeve, right through his shirt, and sliced into his skin. She lifted her arm again, but Frank shoved her away with all of his strength, and she crashed backward through the drugstore window, breaking the glass and knocking over a display of lipsticks and face creams. A carousel of sunglasses fell over, too.

The girl shuddered, and one of her legs kept kicking, as if she were being electrocuted. Frank stepped back, holding his arm. Blood was running through his fingers but when he looked inside his sleeve he saw that the girl hadn't cut him too deeply. He hesitated, grimacing, wondering what he ought to do next. The girl lifted her head a little, but then it dropped back again, and her leg stopped kicking. She was probably dead, and Frank decided to leave her where she was. Whatever Susan Fireman had said, this was still a nightmare, and the Hippocratic Oath didn't apply to nightmares.

He started to jog west toward Lexington, and then southward again to Thirty-seventh. About six or seven blocks downtown he saw sixty or seventy people stampeding across the street, howling and yipping like a pack of hounds, and then he heard the prolonged pop-crackle-popping of gunfire. A woman shouted at him from an upstairs window, "*You! Yes, you, you bastard! Don't you go running away!*" but when he turned into Thirty-seventh Street he was on his own again, and there was nothing but litter and broken boxes and overturned Dumpsters.

Frank could hear the crowds outside the Sisters of Jerusalem from at least four blocks away. Two cars were burning at the intersection of Fifth Avenue and Thirty-seventh, filling the street with black oily smoke, and six or seven people were lying on the sidewalk, their heads covered by coats and blankets, obviously dead. Blood was running across the sidewalk and into the gutter, and a guilty-looking brown-and-white mongrel was lapping it up. People were running in all directions, and what was frightening was how quiet most of them were: Only a few of them were shouting or whimpering, and the rest were all serious-faced and wide-eyed and silent. Even when they collided with each other they seemed not to notice—just stumbled, and carried on. To Frank, it felt as if the whole city had turned into a madhouse.

Outside the hospital the street was so crowded that he had to force his way forward with his shoulders and his elbows; and several times he had to seize people by their clothing and drag them to one side. Every now and then, one of them would suddenly vomit up a fountain of blood, which splashed over everybody around them, but few people seemed to notice, or to care. Here, there was much more screaming and arguing and much more panic, but people were still milling around and bumping into each other as if they had no idea what to do.

Some people were chanting, "*Tatal nostru, carele esti in ceruri . . .*" but not in unison, so that the streets sounded like a vast chicken battery.

After several minutes of struggling, he managed to reach the police barrier. A raging black man in a red woolly hat tried to pull him back into the crowd. "You wait your turn, man! You wait your turn!" but Frank pushed the man's shoulder, and when he staggered backward the man was immediately dragged away by the hysterical crowd, as if he had been swallowed by a raging sea.

Frank ducked under the barrier. As he straightened up, he was confronted by two cops in riot helmets, swinging nightsticks. "Back behind the line, buddy! The hospital's full! Go home, and stay there!"

Frank said, "Wait up! Wait! I'm a doctor, I work here." He pulled out his wallet and held up his ID. "I'm supposed to be on duty."

One of the cops inspected it, and then said, "Okay, doc," and stood back to let him pass. "Honest to God, though—I don't know what the hell you think you can do."

Frank crossed the sidewalk and pushed open the blood-smeared plastic doors. To reach the emergency room, he had to negotiate his way through a shoal of abandoned gurneys, most of them covered in blood and bloody blankets. Inside, the whole world had turned red. Patients were lying six deep in the corridors, noisily bringing up blood. The whole emergency room was plastered in scarlet—the floors, the walls, and even the ceilings. There were red handprints everywhere. Everybody's clothes were soaked in blood, and many of the patients looked as if they were wearing bright red gloves and bright red masks, like revelers at some grisly pagan carnival.

Frank pulled back curtain after curtain, until he found Dean Garrett in a cubicle at the far end of the ER. Dean was bending over a young Puerto Rican woman who was blowing bubbles of blood with every breath. Dean's clothes were soaked in blood, too, and he looked beaten.

"Doctor, I will not die?" the young woman was asking him. "I am so afraid . . . I cannot bear to think that I will never see the sun again."

Dean laid his hand on her forehead, and tried to smile. "You'll see the sun, don't you worry. This time next month, you'll be sitting on your rooftop in your bikini, and I'll come around to make sure."

Frank said, "Hi, Dean."

Dean turned around and blinked at him. "Oh—hi, Frank. Glad you could make it. Mind you, I think we need more priests than doctors." He took Frank's arm and steered him away from the young woman's bed. "They're *dying*, Frank. All of them. They haven't announced it on the TV yet, but this disease is one hundred percent fatal, whatever it is, and there's nothing we can do to stop it."

"Nothing from the labs yet?"

"So far, they're totally baffled. Every victim's blood shows signs of this metallo-enzyme, but they're beginning to think it's a symptom, rather than a cause."

"Where's George?"

"Up on Eleventh, helping with autopsies."

"How many negative outcomes so far?"

"Up until 11:45 we'd admitted seven hundred seventeen patients, which is over ten times our capacity. At a rough guess, I'd say that we've already lost more than half. They seem to succumb much more rapidly, too. It's like a forest fire. Like—the more people that catch it, the faster they die. Round about now, I'd say that most patients are dead within four to five hours of admission."

Frank looked around. He didn't know what to say. Some people were still retching and sicking up blood, but most of them were lying pale-faced and shivering, as if they knew what was going to happen to them, but were too weak even to cry.

"You're bleeding," said Dean.

Frank peered at his elbow. "Nothing serious. Some girl attacked me with a piece of glass. It's like hell out there, believe me. They must be fifty deep, trying to force their way in here."

Dean led the way through to his office. One woman was sitting against the wall and three women were lying on the floor, all of them trembling and muttering. Dean's desk was strewn with blood-stained, crumpled papers. "There's no point in us taking any more in," he said, dragging out his chair and sitting down. "We can't do anything for them, except hold their hands while they die."

"Maybe it'll burn itself out like the Spanish influenza did in 1918."

"The Spanish influenza died out because there was nobody left alive to catch it. I don't know. I don't have any idea what this is, Frank. I can't understand how it spreads and I can't work out why it makes people want to drink human blood."

"Maybe the TV people aren't so far wrong. Maybe it *is* vampires."

"Oh, sure. Nosferatu's Syndrome. Look—you'd better let me put a dressing on that cut."

Frank took off his coat and rolled up his blood-soaked shirt-sleeve. Dean swabbed the cut with alcohol and examined it closely. "You were lucky. A quarter-inch to the left and she would have opened up your radial artery." He applied a nonadhesive dressing and bound it with tape. One of the women on the floor coughed and said, "*Tatal nostru . . .*"

"Has anybody found out what that means?" asked Frank.

Dean shook his head. "We've been overwhelmed, Frank. We're still overwhelmed."

"But they're *all* saying it. Everybody who catches this disease. I mean, don't you think that needs looking into?"

"You're absolutely right, it does. But not by me, and not tonight."

Frank left Dean in his office and took a tour around the ER and all the surrounding wards. In the new-admissions bay, patients were retching and crying out in despair, or furiously babbling to themselves, while exhausted nurses went from one bed to another, trying to keep them as quiet and as comfortable as they could. Until they knew what was causing this epidemic, there was nothing else they could do. Frank stepped carefully over blood-drenched bodies that were packed together in the corridors. Some of them were moaning or praying but most of them were very close to death and were silently staring at the ceiling. Emergency technicians patrolled the corridors, checking the patients who were lying on the floor, shaking them if necessary to see if they were still breathing. Every now and then, one of the technicians would stand up and beckon for the porters, and yet another body would be lifted up and wheeled away to the morgue, draped like a store-window dummy in a bloodstained sheet.

The stench was so strong that Frank had to press his hand over his face. Even though he had been practicing gastric medicine for eleven years, he had never become inured to the smell of decomposing flesh—unlike George, who could happily cut open a slippery gray-green corpse without even wearing a face mask, and whistle *Annie Laurie* while he did it. Frank was always convinced that the smell of death lingered on his hands and in his hair, even after three or even four successive showers. The women in his life had often caught him sniffing his fingers, but he had never told them why he did it. He hadn't wanted them to think that when he made love to them, his hands might still smell like dead men and women.

He gagged, but his stomach was empty, and so he didn't bring up anything but acid-tasting bile. The back of his throat felt as if somebody had forced a carpenter's rasp down it, and his skin prickled. He was so shivery that he began to wonder if he had a temperature. He could feel sweat sliding down his back and into his waistband.

A man on the floor painfully lifted up his head and stared at him. The man had a beard of dried blood and his eyes were unfocused. "*De strigoica, de strigoi*," he said, hoarsely. "*Si de case cu moroi.*"

"What?" said Frank, hunkering down beside him. "What are you trying to say?"

"*De deochetori . . . si de deochetoare . . .*" the man wheezed, but then his head fell back and he lay staring at the dying woman next to him, and gasping for breath.

Frank stood up. He still couldn't work out what language these people were speaking, but he was convinced that it had to be a critical clue. What condition causes people to speak in tongues that nobody has taught them, and nobody understands? Only demonic possession, as far as he knew, and he certainly didn't believe in *that*.

God, he was thirsty. He pushed aside a gaggle of abandoned wheelchairs until he reached the Coke machine. He took out three quarters, but before he inserted the first one into the slot he thought: *I don't want a Coke.* The very thought of swallowing Coke made him feel hotter, and his skin more irritable. *I need something else. Something that will really refresh me.*

A porter went past, pushing the body of a young blonde woman on a gurney. He was short and podgy, with dark circles under his eyes, and his face was waxy with tiredness.

His overall was spattered in so much blood that he looked like a butcher.

"How's it going?" Frank asked him.

The porter stopped, and wiped his nose with his blood-streaked forearm. "We can't help them, can we? All we can do is watch them kick the bucket and then wheel them off to the morgue."

"Here," said Frank. He took hold of the front of the gurney, and helped the porter to steer it along the corridor. If he couldn't do anything to help the dead, he might as lend a hand to the living.

He pushed open the heavy swing doors of the morgue. It was chilly and gloomy inside, and one of the fluorescent lights was blinking on and off. All of the chiller compartments must have been filled by now, because bodies were being wrapped up in sheets with only their faces showing, and then laid out in lines on the floor, as tidily as possible. There was only one morgue attendant on duty—a tall brunette woman with small oval glasses and a Roman nose. She looked as exhausted as the porter, and she had a large red cold-sore on her upper lip.

"Brought you another one," said Frank. "Where do you want her?"

"Any place here is fine," said the morgue attendant, pointing to a row of women's bodies on the right-hand side of the room. "I'm trying to keep the men and the women separate."

"In case of what?" asked the porter. "Post-extinction hanky-panky?"

"Out of respect," said the morgue attendant. "Or maybe that's something they don't teach you in porter school."

The porter left, banging the gurney loudly against the swing doors. The morgue attendant bent over the woman that he and Frank had just brought in, and checked the label attached to her big toe. "Jane Kryzmanski, 1143 West Thirty-eighth Street. Aged twenty-four. God, what a waste."

Frank looked around at the blood-stained bodies. "I don't think I ever felt so helpless in my life."

"You're a doctor?"

Frank nodded. "Frank Winter, gastroenterology."

"Good to know you, doctor. Helen Bryers. We don't have any idea what's causing this yet, do we?"

"No. Whatever it is, it seems to be very difficult to isolate."

"It's a bad dream," said Helen Bryers. "I keep thinking I'm going to wake up, and none of this will have happened."

You and me both, thought Frank. But then maybe he was dreaming her, and she didn't even exist. "How many cadavers do we have here now?" he asked her.

"Three hundred sixty-nine, including this young lady. There's over a hundred out back, in the storeroom. We're going to have to ship them out soon, before they become a major health hazard. I'm waiting to hear about refrigerated trucks."

Frank walked between the bodies. Each of them was a personal tragedy, but right now they were nothing but numbers, and the numbers kept on piling up.

Helen Bryers said, "Could you do something for me, doctor? I hate to ask you, but I haven't had time to go to the bathroom in over four hours."

"You want me to babysit?"

"Both of my colleagues went off-duty and they still haven't come back and I'm not supposed to leave the morgue unattended."

"Just in case one of your charges tries to make a run for it, right?"

She took off her glasses and tried to smile. "It's the rule, ever since that unpleasantness last year."

"I'm sorry?"

"We had some very distressing incidents . . . casual cleaning staff taking advantage of deceased patients. *Intimate* advantage."

Frank suddenly became aware that he was staring at Helen Byers' neck, and at the pale blue line of her carotid artery. He could imagine the warm blood pulsing through her system, pumped by her heart, and the thought was strangely soothing. *Drinking blood . . . it must be like lowering your body into a warm, deep bath.*

He blinked. "Oh—you mean *that* unpleasantness?" he said, abruptly realizing what she was talking about. "Yes, I heard about it. I guess some guys are so lacking in charisma, the only women who are going to fall for them are dead."

"Then it's all right if I—?"

"Sure, go ahead. Take your time. You look like you could use a break."

Helen Byers took her purse and left Frank alone in the morgue. He supposed that he should have refused her request, and returned to the ER to help Dean, or gone upstairs to assist George. But somehow it all seemed so hopeless. No matter what they did, they didn't know how to stop all these people from dying, and maybe they were better off dead. Most people were.

He caught sight of himself in a glass-fronted cabinet, and stared at his reflection as if he didn't recognize himself. *Most people were better off dead?* Why on earth had he thought that? He was supposed to be a doctor. He was supposed to do everything in his power to keep people alive. He rubbed his arm. His skin felt uncomfortably hot, as if he were suffering from sunburn, and his thirst was so fierce that he found it difficult to swallow.

He looked down at the body of a middle-aged woman in a gray-and-white summer dress, stained brown with blood. She was quite handsome, with a well-cut bob, and she had obviously had some cosmetic surgery done around her eyes. Not much use where she was going, thought Frank . . . she should have saved her money. Her eyes were wide open, but all the color seemed to have drained out of them. Whatever she was staring at, it wasn't in this world.

As he turned away from her, he heard a noise in the storage room at the back of the morgue. A clatter, and then a sharp bang, like a stool falling over.

"Anybody there?" he called out. He didn't think it was likely. Helen Byers had told him that she was on her own, and the ER technicians knew what they were doing: They wouldn't have sent anybody to the morgue if they weren't one hundred percent sure that life was extinct.

But then he heard another sound, like a window-bar rattling; and he was sure that he could feel a sudden draft of warm air. The sirens sounded louder, too.

He made his way toward the storeroom, stepping over a row of seven or eight dead men as if he were log-rolling across a river.

"Hey—is anybody there?" he repeated. Maybe somebody *had* been brought into the morgue before he was ready for it. He accidentally stepped on a dead man's hand, and said, "Sorry, feller!" before he could stop himself. The man had white hair and a bulbous nose. He must have been a doorman, because he was still wearing his maroon uniform with gold-braided epaulets. He looked as if he were sleeping, rather than dead.

Frank heard another noise. He stepped cautiously into the storeroom but it was very dark, and he could see hardly anything, except for the window at the very far end, which must have faced the hospital air shaft, because it admitted only a faint, gray light from the night outside. He strained his eyes and he thought that he could a dark figure moving in front of the window, but he couldn't be sure.

"Hey!" he shouted, even though his throat was so sore. "Who are you? What the hell are you doing in the morgue?"

He groped for the light switch, and found it. The fluorescent tubes flickered, and for a split second the storeroom was dazzlingly lit. But then all of the tubes popped at once, and Frank was left half-blinded, with swimming afterimages left in his eyes.

In that split second, though, he had seen something horrifying. The storeroom window was open, and a girl in a bloodstained nightgown was climbing out of it. She was turned toward him, so that he could see how white her face was, and the dried blood around her mouth. Her hair was long and black and wild, and it was flying *upward*, as if it were being blown by a furious wind.

A young man was rising up from the floor to follow her, his green-and-white baseball shirt blotted with blood. He was being helped up by a dark, attenuated figure, which Frank couldn't make any sense of. It was less like a person than a sloping shadow, with an elongated head that rose toward the ceiling, and high, diagonal shoulders. It was leaning at an impossible angle, in the way that only a shadow could.

Yet just before the lights went out, it had snapped its head around, and Frank had glimpsed two black, blurry eyes, and a stretched-open mouth that was more of a *grating* than a mouth. In the darkness, he heard an explosive, hate-filled hiss that sounded like air brakes, and then a high, piercing shriek—a shriek so terrible that he felt as if his brain was being blinded, as well as his eyes.

10

BLOODSHOT

Laticia helped me to drag Ted Busch back up to my apartment. The heels of Ted's sneakers knocked on every stair, all the way up, and *bump-bump-bump*ed along the landing. I was amazed that nobody came out of their rooms to see what the hell we were doing.

We heaved him on to the couch and he lay there with his face all scarlet and blistered and his legs and arms at peculiar angles like a marionette with all of his strings cut. Laticia said, "If I trusted the cops, I'd call for the cops, if I thought they'd come."

"Laticia, he tried to cut my throat."

"Well, you need to wash that blood off of your face and put a BandAid on it at least. Let me do that for you. And if you get scared tonight, with this dead individual lying here, you can always come and share my bed."

"Laticia, you were sent from heaven, FedEx."

"A hundred and twenty-five for all night, mind. Gratuities extra."

* * *

After Laticia had gone back to her apartment, I stood looking down at Ted Busch's body and I felt genuinely sorry for him, and guilty as hell.

"Those *Jeu Noir* cards were dead right about you, buddy," I told him. "They warned you about Imminent Death, didn't they? But you didn't take any notice. Okay, Death was a whole lot Imminenter than either of us thought. But the cards warned you about water, too, didn't they, with the Water Woman? You should never have tried to cut my throat in the bathroom. Well—you should never have tried to cut my throat at all. *Nemo me impune lacessit.* He who steals my clownfish gets a kick in their puny ass."

I opened another can of Guinness. It was my last one, but I needed it. I didn't know what to do next. Singing Rock had given me two letters, "s" and "t." At least I *thought* that he had given me two letters, but I could have been allowing my fevered imagination to run away with me. I had no way of checking if he had really meant "s" and "t." And what was even more confusing, I had no idea how many more letters he was going to give me, or if I'd understand what the word meant when I eventually got them all.

I was pretty damn sure, though, that the blood lust that was affecting so many people in Manhattan was the same blood lust that had led Ted to attack me and try to cut my throat. I was also pretty damn sure that it wasn't caused by any kind of disease, or virus, not in the way that the authorities were talking about it. It was some kind of mass possession, like *The Exorcist* times 8,008,278. This wasn't just one girl talking like Louis Armstrong and throwing the occasional Jesuit out of the window. This was a tidal wave of possession, a spiritual *tsunami*, and it was swamping the city and everybody in it.

And it was genuinely terrifying, on a grand scale. It was September eleventh squared. If so many people had died in a single day, how much longer could the rest of us survive?

I made up my mind. No matter how much Bertie

protested, I would have to talk to Amelia. She was the only person who would believe that Singing Rock was trying to help me from the Happy Hunting Ground, and she was the only person who might be able to persuade the city authorities that I wasn't a fraud or a certifiable lunatic.

At the bottom of my closet I found the old plaid blanket that my dog used to sleep on, and I took it into the living room to cover up poor old Ted. As I unfolded it, I caught the glint of silver around his neck. It was the medallion which he said that the Russian-type girl had given him— the medallion with the spooky face and the eyes that looked as if they opened. I lifted the medallion up and turned it over. The face was still staring at me, grimly, as if it resented my interfering. I hesitated, but then I unfastened the clasp, and took the medallion off. I wasn't intending to steal it, but for some reason I felt that it was some kind of clue, in the way that the letters "s" and "t" were clues.

I drew the blanket over Ted's head and then I turned the AC right down, so that he wouldn't start smelling too ripe. Then I knocked on Laticia's door.

"You change your mind, Harry? You want to stay the night?"

Under normal circumstances I might even have been tempted. Laticia was wearing a purple see-through bra and purple see-through panties with dangling ribbons at the side, and she wasn't unattractive if you didn't mind Prince without the moustache.

"Not tonight, Laticia. I have to go out. I just wanted to tell you that I had to leave Ted on the couch."

"Okay . . . he's not going to bother me, is he?"

"I hope not. If he does, just keep him talking until I get back."

I walked down the stairs, out of the front door and into the street. Khaled's Pakistani Provisions was closed, and its steel shutters had been pulled down. This was highly unusual. Khaled religiously stayed open till 1:00 A.M. at least, seven days a week, in case anybody had an irresistible urge to start cooking *murgh masala* in the weê small hours of the morning.

The night was sweltering hot, and there was an acrid smell of burning in the air, like the days after 9/11. The sirens were still screaming and in the distance I could hear somebody yelling through a bullhorn, something along the lines of "wo-wah-wah-WAH-wah-ba-booh-booh-BAH!" I kept walking westward, turning around from time to time to make sure that there was nobody following me.

As I turned south into Seventh Avenue, I saw two skinny young women with spiky hair crouching on the sidewalk about fifty yards up ahead of me. My first instinct was that they needed help, and I started to walk toward them more quickly. But as I got nearer, I saw that a heavily built man in jeans was lying between them, with his arms and legs spread wide. I also saw that something dark and glistening was running across the sidewalk, like blood. I U-turned smartly and headed back where I had come from.

Just as I reached the corner of Seventeenth Street, I glanced quickly back over my shoulder. One of the spiky-haired young women was getting up onto her feet, and as she did so she turned around and looked in my direction. She must have said something to the other girl, because *she* stood up, too. The heavily built man in the jeans stayed where he was, and I took an educated guess that he wasn't having a nap. The girls hesitated, and then they started walking toward me, and I could tell from the quick, determined click of their heels that they were after me.

I turned into Seventeenth Street and then I sprinted along to Sixth Avenue, and took a right. I could have kept on running, but those girls were at least ten years younger than me and they hadn't been drinking Guinness. Instead, I took another right into Sixteenth Street, and ran as far as the alley next to Feinman's Antique Carpets, and hid myself behind a Dumpster. I waited, and waited. Two people walked past, talking and laughing, but they were both men, and they both seemed as jumpy as I was.

I gave myself five more minutes. The alley was airless and it smelled of weeds and damp brickwork and pee. Across the street, in the window of a discount camping store, I could see the letters RIG in red neon. It flicked on, and then it flicked off. The strange thing was that sometimes it stayed on for almost fifteen seconds, while at other times it flicked on and off almost instantly. RIG. Blank. RIG.

RIG. Maybe Singing Rock was sending me another signal—three more letters for my mystery word. ST plus RIG spelled S-T-R-I-G. But what the flaming Falujah did that mean? I couldn't think of any word that began with STRIG. Maybe it was part of an anagram, like "ostrich." Maybe it was an anagram of a biological term, like "streptococci." But Singing Rock had never had any sense of humor, and he had always been totally contemptuous of white man's medicine, so it was more likely to be something else altogether, like somebody's name.

Eventually, I emerged from the alley and looked left and right to make sure that the spiky-haired girls had gone. From somewhere over by Washington Square, there was a tremendous bang, almost like a bomb, followed by echo after echo. Jesus, this was seriously scary. I could deal with the normal perils of a New York City night—drunks, muggers and assorted freaks—but this didn't feel like New York City any more. I started half-walking and half-jogging toward TriBeCa, staying in the shadows as much as I could, and staying highly alert for people who looked as if they might be hunting for fresh human blood.

I was only a few blocks away from Christopher Street, where Amelia lived, when a man stepped out of a darkened doorway, right in front of me. He had a shaved head and dark glasses and a neck like a section of trans-Atlantic cable, and he was built like a Marine. He was wearing a khaki T-shirt and camouflage pants and about a hundred chains and dog-tags and keys around his neck, and probably a few human ears, too, I wouldn't have been surprised. He was eating a Snickers bar and his mouth was full.

"Hey," he said.

I tried to skirt around him but he double-shuffled to one side and blocked me.

"Excuse me, do you have a problem?" I demanded. "I'm in kind of a hurry here, if you don't mind."

"You know what they say, man. More haste less speed."

I tried to sidestep, but he sidestepped, too. I backed off a couple of paces and he backed off, too, but when I took one step forward, so did he.

I tried to look cool, and bored by all of this waltzing, but my heart was thumping like a basketball and I was beginning to feel very frightened.

He swallowed, and wiped his mouth with the back of his hand. "I gotta know if you're one of them," he said.

"What are you talking about, 'one of them'?"

"Me and my friends, see, we're protecting this neighborhood, and if you're one of them you're not welcome beyond this point."

I looked across the street, and for the first time I saw three other men, waiting in the shadows. At least one of them was holding a rifle.

"My name's Harry Erskine, I'm an herbal visionary."

"You're a *what?*"

"An herbal visionary. I tell your future and then I give you herbal remedies to improve your life prospects."

"Are you trying to be smart?"

"Of course not. It's not your usual nine-to-five job but somebody has to do it."

"Got any ID?"

I showed him my driver's license. "I was also on the front page of *Psychic Weekly*, if you want to know. I'm on my way to visit a friend of mine who's another psychic. And if by 'one of them' you mean who I think you mean, then I'm not 'one of them.' In fact I've been trying to keep well clear of them."

"Okay, Harry. You won't object if I frisk you, then?"

"Frisk me? For what?"

"For anything that you can use to cut somebody's throat."

I lifted both arms. "Go ahead, frisk away."

He didn't hesitate, and he frisked me like an expert. While he was patting my crotch, I said, "The only reason I'm down here tonight is because I think I might be able to stop this epidemic."

"You? What can *you* do?"

"This person I'm going to visit—she and me, well, we've handled some stuff like this before. You remember all those buildings that collapsed, in the nineties? We stopped that."

"Sure you did."

"You don't have to believe me, but it's true. This epidemic, it's not a physical disease, like chicken flu or cholera or anything like that. It's not a terrorist attack, either, like anthrax or ricin."

The man finished frisking me and stood up. "Go on. I'm not stupid. I was with the Rainbow Division in Bosnia. If it's not a disease, what is it?"

"I think it's a spiritual force. Like an evil manifestation from the world beyond."

The man stared at me for almost ten seconds without saying anything. Then he slowly shook his head and started laughing. One of his friends from across the street called out, "What's so damn funny, Gil?"

"Got me a screwball here," said Gil.

"Do I *look* like a screwball?" I demanded.

Gil looked me up and down. "Yes, Harry. You definitely do."

Apart from being moderately drunk, I was still feeling desperately guilty about splashing Clorox all over Ted, and

I was exhausted, and disoriented, and I badly needed to show somebody that I was right about this epidemic. So I said to Gil, "I'll prove it you. I'll damn well prove it you."

"You'll prove it to me? How are you going to do that?"

"If you escort me to my friend's house, she can show you that I'm telling the truth. We'll hold a séance, and you can see for yourself."

"A séance? You're inviting me to a *séance?*"

"What's the matter, you got repetitis? That's what I said, a séance. If we can identify the spirit that's causing all of this chaos, we can do something about it. Exorcize it, or banish it, or send it back to wherever it came from."

Gil smiled, and stepped back to indicate that I could pass. "You just move along, Harry. I think you could do with some strong black coffee and a very cold shower."

"And supposing I get attacked by 'one of them'?" I demanded. "Or '*two* of them,' even?"

"Harry—"

"Supposing I never get the chance to tell the city authorities why all of these people are cutting other people's throats? Thousands more people could die. *Millions*, even. Listen to me, Gil. Without me, this city is doomed. America is doomed."

Gil opened and closed his mouth but didn't say anything. A police squad car came howling past us, followed by another, and another. I heard another explosion: a deep, dull thump, somewhere over by the Hudson River waterfront. I could feel the aftershock right through the soles of my feet, as if the sidewalk was a rug, and somebody had tugged it.

"How far is your friend's house?" asked Gil.

"Four blocks. Christopher Street, that's all."

"Okay, then, I'll come with you to the front door, give you protection, but that's·all. I ain't attending no séance."

* * *

He walked with me southward toward Christopher Street. It turned out that his name was Gil Johnson, and he worked for a company on Twenty-fifth Street that moved pianos. Once, when he had been hauling a Bechstein into an apartment building on East Fifty-seventh Street, a steel hawser had snapped and the piano had dropped nine stories into the street below, flattening a man who had been wanted by the police for rape and armed robbery. "Now was that supernatural justice or what?" Gil had a wife and two teenage daughters and he lived and breathed for the N.Y. Jets. "I love those guys." He had even persuaded Freeman McNeil to be godfather to his oldest daughter.

"We saw the news about people killing people and me and my buddies decided we was going to protect our neighborhood. I'm not having no diseased people cutting my family's throats, no way."

About twenty men and women came running across Charles Street, howling and screaming, but they didn't pay us any attention. They ran off, their footsteps echoing like applause. God alone knew where they were headed, or what they were planning to do when they got there.

"You understand what's going on, Harry?" Gil asked me. "I don't understand what's going on."

"I think I know *what*. But don't ask me *why*."

"I'll tell you something, Harry," said Gil. He showed me his left forearm, which was tattooed with a grinning skull. "I faced death when I was out in Bosnia. I looked death right in his hollow eye sockets. I saw my buddies get shot, and blown up by RPGs, and it was madness out there. But at least we knew who were fighting. We were fighting the Serbs, and the Romanian mercenaries, and the Muslims, no matter how crazy they were. But this—this is like we're fighting everybody and nobody."

"I think that just about sums it up, Gil. Everybody and nobody."

Gil turned around and showed me his right bicep. It was tattooed with the number 10, all wrapped around with razor-wire, and dripping with blood. "That was us, Number 10 Special Detail. One of the toughest details ever. Our job was to penetrate the enemy's positions and grab their senior officers—alive, if we could. Mostly it all went to shit and we ended up blowing their heads off. But that's who I am. I may shift pianos now, but up here in my head I'm still a grunt, and I think like a grunt."

At that moment we were passing a liquor store, and as we did so, a red-and-blue Michelob sign flickered and jumped. I looked into the store window and saw that the number "10" appeared to be dancing on his arm—only it was backward, so that it looked like the letters "OI". A fraction of a second later a great multi-branched tree of lightning crackled over Battery Park, and there was a deafening collision of thunder, *kabooommmmm!* right over our heads.

"*Holy shit*," said Gil.

It shook me, too—but I believed I knew what had caused it. "O" and "I"—two new letters. And, judging by that thunderous punctuation mark, maybe they were the *last* two letters, and I was now in possession of the whole word. I stopped, my face lifted to the sky, turning around and around on the sidewalk. "Singing Rock! *Singing Rock*! Is that you again?"

Gil waited for me, with his hands on his hips.

"You're definitely a screwball, Harry, no doubt about that."

"I wish. Singing Rock is my spirit guide. He's been trying to tell me who started this epidemic."

"Oh, really?"

"Yes, really. The problem is, he has to give me the name in individual letters, a couple at a time. He can't tell me the entire name outright, because if I say it outright, the thing will come after me, whatever it is, and rip my throat out, or something equally undesirable."

"If you say so, Harry."

"Gil, will you just trust me? So far, he's given me five letters—'s' and 't' and 'r' and 'i' and 'g'. Now I looked at your tattoo just then and there was a damn great rumble of thunder which really emphasized what I was looking at, the letters 'o' and 'i.'

I held up my hand and counted the letters off on my fingers. "So far we have S-T-R-I-G-O-I which spells—"

"*Don't say it!*" Gil screamed at me. It was so unexpected that he made me jump.

I stared at him, shocked. "What? I was only trying to—"

"Don't say it, man! I *know* that word! I know what it means!"

"What do you mean you know what it means?"

"They were always using it in Bosnia, the Romanian mercenaries. It was like an insult, only it was worse than an insult. It was what they called somebody they were really scared of."

"You mean *stri*—"

"*Don't say it!* For Christ's sake, it's too much of a coincidence! If people have been killing people and drinking their blood—that's like vampires, man, and that's what it means. It means *vampire.*"

"You're pulling my chain."

"I'm not, Harry, I swear it. You can check it out. That word means vampire and that's what your spirit guide didn't want you to say it out loud. Even in Bosnia they never said it loud, not unless they were all hyped up, and even then it wasn't like they were talking about *real* vampires."

"*Vampires?*" I repeated. "Come on, Gil, is this likely? I know they keep calling it a 'vampire epidemic' on the news, but that's only because people have been drinking blood."

"But why not?" said Gil. "You said yourself that this epidemic was caused by some kind of evil spirits, didn't you? Maybe this is what they are. Real, genuine vampires."

"Gil, I'm not at all sure that I believe in real, genuine

vampires." I put on my Bela Lugosi accent. " '*The children of the night . . . what music they make!*' "

"You believe in spirits, though, don't you?" Gil persisted. "You believe in all of that *Twilight Zone* stuff? Come on, man, you've just told me you have a spirit guide called Singing Rock."

"Listen, Gil, you're supposed to be the skeptic around here."

"Yes, but that *word*, man! Jesus, I haven't heard that word in eleven years but when you spelled it out—that really made my hair stand on end."

"Okay," I said. "I guess it's worth looking into. We can ask my friend about it when she holds her séance."

"You mean *you* can ask her. I told you, I ain't going to no séance, especially if you're going to start talking about vampires."

"You fought in Bosnia and you're scared of vampires?"

"Are you kidding me? I fought in Bosnia and that's *exactly* why I'm scared of vampires."

We reached Amelia's apartment on Christopher Street. She and Bertie lived in a second-floor studio in one of those elegant nineteenth-century apartment blocks that were originally built for the clothing industry, with high windows and decorative columns. The first floor was taken up by Christopher Street Cashmere, which sold strawberry-colored men's sweaters to the kind of men who would pay $400 for a strawberry-colored sweater. And lemon-colored sweaters, too. And pink.

I climbed the steps at the side of the building to the shiny olive-green front door and pressed the shiny brass doorbell marked *Carlsson*. I waited and waited, and eventually Bertie said, "Hello?" through the intercom.

"Bertie? It's me, Harry Erskine."

"For God's sake, Harry, what are you doing here? Don't you know what time it is?"

"Bertie, I have to talk to Amelia. It's incredibly urgent."

"I told you earlier, Harry, I don't want you involving Amelia in any of your problems, whatever they are. Now please go away."

"Believe me, Bertie, I wouldn't bother you if this wasn't critical. But we're talking about thousands of people's lives here. Your life too, and Amelia's, and mine."

"I'm sorry, Harry. I have to think about Amelia's best interests."

But then Gil leaned forward and said, "Excuse me, sir? This is Gil Johnson, Forty-second infantry division, New York National Guard. I believe that we need to give Harry some assistance here."

"National Guard? What do you want from us? I don't understand."

"This epidemic, sir. This gentleman believes that he knows what's causing it, and he needs your good lady's assistance."

"And what if I say no?"

Gil looked at me and winked. "I'm authorized under martial law to arrest you for obstructing the military, sir, and to require your good lady to assist us in any way that she can."

There was a very long silence, and then the door release buzzed. I pushed open the door and we walked into the darkened hallway.

"Are you coming up?" I asked Gil.

Gil pulled a face. "I don't know. I'm not too sure I want to get involved in this."

"Come on, Gil, think about your family, too. I need your authority. If you don't come up, he's not going to believe this martial law thing, is he?"

The two of us squashed together into the tiny elevator and went up one floor. When the door slid back Bertie was waiting for us—a tall, thin man with gray, brushed-back hair and rimless spectacles, wearing a loose beige shirt and baggy beige pants and sandals. I grudgingly had to admit that he was reasonably handsome, even if he looked as if he drank nothing but carbonated spring water and ate nothing but Swedish crispbread.

"So here you are, then, Harry," he said, making no effort to hide his annoyance. "You and your companion had better come in." We stepped out of the elevator and into the living area. The apartment was very Scandinavian, with blond wooden floors and furniture that gave you a serious ache in your butt just to look at it. On the walls hung several huge paintings of blue Scandinavian blobs, and in one corner stood an abstract sculpture of a triangular thing dangling from a skinny rectangular thing. It wasn't easy to reconcile all of this carefully arranged emptiness with Amelia's old apartment in the Village, which had been heaped up with books and armchairs and rolled-up carpets and reading lamps and blotchy old engravings, not to mention a few dirty dinner plates.

"Tasteful," I remarked, looking around.

But then Amelia appeared, crossing the floor in a gauzy, white dreamlike dress. She seemed taller, until I realized that she was wearing wedge-heeled sandals, but she was certainly thinner, and freshly suntanned, and her curly hair was cropped very short. She was no longer wearing glasses, either.

She looked extraordinary, at least ten years younger than the last time I saw her. Her face was still sharply featured, and her cheekbones were still prominent, but she didn't seem to have any wrinkles at all. Her breasts had always been noticeable but now they looked bigger than ever, and firmer, too. She was wearing about two thousand gold bangles on her wrists and a modern necklace made of big lumpy pieces of gold.

"*Harry*," she said. "How wonderful to see you again." She flowed right up to me and put her arms around me, and kissed me, and kissed me again, and again. God, she smelled good. All woman and Chanel. Meanwhile Bertie was pursing up his mouth as if he were trying to suck battery acid through a blocked straw.

"Amelia, you look *fabulous*," I told her. "Whatever Bertie's been feeding you on, it definitely agrees with you."

"*Bertil*," she corrected me. "Yes, Bertil's been taking very good care of me, haven't you, Bertil?"

"I like to think so," said Bertie, trying to smile, although I could tell that he felt like running around the apartment, kicking over abstract sculptures and screaming Swedish obscenities.

"Smorgasbord, I'll bet," I said. "Nothing like those open sandwiches, hey, Bertie? Saves you a fortune, leaving off that top slice of bread, and who really needs it?"

"You're looking tired, Harry," said Amelia.

"Tired, scruffy, down-at-heel, that's right. Well, you know about me and Karen. It was good while it lasted but it was never going to last. She was always going to be too high-end for a mook like me."

"You shouldn't put yourself down, Harry. You have very great sensitivity."

"By the way," I said, "I'd like you to meet Gil Johnson of the Rainbow Division. Gil, this is Amelia, my psychic friend, and this is her husband Bertie."

"Bertil," Bertil corrected me, shaking Gil's hand. "Perhaps I can offer you gentlemen a drink? Tea, or coffee, or a soda?"

"I could murder a beer, if you have one."

"I have Pripps."

"I'm sorry to hear it."

"Pripps is the best-quality Swedish beer, brewed in Stockholm."

"In that case, thanks, don't mind if I do. Amelia—I can't believe how terrific you look. Do you ever hear from MacArthur? What a guy! Do you remember that night that you and MacArthur ran all the way around Washington

Square Park with nothing on but paper bags over your heads? I couldn't touch tequila for about a year after that."

Bertie came back with two bottles of frosty-cold beer, and a frosty-cold expression on his face. "Do you think you could get to the point, Harry?"

I sat down in one of those orthopedic armchairs. Poor Gil remained standing. He was looking very uncomfortable, but he obviously thought it would be impolite to swig his beer down and go. Bertie sat very close to Amelia, with one hand resting possessively on her thigh, giving her an occasional squeeze.

I swallowed beer, and it was so cold that it made me hiccup. "This vampire epidemic, I'm one hundred percent sure that it's being caused by some kind of malevolent spirit. Don't ask me how, or why, but Gil thinks it could even be a *real* vampire."

"A *real* vampire?" said Bertie. "Vampires are in the movies. Vampires can't be real."

"Well, maybe you're right, and we're making fools of ourselves. But Singing Rock has managed to give me the vampire's name, and Gil says it's the same name that Romanians used out in Bosnia, when they wanted to call somebody a butcher or a blood-sucker."

"Singing Rock?" asked Bertie. "Who or what is Singing Rock?"

"He's a Native American medicine man we used to know. He's passed over now, but he still acts as my spirit guide."

"You mean he's dead?"

"In the sense that he's no longer physically with us, yes, I suppose you could say that he is."

"So a dead man has given you a name, and this name is Romanian for vampires, and this is why we must believe that New York has been invaded by vampires?" Actually, he said "inwaded by wampires."

"Erm, yes."

"What's the name?" asked Amelia.

"Oh, for God's sake," said Bertie.

I ignored him. To give the poor fellow some credit, he hadn't come across anything genuinely supernatural before, and I can remember *my* first encounter with things from beyond. I thought it was wall-to-wall bullshit.

"Singing Rock said that I shouldn't say it out loud, because the spirit would hear me, and come looking for me. But if you give me a pencil and a piece of paper . . ."

Amelia passed me a notepad from the Martinez Hotel, in Cannes, France, and a gold mechanical pencil. I wrote down STRIGOI, and pushed it across the glass-topped coffee table to Amelia.

She leaned forward to look at what I had written, but then she immediately sat up straight, staring at me as if I had done something truly appalling.

"Oh my God," she said. "Oh, Harry. Oh my God."

11

BLOOD FEVER

The creature's shrieking went on and on, like a knife scraping on glass, but then it stopped, abruptly; and then there was only the clamor of the hospital, and the roaring of the city outside.

Frank stayed where he was, straining his eyes in the darkness. He thought he could see shadows moving in front of the window, but it could have been the lights of a passing helicopter, criss-crossing down the airshaft.

He cleared his throat and called out, "Who's there? Whoever you are, I'm warning you, I'm calling security."

He wasn't sure that he had spoken loud enough for the thing to have heard him, because it had scared him so badly. It had looked spidery and disproportionate, the sort of creature that appears only in the very sweatiest of nightmares. But although it had been impossibly *stretched*, it had also looked unnervingly human—as if it would be capable of logical thinking, and even talking. In the split-second that he had looked into its eyes, Frank had seen a terrible *knowingness*. And contempt, too, and only humans were capable of contempt.

"I'm going for security now!" he shouted. "Do you hear me? I'm going to have your ass thrown out of here so goddamned fast!"

As he started to edge his way out of the room, however, the lights suddenly *ping*-clicked back on again. He blinked, and shielded his eyes. The window was still open, but the shadow creature had gone. The floor was still covered with rows of bodies, all tied up in sheets, but the young girl who had been climbing out of the window had disappeared, too, and so had the young man who had been following her.

Frank thought he *ought* to call security, but what would they say, if he tried to tell them that he had just seen a stretched-out shadow creature, and dead people who could come back to life? He was already feeling off balance, and he was sure that he was running a fever. Maybe he was still dreaming all of this; or maybe he was sick, and he was hallucinating. There was no way of telling what was real and what was imaginary. He could be lying in bed at home, fast asleep, and none of this was happening, except as a shadow-theater inside his mind.

Cautiously, he made his way toward the window, stepping over bodies as he did so. When he got there, he looked out into the airshaft. The main hospital building went up as far as the seventh story, with a thirty-five-story tower on the northeast corner. All he could see were the lighted windows of the wards and the corridors opposite, and people hurrying to and fro. In the distance, he heard the indigestive grumbling of thunder. He must have dreamed the stretched-out creature, or imagined it. His throat was so sore that he could barely swallow, and his skin was burning.

He was just about to turn away from the window when

there was a dazzling crack of lightning, and the air was so charged with electricity that Frank felt his scalp prickle and his teeth buzz together. There was another crack, and then another. He looked *upward*, toward the sky. And it was then that he saw what had happened to the creature, and the two young people it had been helping to climb out of the storeroom.

They were two-thirds of the way up the airshaft—not just them, but ten or twelve more, all of them still wrapped up in their hospital sheets. They were climbing the sheer concrete walls as quickly as if they were huge white spiders, not even using the window ledges or the drainpipes to help them.

Frank stared at them, appalled. They were dead, those people. That's why they were wrapped up in sheets. And yet here they were, climbing up the airshaft, and disappearing over the edge of the hospital roof. What had Susan Fireman said? *"Any wall can be climbed, Frank, if you have the ability to climb it."* But if you were *dead?*

He watched until the last of the climbers had vanished. Then he slammed the window and turned the security key. He was shaking uncontrollably, and his skin was so sensitive that he could hardly bear the feel of his clothes. He needed to tell somebody what he had seen. But who was going to listen to him, especially with patients dying in every corridor, and hundreds more victims trying to force their way into the hospital?

He left the storeroom and went back into the morgue, and stood among the sheet-swaddled bodies, shivering. He was still there when Helen Bryers reappeared. "Doctor?" she frowned, putting down her purse. "Is everything all right? You really don't look well."

"Keep the window in the storeroom closed," he told her, in a hoarse voice.

"What? It isn't open."

"Not now it isn't. I closed it myself, and locked it. But make sure you keep it that way. There's something around."

She stared at him through her magnifying spectacles. "I'm sorry, doctor. I don't understand what you mean."

"Someone managed to get in. A prowler. I caught him in the storeroom, but he managed to get away. He was—he was disturbing some of the cadavers."

"He did *what?* What are you talking about?"

Frank had to lean against the stainless-steel bench to keep his balance. At the far end of the bench, next to the faucets, lay an open instrument case full of scalpels and lancets. He couldn't help thinking that all he had to do was pick up a scalpel, and slit Helen Bryers' throat. One deep slice would do it, and then all of that warm, refreshing blood would come pumping out. He could clamp his mouth over her neck, and swallow, and swallow, and all of that hoarseness would be eased, and his skin would stop itching, and he wouldn't feel so burningly thirsty any longer.

"Doctor?" said Helen Bryers. "Maybe we should call security. I mean, if there's really an intruder—"

Frank nodded. "You're right, Helen. Maybe we should. I'll go talk to them now."

He pushed his way out of the morgue and into the corridor. He tilted from one wall to the other, and his vision was jumbled like a handheld camera. He could hear people shouting, and the clatter of gurneys, but he felt as if this was all happening to somebody else.

As he made his way through the ER, he heard Dean shouting to him. "Frank! *Frank!* I could really use some help here!" He turned around, and he could see Dean trying to help a young woman who was kneeling on the floor, vomiting up cascades of blood. But he felt too feverish, and he knew that none of these people could be saved. Dean shouted at him again, but he pushed his way through to the entrance, and back out into the night.

What do I do now? he thought to himself. *Where do I go? Maybe I ought to go home and crawl back into bed. Then I can finish this nightmare, and wake up properly, and none of this chaos will have happened.*

The streets outside the Sisters of Jerusalem were packed with struggling people. Some of them were still screaming, and some of them had dropped to their knees, babbling and swaying from side to side. But most of them were silent, although their eyes were staring and they were bearded with blood. "Save my boy!" a black woman called out, holding up a lolling child in bloodsoaked pajamas. "Please, sir, for the love of God, won't you save my boy?"

Frank lifted his left hand to block out the sight of her. From the angle of the child's head, and the gaping wound in his neck, it was obvious that he was already dead. Turning away, Frank tripped on a woman's body and almost fell. The night was so hot that he could hardly breathe, and his skin was burning so fiercely that he felt like tearing off his shirt. Yet he couldn't bear the thought of water. If he splashed himself with water, he was sure that he would be scalded. He needed to slather himself in fresh, warm blood.

He was still stumbling around behind the police lines when somebody came up behind him and gripped his shoulder.

"Dr. Winter? *Dr. Winter?*"

He swiveled around. It was Lieutenant Hayward Roberts. The lieutenant looked tired and grim and disheveled, and the red-and-blue police lights were dancing on his sweaty face. Not far away stood Detective Paul Mancini, talking on his cell phone. Detective Mancini's white shirt was torn and his left eye was half-closed by a glossy crimson bruise.

Lieutenant Roberts had to shout to make himself heard over the sirens and the noise of the crowd. "Glad we found you, doc! We've just been talking to your boss!"

"Oh, yes?"

"We found out what it meant! 'Tattle nostrew!' We

thought—you know—it might help to give us some answers!"

"You found out what it meant?" With a feeling of complete unreality, Frank thought: *Why are you telling me this? I* know *what it means.* He couldn't quite translate it word for word, but he knew that when Lieutenant Roberts explained it to him, it wouldn't come as any surprise.

Lieutenant Roberts took out a damp red handkerchief and wiped his face. Then he leaned forward and said, "I mentioned it to one of our detectives, back to the precinct. He's Romanian, a guy called Cioran."

"Our Father," said Frank.

Lieutenant Roberts stared at him. "That's right. 'Our Father.' How do *you* know?"

"I'm not exactly sure. But I guess when you think about it, it's obvious. The way that everybody was chanting it, it sounded like a prayer, and what's the one prayer that everybody knows by heart? '*Tatal nostru, carele esti in ceruri . . .*' Our Father, who art in heaven."

"So you worked that out already? You could have saved us a journey."

"No, no," said Frank. "It just came to me, I don't know how. But I'm really pleased you made the effort. At least we know for sure." He swayed a little. He felt so hot that he was sure that the skin on his face must be bubbling up in blisters. "Who did you talk to?"

"Your boss, Dr. Pellman; and a couple of your senior medics. But they didn't seem to think that it helped them any. In fact they found it more baffling than ever. Why is everybody who gets sick saying the Lord's Prayer, in Romanian? Like Dr. Pellman said, you can catch the chicken pox, and you can catch the influenza, but you can't catch a language."

"Mass hysteria, maybe," said Frank, thickly. God, he felt bad.

"Well, if it is, it's not like your usual mass hysteria. According to Dr. Pellman, there's been plenty of case histories of people thinking they're possessed by Satan, and cursing, and talking gibberish—and from what he knew, that kind of hysteria can spread pretty quickly, given the right social circumstances. Happened in Pennsylvania in the 1880s, apparently; and in Utah, among the Mormons. But nobody ever started speaking word-perfect Romanian, nor any other language."

Frank said, "Well, no. I never heard of that either. But I can't think why they're doing it, or how. Look—you'll have to forgive me. I'm not feeling too good myself. I was trying to get home."

"That's okay, doc. We can give you a ride."

"I'd be very grateful. I think the stress is beginning to get to me."

Lieutenant Roberts went over to the police lines, and spoke to the sergeant in charge. The sergeant called forward six or seven officers to help them through the crowds toward their car. There was some pushing and shoving and indignant shouting, but nobody became really aggressive. They climbed into Lieutenant Roberts' Buick, and locked the doors. People stared into the windows, and smeared blood all over the glass, but they seemed to be curious rather than hostile, and when Detective Mancini started up the engine and gradually nudged the car through the crowds, they shuffled out of the way and let them through.

"This thing is just spreading and spreading," said Lieutenant Roberts. "Unless you doctors can find out what's causing it, I don't see what we can do to stop it. We've had so many homicides, citywide, people with their throats cut, we've completely lost count. And there doesn't seem to be any logic to it. None at all."

Frank thought of Susan Fireman, back at his apartment. He wondered if she was still there (if she had *ever* been there, and this wasn't a nightmare). Susan Fireman seemed to know what this epidemic was all about. She could climb impossible walls and she knew all about "passing through," whatever that was. *Darkness, and shadows, and closed boxes.* Maybe if Lieutenant Roberts could arrest her, and interrogate her, she might give them the leads that they were looking for.

His hands were burning so fiercely that he clamped them under his armpits to relieve the pain.

Lieutenant Roberts heaved himself around in the front passenger seat and said, "You okay, doc? You're really looking logey."

"I'm okay. Just tired, I guess."

"Hmh! Just so long as *you* don't start chanting that 'tattle nostrew' stuff."

"Me? No, no. I don't think I'm quite that bad." Although he couldn't help thinking, "*tatal nostru . . . carele esti in ceruri . . . sfinteasca-se numele tau . . .*" He could almost hear it sung inside his head, in a high, childish soprano.

"*Si nu ne duce pre noi in inspita . . .* lead us not into temptation . . . *ci ne scapa de cel rau . . .* but deliver us from evil. *Amin.*"

They reached Frank's apartment building in the tree-lined street on Murray Hill and Detective Mancini pulled into the curb.

Lieutenant Roberts said, "Listen, doc, if you think of anything—give me a call. Anything, even if you think it sounds stupid."

"Well . . . there is something. That girl Susan Fireman . . . the first one to get sick."

"What about her?"

"I think I might have been hallucinating, or dreaming, maybe. But she appeared in my apartment."

"She appeared in your apartment," Lieutenant Roberts repeated.

"This was after she died, right?" asked Detective Mancini.

"Yes."

Lieutenant Roberts thought about that for a while, and then he said, "Maybe you need to take some time off, doc. A situation like this . . . well, it can throw you off-balance more than you realize."

"You don't have to tell me that, lieutenant, I'm a doctor. I'm fully prepared to admit that I might have been suffering from exhaustion, or stress, or some kind of mental aberration. But it certainly didn't *feel* like a mental aberration, at the time. And it *still* doesn't feel like it, even now. In fact, I'm ninety percent confident that if I go upstairs right now, she'll still be there, waiting for me."

Lieutenant Roberts puffed out his cheeks, and thought some more. "So what do you want me to do, doc? Ms. Susan Fireman is wanted for multiple homicide, and if she's really hiding in your apartment, then I need to go up there and arrest her. But I know for a fact that Ms. Susan Fireman is deceased, so why should I waste my time?"

"She's dead, yes," Frank admitted. "I was right there in the room when she died. But somehow she came back. She climbed up into my apartment when I was asleep and she—"

"She what, doc?" asked Detective Mancini.

Frank opened the Buick's door. "Nothing. You're right. I must have dreamt it."

"She *what?*" repeated Lieutenant Roberts.

Frank hesitated, but when he saw that they weren't going to leave him until he had given them an answer, he said, "She forced me to have intercourse with her. It was a sex dream, I guess."

Lieutenant Roberts climbed out of the car. "I think I'm going to take a look in your apartment, Dr. Winter. I don't believe for one moment that Ms. Fireman is actually there, but I need to satisfy my insatiable curiosity."

"Believe me, lieutenant—"

"I *do* believe you, doc. I believe that you believe that Ms. Fireman came to visit you after she was deceased, and had carnal relations with you. But I want to know *why* you believe such a thing."

"I didn't steal her body from the hospital, if that's what you're trying to imply. When she climbed into my apartment she was alive, and she was talking, and she was quite capable of forcing me to have sex with her."

"You're saying she raped you?"

"Not exactly. But she was very compelling, and I was afraid of her. Well, anybody would have been afraid of her. She was supposed to be dead. She *was* dead."

Lieutenant Roberts took hold of Frank's arm. "Come on, doc, let's make a quick inspection, shall we? I don't need a search warrant, do I, seeing as how you're inviting me up to your apartment?"

"I don't know—I don't think—I'm really not feeling too good—"

"Won't take but a minute, doc," said Lieutenant Roberts, and helped him up the front steps, gripping his arm so tightly that Frank didn't have a chance of breaking free. Frank found his keys and opened the front door.

His apartment was in darkness, and so he switched on the spotlights. Lieutenant Roberts walked into the center of the living room and looked around, while Detective Mancini went through to the kitchen.

"Very stylish place you have here," said Lieutenant Roberts. He picked up a small chrome statuette of a dancing nude. "Jon Diavolo," he said. "Must have cost you a good few ulcer treatments."

"It was a gift from my sister."

Lieutenant Roberts put it down. He picked up a book of matches from the Red Bench on Sullivan Street, a onetime

Mafia hangout, but now a popular bar for SoHo drinkers who didn't like tourists. "Where did you say Ms. Fireman climbed in?"

"I didn't. But the bedroom window was the only one that was open."

"You want to show me?"

Frank led him through to the bedroom. The sheets were still twisted, and the pillows were scattered across the floor.

"Rough night?" asked Lieutenant Roberts. Frank shrugged, but didn't say anything. He couldn't. His throat was raging, and his skin felt as if he had burned himself sunbathing, and then climbed into a scalding bath.

Lieutenant Roberts inspected the window and then he said, "Beats me how anybody could get in there. Even a contortionist."

"I'm really going to have to lie down," said Frank. Maybe if he wrapped himself up in a sheet and crouched on the bed in the fetal position, his skin wouldn't burn so fiercely. *Oh God, help me*, he thought. *Tatal nostru, carele esti in ceruri.*

"Are you in a hurry to get rid of us?" asked Lieutenant Roberts. He opened up Frank's closet and inspected his neatly arranged shirts and suits. "Very nice threads," he remarked. "Good to see a man who cares about his clothes."

At that moment Detective Mancini came in.

"Nobody?" said Lieutenant Roberts.

Detective Mancini shook his head. "I even checked the laundry hamper."

"Okay, then. It looks like we need to get back to the precinct, and add to the general sense of helplessness. Thanks for showing us around, doc. Why don't you get some rest, that's my recommendation, and maybe something solid to eat."

Through the bedroom door, Frank saw a quick, pale flicker. At first glance he thought that it was Detective

Mancini's shirt, reflected in the full-length mirror that hung in the hall. But as Detective Mancini stepped to one side, away from the mirror, Frank saw to his horror that it was Susan Fireman. She was wearing her simple white gown, and her face was white, too, as if it had been dusted with flour. But she wasn't in the hall.

She was *inside* the mirror, as if the mirror were an open doorway, and she were standing in another room.

Detective Mancini had his back to the mirror, and couldn't see her, even though he was only five or six inches away. "Ready to hit the bricks then, Lieutenant?"

"Mmh-hmh. I'm coming." Lieutenant Roberts was taking a last look under the bed, just to make sure that nobody was hiding there.

Frank shouted out, in a hoarse, breathless voice, "There! For Christ's sake! She's there! Look! Behind you! She's *there!*"

Susan Fireman turned toward him and gave him a wicked, conspiratorial smile.

"*There!*" Frank repeated.

Detective Mancini frowned, and said, "What? Where?"

He started to turn around, but Susan Fireman's arms flowed out of the mirror and Frank saw the sharp glint of steel. With one deep, diagonal cut, she sliced Detective Mancini's throat all the way across, flooding his collar with scarlet. Detective Mancini took one jerky step forward, trying to balance, then another. He looked totally bewildered. But then his head tilted backward and a huge fountain of blood came gushing out of his neck, spurting right up to the ceiling and all across the magnolia-painted walls. He tipped sideways and fell against the hall bureau, knocking his head against the brass handles. He lay on his stomach, his feet jiggling in a desperate little dance.

Lieutenant Roberts said, "What the *fuck*—" He reached inside his coat, trying to pull his gun out, but he wasn't quick enough for Susan Fireman. She stepped out of the mirror and then—*blink*—she was already in the bedroom, as if several frames of her movements had been edited out. Lieutenant Roberts was turning around to face her, his gun half out of its holster, but then—*blink*—she was standing right behind him.

Frank shouted, "*Susan!*" but he was already too late. Susan Fireman slit Lieutenant Roberts' throat so quickly that he didn't even see her do it. Blood burst out from beneath his chin and immediately soaked the front of his shirt.

Without hesitation, Susan Fireman pushed Lieutenant Roberts onto his knees, but then she seized his collar so that he couldn't fall forward onto his face. She looked up at Frank and her pale-blue eyes were bulging. "Here!" she panted. "Here's what you need, Frank! This will make you feel better!"

She gripped Lieutenant Roberts' curly gray hair and pulled his head back, so that the wound in his throat gaped even wider. She had cut incredibly deep, right through his sternocleidomastoid muscle, severing his external jugular vein and his carotid artery.

Frank stared at the wound in horror, and then at Susan Fireman. Her face was almost luminous with excitement. "Look at it!" she told him. You're letting it all go to waste! God almighty, Frank, if you don't have it, then I will!"

As a doctor, Frank had sworn never to hurt anybody. *Above all, I shall not play God.* But Lieutenant Roberts was probably semiconscious by now, and there was absolutely no chance of saving his life. Meanwhile, Frank's skin was burning hotter and hotter. He felt as if he had been doused in gasoline and set ablaze, and his throat was so dry and constricted that his vocal cords had shriveled.

And there was something else, too. A dark and uncontrollable need was rising up inside him like a shark rising to the surface of the ocean, drawn by the scent of blood. Frank had never realized before how strongly blood smelled, even fresh blood, but he could smell it now.

Warm, and metallic, and teeming with life. In spite of his agony, or partly because of it, his penis began to harden, and he began to salivate.

Oh God forgive me, he thought. He hesitated for a moment, looking one way and then the other, but then he knelt down, cupping Lieutenant Roberts' chin in his left hand, and placing his right hand flat on his chest, so that he could tilt his head back even further. Blood was jumping seven or eight inches out of Lieutenant Roberts' carotid artery, and when Frank leaned forward with his mouth open, it splashed against Frank's cheek, and then his nose. For a split second, he thought that he could find the strength to turn away, but then blood spurted across his lips, and when he involuntarily licked it, the taste overwhelmed him.

With a grunt of sheer greed, he clamped his lips over Lieutenant Roberts' wound so that his warm blood would jet directly onto the roof of his mouth. The flavor was astonishing. It tasted like iron, and molasses, and raw meat, and oysters, and the fresh juices of sexually aroused women. He swallowed, and almost at once his throat began to open up, and he felt an extraordinary cooling sensation, starting at the top of his head, and gradually sinking down his body, as if somebody with very cold hands was lightly teasing him from top to toe. He swallowed more, and more. He couldn't swallow enough of it. His penis was so rigid that it hurt, and when the blood flow from Lieutenant Roberts' carotid artery started to weaken, and he had to suck harder, he felt himself ejaculate, and his shorts fill up with sticky wet semen.

But he went on swallowing, and swallowing, and gasping for air, until he suddenly it was all too rich for him, and he retched, and vomited blood all down the front of Lieutenant Roberts' coat.

Slowly, he lifted his head. Susan Fireman was looking down at him with an expression that he had never seen on any human being before. In a way, it reminded him of the slanting shadow-creature that he had seen in the morgue. It was a mixture of contempt, and pity, but relief, too, as if he were a wayward son who had at last decided to come home.

12

BLOOD RELATIVES

"I can't help you with this, Harry," said Amelia. "This isn't your Uncle Walter trying to get his revenge on you because you sold off his precious stamp collection."

"Amelia, I never had an Uncle Walter."

"Of course you didn't. I'm simply trying to tell you that this is way out of my league."

"But you're the best! You're the crème de la milk."

Amelia emphatically shook her head. "When it comes to small-scale stuff, like people's dead relatives, I'm fine, Harry, I can handle it. A wife dies, her husband remarries. The wife's dead but she still feels jealous. She starts throwing pots and pans across the kitchen, or maybe she creates obnoxious smells in the bedroom, when her husband's trying to make love. I can *talk* to a spirit like that, negotiate with her, calm her down. I can make her understand that life has to go on, even though she's passed over. But this is something else altogether. This is one of the reasons I gave up clairvoyance. This is very deep water, Harry, and you could easily drown."

I had picked up my beer bottle to take a swig but now I

put it down again. "Amelia—when Misquamacus was reincarnated—you were amazing. He was the greatest Indian wonder-worker in history, and you were more than a match for him, weren't you? We wouldn't even have known who Misquamacus *was*, or what he was trying to do, if it hadn't been for you."

Bertie cleared his throat. "If my wife does not feel that she can help you, Harry, you will have to accept it."

"But she *can* help us. She has to. I mean, who else is there?"

Amelia picked up the piece of paper with STRIGOI written on it. "Your friend Gil here is absolutely right. This is one of the Romanian words for 'vampires.' I don't know very much about them, only what my friend Razvan Dragomir has told me, but I do know that these are supposed to be real, live vampires, not storybook vampires, and that most Romanians are still very afraid of them—not just peasants, city-dwellers, too—educated people, like doctors and university professors and lawyers."

"So I was right, and we *are* being invaded by vampires?"

"This is absurdness!" Bertie protested. "Just because you can't understand something, you believe immediately that it must be supernatural! Wampires indeed! Are we *children*? There is no such thing as wampires!"

None of us said anything, but we all looked at each other, like students waiting for their angry teacher to finish ranting.

Bertie said, "In a few days, hopefully, the doctors will discover that this epidemic is caused by a pathogen that infects people with a very unpleasing thirst for human blood. The pathogen will be isolated and an antidote will be formulated. It will be straightforward science, my friend. Nothing to do with garlic and crosses and stakes through the heart."

"You think so?" I challenged him. "In that case, how

come I saw Singing Rock and Singing Rock gave me the letters that make up the Romanian word for vampires? That
wasn't straightforward science, was it?"

"No," said Bertie. "It was your fevered imagination, running like a guinea pig in a little wheel."

"Now come on, Bertie—" I began.

But Amelia said, "Harry . . . Bertil simply doesn't believe
in ghosts and demons and things like that. He thinks that
they're caused by a glitch in the human brain."

"In particular, an aberration of the amygdala," said
Bertie, "the center of human fear."

I looked at him in disbelief. "Amelia hasn't told you about
Misquamacus?"

"Of course. Amelia has told me everything about the life
she lived before we met."

"Bertie—Misquamacus was no aberration of the Dalai
Lama, or whatever it is. He was an Indian wonder-worker
from three hundred years ago and he was reincarnated in a
woman's neck. Not just any woman, either, but the woman
I married. We saw it for ourselves. I saw it, Amelia saw it.
Misquamacus almost managed to summon up some of the
greatest forces that the ancient world had ever known.
Storms, lightning, earthquakes, it was unbelievable. He
could have reduced the whole of Manhattan to rubble. If it
hadn't been for Amelia and Singing Rock . . . well, God
knows what would have happened. But that was real."

Bertie nodded and kept on nodding. "I am quite sure that
you *perceived* it to be real."

"You want me to introduce you to Dr. Hughes? He was
there, at the Sisters of Jerusalem, when Misquamacus was
reincarnated, and he lost three fingers to some invisible
lizard. Why don't you tell *him* that he only perceived it?
Eleven cops got killed. Why don't you tell their families that
they only perceived it? Pity their kids can't perceive them
coming home again."

Bertie stood up. "Harry, I am not going to argue with you about the nature of reality. I am simply telling you that Amelia is not going to get involved in this insanity, whether you are right or wrong."

I looked at Amelia. There was an expression on her face that I had only seen once before. It was sadness for something that had gone and that could never be recovered. Maybe it was youth, or happiness, or courage. Maybe it was all three.

"Okay," I said. I was tempted to ask Amelia what *she* thought, but it wouldn't have been fair. Once upon a time she might have been Amelia Crusoe, psychic and clairvoyant, with wild curly hair and jingly earrings, but now she was Mrs. Amelia Carlsson, and I had no right to ask her to be disloyal to her husband, even if he was an asshole.

"Go see Razvan," she said. "He can probably help you. He's written half a dozen books about Romanian witchcraft, and he's probably the greatest expert on vampire legends outside of Bucharest. He's also very sensitive. I met him at a psychic fair in White Plains."

"This is such nonsense," said Bertie, with an abrasive laugh. "Why are you wasting Harry's time like this?"

Amelia wrote down a name and address on the notepad, tore it off, and handed it to me. Bertie gave a dismissive *pfff!* but he didn't try to stop her.

"Thanks," I said. Then, to Bertie, "Sorry. I shouldn't have come around here. I didn't mean to rub your fur up all the wrong way."

"Well, it's forgotten," said Bertie. "It's just that I was brought up to be pragmatic, and to believe in scientific evidence rather than superstition." He put his arm around Amelia's shoulders. "When I met Amelia, I considered it the challenge of my life to show her that no matter how strange events may be, they cannot be explained by magic, or by cards, or crystal balls."

He showed us to the door. Gil said, "Thanks for the beer,

sir," and nodded to Amelia. "Thanks, ma'am. Thanks for try-ing, anyhow."

Outside, on the street, he turned around to face me. "Harry," he said, with great solemnity, "I believe you."

"You do?"

"This epidemic. It *is* vampires, isn't it?"

"Well, I believe so. Or some kind of supernatural force."

"You bet. Did you see her face when you showed her that piece of paper? That was the face of a woman who is truly, genuinely scared shitless. I know. I've seen faces like that before, in Bosnia."

"I'm sure I could have persuaded her to help us, if hubby had let her."

"Well, I don't know about that. But I do know that she wasn't just play-acting. She saw that word and she went *white*. And that's why I believe you. It would have been much easier for her if she had lied to you, because her hus-band doesn't believe in vampires, and he was bound to give her a hard time about it. But she didn't, did she? And if *she* thinks this epidemic is being caused by vampires, and *you* think it's caused by vampires, then I do, too."

At that moment my cell phone warbled. It was Amelia.

"Harry? Listen, I'm so sorry I couldn't do anything more to help you out. Bertil—well, he's very protective, and he's a lit-tle jealous, too, of the people I used to know before we met."

"Don't worry," I reassured her. "Gil and I are going to see your Romanian friend right now. I'll tell you what—I'll keep you up to speed, so that you know what's going on. Maybe you can give us some helpful hints."

"Harry?"

"What?"

I don't know why I said "what?" I knew from the tone of her voice exactly what she meant. It was like meeting an old girlfriend from your teenage years, and picking up her big fat kid and saying, "he's terrific, isn't he?" when what you're really trying to say is, "remember those times, lying on the grass, with the sun shining through the trees, and we didn't care about anything but us?"

Gil looked at his watch and said, "Listen—I should go check back with the other guys, tell them what I'm doing."

"You can use my cell phone if you like."

"I have my own," said Gil, holding it up. "But I think this is something I have to explain to them face-to-face. Besides, I need to see my family. My wife, my little girls. I ought to make sure they're safe."

"Okay, then, sure. Why don't I go see this Romanian character, and you catch up with me?" I peered at the piece of paper that Amelia had given me. "Sixty-one Leroy Street, that's only three blocks from here. You should recognize Leroy Street—that's where they shot the exteriors for *The Cosby Show*. Put my number into your phone, so that we can keep in touch."

Gil started to make his way back toward Houston Street. He had only walked half a block, however, when I heard whooping and screaming, and the rushing noise of dozens of pairs of feet. Around the corner came fifty or sixty people, their eyes staring, their arms waving, their clothes drenched in blood. They were mostly men, but I saw at least six or seven women, one of them with her ginger hair stuck up with dried blood like a Native American headdress, and another one bare-breasted with scores of crisscross cuts all over her breasts.

They ran toward Gil and Gil immediately turned around and started running back toward me. I saw the flashing of knives and I knew exactly what they wanted, and so I started running, too.

"*Harry!*" Gil yelled at me.

It didn't take long for Gil to catch up with me. He was at least five years younger than me and I doubt if he drank seven cans of Irish porter every day. Together we pounded back along Christopher Street, with the screaming crowd close behind us, and believe me I was so panicky that I could hardly catch my breath.

We turned south on Bedford Street, crossing Grove Street and Barrow Street, still running flat out. But as wild and disheveled as it was, the crowd was catching up with us. I didn't want to look back but I could hear the *slap-slap-slap* of their feet echoing from the buildings close by, and I guessed that they were only half a block behind.

"Maybe—we should—split up!" I panted.

"No!" Gil retorted. "We're going to have to face them!"

"Are you—nuts? They'll cut us up—like—carrots!"

"There!" said Gil. "Building site!"

"*What?*"

But Gil didn't answer me. Instead, he headed diagonally across the street to the corner of Houston and Morton, where the front of a nineteenth-century warehouse was being restored. The front of the building was covered in scaffolding and placards announcing a new TradeWinds Fashion Store, and there were two builders' Dumpsters parked in the street outside.

Gil jumped up onto one of the Dumpsters and pulled out a short length of scaffolding pole. "Here!" he said, and threw it to me. Then he dragged out a six-foot length of timber, with razor wire wrapped around one end.

"We have to stand back-to-back!" he told me. "And don't think about them as people! They want to kill us, and they will, unless we kill them first!"

We stood back-to-back in the center of Morton Street as the crowd ran up to us. I swung the scaffolding pole from side to side, and did some fancy figure eights with it, like Tom Cruise in *The Last Samurai*. Gil stood still, with his feet planted wide apart, gripping that length of timber in both hands, and looking as if he were ready to take on the combined hordes of Genghis Khan and Attila the Hun.

"Whatever you do, stay close," Gil told me. "Don't allow those freaks to get in between us, or we're finished."

The crowd had slowed down now, and they were approaching us very cautiously. All of them were carrying knives or machetes or sickles, and all of them had a stareyeyed expression on their faces. They were all very white, too, as if all the blood had drained out of them. Some of them were moaning, and others were sobbing in pain, and I realized that they must all be feeling the same burning sensation that had driven Ted Busch so crazy, as if they were being cremated alive.

"Listen!" Gil shouted at them. "We know that you're all feeling pretty sick, and that you're thirsty for blood, but this is a big mistake! Me and my friend here, we're looking for a way to cure you, to give you your normal lives back! Haven't you ever seen a vampire movie, for Christ's sakes? If you kill us, you'll need to drink blood forever!"

I don't know whether they could understand him or not, but they took no notice. They kept edging forward, their knives and their sickles raised up, watching us closely for any sign that we were going to lose our nerve and make a run for it. Apart from their blood-spattered clothes and their staring eyes, they looked just like regular everyday people. I saw a man who could have been my accountant, in a red polo shirt and glasses; and a fiftyish-looking guy in a bus driver's uniform. I saw a woman who looked like Lucy's grade-school teacher, and another woman in a white silk blouse and pearls. They were ordinary men and women, the same men and women that you would pass every day in the street and never even glance at—but because they were so ordinary, they were ten times more scary than zombies in decaying tuxedos, or vampires wrapped up in tattered winding-sheets.

"How are we going to play this, Gil?" I asked him, trying to confident.

"There's only one way, Harry," said Gil. "Them or us."

"Hmm. 'Them or us.' You know, I never really understood

what that meant. I mean, if it's 'them,' does that mean that *they* win? And what happens if it's 'us'?"

Gil said, "Just hit the bastards and keep on hitting them until they stop moving. You can worry about the grammar afterward."

Without any warning, the man in the red polo shirt and glasses came running toward me, screaming. I had never taken any classes in martial arts, but I crouched down and whirled my scaffolding pole like a kendo thingy, and shouted out, "*Hai! Ahaki! Ahaki-waki-baki!*" Then I swung my scaffolding pole and hit the man on his upraised elbow.

It could have been a lucky swing, but it struck him so hard that his craft knife went flying and I think I might even have broken his arm. He dropped sideways onto the ground, making a high, piping noise, like a run-over squirrel.

"*Finish him!*" Gil shouted at me.

"He doesn't need finishing! He's finished already!"

"Finish him! If you don't finish him, the others will think that we don't have the stones!"

"For Christ's sake! I can't murder him!"

"Keep your back against me!" Gil ordered.

"What?"

Gil nudged me with his left shoulder, hard. Then he edged his way around until *he* was facing the man in the red polo shirt. I didn't have any choice but to edge around, too, to protect his back. With no hesitation at all, Gil hefted up his length of timber with both hands and whacked it into the man's face. It made a dull, wooden bang, and a nasty crack, too, which must have been the man's skull breaking. Gil pulled the timber up again, and the razor wire dragged half of the man's face with it, including his right eye and his upper lip. The man was screaming in a piercing falsetto, but Gil whacked him again, and then again, and then again, and bloody shreds of his face were flying around everywhere.

I was thinking: *Jesus!* But I didn't have time to think anything more. A bald-headed man in a sweaty gray T-shirt came ducking and weaving toward me, closely followed by a frizzy-haired woman waving a straight razor, of all things. I swung my scaffolding pole from side to side, trying to look threatening, but the two of them suddenly rushed at me, with two other men close behind them, one of them brandishing a carving knife.

Now I knew what Gil meant by "them or us." I shouted out "*hakamundo!*" and struck the woman on the side of the head. She screamed and dropped to her knees, with her left ear smashed into scarlet gristle. The bald man stepped back in surprise, and as he did so I brought the scaffolding pole right down on the top of his skull, as hard as I could. The pole *rang*, like a bell, and I could feel the shock of hitting him all the way up to my shoulder joints.

The man fell facedown in front of me, dropping a horn-handled camping knife with a clatter.

One of the other men lunged at me, but I brandished my scaffolding pole in a furious criss-cross pattern. He managed to touch it with the tip of his knife, so that it went *ting!!* But then he backed away, and kept on backing away, and the crowd behind him started to back away, too.

Gil was still furiously waving his length of timber, but after they had seen what he had done to the man in the red polo shirt, the rest of the crowd had clearly lost its appetite. Part of the man's nose was still dangling on the razor wire, and whatever pain these people were going through, and no matter how much they thirsted for blood, they didn't seem to think that it was worth losing their schnozzes for. They stepped back—grudgingly at first, one step at a time, but then Gil screamed, "*Come and get it! Come on, you freaks! Come and get it!*" and took two or three steps toward them. Without any more hesitation, they all turned around and hurried away down Houston Street, their feet pattering urgently on the tarmac. At the corner, one of the women let out a hair-raising, vixen-like shriek, but I think she was crying out in pain rather than frustration. These people were hurting too badly to waste any more time on Gil and me: They needed blood and they needed it quickly, before their burning became unbearable.

Gil threw down his length of timber and said, "Good job, Harry."

I was sweating and shaking and I could hardly keep my balance. I had never had to fight for my life like that, not hand-to-hand. In fact I don't think I had ever hit anybody since Jimmy Ruggio in the second grade. But I managed to give my scaffolding pole a last defiant flourish in the air before I threw that down, too, with an echoing clang. "Them or us, Gil," I told him. "Them or us."

It was well past eleven o'clock. "Why don't you go back to see your family?" I suggested. "Give me a call before you come back out again. If this Romanian guy isn't home, or if he doesn't want to talk to me, you don't want to risk running into those ghouls again, do you?"

Gil gripped my shoulder so hard that it hurt, although I didn't let on. I've never had too many friends, especially friends who were capable of beating the crap out of people, but that night I believed that I had found a friend in Gil. I really liked his straightforwardness, and his complete lack of cynicism. He was GI Joe, right out of the box. But most of all I liked him because he had shown me that *I* could beat the crap out of people, too, if I really needed to. He had made me feel brave.

He said, "Okay then, I'll catch you later." Then he turned and walked back toward Seventh Avenue and I walked off in the direction of Leroy Street, although I had to stop on the corner, and drag out the tail of my shirt, and wipe my face with it.

Along this stretch of Hudson Street, every store window and restaurant had a smashed frontage. Only one fluorescent light was still flickering, the lettering outside the Hudson Street Grill, and out of those only three letters were left unbroken—the "l" of "Grill" and the "up" of "Suppers."

I stopped and stared at it for a few moments, but Singing Rock had already given me my message, so I didn't think that "l up" could mean anything.

Razvan Dragomir's house was a tall, narrow brownstone in the row between Washington Street and Greenwich Street. Two well-clipped bay trees stood in huge ceramic pots on the front steps, secured with chains that you could have used to dock the *Mauretania*. I looked up and down the double row of shiny brass doorbells until I found a bell marked *R. Dragomir* in mauve ink, right at the top, and pushed it.

There was no answer, so I pushed it again. It would be just my luck if Amelia's friend was out of town. When people try to save the world in movies, everybody they ask for help is always at home. But in real life it never works out that way.

I had already turned around, ready to leave, when the intercom made a popping noise and a woman with a strongly accented voice said, "*Da?* Who is it who is there?"

I jumped back to the door. "Oh! Hi! Sorry to disturb you! My name's Harry Erskine, I'm a friend of Amelia Crusoe. Well, Amelia Carlsson, as she is these days. I'm looking for Mr. Razvan Dragomir."

"Oh, yes. Mrs. Carlsson called earlier to say that you might be coming. I'm sorry but my father is away for two weeks in Bucharest."

"I see. Is there any way I can contact him? I really seriously need his advice."

"Mrs. Carlsson explains this all to me. About this epidemic, the people who are dying. I can help you."

"*You* can help me? Really?"

"I am my father's daughter. What my father knows, I know. Wait, I will let you inside. Top floor, take the elevator."

The door release buzzed and I pushed my way inside.

The hallway was gloomy and smelled of lavender polish and musty old plaster and mold. I turned around and saw this scruffy-looking deadbeat standing right next to me, and almost had a heart attack, but it was a mirror, hanging in an alcove.

At the end of the hallway I found a rickety old elevator with one of those handles that you swung up for "Up." It slowly cranked me to the fourth story, although I was sure that I could hear the wires twanging, one by one. When I forced open the door and stepped out, I found myself in large apartment, dimly lit by pierced brass lamps. There was nobody there to meet me.

The deadbeat that I had encountered in the lobby had come up with me, because there he was again, reflected in a huge full-length mirror opposite the front door. The mirror had a dark mahogany frame that was carved with all kinds of fruit and vegetables, apples and cabbages and summer squash.

"Hallo?" I called out. I could smell cloves, and stale tobacco, and something sickly sweet, as if somebody had burned a panful of condensed milk.

I slammed the elevator door. The Dragomir apartment looked like a Romanian folk museum. It was crammed with blood-red velvet couches and blood-red velvet chairs and embroidered footstools. Every wall was hung with gilt-framed mirrors and Oriental rugs, and between the mirrors and the rugs hung oil paintings of frowning men with magnificent moustaches and felt hats with peacock feathers spouting out of them; and dark-eyed women in white lace headscarves and richly decorated blouses. The place was knee-deep in shining brass-topped tables crammed with ornaments and family photographs, and shining brass storks, and feathery ferns in shining brass vases.

"*Hallo?*" I repeated.

"Welcome, Mr. Erskine," said the strongly accented voice. From behind a heavy velvet curtain that was draped over one of the doorways, Razvan Dragomir's daughter appeared, as if she were making an entrance in a 1930s horror movie.

She was tall, over six foot one in her shoes, at least as tall as me and probably taller, with short, black glossy hair that was severely cut around her face, Vidal Sassoon-style. Her eyes were slanted and deep set, and she had high, sharply defined cheekbones, and belligerently pouting lips. She was wearing a very short black shift, with red embroidery on it, and puffy little sleeves that accentuated her very wide shoulders, and her legs went on till next Labor Day. Her breasts were huge, but far too heavy and complicated in their movement to be anything but natural. In her cleavage hung a five-pointed gold star, studded with garnets.

She held out a hand with rings on every finger, including her thumbs. "My name is Jenica Dragomira, but of course you can call me Jenica."

"Harry Erskine, but of course you can call me Harry."

"Mr. Harry, you have hurt your face. It is bleeding."

"Oh, that, yes." I touched the plaster that Laticia had stuck on my cheek. It was soaked with blood, and hanging half off. The cut must have opened up again when I was fighting with the crowds in the street.

"Here, Mr. Harry, come with me," said Jenica. She drew back the curtain again and indicated that I should walk through. I hesitated for a moment, but then I did as I was told. As I passed her, my arm brushed against her breasts and I breathed in her perfume, which was like crushed roses and Turkish Delight, combined with that musky aroma of warm hair. I don't think I could have dated Jenica, even if she had agreed to go out with me. I would have spent the whole evening trying to hide my hard-on.

"This way." Jenica ushered me along a narrow, wallpapered corridor. At the very end, she opened another door, and then she took my hand as if I were a child and led me inside. I found myself standing in the most amazing bathroom that I had ever visited. It was decorated like a Moorish temple, with pillars and arches and peacock-blue mosaic tiles, and it had green stained-glass windows with herons and leaping fishes on them, and it echoed. Jenica opened up her elaborately carved medicine cabinet and took out some cotton pads and a bottle of lurid yellow antiseptic.

"You are brave?" she asked me.

"A little pain never hurt anyone," I told her, gritting my teeth.

She dabbed my cut with antiseptic and it stung so much that I couldn't help yelping.

"You will have to very, very brave to face *strigoi*," she murmured.

I looked at her cautiously. "You said the word. You said it out loud."

"Of course. Some ignorant people think it is dangerous to say the word *strigoi*. But it is only dangerous to speak the name of any particular *strigoi*."

"I see." I realized then that I hadn't yet received the whole message. Singing Rock had told me that I was looking for a vampire, but I didn't yet know *which* vampire.

Jenica and I stared at each other and we both knew that we weren't really looking into each other's eyes. We were staring into the abyss.

13

BLOOD HUNT

Frank couldn't stop shivering. The thermostat on his air-conditioning unit said that it was 94 degrees in his bed-room, and he was basted in sweat, but he felt chilled to the very core, as if his skeleton had been taken out of his body and stored in the freezer overnight, and then put back. Even his teeth felt as if they were frozen.

He didn't know what time it was but he knew that some-thing nightmarish had happened. Every time he swallowed he could taste metal, and the roof of his mouth felt as if it were thickly coated in congealed fat. He had a jumbled memory of somebody shouting, and blood, and struggling, but his brain refused to focus on it in any detail. It occurred to him that he might have been involved in a serious acci-dent, and that he was suffering from shock.

It didn't occur to him that he was dying.

He tried to sit up. After two attempts, he managed to prop himself up on one elbow. It was then that he saw Susan Fireman sitting on the end of his bed watching him. It was still dark outside, although the city sounded much quieter than it had before. No helicopters, and only an occasional siren.

"I feel cold," he croaked.

Susan Fireman stood up and moved around the bed with a strange gliding walk. She looked down at him and she was smiling. "It won't be long now," she told him. "You took care of me, and now I'm taking care of you."

"I feel so cold. Why do I feel so cold?"

"You won't feel cold for much longer, Frank."

He lay back down on the bed. "What's happening to me?" he asked her.

She stroked his sweat-beaded forehead with her fingertips, and then sucked them, one after the other. "The greatest adventure that can happen to anyone."

"I don't understand."

"You will, Frank, once you pass over. It will all become shining clear to you, as if the moon has come up."

"The moon?"

"Of course. You can never see the sun again."

Frank slept, and dreamed that he was running through the dunes at Hyannis, on Cape Cod, where he used to live when he was a boy. The wind was fluffing in his ears and the long grass was whipping his legs. In his dream he was aware that something was badly wrong but he didn't know what. He turned his head to see if anybody was running after him but there was nobody there. Only the dunes, and the clouds, and the slowly circling seagulls.

The sky was so blue that it was almost black, like night.

As he climbed the dunes toward the roadway, he saw a dazzling flash of light. It flashed again, and it was so bright that he had to lift his hand to shield his eyes. He struggled up through the deep, soft sand until he reached a white picket fence. An old black Mercury Marquis was parked about fifty yards away, its side panels smeary with wax. It looked at first like the same car that had once belonged to his grandfather, but then he realized that it had been converted into a hearse, and that there was a gray metal casket lying in the back. His grandfather, Stephen, was sitting in the driver's seat, his white hair combed so that it was shining like a halo. He was staring out toward the ocean.

Not far away from the front of the car stood Susan Fireman. She was naked except for a strange hat that looked as if it had been folded out of stiff black paper. Beside her was the cheval-mirror that usually stood in the corner of his bedroom, and she was deliberately angling it into his eyes.

He reached the tarmac and started to walk toward her. The sand crunched under his shoes. "What are you doing here?" he shouted at her, although his voice sounded flat and muffled, as if he were shouting into a metal bucket.

She didn't answer, so he walked right up to her. She lifted her head and smiled at him, and both of her eyes were totally crimson.

"What's happening?" he asked her.

"You can't go out in the sun any more," said Susan Fireman. "I thought you would like to see its reflection, to remember it by."

Frank turned around. Behind him, it was nighttime. The sky was dark and the ocean was nothing but a thin, phosphorescent line of foam. Inside the cheval-mirror, however, it was still daylight, and the sun was shining on the sand.

"What's happening?" Frank repeated.

"Don't you know, Frank? You're passing over. The sun will be coming up soon. Why don't you step inside the looking glass, where it's bright? You can be safe there, until it's dark."

"What do you mean, 'step inside the looking glass'?"

"A looking glass is a *door*, Frank. It's not a wall. A looking glass is a way through."

"I can't step inside, it's impossible."

"Come on, Frank. You're one of the pale people now. You can do anything you want. Climb walls, step into mirrors."

Susan Fireman walked around so that she was facing the mirror. She turned to look at Frank and then she stepped straight into the glass, so that she joined up with her own reflection, like two brightly colored shapes in a kaleidoscope. The next thing Frank knew, she was standing *inside* the mirror, in the sunshine, and she was no longer beside him, in the dark. She laughed, and he could hear her, but she sounded as if she were laughing on the other side of a closed window. Alarmed, he looked around. The wind was rising and he was alone. His grandfather had gone, too. The black hearse stood empty, its chrome spotted with rust and its windows all milky.

"Come on, Frank," said Susan Fireman. "It only takes a single step."

"I'm not coming," he told her.

"You have to, Frank. You don't have any choice."

"I told you, I'm not coming!"

It was then that he saw something on the shoreline, about a half-mile behind Susan Fireman, right at the ocean's edge. It was tall and dark and angular, and it was striding toward her. It reminded him of the mirage in *Lawrence of Arabia*, the black-robed Arab gradually approaching Lawrence across the desert, except that it was so stretched-out and disproportionate that it looked more like an ungainly combination of horse and man, or something else altogether, something totally monstrous.

As it came nearer, he saw that it was the same creature that he had encountered in the storeroom at the Sisters of Jerusalem. He saw its face, first leaning one way, and then the other, and its eyes, constantly shifting and changing, from the stone eyes of a garden statue to the glassy amber eyes of a tigerskin rug.

It approached Susan Fireman at extraordinary speed,

growing larger and larger, and as it came nearer a high trail of sand was whipped up behind it, and whirled away by the wind.

"Hurry up, Frank!" Susan Fireman urged him. "He'll come after you anyhow, whatever you do!"

Frank turned around. He thought about running, but he knew that he was dreaming and that he could never run fast in dreams. The dark attenuated creature was so close now that it would probably catch him before he could reach the dunes.

There was only one thing he could do. He took three steps back, and picked up a broken brick from the parking lot wall. Gripping it tight, he walked right up to the mirror and hit it, hard, right where Susan Fireman's face was. The mirror cracked from side to side—but he smashed again, and again, and again, until there was nothing but a glittering heap of glass and an empty oval frame.

He dropped the brick, and stood back. He was so cold that he could barely think, but he felt that he had saved himself, at least for now. He was still standing there when the moon rose, and shone through the empty oval frame like the face of a long-dead friend.

He opened his eyes. His bedroom was filled with blurry sunlight. He lay staring at the wall for a very long time, feeling so cold that he was unable to move. If he moved, he felt that his knees and elbows would probably break, and his finger bones would crackle. But at least he was sure that he wasn't dead.

Eventually the sun inched its way across the lower part of the bed. It burned his toes, blistering the skin and actually sending up wisps of smoke, but at least his feet felt warmer.

He knew now that everything that had happened to him was real. Susan Fireman, the blood-drinking epidemic, the morgue filled with corpses. The people in winding-sheets climbing out of the hospital window and over the rooftops. The dark, angular figure with eyes that changed from glass to stone. It had really happened, and it had happened to him.

It was then that he remembered last night's dream—the beach at Hyannis and the shattered mirror. Slowly, with a grunt of pain, he managed to lift up his head, and look toward the far corner of the room.

"Oh, Jesus," he whispered. General Grant's cheval-mirror was nothing but an empty oval frame, with a heap of sparkling fragments all around it. Close to the wall lay a heavy black onyx box that Christina had given him for his thirty-second birthday, the only gift that he had ever liked.

He shifted himself around, so that he could see through the open doorway, into the corridor. At first he couldn't understand what he was looking at, but then he realized that somebody was sprawled on the carpet. He could see a pair of shiny black shoes, and a pair of legs, dark-trousered, and a hand, with a heavy signet ring on it. He lifted his head a little more and saw that it was Lieutenant Roberts, whose blood he had swallowed, warm and thick, directly out of the spouting wound in his neck.

"*Errkk*," he choked. The sudden recollection of it made his stomach muscles cramp up, and he retched, again and again, until his throat was so sore that he couldn't retch any more.

His head dropped back and he lay on the bed for almost another hour, exhausted and feverish. Then he thought to himself: *I have to get up, I have to get out of here. I have to find help.* Otherwise another day would pass by and darkness would return and he didn't have any doubt that Susan Fireman would be coming back for him. And she would bring that angular shadow-creature, too, whatever that was.

Slowly and painfully, like a man twice his age, Frank

managed to sit up, and ease his legs off the bed. His bed was like some grotesque piece of modern art. The sheets were covered in hardened blood and twisted into strange shapes, like tortured faces. He gripped the head of the bed and pulled himself up, so that he was standing. For a moment, he felt as if all the blood had dropped out of his head and he was going to faint, but he took five or six very deep breaths, and steadied himself.

He walked stiffly out of the bedroom, stepping over Lieutenant Roberts' body on the floor. The wound in Lieutenant Roberts' neck was gaping so wide that Frank could see into his open windpipe. Lieutenant Roberts was staring at nothing at all, and his face was gray, as if had been dusted with ash from a crematorium. Frank looked down at him, and said, "Sorry, pal. Rest in peace." He didn't know what Lieutenant Roberts' religion had been, and he couldn't think what else to say.

Further along the corridor, on his back, lay Detective Mancini. His eyes were closed but he still looked terrified. His arms and legs were sticking out at awkward angles and his mouth was caught in mid-gag, as if he were choking on a fishbone. His neck was cut wide open, too, like Lieutenant Roberts', and it was obvious from the pallor of his face that he had been exsanguinated. There were only a few brown squiggles of blood on the carpet, so Frank guessed that Susan Fireman had drunk the rest of it.

The thought of that made him feel nauseated again. He walked through to the kitchen and hung over the sink, and vomited lumps of half-digested blood. It was black, like raw liver, and it slid down the drain as if it had a life of its own. He hunched there for almost five minutes, his stomach muscles clenching and unclenching, but at last he managed to straighten himself up, tear off a sheet of paper towel, and wipe his mouth.

God, he thought, *physician heal thyself.* He didn't want to die, especially if it meant that he was going to be reincarnated like Susan Fireman, or any of the other people who were roaming the city, thirsty for human blood. He knew he was very sick, but if this was an illness, there had to be a cure for it.

He dragged out a chair and sat down at the kitchen table. His tongue felt as if it had been sandpapered, and he desperately needed a drink, but even the thought of running water gave him the dry heaves.

The Death Troll was wrong. This disease wasn't at all like hemorrhagic dengue fever. It was much more like rabies. Just like rabies, it started with irritability and feverishness, and soon afterward, the sufferer started to have nightmares, and irrational terrors. Just like rabies, it was characterized by an irrational dread of water, which was why rabies was often called "hydrophobia."

Unlike rabies, however, this disease didn't seem to be transmitted by animal bites, or by bites of any kind. If Frank's own experience was anything to go by, it was communicated through the exchange of bodily fluids, like HIV.

He didn't know how Susan Fireman had persuaded him to have sex with her. His memory of it was nothing but a jumble of pornographic images. But she had done it somehow, and dug her nails into his scrotum while she did it, and so the chances were that he had contracted the disease through his open scratches. Just to make sure, she had made him swallow a drop of his own infected semen.

He guessed that a man could probably pass the disease to a woman in much the same way—through vaginal lacerations, or maybe by ejaculating into her mouth.

One thing was plain: once they were infected, victims quickly began to feel an unbearable burning sensation all over their skin surface, and a raging thirst for human blood. They also showed symptoms that violent and radical changes were taking place in their metabolism. They became "pale people," so highly charged with adrenaline that they could climb near-vertical walls and contort their bodies—as Susan Fireman had done—into near-impossible knots. They started to have suffocating nightmares of being shut up in boxes, and speak in foreign languages, although Frank couldn't even begin to understand how this could happen.

Although their thirst for human blood was so overwhelming, it was obvious that the "pale people" couldn't digest it in any great quantities, which led to them vomiting most of it back up again. But once they had died, or "passed over," as Susan Fireman had called it, they seemed to be able to drink copious amounts of blood, and keep it down.

Frank looked down at his hands. His skin was burning so painfully that he had to curl his fingers, and he bit his lips to stop himself from sobbing out loud. But he knew that sobbing wouldn't do him any good. He needed to think. *Think, Frank.* He was a doctor. He needed to find out where this disease had originated, and how it was being spread so rapidly. He needed to find out how to cure himself, before *he* "passed over," too. And then he had to work out a way to inoculate the rest of the city's population.

Before he did anything, he knew that he had to accept one impossible fact: People who were infected by this disease could walk and talk after they had appeared to be clinically dead. Susan Fireman had died, and yet she had managed to climb into his apartment and kill Lieutenant Roberts and Detective Mancini. Already, the city streets must be crowded with people like her. Dead people—or technically dead people—walking.

He searched his apartment, room by room. He opened cupboard doors and even checked under the sink. There was no sign of Susan Fireman anywhere, so she must have left. But what had she asked him, in his dream?

"Why don't you step inside the looking glass? You can be safe there."

He went back to the hallway. It suddenly came back to

him now. Susan Fireman had been standing *inside* the mirror. Not her reflection—*her*, behind the glass. Detective Mancini had backed toward her, and she had reached out of the mirror and cut his throat.

Frank stepped over Lieutenant Roberts again. There were bloody smudges all over the carpet, in every direction. The pile was too thick for them for them to be clearly identified as footprints, except in the bedroom, around the spot where Susan Fireman had actually cut Lieutenant Roberts' throat. Here, there was a huge dark patch of blood that was still wet, and small bare footprints crisscrossing right through it. On one side, however, the footprints headed directly toward the cheval-mirror. Where they finished.

Shaking with pain, Frank knelt down on the carpet and carefully picked up a handful of shattered glass. At least two of Susan Fireman's footprints were underneath the glass, so the mirror must have been smashed *after* she walked up to it. But there were no footprints heading away from it.

So maybe his dream hadn't all been illusory. Maybe Susan Fireman *had* stepped into the cheval-mirror, and maybe she *had* beckoned him to follow her inside. And maybe the half-brick hadn't been a half-brick, but his onyx box.

He suddenly thought to himself: *vampires can't survive in sunlight, can they? Not in the legends, at least. That's why they return to their coffins, when dawn breaks. But what if they can't find coffins to hide in, or seamlessly dark places? Where do they go?*

It seemed impossible, but maybe there *was* a hiding place for vampires. A hiding place that was always bright, but which no light could ever penetrate. The world of mirrors.

Frank went into the kitchen, opened the cutlery drawer, and took out the hammer that he used for flattening steaks. Then he walked around the whole apartment, smashing every single mirror, even the shaving mirror in the bathroom. Maybe he was losing his mind, but mirrors could be replaced, and if he was right, he might have found a way to protect himself from Susan Fireman and her shadow-creature. If they hid inside mirrors during daylight hours, then breaking mirrors was as good as bricking up doors.

He looked at the square black Italian clock in the livingroom. It was 7:37 in the morning. He needed to get back to the Sisters of Jerusalem and tell the Death Troll what he had discovered. He was sure that if the hospital's pathology team knew what they were really up against, they could isolate the cause of this epidemic much more quickly. He lifted one arm, and sniffed. He stank of blood and stale sweat, but he couldn't face the idea of taking a shower. Instead, he went back to the bathroom and pulled down the blind. Then he took off all of his clothes, and carefully wiped himself all over with a facecloth soaked in Dolce & Gabbana aftershave—face, neck, chest and underarms. He winced when he wiped the scratches on his scrotum, but he needed to feel clean and sterilized all over.

When he was finished cleaning himself, he smothered his face with a thick layer of sunscreen, factor 30, which he had bought for his skiing vacation last year in Vail. Then he dressed in a pair of black jeans and a black turtleneck sweater, and gloves. Finally, he pulled a black ski hood over his head, and put on a pair of Ray-Bans. He looked like the Invisible Man.

Before he opened his front door, he stood with his hand pressed against it, breathing deeply to control his pain. His skin was on fire, and his thirst for blood was so fierce that he felt like one of the addicts who were brought into the Sisters of Jerusalem, quaking with need, all of their humanity lost to their addiction. They would kill for drugs, most of those addicts, and he was sorely tempted to forget about the Sisters of Jerusalem, and do the same.

"*Tatal nostru*," he whispered, "*carele esti in ceruri*."

The sun blinded him as he came down the front steps of his house, even though he was wearing dark glasses. He hadn't imagined how much the sun would burn him, even through his clothes, and he let out a staccato cry of agony that was almost a laugh. But he managed to cross the street into the shadow of the houses opposite, and he found that if he kept himself out of direct sunlight, the burning was nearly bearable.

"*Tatal nostru*," he repeated. "*Carele esti in ceruri*." For some reason the words gave him hope that everything was going to turn out for the better, and that his agony would soon be over.

Murray Hill was deserted. In the distance, uptown, Frank thought that he could see people hurrying down Third Avenue, and the sharp glint of an automobile window, and from over on the West Side he could hear the *wok-wok-wok* of police sirens. But here, midtown, the streets were almost completely silent, and there seemed to be nobody left alive. A burned-out Lexus lay halfway across the street, and two or three blocks away Frank thought that he could see bodies lying on the sidewalk, surrounded by squabbling crows, but the glare of the sun was too bright for him to see how many there were.

"*Tatal nostru*," he whispered.

He hurried across Third Avenue and Lexington and Park. He felt as if he were the only person in New York City left alive. Up above him, the sky was cloudless, except for a few streaks of mares' tails toward the northwest. Some of the debris that was lying in the streets was so strange that he couldn't imagine who had left it there, or why. On Lexington, a grand piano was standing in the middle of the road, and on Park he came across piles of men's tuxedos, strewn across the sidewalk. It looked as if an orchestra had been attacked by marauding Indians, and this was all that was left.

By the time he reached Fifth Avenue, he was close to collapse. His legs were blistering underneath his jeans, and his lips felt as if he had kissed a hot electric iron. Maybe he should turn back. Maybe he should try to find somebody whose blood he could drink. A down-and-out, maybe, somebody whose death wouldn't really matter. After all, he was much more important than some bum, wasn't he? If he were to die, nobody would find out the truth about the epidemic, and thousands more people would be killed.

By the time he reached Thirty-third Street, he had almost persuaded himself to go in search of a victim whose throat he could cut. But as he hurried around the corner, he was suddenly faced by two police cars, and six or seven police officers with dogs and riot shields.

"*Stop!*" shouted one of the cops. "*Hit the sidewalk, face down!*"

Frank didn't hesitate. He turned and ran. He knew what would happen if they caught him. They would take off his sunglasses and his hood and the sunlight would incinerate him, right in front of them. That's if they didn't shoot him first.

He ran and ran and kept on running, dodging from one street to the next, and cutting through alleys whenever he could. He heard one of the police cars coming after him, its tires squealing as it slid around the corner. He even glimpsed it, momentarily, as it flashed across Twenty-eighth Street, but he dodged into the doorway of a dry cleaner's, and stayed there, gasping for breath, until he was sure that it wasn't going to come doubling back.

"*Tatal nostru,*" he panted. Smoke was pouring out of his sleeves. "*Tatal nostru, nu ne duce pre noi in ispita . . .* but deliver us from evil, amen." Then he started running again.

For a while, a mongrel ran alongside him, barking, but

when he reached Washington Square it caught sight of a brindled bitch, and tore off after it, between the trees.

He slowed to a walk. He was burning so badly now that he hardly cared if they caught him. Maybe he should allow himself to die, so that he could join Susan Fireman in the world of mirrors, and absolute darkness. Anything had to be better than this. Even if he could help to isolate an antidote, there was no guarantee that he was going to be able to cure himself.

He stumbled on and on, crossing street after street. He had completely lost his sense of direction. He didn't know where the Sisters of Jerusalem was and he no longer cared. He just wanted the pain to stop.

Halfway across Barrow Street, he dropped to his knees. He stayed there, with his head lowered, trying to summon up the strength to carry on. *Our Father, which art nowhere to be found, please rescue me.* Gradually, however, he became aware that somebody was standing in front of him. He looked up, slowly, and saw a muscular young man in a khaki T-shirt and Desert Storm pants. The man was holding a pickax handle in one hand, which he kept slapping into the palm of his other hand.

"Don't think you're coming any further, fella," the young man told him, flatly.

Frank coughed, and coughed, and spat blood. "I don't think I could come any further if I tried."

"This area is off-limits to bloodsuckers. Maybe your problem isn't your fault, but we don't want you around here. So I suggest you turn around and stagger back the way you come."

"I'm a doctor," said Frank.

"What?"

"I'm a doctor. I've caught the virus, but I haven't cut anybody's throat yet, and with any luck I won't have to."

He tried again to climb to his feet but the young man jabbed him in the breastbone with his pickax handle, so that he dropped back onto his knees. "You stay away from me, man. You hear me? You stay well away. I don't want to catch that thing, too."

"I don't think that's very likely," said Frank. "It's a sexual disease . . . it gets passed from person to person through the exchange of bodily fluids."

"You mean like AIDS?"

"Exactly like AIDS."

"So how do you know that?"

"Because I'm a doctor. And because that's the way *I* caught it."

"Through having *sex?*"

"That's right, through having sex. Now I'm trying to get back to the Sisters of Jerusalem. I can't call them because all the phone lines are dead, and my cell phone won't work, and my computer server's down, too. But they need to know what I've discovered."

"If you're trying to get to the Sisters of Jerusalem, man, you're way off. Do you know where you are?"

Frank looked around. His eyes were blinded by the sun and his head was throbbing so hard that he could barely think.

"I don't know . . . Seventh Avenue, in the twenties?"

"You're way down in the West Village. Hudson Street, at Barrow."

Frank managed to get up on one knee. "I have to get to the Sisters of Jerusalem."

"I don't care where you have to get to, buddy, so long as you turn yourself around and head back exactly where you came from."

"But nobody else understands. They're *vampires*, that's what they are. Not just ordinary people sucking blood. They're real, genuine vampires. They call themselves *strigoi.*"

The young man stared at him acutely. "Did you just say what I thought you just said?"

Frank felt confused. His head was throbbing more painfully than ever, and he was sure that he could smell his body hair burning. "What? I don't know what I said."

"You said *strigoi*. You know about *strigoi*?"

"Well, no—not very much. But I know what they are, and I know where they hide when the sun comes up. At least, I'm pretty sure I do. And I think I know how to stop them coming back, when it gets dark."

"But you're one of them."

"Not yet. I've been infected, yes, but I haven't passed over."

The young man didn't seem to know what to do. He looked left and right, and then he said, "You can't go back to the Sisters of Jerusalem."

"Why not?"

"No point. The last I heard, the place was overrun, and it was on fire."

"I still need to find somebody in charge. Somebody from the city health authority, or the CDC."

"I don't know, man . . . the whole damn city's turned into a nuthouse."

Frank coughed up more blood. The young man watched him for a while, and then he said, "Listen, I met this guy, and he knows something about these *strigoi*, too. I think the best thing you can do right now is come to meet him."

"You're sure?"

"Not really, but what else am I going to do?"

Frank looked up at him, shielding his eyes with his hand. "You may as well know that I have a raging thirst for human blood. I can't pretend that I don't. My skin feels like it's on fire, and if you take me with you, then I can't give you any guarantees that I'm not going to cut your throat and drink your blood."

"What's your name?" the young man asked him.

"Frank Winter, MD."

"Well, doc, my name's Gil Johnson, and I'm a National Guardsman with the Rainbow Division, and if you even *look* at my throat, I'm going to take this pickax handle and I'm going to beat your brains into raspberry Jell-O."

Very unsteadily, Frank stood up. "Believe me, Gil, that would probably be a blessed relief."

14

BLOOD OF DRACULEA

Jenica poured us two glasses of sweet white Romanian wine, and offered me a plate of almond biscuits that tasted like very fine sand. She sat next to me on the velvet-upholstered couch, close enough for our knees to keep touching.

"My father telephoned me from Bucharest as soon as he heard what was happening in New York. His very first word was, *strigoi*."

I coughed on my biscuit. "Singing Rock specifically warned me not to say that name out loud. You know, in case they heard me saying it, and came after me. He said they would tear me to pieces."

"No, no," Jenica reassured me. "The word *strigoi* alone is not enough to alert them. *Strigoi* is just general name for vampires, not any special vampire. Your spirit-guide was warning you, yes, but he must have told you another name, too. A special name."

I shook my head. "If he did, I didn't pick up on it."

"Well, if he has not told you yet, he will very soon,"

Jenica assured me. "If so many *strigoi* are suddenly loose in New York, they must have come from a nest."

"I don't follow you."

"A nest is many *strigoi* who are hiding together, or perhaps sealed up by vampire-hunters. Sometimes they remain concealed for centuries, waiting to escape. My father studied *strigoi* when he was in Romania, at the university in Babes-Bolyai. He was always convinced right from beginning that there was a nest hidden someplace in New York. He has searched for it for many years, ever since he first came to America. He has visited many libraries and studied many old maps and diaries, but he could never locate them."

Jenica took hold of my hand and began to emphasize what she meant by tracing patterns on my palm—a sensation that was strangely erotic. "A nest of *strigoi* will always be guided and controlled by a very powerful vampire spirit, one of the *svarcolaci*. In English I suppose you would translate one of the *svarcolaci* as a *dead* vampire. He does not inhabit his physical body any more, like one of the *strigoi*, who are the undead. He is what you would call a ghost, or a wandering soul."

"*Svarcolaci*? I never heard of *svarcolaci*. Mind you, I never heard of *strigoi*, either, before today."

"In Romanian folk stories, another name for one of the *svarcolaci* is Vampire Gatherer. Once the *strigoi* from the nest have infected people, the Vampire Gatherer goes out searching for them, and leads them back to the nest. There he teaches them the ways of the night, so that they become *strigoi*, too.

"I am sure that it was one of the *svarcolaci* that your spirit guide was warning you about, because a Vampire Gatherer can hear his name called, at any distance, even in a whisper . . . even if you say it in your dreams. Sometimes you only have to *think* his name, and he will prick up his ears and come after you."

"So—uh—what are they like, these Vampire Gatherers?"

"They take many different shapes, Mr. Harry, and many different faces. But mostly people call them the Slanting Ones, because they always appear like shadows, leaning away from any source of light. I will show you."

Jenica walked across the living room, and brought back a small red leather-bound book from one of the shelves. She opened it up and handed it to me. The text was all in Romanian, but the engraved illustration didn't need any translation. It showed two small children sleeping in a wooden bed, with a guttering candle on their bedside table. Above them stood a sloping, dark, impossibly stretched-out figure, exactly like the figure that had appeared in my apartment when I was reading Ted Busch's fortune. I felt a chilly, sinking sensation in my stomach—the feeling you get when you know that things are going badly wrong and there's nothing that you can do but sit and wait for the worst to happen.

"I've seen him," I told Jenica, handing the book back. "I've seen this sucker for real. Singing Rock showed him to me, in my apartment. This is him, or something very much like him."

"Then now we are absolutely sure what we are dealing with," said Jenica. She studied the picture for a moment and then she closed the book tightly and put it down on the table, with a heavy glass paperweight on top of it, as if the Vampire Gatherer might find a way to escape from between the pages. "There are many *svarcolaci* and I think my father knows them all, but of course I cannot contact my father yet, until the phones are back."

"But your father really believes that there's a nest of *strigoi* here in New York?"

"He is completely sure. He found some letters from the nineteenth century and also some bills of lading from a shipping company. Some of the letters were written in a kind of code, but it was not a difficult code to break."

She poured me another glass of wine. I didn't really want

one, especially since it tasted like sweaty leather watch-bands. But it was well past 2:00 in the morning and even though I felt exhausted and bruised and more than ready for bed, my brain was still jumping. Maybe the wine would act as a sedative, and maybe it would stop me from dreaming, too. Believe me, the last thing I wanted to do tonight was dream.

Jenica said, "In 1869, two of the richest men in New York were Charles Redding, from New England, and Gheorghe Vlad, from Cluj-Napoca, in Romania."

"Sure, I've heard of them. Well, Charles Redding, anyhow. He founded Redding's Department Store, didn't he? And he built some incredible Greek-style mansion right next door to the Astors on Fifth Avenue."

"That's right. Charles Redding and Gheorghe Vlad were business partners. Together they made millions of dollars by importing luxury goods from Europe and the Middle East—women's fashions and furniture and carpets and glassware. Charles Redding was satisfied to stay in New York. But Gheorghe Vlad believed that they could become a hundred times richer if they opened department stores all over America—first in Denver, in Colorado, and then others in California. He traveled to Denver, and found a site for a new store, and then he sent back to New York for his wife and his six young children to join him. On their way across the Plains, though, his family was attacked by a war party of Teton Sioux, and all of them were tortured and killed, even his newly born baby.

"Vlad swore an oath in front of God that he would have his revenge on the Indians, and that he would wipe out the Sioux—men, women and children, just as they had wiped his family out. He took his family's remains back to Romania, and arranged a traditional funeral. But my father discovered that he arranged something else, too. He went to a village near Borsa in Transylvania, and arranged to take two hundred coffins from the vaults of the local churches, where they had been sealed since 1767 for safekeeping. According to the letters that my father found, these coffins contained *strigoi*, the undead, as well as a special iron sarcophagus containing one of the *svarcolaci*.

"Gheorghe Vlad's intention was to ship them to America, and then to have them carried to Sioux territory, where he would revive them, and they would exterminate every single Sioux they could find."

"Jesus," I said. "That was a hell of a plan. But even in those days, how did he think that he was going to get away with it? I mean, anybody who wanted to cart two hundred dead bodies into Indian country wouldn't exactly have been inconspicuous, would he?"

"Of course. But there is some documentary evidence that Gheorghe Vlad was actually given support by the U.S. military, and even an offer of wagons. The Army saw it as an opportunity to defeat one of the most warlike of all the Indian tribes without having to risk any casualties among their own troops."

"But letting all those *strigoi* loose—that was a pretty risky idea, don't you think? Once they'd wiped out the Indians, who were they going to feed on then? They would still have been looking for a regular diet of human blood, wouldn't they?"

"I don't know for certain," Jenica admitted. "Maybe Gheorghe Vlad had thought of what he was going to do with all of those *strigoi* once he had taken his revenge. Maybe he hadn't. But you have to understand that he would have had very strong control over them, through the Vampire Gatherer. The Vampire Gatherer is a *dead* vampire, remember. He would not have been able to come back to life until Gheorghe Vlad had performed the appropriate rituals to revive him, and once he was revived, he would have had to obey Gheorghe Vlad's wishes, whatever they were. It is like the story from the *Arabian Nights* of the genie in the lamp. Whoever revives the Vampire Gatherer controls the vampires."

"But Gheorghe Vlad *didn't* wipe out the Sioux, did he? I mean, the U.S. Army did it in the end."

"Well, you are right. The ship carrying the coffins arrived safely in New York harbor . . . my father found a written record of that. Unfortunately for him, Gheorghe Vlad died of a stroke an hour before the ship docked. So here were all these coffins in the ship's hold, but nobody knew what was in them, or why they had been shipped all the way from Romania. Apart, that is, from the clerics in Borsa, in Romania, and two or three senior officers in the U.S. Army. Once Gheorghe Vlad was dead, of course, nobody from the Army was going to come forward to requisition the coffins. Even if any of their officers had known how to revive the *strigoi,* which they didn't, somebody in authority would have asked what they wanted them for, and they wouldn't have been prepared to admit that they were planning on genocide."

"So what happened to the coffins?"

"Charles Redding ordered them to be stored in the basement of Redding's Department Store until he could find out why his partner had brought them across the Atlantic. He thought that maybe they were the remains of Gheorghe Vlad's relatives, and that Vlad had wanted them all to be buried in America, where he could pay his respects to them and tend their graves. He sent letters of inquiry to Bucharest, but he never received any replies, and only five months later, in the winter of 1871, he himself died, of pneumonia.

"Redding's Department Store almost went bankrupt after his death, and it was bought by Green's, and then by Bloomberg's, and nobody knows what happened to the coffins. Presumably they were bricked up and buried in the foundations when Redding's Department Store was demolished in 1907."

"But now it looks like they've showed up?"

"Yes. My father and I, we both believe that these *strigoi* have come from Gheorghe Vlad's nest. But there is a big question. Who has revived them? They must have been discovered by somebody who knew how to bring the Vampire Gatherer back to life."

"There can't be many people who would know how to do that."

"Of course. But we have no ideas who it is. Somebody who knows old Romanian legends perhaps."

"So what's the plan?"

"I don't know. If we want to stop this epidemic, we have to find out where is the nest, and where is the Vampire Gatherer, and who has revived him."

"And *why* he revived him, surely? I mean, whoever knew how to do it, they must have had some idea of what the consequences would be."

"Of course. So we are looking perhaps for a terrorist. Or maybe somebody worse than a terrorist. A complete madman, maybe."

"That's encouraging."

I tried my cell phone again, but it was still dead. I listened, but for now the city seemed to be weirdly silent. No sirens, no helicopters, no traffic.

"Do you want to come to bed?" asked Jenica.

"Excuse me?"

"You can sleep in my father's bed if you wish. There is nothing more we can do tonight."

"Oh, right. That would be great. And I could really use a toothbrush, if you have one. My mouth feels like I've been French-kissing an armadillo."

Jenica smiled. "That is Romanian wine. They say it gives a man such breath that he can knock down a house made of brick."

I was woken up by somebody touching my shoulder. I thought it was Karen at first, and I batted her away.

"*Sleep*," I protested.

"Mr. Harry, I have brought you tea."

I opened one eye and tried to focus. Jenica was standing over me, wearing a silky fuchsia-pink robe, very loosely tied. I lifted my head and looked around, and realized that I was lying on her father's cement-slab four-poster bed, in his gloomy museum of a bedroom, and that I was fully dressed, apart from my shoes.

I sat up. I could see myself in a blotchy mirror on the opposite side of the room. My hair was sticking up like Erskine the Mad, and my left cheek was embossed with Oriental patterns from the cushion that I had used as a pillow. There was a hole in my fawn-colored sock, and my big toe was poking out of it.

"What time is it?" I asked her.

"Six."

"Six? Oh, wonderful. Almost three-and-a-half hours' sleep."

"Yes, but now the sun is bright we can begin to search for the *strigoi*."

Strigoi. It was the crack of dawn and she wanted to go looking for *strigoi*. She placed a glass on the table beside me. "Would you like breakfast?" she asked me. "I have yogurt and honey and farina with dried apricots."

"Oh, no. I'm fine, thanks. I make it a rule not to put anything solid into my mouth until I'm officially awake, and I'm not officially awake until noon."

I picked up the glass and took a sip of tea. I'm not a tea person, as a rule. As far as I'm concerned, a drink should (a) wake you up or (b) nourish you or (c) knock you unconscious, which is why I stick to strong black coffee and Guinness and Jack Daniel's. Tea is just leafy water, and you can find leafy water in the woods.

Jenica looked pleased with herself. "I have looked through my father's library and found his book of all the *svarcolaci.* It was compiled by a special brotherhood of priests in the late 1700s, the Black Purifiers. In those days, vampires were spreading through Transylvania and Wallachia faster than a plague, and so the bishops of the Romanian Orthodox Church demanded a purge of every *svarcolaci* and *strigoi* and *moroi.*

"The Black Purifiers searched every cellar and every steeple, and they impaled every vampire they found, or beheaded them, or burned them alive; or else they sealed them up in caskets and sarcophagi. The book has the pictures and names of every known *svarcolaci* that they managed to track down."

"That's terrific. Maybe you can give me a couple of minutes for my eyes to focus, and then I can take a look at it."

"You would like more tea? It is bison grass tea. It is supposed to make men have the more virility."

I peered short-sightedly into the depths of Jenica's cleavage and thought that the last thing I wanted right now was to have the more virility.

"I hate to be ungrateful," I said, "but do you think there's any chance of some coffee?"

"Of course. Wash, and I will make you coffee. I have laid out towels."

I limped into the Moorish bathroom and climbed into the shower. It had a baffling array of old-fashioned faucets, and I blasted myself three times with freezing cold water before I managed to adjust it to a heavy, tepid downpour, the kind where you have to hold your breath to stop yourself from drowning.

I was toweling myself dry when Jenica walked into the bathroom as unself-consciously as if we were married. "You would like cake?"

"No, no. Just coffee."

"Always I used to think that it was not really true, about the *strigoi* in New York, even though my father was so sure.

Who would believe that it was true? Who would believe that we would have to hunt the *strigoi*, you and I?"

"We don't *have* to hunt them, you know. We could always barricade ourselves in and wait until they've gone away."

"You are losing your nerve, Mr. Harry?"

"Of course not. I'm just saying that we're not actually *obliged* to go out looking for them. Nobody's going to think any the less of us if we don't."

Jenica shook her head. "*We* will think less of us. Besides, the *strigoi* will never go away until they have drunk the last drop of human blood in the city. Then, this will only be a city of the night, and there will be no people here by day. It happened before, in Tirgu Mures, in Romania. It can happen here."

The trouble was, I knew she was right. It seemed impossible that the most important city in the United States was being overrun by blood-sucking creatures from the Dark Ages. In fact, it seemed insane. But on September 11, 2001, New York's two tallest buildings had been brought down by a handful of nut jobs armed with nothing more than box cutters, and more than three thousand of its citizens killed, and on the evening of September 10, who could have imagined anything more insane than that?

It's always hard to believe that anybody can hate you that much, for no reason at all. Once I was dressed, I went through to the living room and found Jenica poring through her father's book. It was a very thin book, bound in cracked tan leather that had the texture of dried human skin, with some kind of mystic symbol on the front, an oval with an eye in the middle. On each page there was a finely rendered woodcut of a man's face, and a few paragraphs of dense handwritten text.

"Here is your coffee," said Jenica, and passed me a tiny blue porcelain cup that she must have burgled from a doll's house. I peered into it and it was only a third full. But it had a rich nutty aroma, and when I tipped it back and swallowed it, I felt as if I had instantly grown a thick black beard, and I was quite surprised when I didn't start talking like James Earl Jones.

"Perhaps soon your Singing Rock will give you the name of your Vampire Gatherer," said Jenica.

"I guess I could try asking him, although I doubt if he will. I think there's a strong possibility that he might have given it to me already and I just haven't realized it, and he's kind of huffy about doing things twice."

Jenica said, "It is most important for us to have this name. We need to know which of the *svarcolaci* we are looking for, because a different ritual is necessary to dismiss each one of them. This ritual is what you would call the disenchantment, and it is supposed to force the *svarcolaci* to return to their coffins and to seal them up until they are summoned again."

I peered at the page she was pointing at, although I couldn't understand any of the words, let alone pronounce them. "*Ci, ii dracul cu dracoaica, striga cu strigoiul, deochiu cu deochitorul, pocitura cu pocitorul, potca cu potcoiul. . . .*"

But then I looked more closely at the woodcut. It depicted a man, smiling, with his eyes closed. Around his face was a decorative border of toads and dragonflies and tiny flowers. Although the man's face was different, and the border was different, the design bore a strikingly close resemblance to the medallion that I had taken from Ted Busch. I wedged my hand into my back pants pocket and dragged the medallion out.

"Here," I told Jenica, holding it up. "I took this from the young guy I was telling you about last night."

Jenica held it in her hand, and peered at it closely. Then she looked at me with those dark, liquid eyes as if I was the village idiot. "Why did you not show me this before?" she demanded.

"I don't know. I forgot about it."

"How could you forget about it? This is one of the *svarcolaci.*"

"Well, I know that *now*."

She turned it over. "The inscription on the back, this is a kind of protection. *From vampires and from a home with vampires, from those who cast the evil eye, keep me safe.*"

"The poor guy said that it was given to him by a Russian-looking girl."

"Hmnh," said Jenica, dismissively. "I would be sure that she was Romanian, probably, and she was the *strigoica* who infected him. You see, she would have given him the medallion to keep him safe from other vampires who wanted to cut his throat and drink his blood. She must have liked him, and wanted him to become *strigoi* like her, one of her lovers."

"How about the face?"

"We have to look through the book."

I stood close beside her as she carefully turned each page. There were over eighty *svarcolaci* and most of them were very similar—handsome, in a Slavic way, thin-faced and pointy-nosed, although some were very swarthy-looking and some were sporting huge moustaches and enormous beards. Maybe they'd been drinking Jenica's coffee. Each *svarcolaci*, however, had a different decorative border drawn around his face—everything from song-birds to razors to mulberry leaves.

"Here," said Jenica, suddenly. "This, I am thinking, is our Vampire Gatherer."

I was thinking that she was right. The man in the wood-cut was wearing a striped turban wound around his head, and one elaborate earring, but it was definitely the same man whose likeness was embossed on Ted Busch's medallion. The border was the same, too—snakes intertwined with each other, and stars. His expression was grim, as if he were seriously pissed that we had discovered him.

The name below the picture was *Vasile Lup*. Jenica immediately covered it with her hand and said, "Do not read this out loud. This could be the name that your spirit guide was warning you about."

"My lips are sealed, believe me."

Jenica took her hand away and began to translate. "His name means The Wolf. It says here that he was a cousin of Vlad Tepes, known as Vlad the Impaler, or Draculea."

"You're kidding me. Draculea as in *Dracula?*"

"Well, of course. But Draculea himself was only a man of very extreme cruelty, the *voivode* of Wallachia."

"The what of where?"

"He was like a prince, in the southern part of Romania. But he was never a vampire."

"But this guy *was?*"

"That's right." Jenica's fingers traced along the thick black lines of Romanian script. "It says here, 'Late in September 1457 when he was hunting in the mountains for wild boar'—well, I shall say 'The Wolf' each time, instead of his real name—'The Wolf became hopelessly lost, and he was forced to spend several nights sleeping in the forest. Each night as soon as it grew dark he was approached by swarms of *strigoica*.' These were the female vampires who were always looking for male lovers, so that they could turn them into *strigoi*.

" 'There were too many *strigoica* and The Wolf's efforts to keep them at bay were hopeless. He became one of the un-dead himself. When he eventually found his way back to Draculea's castle he would say nothing of what had happened to him, although after his return from the forest he was never seen abroad during the day and he became very secretive in his behavior.' "

"That doesn't surprise me. I think I'd be pretty secretive if I was dead."

Jenica frowned at me. She was so serious about all of this *strigoi* stuff that it was hard not to believe that it was all true—even though, *hello?* we were talking about Dracula here, and real live dead people who were five-and-a-half centuries old.

" 'The Wolf began to gather around him some of Draculea's many disaffected courtiers with the intention of assassinating Draculea and taking over as *voivode*.' In those days, you see, assassination was the usual way to seize power, even amongst sons and brothers. 'But Draculea had many spies and discovered what The Wolf was plotting. When The Wolf was dragged from his bed, and exposed to daylight, Draculea immediately realized that he was one of the undead. He ordered him to be impaled on a high pole, which was the usual way in which he dealt with traitors and liars and people who displeased him. On one occasion Draculea had impaled three thousand people in a single day. The pole was blunt and very well oiled, so that The Wolf would not immediately die of shock, and it was pushed into The Wolf's buttocks until it came out of his mouth. It was then erected in the shadow of the castle walls, so that The Wolf would not be incinerated by the rays of the sun, and would suffer great agony for days on end.' "

I was tempted to say something about right royal pains in the ass, but decided against it.

Jenica turned the page. " 'However Draculea's mistress, Lenuta, who had once been The Wolf's wife, and had been forcibly taken by Draculea, took pity on him. She shone her hand mirror from the battlements so that the rays of the sun set him on fire, and cremated him to ashes, and so delivered him from his pain. The Wolf thus became a dead vampire, or a *svarcolaci*. Draculea discovered what his mistress had done, and had her stomach cut open, so that everybody could see where he had been. The Wolf had to wait many years to take his revenge on Draculea, but eventually did so. On the second night of the Battle of Bucharest in December 1476, five *strigoi* entered Draculea's tent. They slit his throat and drank his blood, and then they cut off his head and mounted it on a pole, so that the victorious Turks would discover it in the morning, when the sun rose."

"Well, that's not exactly bedtime reading, is it? Does it say how The Wolf was caught by the priests?"

"Only briefly," said Jenica. "In 1767 the Black Purifiers tracked down The Wolf and his nest of *strigoi* to a house near Borsa in Transylvania. The priests diverted a stream so that the house was surrounded on all sides by running water, which vampires are unable to cross, and then they tore the house down so that the vampires were exposed to sunlight." The Wolf, of course, could not be killed, but it says here that "he was wound around with a mile of silver wire and then he was shut up in an iron casket lined with silver, which was sealed with wax made from melted church candles mixed with crushed garlic. Or rather—"

Jenica frowned, and read the words again.

"Something wrong?" I asked her.

"I do not completely understand this. It does not actually say that The Wolf himself was bound with silver wire and shut up in a silver-lined casket. If you translate the words literally, they mean '*his perfect picture*.' Or maybe '*his exact likeness*' would be more accurate."

"Well," I suggested, "he was a spirit, wasn't he, rather than a walking dead person? And spirits can assume all kinds of really strange shapes. When Singing Rock brought him into my apartment, he was all stretched out—more like a shadow than a person. Maybe the priests were trying to say that whatever shape he was, it was definitely him. *His exact likeness*."

"I'm still not sure," said Jenica. "But anyway, the casket was taken to Borsa, and bricked up in the vaults of the Chapel of St. Basil, and that must have been where Gheorghe Vlad found it."

"So this is the Vampire Gatherer we have to go looking for?"

"That's right. Although I do not know how we are going to find him. The *svarcolaci* are notorious for concealing themselves so that not even the most skillful purifiers can discover their hiding places."

"Maybe I should try saying The Wolf's real name. That way, he'd come looking for *me*."

"No! You do not know what are you suggesting, Mr. Harry. If the *svarcolaci* becomes aware that you are hunting for him, he will always make sure that you are dead before the next sun rises. And yes, your spirit guide is right. You will be ripped to pieces so that there is nothing left to bury of you but human rags."

"Okay, then," I said. "So what's Plan B?"

"I will look through my father's books, and see if I can discover how it was that the Black Purifiers discovered where The Wolf was hiding."

"Very good idea. You're not just an extraordinary looking woman, are you?"

She stared at me, as if she were waiting for me to say something else.

"What do you want me to tell you?" I said. "I think you're beautiful, and if you don't know that you're beautiful, then you've been looking in the wrong mirrors."

"Mr. Harry, we are looking for a Vampire Gatherer."

"Yes. I'm sorry. But I just thought I'd let you know that I'm not completely impervious. You know, to the way you look. And that tickly thing you did, on the palm of my hand. And you walked into the bathroom, didn't you, when I was taking a shower?"

Jenica looked totally baffled. You can't even imagine how relieved I was when the doorbell rang.

15

COLD BLOOD

We drew the velvet drapes together as tightly as we could. Apart from a few triangular chinks of sunlight, it was so gloomy that we could hardly see each other, but Dr. Winter still couldn't stop shivering. Gil had given him a gilded, straight-backed dining chair to sit in, but the poor guy kept doubling forward in pain. His face was thick with yellowish-white sunblock, and there was dried blood on his chin, like a beard. His black pants were filthy and one of his sleeves was torn.

"Maybe I shouldn't have brung him up here," said Gil.

"No," I said. "I think you did right."

Jenica was pacing up and down. "What if The Wolf sent him here to tear us to pieces? How can we know for sure that he will not turn on us, and cut our throats, and drink all our blood?"

The answer was, um, we couldn't. But for some reason I felt that we could trust him, at least some of the way. He didn't have the same unhinged stare as those people who had attacked Gil and me in the street. He was very sick, no doubt about it, but it was obvious that he was struggling hard to keep his sickness from overwhelming him. And he was a doctor. Once upon a time he had taken an oath to save people's lives, for what that was worth.

I sat on the couch next to him. "It's Frank, isn't it, doc?"

Frank lifted his head, and attempted a smile. "I want to thank you, for taking me off the street. I think I'd be dead by now, if you hadn't."

"Gil says you've been infected."

"That's right. It was a girl called Susan Fireman, a patient of mine. She died, or at least I thought she was dead. She climbed into my bedroom the night after she was taken to the morgue. We had sex."

"A dead girl climbed into your bedroom and you actually managed to have sex? Jesus. I'd have been halfway to the Canadian border, leaving a brown trail behind me."

Frank coughed, and nodded. "It was like a dream. Well, more like a nightmare. I can't really explain how it happened. But I'm pretty sure that's how the vampires pass their infection on, from one person to another, through the exchange of bodily fluids. It's perfect . . . the quickest way to spread an epidemic, bar none. You should see how the HIV virus was spread in India . . . by long-distance truck drivers, using roadside prostitutes. Millions got infected. Five million, in a few months, all across the continent. The same thing's going to happen here, with this."

"So you think it's a virus?"

"It's some kind of viral-type infection. Our pathologists at the Sisters of Jerusalem were trying to isolate it, but from what your friend tells me—"

"The Sisters of Jerusalem was burning, the last I heard," Gil put in. "St. Vincent's too, and Bellevue."

I turned back to Frank. "So how do you feel? Do you think you're going to be able to beat this thing, or what?"

"I don't know. My skin's burning. I feel like a pig, to tell you the truth, roasting on a spit. I'm so thirsty I can hardly swallow, but even *thinking* about water makes me sick to my stomach. All I can think about is human blood. It's worse than being an alcoholic and needing a drink."

"Are you hungry? When was the last time you ate?"

"I can't remember. Yesterday morning, I think."

"Do you think you could manage to eat something?"

"I don't know. Some raw meat, maybe."

"Jenica?" I asked her.

"I have some chopped liver in the fridge," she said, although she didn't make any effort to hide her disgust.

"Well, I'll tell you what we'll do, we'll blend some chopped liver with some Romanian wine, and we'll see if you can keep going on that. If you don't drink any human blood, Frank, maybe you can beat this infection, you know?"

"I'll try," said Frank.

I scraped the chicken livers out of their bloodstained paper into Jenica's Waring blender. Then I poured in half a bottle of Feteasca Neagra, and blitzed the livers into a smooth, dark-brown glop. It smelled appalling, like a rabbit that had died after a weekend on the booze, but Frank needed feeding and I couldn't think of anything else that he might be able to stomach.

Gil came into the kitchen while I was making it, and between blitzes I told him everything that Jenica and I had found out about *strigoi* and *svarcolaci*.

"Most important of all—we think we've found out the name of the actual Vampire Gatherer who's here in New York. Back in Romania they used to call him The Wolf."

"So what's his real name?"

I scraped the brown glop into a cereal bowl and rooted around in the cutlery drawer, looking for a spoon. "We daren't say his name out loud, in case he picks up on it, and comes looking for us. And from what Jenica tells me, he doesn't take prisoners."

Gil said, "Shit, man, we really have to take some action. And I mean, like, *now*. Outside in the streets—it's like a goddamned war zone out there. Bodies lying everywhere. Men, women, kids. It's worse than Kosovo."

Gil had managed to shower and shave when he was home, and he was wearing a clean khaki T-shirt and clean Desert Storm-style pants. But he had haunted, dark circles under his eyes and I could tell from his disconnected speech how exhausted he was.

"Is your family okay?" I asked him.

He nodded. "I've barricaded them into our apartment, and they're pretty well supplied with food and bottled water. I've left Marie my gun, too, and she knows how to use it."

"That's good."

"Yes—but we still need to *do* something. We can't just sit on our duffs talking about it, for Christ's sake."

"We're not going to," I reassured him. "For starters, we're going to go looking for the nest."

"Then we can frag it, right?"

"I don't think you can beat these suckers by fragging them. They're undead, remember, which means they're dead already. What we have to do is, identify which casket belongs to the Vampire Gatherer. He's in charge of all of the rest of the vampires. Jenica has a book, and it has the ritual in it for sealing him up again. So if we can catch the Vampire Gatherer during the day, while he's hiding in there, we can stop him from ever getting out again."

"So where do we start looking?"

"Well, I'm not sure, exactly. I was hoping that the doc might have some ideas. I mean, he's halfway to being one of *strigoi,* isn't he?"

"And what if he doesn't? If Jenica's old man hasn't been able to find it, after all these years, what hope do we have?"

"I don't know, Gil. Maybe we'll have to put our faith in the Lord."

I carried the brown glop back into the living room. Frank

took it, and sniffed it, and prodded it with his spoon. But then he tried a little, and managed to swallow it.

"How is it?" I asked him.

"Don't ever try to open a restaurant, but I think I can keep it down."

I sat beside him as he tried to eat. I had to admire the guy. He was obviously going through seven kinds of hell, but he was trying very hard to hold on to his humanity— even to his sense of humor. All the same, there was something in his eyes that told me that he was fighting a losing battle. A kind of *looking inwards*. I had seen that expression before on people who knew they were soon going to die. Like, how can the world be so heartless as to leave me behind?

"We need to find the place where the vampires' coffins are hidden," I told him. "I was wondering if you had any ideas."

"My father always believed that they were still downtown someplace," put in Jenica. "But we have no records of where they might be. Maybe you have some special intuition."

Frank attempted a smile. "I'm not one of the undead yet," he remarked. "But I'll tell you something—from what I've seen, the *strigoi* don't need coffins to hide during the day. This was what I wanted to tell the pathology people at the Sisters of Jerusalem. It sounds crazy, I know, but they can hide inside mirrors."

"What?"

"They can walk into a mirror just like it's a door, and they can stay there until it gets dark."

"How the hell do they do that?"

"I'm not sure. But the early tests we did at the hospital showed that they had an enzyme in their bloodstream with a silver element attached. In some way, they seem to have a metabolic association with silver, and maybe this allows them to penetrate the reflective surface of a mirror and pass through to the other side." He coughed. "Or maybe it doesn't. Maybe it's black magic, who knows?

He managed another spoonful of liver and wine. "This is truly disgusting," he said.

"I'm sorry," I apologized. "But it should help you to keep your strength up."

Little by little, as he ate, Frank told us what had happened in his apartment. He explained how Susan Fireman had climbed in through the window, even though she was clinically dead, and how she had reached out of the mirror in the hallway and cut the detective's throat. "There was blood just about everywhere."

"Weren't you at all . . . *tempted?*" asked Jenica. She was a sharp one, no question about that.

"Tempted?" Frank shook his head, but as he did so he gave me quick, shifty glance, and I strongly suspected that he was lying. But who was I to judge? He was infected with a virus that had already turned hundreds of people into murdering blood-drinkers, and nobody knew how to cure it. He was a victim, too.

"I had a dream that Susan Fireman stepped into this tilting mirror that I have in my bedroom," said Frank. "Well—it may have been a dream, or maybe I was hallucinating. In any case, I refused to follow her. I smashed the mirror to stop Susan Fireman from coming back through, or the Vampire Gatherer from coming after me, and when I woke up, I found that I had broken my mirror for real. I think that's the only thing that saved me.

He had another fit of coughing, but then he said, "The reason I was trying to get back to the Sisters of Jerusalem—I needed to talk to our chemists. If they can find some agent that can break down this silver enzyme— maybe we could inject people with it when they first show signs of infection."

"But would that stop them from turning into *strigoi?*" asked Jenica.

"I doubt it. But it would probably stop them from escaping into mirrors. When the sun came up, they wouldn't have anyplace to hide, and they would burn up, and die for good. Eventually the *strigoi* would stop spreading so fast, and we could hunt them down and get them under control."

"That's kind of extreme," I told him. "That's like stopping a forest fire by cutting down the forest."

"Do you have a better idea?"

"Well, like I said, I think we need to find out where these freaks are hiding and hit them where they live. Or where they're *undead*, rather. That would be a start. But we also have to find out who revived the *strigoi*, and why, and we have to get rid of *him*, whoever he is."

"Of course, Harry, this is the best plan," Jenica put in. "But this is not going to be such a simple proposition. For all of his adult life my father has been searching for the Vampire Gatherer and his nest of *strigoi*, and he could never find them. Besides, we must be rational. The *strigoi* are surrounded by myths and legends, remember, not established facts."

"You think so?" said Gil. "The way I see it, all those dead people in the streets, they weren't killed by myths and legends—but if they *were*, then the myths and legends must be pretty much true. Like the doc says, this is either some complicated kind of bio-chemistry, or else it's black magic. Dead people can't climb up buildings, and nobody can hide inside mirrors, whether they're dead or alive. But, hell—here they are, *doing* it. So if all the intelligence we've got to go on is myths and legends, that's still better than no intelligence at all, believe me. In Bosnia once I had this superstitious feeling that the Serbs had set up a booby trap inside a children's hostel, and that superstitious feeling saved me from getting my ass blown inside out.

He paused, and then he said to Jenica, "You don't have any kind of candy bar, do you?"

"What?"

"I think my blood-sugar level is dropping."

"Well . . . I have Romanian chocolate. Romania is famous for chocolate."

"Sure, anything. This morning I ate four Snickers bars one after the other, and that was my breakfast. Once I start getting hyped up, I have to have candy."

I have to admit that our whole situation looked slightly worse than totally hopeless. I mean, what a bunch of clowns—what could *we* do to save New York City, the four of us, sitting in this stuffy downtown apartment with the drapes drawn? Shivery, Sleepy, Superstitious and Sexy.

There was Frank, with his face as white as a papier-mâché mask, shivering and coughing and grunting every two or three minutes because he felt like he was burning up alive. He was a doctor, sure, but right now his medical expertise wasn't much use to anybody, least of all himself. Then there was Gil. He was a trained soldier, but he was so tired and wired by what he had seen in the streets that he was eating chocolate with his eyes closed. Me—I had some practical experience of malevolent things from beyond, but I didn't have the slightest idea how to deal with real live vampires, and I wasn't at all sure that I was brave enough or public-spirited enough to go out and try. And Jenica—well, she was highly academic, and she was very sexy, but in my opinion it was going to take more than a deep cleavage and a Ph.D. to handle a 550-year-old *svarcolaci.*

More to the point, did any of us have the strength or the guile or the know-how to fight whoever had raised The Wolf up out of his casket, and defeat him? Or *it?* Or whatever it was? Remember that I once saw a mythical lizard appear out of nowhere and bite a doctor's fingers off, so I was prepared to believe in anything at all—and *you* should be, too, because that kind of shit happens, no matter how much you don't want to believe in it.

In the end, though, Gil was right. We might have been clowns, but we had to do *something*, because it didn't look as if anybody else in New York City had our unique combination of peculiar knowledge and contacts with the spirit world.

I snapped off a piece of Gil's chocolate while he still had his eyes closed. "So, okay," I said, "where exactly are we going to start looking for these vampires? If they can hide in mirrors, we don't stand a chance, unless we break every mirror in Manhattan."

"We still need to find the nest," said Jenica. "*Strigoi* need to gather together from time to time. They are very vicious, but their emotional strength is very brittle. They are thousands of miles away from their homeland, remember, and they have outlived their friends and their loved ones by hundreds of years. My father always says that they are dangerous, but very lonely, and perhaps their loneliness makes them even more dangerous still."

"Okay, then, let's use some logic. If your father couldn't find the nest, *why* couldn't he find it?"

"He has several suspicions. He has always been sure that when Redding's Department Store was demolished in 1907, the coffins could not have been taken very far away. It would have been too expensive to carry them far, and who would want to pay for dead people they did not even know? Also, there is no mention in any of the newspapers of so many coffins being transported out of New York, or sent back to Romania, and that would have been a newsworthy item."

"Maybe they were taken to a cemetery and buried?"

"Perhaps. There is a Romanian Orthodox Cemetery in New Jersey, but the records show that they were not interred there. In fact, no cemetery of any faith within two hundred miles of New York City has records of so many coffins being interred in one day—even Potters' Field on Hart Island, where the city's paupers were buried."

"What would you logically do with two hundred coffins?" I wondered. "If you weren't going to have them cremated, and if you didn't bury them in a cemetery, where would you stash them?"

Jenica said, "I will show you a map." She went over to the bookcase and came back with a large-scale street map of downtown New York in 1914, which she spread out over the coffee table. It was yellowed with age, and the creases had been reinforced with Scotch tape to prevent it from falling apart. A sheet of tracing paper was fastened over the pages that showed Wall Street and Battery Park, on which her father had penciled the location of Redding's Department Store on Cortlandt Street, and several other locations where he had obviously thought that the coffins might have been buried, or re-housed.

"Of course this map was drawn seven years after the coffins were moved, so many of the buildings would have been different. In those days, everything in the business district was being torn down and rebuilt, almost constantly. The streets were always filled with rubble. Every bank wanted a grander headquarters, every stockbroker wanted a taller office. Private houses were disappearing and moving uptown, new factories were opening and closing."

"So—if the buildings were changing so often, it's unlikely that the coffins were stored in a warehouse, or an attic? They would have been easily discovered, if they were."

"So you're thinking cellar," put in Gil, without opening his eyes.

"Cellar, or wine vault, or sewer maybe. But someplace underground, that's my guess. Even if the building above it was torn down, a cellar could have stayed intact."

Frank eased himself out of his chair and came across to the couch to sit beside me. He stared at the map for a long time, trying to suppress his coughing, and then he said, "What's this? St. Stephen's Church?"

"That's right," said Jenica. "St. Stephen's Romanian Orthodox Church, on Cedar Street. It was opened in 1916, but it stood right at the foot of the World Trade Center. When the South Tower collapsed, it was totally demolished."

"Yes, of course, I remember seeing it on TV. The streets on this map are all so different, I didn't realize that this was the same church. But *Saint Stephen*—that's very strange."

"Why is it strange?"

"In my dream, I saw my grandfather. He was sitting in his old black Mercury Marquis, only it was converted into a funeral car. What I really noticed was that my grandfather's hair was shining like a halo, and I thought: *He looks just like a saint.*"

"This was the dream with Susan Fireman?" asked Jenica. "The dream when she was trying to persuade you to go through the mirror?"

Frank coughed, and cleared his throat. "Yes, but I'm beginning to believe that it wasn't a dream at all. It was more like a hypnotic trance. She was inside my head, just like a hypnotist. She was conjuring up my childhood memories so that I would feel that everything was fine and there was nothing for me to worry about. I could walk through the mirror, I could die, I could turn into one of the *strigoi*, everything would be wonderful. It *looked* like my world, but it was entirely controlled by *her*."

"I don't follow you," I told him.

"Everything in that dream had some kind of significance. The beach, the mirror, everything. So what was my grandfather doing there? And why was he sitting in a hearse? And why did he have a halo? I keep on turning that over and over in my mind, and the more I think about it, the more sure I am that Susan Fireman was trying to show me something in a way that I would understand it. *My* memories, but *her* meanings. You're going to meet an elder, and you're going to respect him, the same way you used to respect your grandfather, and you're going to love him."

"Your grandfather looked like a saint," said Jenica, nodding her head as if she was beginning to understand what Frank was getting at—which was a damn sight more than I was. "What was your grandfather's name?"

"That's the whole point. His name was Stephen."

"So, in this dream you saw Stephen, looking like a saint, and sitting in a funeral car?"

"That's right."

"Did the funeral car have a casket in it?"

Frank closed his eyes, and thought for a moment. Then he said, "Yes . . . yes, it did. A big gray casket, made of metal. But it was very scabby and corroded, as if it had been buried underground for hundreds of years."

"And were there any flowers around the casket?"

"No, no flowers—but now I come to think, there was something twined around it. Like branches, silver and green—only they were shiny, and I could swear that they were *moving*."

"*Snakes*," said Jenica.

"Snakes?" I asked her.

"Of course. This young *strigoica* was trying to persuade Frank to join her in the place where the *strigoi* were hiding, yes? She was thinking so strongly about it that her thoughts appeared in Frank's dream, or trance, or whatever it was. But they appeared in the way that thoughts always appear in dreams—as symbols, or riddles."

"So Frank's grandfather Stephen looked like a saint?" I asked her. "And the saint was looking after the casket with the Vampire Gatherer in it."

"Yes. But Saint Stephen is not a man . . . St. Stephen is a *building*. St. Stephen is St. Stephen's Romanian Orthodox Church."

"But the church was flattened on 9/11."

"Yes. But maybe not the vaults underneath it."

"Your father—didn't he ever *search* St. Stephen's Church?" I asked Jenica. "It seems to me like the first place he would have checked out. Not only that, it's only three blocks away from Redding's Department Store."

"Of course. He searched it in the 1960s, on the pretext that he was a student of religious architecture, but he found nothing at all. I know this, because he mentioned it to me after we heard that St. Stephen's had been demolished.

"He said that he tried to search it again in the 1970s, after there was a documentary on TV about the building of the World Trade center towers. It showed them excavating the foundations, and my father realized how soft the soil was, because it was all landfill, and how easy it was to dig so deep. I remember him wondering if St. Stephen's Church had vaults beneath vaults, like some of the older churches in Translyvania and Wallachia. Most of them used to have catacombs and tunnels that ran deep below the Carpathian mountains, and this is where they hid all their art and their treasure during the time of the Ottoman empire.

"My father asked the church authorities if he could make another search, but by this time they knew from articles in the newspapers that he was trying to find *strigoi*, and they refused. The Orthodox Primate of New York was not going to allow the media to say that he had welcomed a vampire-hunter onto the premises!"

"Well, I may be barking up the wrong building," I said, "but if your father thought that St. Stephen's Church was worth a second look, I think we ought to do just that."

Frank coughed, and nodded. "I have an intuition that you may be right, Harry."

"Are you okay?" I asked him. "You don't want me to make you another liver-and-wine smoothie?"

He couldn't speak at first, but he vigorously shook his head. Eventually, he managed to choke out, "Harry—I'd rather die first."

*   *   *

After a brief and bad-tempered argument, we agreed that we would *all* go looking for the vampire's nest. Jenica thought that it was far too risky to take Frank along with us. He was so sick, and he would slow us down, and supposing he was already much more infected by the *strigoi* virus than he was letting on, and led us into a trap? But Gil was confident that he could handle Frank, even if Frank did try to double-cross us. As for Frank—Frank was desperate not to be left behind on his own, coughing his lungs all over the carpet and waiting for the Vampire Catcher to come for him.

"What do you think, Harry?"

"I think he should come with, if he's feeling up to it. This situation can't be any more suicidal than it is already."

Out on the streets it seemed twenty times hotter. The sky was a weird shade of laurel green, as if we were on another planet, and there was a noticeable absence of shadows: as if they, too, were hiding away from the vampires. The back of my shirt was soaked in sweat before I had even walked down the front steps of Jenica's house, and I had to keep wiping my face with a balled-up Kleenex.

Frank wore oven gloves and a hood and he had thickly smeared his face in even more Ambre Solaire. Jenica had draped a net curtain over his head to strain out as much light as possible, so that he looked like a medieval leper. Even so, when he took his first step into the sunshine he sucked in his breath, like, *ittthhhhh*! and for a moment I thought he was going to turn around and stumble back inside.

"Frank? *Frank?* Think you can make it?"

"I'm a survivor, Harry, don't you worry about me. I'm not going to die. And besides—" c*ough!* "—I'm damned if I'm going to let that goddamned wife of mine take all of my property."

I turned to Gil with exaggerated wonderment. "Did you hear that? This must be the first vampire who's more worried about his divorce settlement than he is about drinking blood."

"Same thing, from what I've heard."

Jenica was still acting sulky, but I happen to like petulant women. She was wearing a short linen dress, in a natural color, with blue and yellow flowers embroidered across the yoke, and soft cream leather boots. She carried an embroidered bag across her shoulders, which contained her vampire-hunting kit. This consisted of a large crucifix, set with amber and bloodstones, which had been given to her father by the Orthodox monks from Maramures Monastery in Romania, and which he had always taken with him when he went looking for *strigoi*; as well as a round brass bottle of holy water, several sticks of pale green sealing wax, and a screwtop jar full of garlic paste, thickly mixed with silver filings from a maker of religious icons. Most important of all, though, she had the book of *svarcolaci*, and the words that could seal the Vampire Gatherer back in his casket—hopefully, for another five hundred-fifty years.

Gil had brought all the practical equipment, most of it hung around his waist. Two flashlights, a large screwdriver, a hunting knife and a baseball bat.

The streets were uncannily silent, like an abandoned movie set, but there were bodies everywhere, and in the heat and humidity they were beginning to stink. Every block was cluttered with wrecked and burned-out cars and trucks, and almost every vehicle contained a corpse, either incinerated into a black matchstick person, or hugely bloated with gas, like a blown-up doll. At one intersection there was a whole bus full of blown-up dolls, all of different ethnic origins.

I saw three small children lying on the sidewalk next to a dumpster, hand-in-hand, and their bodies were glittering with blowflies. I saw a middle-aged woman in a red-and-yellow dress, curled up next to a fire hydrant. I thought she was winking at me, until I realized that maggots were dropping from her forehead into her empty eye socket.

"What did I tell you?" said Gil. "This is like the end of the frigging world."

We kept on walking, although my stomach made a horrible gurgling noise, and I would have given anything to go back to Jenica's apartment and slam the door behind me and lock it, and wait for somebody to tell me that it was safe to come out.

Almost all of the victims had their throats cut—some so severely that their spines were practically severed—although there was very little blood on the pavement. "*Strigoi* did this," said Jenica. "They cut, they drink their fill. And you see how many bodies? They must be multiplying very, very fast."

The stores were deserted, even though many of them had their windows smashed and their doors had been left wide open. Some of their stock had been strewn around across the sidewalks, but it didn't look as if anything much had been stolen. The *strigoi* had been looking for fresh human blood, not microwave ovens.

We looked into a Greek delicatessen. A young woman lay dead on the black-and-white tiled floor, her face covered by her upraised dress, her legs wide apart. "Hold up a minute," said Gil. I waited on the sidewalk while he went inside. He bent over the young woman's body and tugged down her dress to make her decent. Then he covered her face with a red-checkered napkin, and crossed himself.

He came out again, saying nothing, but I understood then why he was helping us to find the vampires. He believed in human dignity, and he understood the true value of human life. He had seen for himself what happens when men become devils.

We walked six blocks and we saw no signs of life, except for a curtain listlessly waving in a fifth-story window. No traffic, no sirens, no helicopters, no ships whooping in the harbor. No *dogs*, even. Only bodies, some of which were so repulsively mutilated that they didn't looked human. A man was wearing his own fleshless ribcage like a massive helmet. A young boy of maybe three or four had been run over by a truck, and his head was completely flat, and nearly two feet wide.

At last we reached Ground Zero, where the World Trade Center towers had collapsed, and where the Freedom Tower was already starting to rise. Again, there was nobody here—nobody alive, anyway. The construction huts were all deserted, and the heavy machinery stood silent, back-hoe diggers and bulldozers and concrete mixers. I saw a man's body suspended from a crane, twenty or thirty feet in the air, like a lynching, with two or three seagulls picking at it.

This site had stirred up enough emotions when I had come downtown to view it after September eleventh. But that had been right in the middle of the cleanup, and it had been noisy and busy and bustling with purpose. This morning it was just plain eerie, a deserted construction site in a city populated by rotting corpses, and undead people who could only come out when it was dark. The crane clanked, and clanked, and one of the seagulls screamed in frustration.

"Where's the frigging federal government?" Gil demanded in a sudden burst of frustration. "Where's the rescue teams? Where's the frigging marines? Don't tell me they've just abandoned us. You can't just abandon a whole frigging city!"

Frank leaned against a barrier and coughed. "You can if it's contagious."

"You mean they've put up the shutters and left us here to die?"

"What would *you* do? Like Harry says, this thing could spread across the eastern seaboard like wildfire."

"But there's no helicopters even!"

Frank coughed again. "They probably don't want to give us any false hopes," he said, wryly.

At that moment Jenica called out, "It's here! St. Stephen's Church!" Her voice sounded flat, like someone shouting in a dream.

We gathered around 155 Cedar Street, where St. Stephen's Church had stood. The layout of the street was being changed, and there were metal fences everywhere, and rubble, and long coiling hoses, and portable generators. A narrow trench had been excavated along the side of the street, where new utility pipes were being laid, and this was heaped with bodies, too, although I couldn't count how many, and I didn't want to look them too close. One man's face was already looking runny.

Frank straightened up, and sniffed the air, as if *strigoi* gave off a detectable smell.

"Well?" I asked him.

"I can feel something, but I'm not sure what. A kind of emptiness."

"*Emptiness?* What do you mean?"

"It's like when you're moving out of a house—and you take a last look around—just to make sure you haven't left anything behind—but really you're trying to remember everything you did there—but you can't—"

"What about *strigoi?*" said Gil.

"I don't know. But there's *something* here. My skin's burning. And my teeth are aching. Believe me—they really, really hurt, right down to the roots."

Even through the folds of the net curtain I could see that he was suffering. "Do you want to go back?" I asked him.

"No," he said, emphatically. "This is where the nest is, I'm sure of it. Let's go find these bastards and finish them off."

16

BLOOD HEAT

I squeezed around a metal fence and walked across the construction site. St. Stephen's had been only a tiny building, with a street frontage of only fifty feet and a depth of no more than seventy-five feet. The site had been completely scraped down to floor level, and the mosaic flooring had now been cleaned and swept and covered in heavy-duty plastic sheeting, to protect it. I looked down and there was St. Stephen staring up at me through the vinyl, dark-skinned and sad-eyed, with a tarnished gold halo.

The buildings on either side had been less seriously damaged, so the site was like a gap where a molar had been extracted, and we stood deep in shadow.

Gil and Jenica followed me as I picked my way to the very back of the building. Here, there were two raised platforms, where the altar had once stood, and off to the left I could see a three-foot space in the mosaic where the door to the vaults must have been. The stairs leading downward were covered over by rusty metal sheeting, but it looked as if somebody had shifted it, just enough to allow somebody very thin to creep in. Or maybe creep *out.*

Frank came to join us. "I can feel that emptiness even more strongly. It's almost—I don't know—*sad.*"

"Okay, let's go down and see what St. Stephen has been hiding from us all these years."

Between us, Gil and I managed to manhandle the metal sheeting away from the staircase, even though it felt like it weighed half a ton, and after we had moved it I had to walk around in a circle like Groucho Marx, until I straightened myself up. The staircase was wooden, and very dusty. After six or seven steps it took a sharp turn off to the right, toward the back of the construction site, and was swallowed by darkness.

Gil switched on the larger of his two flashlights. "I'll go first. Jenica—I think you should maybe come next. You have all the vampire-hunting gear. Harry—you should take up the rear."

"Don't trust me?" asked Frank.

"I'm a grunt," said Gil. "Grunts don't trust nobody, never."

Jenica said, "We should be safe, if the *strigoi* are sleeping. But like I told you before, we know about them only through myths and legends, and we cannot be absolutely sure that they will not attack us."

"That's a risk we'll have to take," I told her. "Come on—we're dealing with the supernatural here, and when you're dealing with the supernatural, you don't get a manufacturer's warranty."

She looked at me, and there was something in her eyes that made me feel as if the ground was sliding sideways, underneath my feet. "Of course," she said. "Life is full of unexpected terrors."

Gil tested his weight on the top step of the staircase. "Seems okay," he commented. Then he went down the next step, and the next. "It's a little creaky, but otherwise I think it's sound."

He disappeared around the bend in the stairs, although we could still hear his voice. "It's pretty dusty down here, but it's dry. There's another bend in the stairs, and then there's an archway. Are you coming on down?"

Jenica took her eyes away from me and followed Gil down the stairs, her boot heels going *clomp, clomp, clomp* on every tread.

"Are you going to be able to manage this?" I asked Frank.

Underneath his net curtain, he nodded. "This is the only way. If I don't do this, I'm going to die. Worse than that, I'm going to die and I won't be dead."

"Keep fighting it, Frank."

"I'm trying, Harry, believe me. Do you know something—I've treated patients with stomach cancer, and they've taken hold of my sleeve, and they've begged me to kill them. Begged me, with tears in their eyes. *Kill me, doc! Kill me!*

He paused, and then he said, "I never knew what they were suffering, not until now. But you can't get your revenge on cancer, can you? I think those people would have wanted to go on living, if they could, no matter how much pain they were going through."

"Look, if this gets too much for you—"

"Harry, I'm a doctor. I'll know when it's time to pull the plug. But, thanks."

"Right, then. Let's go."

Frank felt his way down the staircase and I followed close behind him, giving a quick glance around the construction site to make sure that nobody was watching us. I'd seen too many of those movies when Dr. Van Helsing goes into Dracula's cellars to put a crucifix and a bunch of garlic in his coffin, only to be caught by the vampire coming back home from a night's blood-sucking.

We had to duck our heads to go around the corner in the staircase. It was narrow, and it was very low. As Gil had warned us, we had to negotiate another bend, and then we found ourselves in a cellar, with red brick arches, and a red brick floor. It was obvious that it had been completely swept clean, probably by the N.Y. Department of Environmental Protection, after September eleventh. It smelled of nothing but brick dust, and there was nothing stored here—no boxes, no religious paraphernalia, and definitely no coffins.

Gil went over to the far side of the cellar, so that the arches hid his head. He flicked his flashlight left and right, up and down, but then he came back and said, "Looks like we've drawn a blank. I can't see any trapdoors, or secret passages. Maybe the vampires *were* here, they're not here now, and that's for sure."

"I could *feel* them," Frank insisted.

"You felt emptiness," I reminded him. "And whatever you say about it, this is emptiness."

"Anyway, we will have to think again," said Jenica. "If they are not here, then where are they? If only I could talk to my father, he would have more ideas where we could look."

I borrowed Gil's spare flashlight, and took a slow walk around the cellar, peering at every crack between the bricks.

"You're wasting your time, Harry," said Gil. "If there *is* another vault, underneath this one, my guess is that it was sealed up years ago. Remember this part of downtown gets flooded pretty often. That's why they had to build the World Trade Center in kind of a concrete bathtub."

I had almost completed a circuit of the cellar when I noticed that the shadow to the left of one of the arches appeared to be slightly wider than any of the others. If you had been giving the cellar nothing more than a quick, superficial search, you never would have seen it. In fact, unless you were specifically looking for a concealed entrance, you never would have seen it at all.

Jenica was already making her way back up the staircase, but I called out, "Hey! Wait up!"

"You got something?" asked Gil.

I had to go up really close to the arch before I realized why the shadow was wider. There was a niche there, but it was only about eighteen inches wide, if that, and it was cleverly concealed by protruding brickwork. But when I shone the flashlight directly into it, I realized that it ran right behind the arch. After about five feet, I could see narrow brick steps. The steps led downward, and then turned sharply and steeply to the right, so that they disappeared below the building next door.

"This is it," I called out. "Here's the way down."

Gil came around to look at it. "Jesus, that's skinny. Nobody over a hundred and eighty-five pounds need apply."

"No claustrophobics, either."

Jenica and Frank joined us. Because there was no sunlight down here, Frank had pulled off his net curtain, and his hood. Frank said, "I knew it."

Gil said, "Let's be realistic about this. If we go down there, and we get ambushed, it isn't going to be easy to get out."

"Do we have a choice?" I asked him.

Frank said, "Why don't I go first? If we don't find these bastards, I'm going to die anyway. And maybe they won't attack me, if they think that I'm one of them. Or *nearly* one of them."

"That is what frightens me," said Jenica. "Supposing you have been leading us into an ambush, all along?"

"Well, I don't feel well enough to make an issue of it," said Frank. "I'm just saying that if you want me to go first, then I will."

"I trust him," I said. In reality, I wasn't entirely sure that I did, but I was entirely sure that I didn't want to go first.

Gil shrugged. Then he took a pack of Fruit Loops out of one of the patch pockets on his pants, shook out a handful, and crammed them into his mouth. "All right by me," he said, indistinctly.

I gave Frank my flashlight and he edged his way into the

niche. He had to go in sideways, and to hold his breath, too. The flashlight shone upward into his face, which made him look even more ghoulish than he did already. "It's not too bad," he said, but then he started coughing, and he was forced to stop.

"Do you want to come back?" I asked him, but he managed to clamp his hand over his throat.

"I'm okay. I can make it."

He inched his way toward the steps, and then gradually he disappeared out of sight. We could still see his flashlight dancing on the brickwork, and we could hear his shoes scraping on the steps, but that was all. Then the flashlight disappeared, too, and there was darkness, and silence.

"*Frank!*" I called out.

Still silence.

"Frank, are you there? What do you see?"

More silence, but then a distorted, echoing voice. "*It's incredible! It's incredible! You got to come down here!*"

"Frank? Is everything okay down there?"

"*Come see for yourself!*"

"Are there any *strigoi* down there?" asked Jenica.

"*Come see.*"

"It's a trap," said Jenica. "I am sure that he is trying to trap us."

"I still trust him," I told her. "And he doesn't sound like he's in any kind of trouble."

Gil lifted up his baseball bat. "I'll go down first. If you hear me shout, just get out of here as quick as you can."

He squeezed himself into the niche, and worked his way sideways down the steps. I get panicky in confined spaces. My sister locked me in the linen closet when I was four years old, and I didn't stop screaming for three days. Well, my mom said that it *felt* like three days. This was even worse. First I had to exhale, and then I had to pull my stomach in, and even then it took a whole lot of effort to force myself along. The brickwork was scraping at my belt buckle, and I seriously began to think that I was going to get stuck here, and starve to death. It didn't help that I was starting to hyperventilate.

"You can go faster," Jenica scolded me. She may have been bosomy, but she was a whole lot slimmer than me.

"I'm going as fast as I can, okay?"

"And what if we have to escape?"

I didn't answer. I was too busy struggling round the corner. I had never felt so panicky in my life, even when Misquamacus had brought down hordes of giant rats from the Great Beyond, and I hated rats almost as much as I hated confined spaces.

After I had turned the corner, however, I found that the niche began to widen, and that the ceiling was higher. The last twenty steps were very steep, but they led down into a huge, dark vault, with massive cast-iron pillars to support it. Gil was there, and Frank, too, and they were criss-crossing their flashlight beams in all directions.

Between the pillars lay hundreds of coffins, *hundreds*, and they were all lying open, with their lids tilted. Further back, the flashlights picked up the glitter of water, where part of the vault was flooded, and some of the coffins were afloat.

"*Strigoi*," whispered Jenica, as she came down the last step, and joined us.

Frank approached the nearest coffin. It looked like oak, and it must have been varnished black when it was made, but now the varnish was blistered and faded. Inside, the fabric lining was yellow and stained, and spotted with mold, and there was a clear impression of somebody's body. There were even a few dry brown hairs on the pillow, and Frank picked them up, and rubbed them between his fingers.

"Frank?"

He turned to me, and he looked totally shattered, even beneath that thick mask of sunblock. "It's true," he said.

"They really exist. The undead. I haven't been dreaming, have I?"

I didn't know what to say to him. He turned away, and went from one coffin to the other, as if he were searching for evidence that this was all some kind of monstrous fake. Some of the coffins had nameplates on them, and he read them out.

"Naum Ciomu, Valeriu Erhan, Ioan Stefanescu . . ."

Jenica was over on the other side of the vault with Gil, but when she heard Frank reading out the names she called out, "Harry! Tell him to stop! Some of the *strigoi* might be able to pick him up!"

"Frank," I warned him, and he held up his hand and said, "Okay. I heard her."

He came back and stood next to me. "She really doesn't trust me, does she?"

"No. But she knows a whole lot more about vampires than we do, and maybe they *can't* be trusted, as a rule."

"I'm not a vampire, Harry, and I don't intend to become one."

I watched Jenica climbing over a row of empty coffins, with Gil close behind her. "Maybe she had a bad experience with vampires, who knows?"

"*She* had a bad experience with vampires?"

I looked at him. I didn't know what to say. I could only guess what agony he was suffering.

"Who would have thought that this was all true?" he asked me. "All those horror comics we used to read when we were kids . . . all of those Dracula movies. All of that stuff about the vampire Lestat. And all the time, it was true."

It was then that Gil waved his flashlight in our direction, and Jenica called, "Harry! Harry, we've found it! The Wolf's casket, it's over here!"

The Vampire Gatherer's coffin was enormous, like a 1940s sedan, and it had been propped up on bricks to keep it clear of the water. Just like the coffin that Frank had described in his dream, it was forged out of iron, and it was thick with overlapping scales of dirt and corrosion. It had six huge handles in the shape of shaggy wolf heads, holding rings in their jaws, and its edges were thickly decorated with intertwined snakes.

In common with all the other coffins, its lid had been lifted off and tilted aside, although it was raised up so high that we couldn't see if there was anybody lying in it.

Gil immediately genuflected in front of me and cupped his hands. "Here—I'll give you a boost up."

"Just a goddam minute," I protested. "What if he's *in* there?"

"If he's in there, I don't know. You hammer a stake through his heart."

"We don't have a stake."

"It would do no good, anyway," said Jenica. "The Wolf is already dead. His heart is buried in Wallachia."

"So if he's in there, what *do* I do?"

"You say nothing. You stay silent. I will cross him with holy water, and read the dismissal from the book of *svarcolaci,* and then we will close his coffin with wax."

"And that will seal him up again, for good?"

"As you say, Harry, this is the supernatural. It does not arrive with a manufacturer's warranty."

I put my foot into Gil's cupped hands, and gripped his shoulders. He said, "Ready?"—but before I could tell him that I wasn't, he was heaving me upward, with my arms wildly waving to keep my balance.

I managed to catch a glimpse inside The Wolf's casket before I teetered sideways and had to jump back down to the floor, but only for a split second. He wasn't in there, thank all the saints of Wallachia. I saw a filthy gray pillow, and lace ruffles that had turned yellow with age, but that was all.

"You want to try again?" asked Gil.

"Forget it, it's empty."

"He's probably hiding in a mirror someplace," said Frank. "In fact, I'll bet *all* of them are."

"I would like to look in the casket for myself, please," put in Jenica.

"Okay," said Gil, and knelt down again. Jenica placed her booted foot into his interlaced hands, and I stood next to her, holding her elbow, to help her to keep her balance. Gil lifted her up, and we both made a serious effort not to look up at her thin white lacy thong. She peered over the edge of the coffin, and confirmed, "Yes, he is gone." But just when Gil was about to lower her back down, she said, "Wait—wait up a second! There is something here!"

When she climbed down, she was wielding something that looked like a thick brown stick, a little over a foot long, with a knob at each end. It was only when Gil shone the flashlight on it that we realized what it was. A very old bone, heavily decorated with all kinds of zig-zag patterns, and with a hole drilled through one end, with feathers attached.

Frank coughed, and said, "That's a shinbone. A human tibia."

"You sure about that?"

"Trust me, I'm a doctor."

I took the bone from Jenica and peered at it closely. I couldn't think why, but I found it oddly evocative, like some smell that you haven't smelled in years, or some song that you can't quite remember. "Do you know what this is used for?" I asked Jenica. "I mean, is it part of any vampire ritual?"

Jenica shook her head. "It is not Romanian, I don't think."

"So what's it doing in the Vampire Gatherer's casket?"

Frank approached the casket and touched it with the fingertips of both hands. "You know, I can almost feel this guy," he said, hoarsely. "That *emptiness* I was talking about.

It's very, very strong." He traced one finger across the corroded plaque on the end of the casket. "I think I can see some letters here."

I said, "Here," and shone my flashlight onto them, and Frank slowly read them out. "N—U—M . . . E—L—E . . . M—E—U—E—S—T . . . and then there's an E . . . what does that mean in English?"

Jenica said, "Can you repeat that?"

"N—U—M—"

"That's all right, I understand it," Jenica interrupted him. " '*Numele meu este.*' It simply means 'my name is—' "

"*Vasile Lup,*" Frank whispered.

We stared at him, stunned. "You *said* it," said Gil.

"What?" said Frank, blinking at us.

"You *said* it, man. You said the fucking name! You're not supposed to say it, otherwise he can pick it up on his radar and he can tell that you're looking for him."

Frank looked distraught. "I know that, I know. But I didn't mean to, I swear it. I just—"

"You didn't *mean* to?" snapped Jenica. "Harry! Didn't I *warn* you that he couldn't be trusted! Now he has spoken the Vampire Gatherer's name and the Vampire Gatherer knows that we are trying to find him! He will find us first, believe me, and he will kill us all!"

Frank said, "Listen! I really didn't intend to say it out loud. I don't know . . . it just kind of came out."

"Oh! So you think we are fools? You are already one of the *strigoi!* You wanted to stay with us just to make sure that we were all trapped, and torn into pieces!"

Frank started to cough. "I didn't mean to say the goddam name, okay? I want to see this son-of-a-bitch get his comeuppance even more desperately than you do!"

"You will have your wish, sooner than you know!"

I said, "Hey, come on, Jenica, take it easy. You said yourself that most of this vampire stuff is only myths and legends. So all this stuff about saying the name, maybe that's just mythical, too. Gil thought you only had to say the word *strigoi*, didn't he, and the vampires would come and hunt you down? And like, think about it. How could this Wolf character hear Frank whispering his name, when *we're* right down in this cellar, right, and *he's* probably twenty blocks away, in some multi-story parking lot, hiding inside somebody's rearview mirror?"

But Jenica wouldn't lighten up. "There is so much historical evidence," she said, stalking backwards and forwards. "People have spoken the name of a *strigoi* or a *svarcolaci*, and next day their bodies are scattered over the fields, for the crows to feed on! The famous historian Alexandru Dutu, that happened to him in 1954, in Bucharest! He gave a speech at the university, and he said out loud the name of a *svarcolaci*. That night, they say that his blood came down on Presei Libere like rain!"

"Okay," I acknowledged. "But even if Frank did say the name deliberately, which I don't believe he did, maybe he's saved us all the trouble of looking for this character. Come on, Jenica. We have to face up to him sooner or later."

"In the daylight, yes, when we have the advantage! But later—"

"I know. *In the night, in the dark.*"

"You mock me, Harry."

"Jenica, I wouldn't dare."

At that moment, however, we heard a splash, and then a quick, sharp patter. Over in the far corner of the vault, three or four of the floating coffins started to knock together, like canoes. Gil raised his flashlight and tracked it slowly from side to side. There was another patter, and another splash. Then more coffins began to sway.

"Oh my God," said Jenica. "Look!"

I lifted my flashlight, too, and it was then that I saw them. *Rats*—there must have been thousands of them, swarming over the coffins like giant gray lice. Some of them were struggling in the water, drowning, while scores more of them were running over their backs. Their eyes glittered bright yellow and the vault was suddenly filled with their chittering and squeaking.

I could *smell* them, too, in a nauseating wave of long-confined air. They stank of raw sewage and something a whole lot worse.

"I think we need to get out of here," said Gil.

He didn't have to repeat himself. Jenica was already climbing the steps, and Frank was close behind her. "Go on, Harry," Gil told me, lifting up his baseball bat. "I'll hold them off." I hesitated for a moment, but then I turned and started to make my way back up.

"Come on, rodents!" Gil shouted. "Come and get your teeth knocked out!"

It took me only a few seconds to reach the bend in the steps, where they narrowed into a niche. When I glanced back, however, the rats had already poured over every coffin in the vault, and they were rushing toward Gil in a tidal wave of greasy gray fur.

Jenica had made it through the niche, but Frank was stuck. He had managed to squeeze himself a little way in between the bricks, but now he was coughing with pain and panic, and he couldn't go any further.

"Frank!" I shouted at him. "Try to relax! Take a couple of deep breaths!"

"I can't, I—*cough!*—I can't breathe—*cough!*"

I looked back down again. The rats had already reached Gil's feet and he was whacking at them left and right with his baseball bat. He had killed at least ten of them, but three of them were already clinging to his back, and more were starting to run up his legs. He swung his bat again and again, and pieces of bloody rat went flying across the vault, but one rat managed to jump up and grip his sleeve with its teeth, and even while he was swinging at the other rats, it dangled from side to side, refusing to let go, and more rats kept jumping up to join it.

I turned back to Frank. "*Frank!*" I shouted at him. "If you don't dislodge yourself, dude, we're all going to die! For God's sake force yourself!"

Frank still couldn't stop coughing and his face in the jiggling flashlight was almost maroon. I put my shoulder up against him, and I pushed him—I literally forced him into that niche, and then I shouted up to Jenica, "Take Frank's hand! Take his hand and pull him through! He's having a panic attack!"

He wasn't the only one. My heart was banging and I could hear the blood rushing in my head. Gil was still furiously beating at the rats, but now he had four or five or them hanging from each arm, and they had climbed right up on top of his shoulders so that he looked like a hunchback. With each blow, rat blood sprayed everywhere, and a bristly rat head hit me in the cheek. But the vault was heaving with vermin now, from one wall to the other, and all up the cast-iron arches, and more were still pouring in, and I could see that they were going to bury us.

"*Gil!*" I screamed. "*Get back up the steps!*"

He turned around and saw me, beating two rats off his shoulders as he did so. But one of them had already savaged his left earlobe, and three more were climbing up his back and tearing at his T-shirt. He tried to climb the steps, but he staggered and fell sideways, and the rats immediately saw their chance. They seethed over him, until he was covered in rats, and the massed weight of their bodies made it almost impossible for him to stand up again. He tried. He was like a monstrous rat-man, covered entirely in gray fur and writhing tails. I heard him shout something indistinct, maybe it was "*mom!*" but then he dropped back down again, and so many rats scrambled over him that I couldn't even see where he was.

Now the rats came after me, too. Frank had disappeared into the niche and I could only pray that he had made it through to the other side, and wasn't stuck halfway. *Please God, if I never ask you anything, ever again, let Frank not be stuck halfway.* If he was, he and I were going to be trapped together between those two brick walls with scores of rats tearing us to shreds. Maybe Jenica had been right. Maybe this was Vasile Lup's way of destroying us, and ripping us into so many pieces that we wouldn't be worth burying, even if there was anybody in New York left to bury us.

A huge gray rat ran at my ankle, and bit at the cuff of my pants. I kicked at it, and kicked again, and then I swung the bone at it—the shinbone that Jenica had found in the Vampire Gatherer's coffin. I didn't even hit it, but the rat abruptly tumbled over. I was going to swing the bone again and smash its head in when I realized that it was already dead—or apparently dead. Its eyes were closed and it was lying sprawled on the step with its pale gray belly exposed. Blood was leaking from its anus.

Another rat scurried up, and then another. I swung the bone again, and both rats flopped over and rolled back down the steps. I couldn't believe it. I swished the bone from side to side, and as I did so the rats fell dead, in their dozens. Swish, and they collapsed to the right. Swish, and they collapsed to the left. They dropped into the empty coffins, with hundreds of muffled thuds. They dropped from the cast-iron arches, into the water.

I advanced on them, swinging the bone, and it was a massacre.

By the time I reached the heap of rats that was wriggling on top of Gil, I was squashing and sliding over so many dead and half-dead rats that I could hardly keep my balance. But I managed to swing the bone right over the top of them, one way and then the other. The rats toppled off him in heaps, until he reappeared. He was crouched down on his knees and elbows, his hands clamped over his face. His scalp was bloody and both of his ears were ripped. But he was still alive, and he was gasping for air.

"Gil! Gil, it's Harry! You can get up!"

"*Harry?*" He slowly took his hands away from his face and looked up at me in disbelief. His upper lip had been bitten and he could barely speak. "Harry, what happened?"

I held up the bone. I didn't have to swing it any more. All around the vault, the rats were rushing away, running between the coffins and into the water. In only a few minutes, almost all of them had disappeared, except for their hundreds of dead. The vault was silent, although the musky smell of rats made my eyes water.

"I think I got the power of the voodoo," I told Gil.

17

BLOOD-RED MOON

Jenica did her Girl Scout bit and patched us up. She stuck Band-Aids all over Gil's scalp, in criss-cross patterns, and she even managed to sew back a torn flap of flesh that was dangling from his right earlobe, using nylon button thread. Throughout the operation, Gil sat on the dining chair, whistling tunelessly between his teeth, but when she was tying the thread into a knot, he allowed himself a single, "*Shit.*"

Gil and I had suffered not much more than scratches and bruises and rat bites. But Frank was growing steadily worse. He had retreated to one of the Dragomirs' spare bedrooms, and he was lying in the dark, shivering and mumbling with pain. His temperature was way up, and his eyes kept rolling up into his head, and we were beginning to worry that he wasn't going to last out the night.

The power was completely out now, so we couldn't even make ourselves anything hot to eat. I opened up a can of frankfurters and served them with crackers and cheese and overripe bananas. The water supply was still working, and the water seemed to be clean, but all the same I filled up the bathtub, just in case the faucets ran dry.

After we had eaten, we sprawled in the overstuffed armchairs in Jenica's over-decorated living room and Jenica poured us another huge glass of death-breath Romanian red wine. The sun was beginning to sink over the Jersey shore, and her face was illuminated in bright orange, so that she looked like a medieval painting of herself. St. Jenica of the Vampires.

"I hate to speculate on this," said Gil, "but what do we do if Frank buys the farm?" I hadn't liked to say so, but that was exactly what I was wondering, too.

Jenica shielded her eyes from the setting sun. "If he dies from this infection, then of course he will become one of the *strigoi*. We will have to dismember his body and burn it and we will have to keep his heart in a jar filled up with holy water."

"We have to cut him up?" I asked her. "Jesus, I can't even skin a chicken without barfing."

"We will have no choice, Harry—not just for our own protection, but for *his* sake, too. To become one of the undead . . . that is the greatest curse that anybody can suffer. What Frank said about emptiness . . . that is all the undead can ever feel, because they have no loved ones any more, nor homes to return to, and as each century goes by, they grieve ever more deeply for the life that they have left so far behind."

Gil sipped his wine and sniffed. "You're almost making me feel sorry for the bastards."

"Well, don't," said Jenica. "They feel sentimental for themselves, but not for you or me. You think the dead hate us? The undead hate us even more. They resent us beyond anything you can imagine, and they never have any guilt about drinking our blood."

The shinbone that Jenica had found in the Vampire Gatherer's casket was lying on the coffee table in front of me. I picked it up and waved it from side to side. "So what do we think this is, apart from the best rat-exterminating device known to man? I'll tell you something, if we get out of this in one piece, I'm going to patent this sucker. Erskine's Amazing Rat-Zapper, two for $14.99, and I'm going to sell them on the shopping channel. I wonder if they work for mice. Or roaches, even."

Jenica said, "It is not Romanian. I have never seen anything like it before."

"But what was it doing in the The Wolf's coffin? I mean, it looks kind of ritualistic, doesn't it? Maybe it was part of the ceremony that brought him back to life."

"I don't think so," said Jenica. "In the book of *svarcolaci*, it says that the way to revive a dead vampire's spirit is to use salt and silver and drops of your own blood, and to recite the Seven Red Prayers. There is no mention of bones, or feathers."

I finished my glass of wine and then I went into the bedroom to see Frank. We had wiped off the sunblock, but his face was so white that I thought for a moment that he was already dead. When I sat down on the bed next to him, though, he opened his eyes and tried to focus on me.

"Think I'm passing over, Harry."

"No way, Frank. You stick with us."

He gave a barely perceptible shake of his head. I was convinced that I could see smoke seeping out of the collar of his shirt. "I'm burning, Harry. I'm burning alive. Now I know why they jumped, those people."

"Who people?"

"Nine-eleven. Those people who jumped from their offices. It's unbearable, Harry. I never knew that pain like this could even *exist*."

I tried to touch his hand but he twitched it away. "You'll

get through it, Frank," I told him. "All you have to do is grit your teeth and hold on."

"I don't think so. Maybe I'm getting what I've always deserved."

"What are you talking about? Nobody deserves this."

"I don't know. I've always been so—arrogant, and self-opinionated. I've always behaved like I'm God."

"Well, you're a doctor, Frank. To some people, you *are* God."

He licked his lips, and coughed up blood. "I'm going to make you a promise," he said. "No matter what happens to me, I took an oath to preserve human life. If you need me, and if it's possible that I can help you, then I will."

"I appreciate that, Frank. But the only thing that's going to happen to you is that you're going to get better. We'll have you back on your feet before you know it."

Frank almost managed a smile. "Don't try to kid a kidder, Harry. I've used those very same words more times than you can imagine. A doctor says you're going to get well—you mark my words, that's the time to start panicking."

While Frank slept, Jenica and I searched through Razvan Dragomir's bookshelves, trying to find anything informative on mirrors and vampires. All the time the sun was hurrying down, until the living room was so gloomy that we could hardly see each other. Jenica lit dark red candles that smelled like spices.

The *strigoi* might have abandoned their coffins at St. Stephen's, but there was nothing in any of Razvan Dragomir's books to suggest that Frank might be right, and they were able to hide inside mirrors instead.

I used to be pretty skeptical about the supernatural. After all, I peddled it for a living. But once I realized that there *is* a spirit world, and there *are* such things as demons, I guess I accepted every strange phenomenon without too much critical thought about it. Jenica, on the other hand, believed in vampires only because her father had given satisfactory proof of their existence, and on the whole she was much more skeptical than I was, and much more analytical. She thought that the vampires could have concealed themselves in cellars, or down in the subway, anyplace that the sun could never penetrate. She even suggested that they might have gone to funeral homes, and shut themselves in unsold coffins during the hours of daylight.

But mirrors? "In all of Romanian legend, there is nothing about *strigoi* hiding in mirrors."

I was finished with *Legends of Moldavia* and so I started leafing through a musty old book on *Romanian Folk Beliefs*, 1886. It had dozens of engravings of naked women in it, which led me to believe that it hadn't been published entirely in the interest of anthropology. In fact it was more of an academic stroke book. But halfway through I came across a picture of a deathbed with a woman's empty nightgown lying on it. The nightgown was beautifully arranged, as if its owner had managed to take it off without disturbing it at all. Its embroidered sleeves were neatly crossed over the bodice, and white lilies were spread on top of it.

The shock of the picture was the woman herself, who was stark naked, and who was climbing into a large mirror that was hanging above her bedroom fireplace. One of her arms, like Alice's, had already penetrated the glass, and could dimly be seen inside the reflected room. She was looking back regretfully at her real bedroom and saying (according to the caption) "Farewell, My Mortal Existence."

On the facing page, there was a paragraph that said, "In rural communities in Romania, when a family member lay dying of certain ailments, looking glasses were turned to face the wall, in order that, upon death, the spirit should rise unimpeded to Heaven, and that the deceased should not be tempted to pursue physical immortality by entering the world of reflections. In the world of reflections, it was believed, one can live for all eternity. But the price of living for all eternity is eternal misery, since those who choose to enter it can never walk again in daylight, and can never find that perfect peace and spiritual contentment which only the Lord can offer us."

Jenica read it, but then she passed it back to me with a shrug. "This tells us nothing."

"It doesn't tell us a whole lot, I'll grant you. But it does kind of suggest that dead people *might* be able to pass through mirrors, doesn't it? Or *some* dead people, depending what they died of."

"Perhaps. But there is no specific mention of *strigoi*, is there?"

"No—but it does say *certain ailments*, doesn't it? One of those ailments could be the vampire infection."

"Yes, Harry, but this is always the problem with myths and legends. It is so easy to use them to support any theory you want them to."

"But Frank saw this Susan Fireman woman stepping out of a mirror, and what do we have here? A woman stepping *into* a mirror."

"I am not saying that you are wrong, Harry. Maybe this woman in the picture is *strigoica*. But it does not categorically say that she is. Also, it does not explain how you can discover if *strigoi* are hiding inside a mirror; or how to stop them from coming out of it; or if it is possible to follow them into this world of reflection, to pursue them, and destroy them."

"Well, this is a book of popular beliefs, that's all. But at least it shows that there's a folk story about people going into mirrors. What you're talking about is a technical manual for hunting down vampires—you know, like the Catholics have for exorcizing demons."

She shook her head. "I doubt if anyone has ever written such a book. Most Romanian clergy deny absolutely the existence of *strigoi*, even in the face of all the evidence. They prefer to be sweeping it under their carpets. Only the Romanian Tourist Board insists on keeping alive the legends of vampires, and what *they* are doing is ludicrous, with their balloon rides over the Transylvanian mountains and champagne breakfasts in Dracula's birthplace."

"All the same," I said, "I still think that Frank is telling it like it really happened, and that Susan Fireman *did* come out of the mirror."

"I'm not too sure," Gil put in. "I wouldn't go so far as to say that he was deliberately falsifying, but you have to admit that he was pretty delirious. I seen men like that before, in Bosnia. They used to rave about all kinds of things."

"He's sick, for sure but—"

"He is much more than *seek*," Jenica interrupted. "He is one of the pale people, not yet dead but already half *strigoi*."

"But that's exactly why I believe him. He could have jumped on us at any time, couldn't he? He's burning up, and he'd do anything to drink our blood, but he's fighting it. He might be half *strigoi* but he's still half human, and that's what he's trying to cling on to. Why else would he warn us that the vampires can hide in mirrors? He doesn't want us to be taken by surprise, that's why. He's trying to protect us. He thinks it's the final human gesture he can make before he passes over, and becomes one of them."

Outside, the last gleam of crimson sunset had been swallowed up by darkness, like the lining of Bela Lugosi's cloak. Gil looked up at the gilded clock and said, "Nine-thirty. I guess it won't be too long now before we find out what's really real and what really ain't."

Jenica opened her embroidered bag and took out her

vampire-hunting paraphernalia—her crucifix and her holy water and her garlic paste. "All we can do now is to pray that the legend is wrong, and that the *svarcolaci* are deaf to their names being spoken."

"How about a game of Hold 'Em'?" asked Gil.

I don't remember when I fell asleep, but I suddenly jerked awake and all of the candles had burned down except for one, and that was dipping and winking and just about to go out. I looked up and the hands on the gilded clock were pointing to twenty-five after one.

I was sure that something had woken me, but when I listened the night outside was absolutely silent.

"Gil?" I whispered. Gil was leaning sideways in his chair, snoring like a duck. Jenica had stretched out on the couch with her dress hitched up, and I could see her bare hip shining in the candlelight.

I eased myself out of my chair and walked across the living room to the shelf where we had left our flashlights. I switched one of them on, but I kept the beam aimed at the carpet. I didn't want to wake up Gil and Jenica unless I really had to.

Out of the window, I could see that the city was in total darkness. The buildings looked like monuments in a massive cemetery. The heat and humidity were overwhelming, and sweat dripped off the end of my nose. For the first time since this vampire epidemic had broken out, I began to be convinced that—sooner rather than later—we were all going to die.

I tippy-toed into the corridor and along to Frank's bedroom. He was lying on his back, staring at the ceiling. I shone the flashlight in his face and whispered, "Frank? Frank, are you still with us?"

He didn't answer and he didn't move. I came up closer and I could tell at once that he was dead. He wasn't staring at the ceiling at all. He was staring at infinity.

"Safe journey, Frank," I told him. "I think God's going to forgive you for playing God. It's better than playing the devil."

"Sweet words," said a woman's voice, right behind me.

My heart jumped up and practically hit me under the chin, and I dropped my flashlight onto the bed.

"Jenica! You scared the shit out of me!"

But almost instantly I knew that it wasn't Jenica. It didn't sound like Jenica and Jenica wasn't wearing white and Jenica was six foot tall. I scrabbled for the flashlight and shone it directly into the woman's face.

She made no attempt to cover her eyes. She was small-boned and very pale and her dark brown hair was tangled and knotted. She was wearing a plain white linen smock, more like a shroud than a dress. The front of it was splattered with brown and yellow stains, and there were burrs and thistles sticking to it, as if she had been walking through a waste lot, or a railroad yard.

"What are you doing here?" I garbled. I don't think I was even speaking English. "How the hell did you get in?"

"You shouldn't be frightened," she told me, and she actually smiled. "I've come to collect Frank, that's all."

"You've come to do what? Frank's dead."

"No, no. Frank's passed over, that's all."

"Listen, I don't know who you are, but you need to get out of here now."

"Don't tell me that Frank didn't mention my name? Susan Fireman. Frank and me, we're very good friends."

I edged carefully around the side of the bedroom, keeping the flashlight pointed at her face. Susan Fireman, shit. She didn't even blink.

"*Jenica!*" I shouted.

"What's the matter?" Susan Fireman asked me. "You shouldn't be frightened. I won't hurt you."

"Oh, like you never—like you never hurt Frank?"

"Frank's been stubborn. If he hadn't been so wilful, he wouldn't have suffered at all."

"*Jenica!*"

Susan Fireman touched her fingertip to her lips. One second she was standing by the door and then *blink* she was standing right in front of me, and I hadn't even seen her move. "There isn't any point in calling for help," she said. "There are too many of us now, and every minute there are more."

"So what are you going to do, Ms. Fireman? You're going to drink my blood?"

"Of course not!" She paused, and then she said, almost seductively, "Not unless you want me to."

"Jenica! I need you in here now, Jenica!"

Susan Fireman turned and *blink* she was standing on the opposite side of the bed, leaning over Frank, and stroking his forehead.

"Frank," she whispered. "Frank, it's Susan. We've come to take you home with us, Frank."

At that moment, Jenica appeared in the doorway. She looked almost as pale as Susan Fireman. Gil was close behind her, with his baseball bat.

"Who is this person?" Jenica demanded. Susan Fireman didn't even look at her. She carried on stroking Frank's forehead, and breathing over his face. "Wake up, Frank. All of your pain is over now. The long, long night is just beginning."

Jenica took two more steps into the room. "Harry, who is this? What is she doing here? How did she get in?"

"Susan Fireman," I told her. "Frank's dead, and she says that she's come to take him home."

"*Strigoica,*" breathed Jenica. Then she screamed out, "*Strigoica!* Get out of my house!"

Susan Fireman looked up at her. "Quiet. You don't have to get hysterical. You'll only make things worse for yourselves."

"Hold up a minute," said Gil. He disappeared, and I heard him going from room to room throughout the apartment, banging doors.

Susan Fireman said, "I don't want to do you any harm. I

want to leave here with Frank, that's all. Frank's new life is waiting for him, don't deny him that."

Gil reappeared. "Kitchen window, that's how she got in. Though Christ knows how she climbed up there. It has to be eighty feet, minimum, and not even a rainwater pipe to hold on to."

I slowly approached the bed. "You listen to me, Ms. Fireman. This isn't what Frank wanted. Frank struggled hard to stay human, and when you're human, dead means dead. So he's not going anywhere, except a crematorium."

"You don't know *anything*, do you?" said Susan Fireman.

"I know one thing for sure. I'm not going to let you take Frank."

I heard a noise in the kitchen, a pan being knocked over. Gil turned around and said, "Jesus! There's more of them!"

A tall, white-faced man appeared in the hallway behind him, dressed in a heavily bloodstained sweatshirt. He was closely followed by a young woman with wild red hair, and another man, shaven-headed, in dirty mechanics' coveralls. I caught the shine of knives in their hands.

Without any hesitation, Gil tilted back against the wall and hit the white-faced man with his baseball bat. The man collided with the girl behind him, and as he was trying to regain his balance, Gil hit him again, and again. I heard a sharp crack and the man's forehead suddenly split apart, and blood sprayed across the wallpaper.

I took hold of Jenica's sleeve and pulled her back behind me. Then I frantically looked around the bedroom for something to use as a weapon. All I could see was a three-legged stool, so I picked it up and swung it around my head. One of the legs hit me on the forehead and I almost concussed myself.

Susan Fireman—*blink*—was back on the opposite side of Frank's bed. She knelt on the floor and cradled his head in her arms. But right now I couldn't worry about Frank.

The white-faced man had collapsed onto the carpet in the hallway, but the red-haired girl was lunging at Gil with a ten-inch kitchen knife, and the man in the coveralls had blinked himself into the bedroom, waving a craft knife at me. I could see another man making his way toward us, and then another two women, one of them gray-haired and wild-eyed, like a lunatic Gloria Steinem, and another one smothered in dried blood, so that her hair stuck up like a punk.

They were all making a low, needy noise—*urrrrhhhh, urrrhhhh, urrrhhhh*—as if they couldn't wait to cut our throats and start drinking our blood.

Partly out of anger, but mostly out of panic, I started to lose my self-control. I lifted the stool clear over my head and struck the man in the coveralls on the shoulder. He dropped his craft knife and I struck him again, right on the bridge of the nose. I hit him again, and then again, and then again, until he was down on his knees, and then I swung the stool sideways and caught him in the side of the head, and this time *blink* he was out of the bedroom and crawling back along the hallway toward the kitchen.

Together, screaming with rage and terror, Gil and I began to beat the *strigoi* back toward the kitchen. They were panting for our blood, but both of us were in a frenzy, and right then I don't think that there was anything natural or supernatural that could have stood up to us. I hit the Gloria Steinem woman straight in the face, and she staggered backward, bringing down the blood-covered girl behind her, and then I went mad on both of them, hitting their arms and their legs and their heads until they were mewling in pain.

When we reached the kitchen door, we found that it was crowded with twenty or thirty *strigoi*, and more were climbing in through the window. It was only open about six inches, but somehow they managed to slide through it,

"*The door!*" shouted Gil. We kicked two *strigoi* away from the door, and then we slammed it shut, and Gil twisted the key. Immediately the vampires threw themselves at the other side of the door, and we heard the panels crack. We probably wouldn't be able to hold them in there for long, but a couple of minutes would give us time to get away.

Jenica was close behind us.

"What's happening to Frank?" I asked her.

"I don't know! I didn't see! We have to leave quick, and find someplace to hide ourselves! The Vampire Gatherer is after us!"

"I'm not leaving here without Frank!"

"He's *dead*, man!" said Gil. "There's nothing you can do for him now!"

There was another thunderous crash against the other side of the kitchen door, and this time the frame began to come away from the plaster. I could hear something else, too. The same cathedral-like whispering that I had heard in my bedroom, when Singing Rock had first conjured up the Vampire Gatherer for me. Scores of voices, *hundreds* of them, and all of them chanting for our blood.

"Let's just get the hell out of here!" said Gil.

But Jenica said, "No—there will be many more waiting for us outside. We won't stand a chance!"

"Then what?"

"I need my crucifix, and my candles, and the book of *svarcolaci*. These strigoi are only Vasile Lup's children, but Vasile Lup himself will be coming for us, and our only chance is to send him back to his casket!"

Crash! The kitchen door began to splinter, and dust sifted down from the ceiling. *Crash!* One of the center panels broke, and two or three knives started furiously chopping at it from the other side.

We turned toward the living room, but as we did so Susan Fireman abruptly appeared from the bedroom. She stood in the hallway and there was something about her that electrified me with dread. She was staring at us wide-eyed and her irises were so pale that it looked as if she had no irises at all. But she looked triumphant.

"Come," she said, and made a beckoning gesture. Not to us, but toward the bedroom.

"Oh, Christ," said Gil. "Tell me this isn't true."

But we had to believe it, because he came out of the bedroom and he looked just the same as he had when he was alive. Frank, his cheeks drained of color, just like Susan Fireman's, his eyes unfocused, but walking, and obviously conscious.

"Frank," I said. "Frank, can you hear me?"

He turned his head slightly and stared at me. At that instant, *crash!* the kitchen door was shaken yet again, and this time another panel was kicked right out. Three or four hands came struggling through, trying to find the key.

"I can hear you, Harry," said Frank. "I might be dead but I'm not deaf." His voice didn't sound any different, except that it had a kind of *empty* quality about it, as if he were reading his words from a script, and didn't really understand what he was saying.

"Frank, you should stay here, Frank. The *strigoi* want to take you away, but you're better off dead, believe me."

"I have to go, Harry. I don't have any choice."

"My *book*," Jenica muttered. "My *book*, and my crucifix, and my holy water."

She went into the living room. As she did so, one of the lower panels of the kitchen door was kicked out. Gil started to beat at the vampires' feet with his baseball bat. It was only going to be seconds now, before they came through—and then I knew that we were finished. There were too many of them, and they were thirsting for our blood too badly.

"Come on, Frank," said Susan Fireman, taking his arm. "Vasile is ready for us. Come."

The two of them took a step toward us, and the second they did so, *snap*, the entire hallway was flooded with blinding sunlight. It lit up everything—the draperies, the oil paintings, the dusty chandeliers. I turned around, and saw that the huge full-length mirror opposite the front door wasn't showing a reflection any more, but a sunlit beach, with dry white sand, and blowing grass, and white-painted summer houses, and clouds.

Gil said, "Shit. It's the *mirror*, man. Frank was telling us the truth."

Susan Fireman led Frank along the hallway, arm in arm. I stepped right in front of them and said, "Stop."

But Susan Fireman simply smiled. "You can't stop us, not now. You should know that—*you*, of all people."

"Me? Why me?"

"Because it was you who gave Vasile the power to come back."

"*I* gave him the power? How did I give him the power? What are you trying to say to me?"

She didn't answer. She was looking right past me, toward the mirror, and the windy seashore. I looked around, too, and in the distance I could see a dark figure walking quickly toward us, with a long, determined stride. It was the same figure that Singing Rock had shown me, in my bedroom. It was slanting, and distorted, and it always seemed to lean away from the sunlight, as if it were a collection of shadows, rather than a man.

All the same, I could see its face—or *faces*, rather, because they appeared to shift with every step it took. One second it was thin and wolf-like, the next it was nothing but a white oval, with slits for eyes. It approached faster and faster and I had never seen anything so frightening in my life.

I turned back to Frank, but suddenly Frank and Susan Fireman had *blinked* along the hallway until they were facing the mirror. Inside the glass, the sand was blowing and the grass was whistling and the sea was all churned up, but I couldn't feel any wind inside the apartment, and I couldn't hear the surf. Here in the hallway, it was hot and airless, and I was deafened by the sound of Gil beating at the kitchen door, and the cracking of the door frame, and the feverish whispering of all those thirsty *strigoi.*

"*Frank!*" I yelled at him. Then, much more quietly, "Frank, don't do it!"

Frank looked around. I couldn't make out if he was feeling regretful, or resigned. The next thing I knew, he was taking a step toward the mirror, and he walked clear through the glass as if there was nothing there at all. His image was momentarily *warped*, as if I was looking at him through water. But then I could actually see him standing three or four feet away, on the sand, with the wind ruffling his hair. The dark slanting creature was less than a hundred feet away from him now, and it was still loping toward us.

Susan Fireman hesitated for a moment. "Bring him back," I asked her.

"I can't do that. He's one of us now, and he always will be. He's mine."

"You like him, don't you?"

But again she didn't answer me. She turned her back on me and stepped right into the mirror. There was that momentary distortion, and there she was standing right next to Frank.

I thought for a split second that the mirror was going to darken again, and go back to being a normal mirror. But it stayed brightly sunlit, and Frank and Susan Fireman began to walk away, quite quickly, in the direction of the dunes, and the distant summer houses; while Vasile Lup the Vampire Gatherer continued to advance on us.

I suddenly remembered what Frank had told us about Susan Fireman coming out of the mirror and cutting that detective's throat. Vampires could step in and out of mirrors as if they were doors. And this one, the arch-vampire, the *svarcolaci*, was heading straight for us. Now it was less than thirty feet away, and its pace was even quicker than before. It was almost running. It was coming for us.

"Jenica!" I dodged into the living room and almost collided with her. She was coming out with her crucifix and her bottle of holy water, with her book open at the page on Vasile Lup.

At the same time, Gil shouted, "*Harry!* Help me, man! They're breaking through!" The *strigoi* had smashed all of the panels out of the kitchen door, and all that was holding them back were the central cross rails. Gil was beating frantically at their groping arms, but it was clear that he couldn't hold them off for much longer.

I picked up the nearest weapon I could find—the decorated bone which we had found in the Vampire Gatherer's casket. I went back into the hallway just as the Vampire Gatherer himself was materializing out of the mirror. He was huge, dark, and slanting, with a hundred faces, and he was so cold that he made me gasp. The temperature in the hallway must have dropped twenty degrees in a matter of seconds.

Jenica lifted up her jewel-studded crucifix. I knew that she was just as terrified as I was, but there was a look of elation on her face, as if she had been born to do this.

"I dismiss you, Vasile Lup! I send you back to your sarcophagus! Let the earth take back the flesh it has given you, and the wind take back the breath it has given you, and the rivers take back their blood! Let the ashes of your soul be scattered like the ashes of your body!"

The apparition opened its mouth, and then another mouth, and yet another mouth. I saw black, ribbed palates and rows of razor-sharp teeth. It let out a noise that was like the whole of existence being twisted, a groan that made me feel as if every organ in my body was being displaced, and I was going mad.

18

BLOOD BROTHER

Gil clamped his hands over his ears, and I fell back against the door frame, stunned, but Jenica held her ground. The Vampire Gatherer was looming over her now, its slanting head almost touching the ceiling, and its face had taken the form that I had seen in the book of *svarcolaci* . . . handsome, but very Romanian, with a thin hawklike nose and heavily lidded eyes.

"I dismiss you, Vasile Lup!" Jenica repeated, and now she flung holy water at him, in the sign of the cross. "May your memory be dispersed with the dust; and your name erased from the tongues of all who ever spoke it. May the stars forget that they ever foretold your destiny; and the moon deny that you ever walked beneath her."

Vasile Lup threw back his head so that it disappeared into the shadows of his shoulders, and let out another terrible groan. This time, his cry was taken up by the *strigoi* who were crowded in the kitchen, and they kicked and kicked at the cross bars until the door gave way. They poured out into the hallway, bloody and bedraggled, both men and women, and all of them carrying knives or razors or shards of broken glass.

Gil backed away, brandishing his baseball bat two-handed. The *strigoi* edged forward, panting *urrrhhhhhhh, urrrrrrrhhhhh, urrrrrhhhhh*, until Gil and I were pressed close together, right behind Jenica. She looked around quickly, to see what was happening, but she didn't catch my eye, or give me any indication that she was frightened. She was too busy concentrating on Vasile Lup.

"The seal that was put upon you was more than a seal of wax," she recited, although her voice was beginning to waver. "It was a seal of the spirit, and its influence remains. The seven prayers that were said upon your incarceration were more than words, and their influence remains. You are disenchanted, Vasile Lup, until the Day of Judgment, and only then can your soul take shape again, so that you may raise your face to the Lord and pledge Him your obedience."

Gil said, "This is bullshit, man. This is bullshit. These motherfuckers are going to cut us to pieces."

He shouted, "*Back off!*" and made a sudden thrust at the nearest two *strigoi*, his bat clanking against their knives. They lifted their arms to shield themselves, but then they started advancing on us again. Two ordinary looking men in torn and bloodstained shirts. One of them was a bus driver and the other was probably an office worker of some kind, and there was a pasty-faced girl behind them who reminded me of the girl who served in my local coffee shop.

"I said back off!" Gil repeated, and this time he struck the bus driver on the shoulder. The bus driver retaliated by slashing at Gil's arm, and cutting the heel of his hand.

"*Motherfucker!*" Gil swore at him, and started to beat wildly at the *strigoi*, left and right, with his blood spraying up the wallpaper.

At the same moment, the Vampire Gatherer seemed to rise up higher and higher, his shadow covering the ceiling, and the hallway had grown so cold that our breath steamed. Jenica took a step back, still holding up the crucifix, but freezing vapor was pouring out of the darkness and covering her with sparkling particles of ice. It was in her hair, and on her eyebrows, and on her lips. Some of it fell onto my face, too, and it was like being breathed on by a Polar bear, cold and fetid and wet.

"*I dismiss you, Vasile Lup!*" Jenica screamed at him. "*I dismiss you in the name of the Father, and of the Son, and of the Holy Spirit!*"

The ice particles fell thicker and thicker, until they were blinding, and my hair was encrusted with them. The Vampire Gatherer appeared to open its arms, or its wings, and lean down toward Jenica as if were trying to embrace her. They weren't really arms, or wings, they were shadows, but I could guess what would happen if Jenica got folded up in them.

I struck out at the Vampire Gatherer with my decorated leg bone, and shouted out, "Get off her, you bastard! You've been exorcized!"

Something very weird happened then. I felt as if the leg bone had been plugged into the mains. It felt electric, and alive, and it almost *hummed*. I held it up, and I felt as if I was holding up the most powerful weapon in the world, more powerful than any sword. Suddenly, I didn't feel afraid any more. I was calm, and I was strong, and *I knew my enemy.*

I heard myself speaking. It was my voice, but the words were somebody else's. It was extraordinary. My tongue was moving as if it didn't belong to me, and I didn't even know what I was going to say next.

"So you have managed to come back to us, O worker of magic and miracles, and this is where you have been concealing yourself! A spirit concealed within a spirit, concealed within a reflection! I should have known it was you. Only you could be so vengeful. Only you could have such wholesale bloodlust!"

Jenica turned and stared at me but all I could do was shake my head. "It's not *me*," I told her.

She stared up at the Vampire Gatherer. The shower of ice particles was already easing off, and the shadowy creature seemed to be edging away from us. Its face changed to an expressionless mask, like a Japanese *noh* player, and then it flickered through twenty or thirty different changes—so quickly that I could barely see them.

"It's no use trying to hide yourself," I told him. "Now I know who you are, I know how to hunt you down, and defeat you. I have done it before and I will do it again—but this time I will make certain that you are banished from this earth for all eternity!"

The Vampire Gatherer let out yet another groan. It felt as if the fabric of the whole apartment block was being moved, brick grinding on brick, floorboards squealing against floorboards, joints straining against joints. Jenica was shaking her head from side to side and Gil was roaring *"Shut him up! For Christ's sake, shut him up!"*

But then there was silence. The Vampire Gatherer whirled around in a complicated counterplay of shadows, and stormed back through the mirror, onto the sand, and started to walk away from us. Above him, in the mirror world, the sky began to darken. Black clouds rolled over from the ocean, as quickly as a speeded-up movie, and seagulls were tossed in the wind like sheets of newspaper.

Behind me, I heard murmuring, and shuffling, and when I turned around, I saw that the *strigoi* were beginning to retreat back into the kitchen. Gil prodded them with his baseball bat, harder and harder, and they struggled back through the doorway, pushing and jostling each other. They were snarling at Gil with frustration, but for some reason they seemed to have lost their appetite, and their nerve.

Jenica took hold of my wrist. "*Look*," she said. Back in the mirror world, the Vampire Gatherer had stopped, and was staring at us.

His shadows slanted sideways, away from the wind, at an increasing angle. Forty-five degrees, and then fifty, and then sixty. No human being could have stood at an angle like that. But as the shadows slanted, they revealed a figure standing in the middle of them—a figure who stood tall and upright.

"Oh God," I whispered.

"What?" said Jenica. "What is it?"

I took a step toward the mirror, and then another, and then all I could do was to stand there, staring into a world that I could never enter, at the man who had turned my whole life into pain and turmoil.

He looked exactly like his photograph, the one taken at Pyramid Lake in 1865. His face was like chiseled granite, his cheeks embossed with magical scars. His eyes were as cold and glittering as ever. Now, however, he was wearing his full war bonnet, a huge headdress fashioned from the skull of a buffalo, and hung about with crow feathers and strings of beads, and crawling with shiny black beetles, thousands of them, which dropped onto his shoulders and scuttled over his cloak.

His cloak was sewn with hundreds of crow skulls, and dried ribbons of human flesh—pieces that his followers had cut from their own bodies and given to him in homage. There were ears, and strips of thigh muscle, and fingers, and even penises, all shriveled up and orange with age.

He stood very tall, but the fierce wind that was blowing across the sand seemed to make his figure sway slightly, as if he were standing two or three inches above the ground.

I was afraid of him. I couldn't pretend that I wasn't. I had seen how cruel and ruthless he could be, and I knew that his hatred for the people who had swarmed all over his land was deep and dark and utterly bottomless—as bottomless as the world of death that exists below our feet, the Happy Hunting Ground.

He said nothing. He didn't need to. Although I had no

idea how he had managed to resurrect himself, I knew why he was here, and what he wanted to do. He wanted to see the pages of history turned back six hundred years. He wanted to see every American city deserted, and strewn with dead, whether they were white or black or Hispanic or Oriental. He wanted the crows to circle, and pick our bones.

Above all, he wanted to see Indians riding across the plains again, so that they could come to the top of a rise, with the wind lashing the grass all around them and lightning dancing on the distant hills, and know that this land was theirs, all of it, forever.

He was probably the last remaining Native American who refused to admit that there was no such thing as "forever." But then his name was Misquamacus, and he was the greatest wonder-worker who had ever lived, and died, and lived again, and been dispersed to the elements. And here he was again, and for all the pompous words that had magically come out of my mouth, I knew that we were royally screwed.

In the mirror, the sky grew blacker and blacker, until I found myself staring at nothing but my own reflection. I turned round and Jenica was standing close to me, with about six different expressions on her face.

"Who was that?" she asked. "Do you know him?"

Gil came out of the kitchen and laid his baseball bat down on the hallway table. "They've gone," he said. He had wound a tea towel around his hand, but it was already soaked with blood.

Jenica said, "Here . . . let me see that."

"It's not too bad. At least it's clean." He looked back into the kitchen as if he couldn't believe what he had witnessed. "You should have seen them hightailing it out that window . . . like roaches when you switch on the light. And they climbed right down the wall, like, *headfirst*, man. How do you climb down a wall headfirst?"

"Count Dracula did it, in the original novel," I told him.

Jenica said, "They defy gravity, the *strigoi*, because they are no longer alive."

I lifted up the decorated bone and looked at it again. I had no idea what its origins were, or what the symbols on it might have meant, but it definitely contained some extraordinary power, and not Romanian-type power, either.

"I could sure use a drink," said Gil. "How about opening another bottle of death-breath?"

"There is one thing I must do before that," said Jenica. She picked up Gil's baseball bat, went up to the mirror, and hit it as hard as she could. Her first blow only starred it, but then she swung the bat again, and this time the glass dropped onto the floor in a sparkling heap, and there was nothing left in the frame but a plain wooden backing. "I think I owe Frank an apology," she said. "And you too, Harry, for doubting you."

"Little bit late for Frank, I'm afraid."

We went into the living room and sat down. Jenica said, "I think my father would understand if I open his *palinca*."

"Excuse me?"

She held up a clear glass bottle. "Plum brandy, from Transylvania. Very strong."

She poured us each a large measure, and we took a swallow without making a toast.

"Jesus wept," said Gil, gasping for breath. "You could dissolve diamonds in this."

"My father says that every person who drinks *palinca* becomes in their heart a Romanian, whatever their passport says."

I took another swallow. I don't know what it was doing for my nationality, but it was certainly doing my *cojones* good. I reckoned that after half a bottle of *palinca* I could probably fight a whole legion of *strigoi*, and any *svarcolaci* you cared to bring on.

"So what exactly happened out there?" said Gil. "I don't understand why those *strigoi* suddenly turned tail."

"I am not so sure, either," said Jenica. "I spoke the ritual for disenchanting the Vampire Gatherer, and at first I thought that it had not worked. Yet suddenly he turned around and returned to the mirror world, and when he did that, all of the *strigoi* left, too." All the time she was looking at me, because she wanted to know who that figure in the war bonnet was, and she knew that I knew.

"That creature . . ." I said, "that shadow thing . . . that *looks* like the spirit of Vasile Lup, and it *is* the spirit of Vasile Lup, mostly. But he's like somebody who gets possessed by a demon . . . you know, like Regan in *The Exorcist*? Outwardly, you know, they *seem* to be the same person. Their appearance is the same, but they're not in control of their own personality. It's the demon who's taken charge of everything they say and everything they do."

"So what are you telling us?" said Gil. "That Vasile Lup's spirit is possessed by another spirit? How does that work?"

"Spirits are just the same as living people. Some of them are leaders and some of them are followers."

"Vasile Lup must be a pretty dominant character, though, if he was able to rouse up all of these vampires. And he not only roused them up, he got them to spread themselves all over the city in less than forty-eight hours. Think about it. A couple of hundred vampires have managed to do in two days what even al Qaeda could never have done, even with a nuclear bomb. They've killed thousands of people and they've recruited thousands more to do the same, so the killing is spreading, like, exponentially."

"Sure," I said. "But Vasile Lup didn't start this epidemic himself. Somebody had to rouse *him,* didn't they? That's why I think that he's been possessed by some spirit that's even more powerful than he is."

"You know who this spirit is, don't you?" said Jenica. "It was that man with the headdress on. The one you saw in the mirror."

"You actually know who that was?" said Gil.

I nodded. "He's a Native American wonder-worker called Misquamacus. He was the greatest medicine man of his time—or any other time, for that matter. I've had a couple of run-ins with him before. I thought I managed to destroy him. Well, I thought I managed to destroy him four times over. Three times he came back, but the last time I thought was for keeps."

"A Native American wonder-worker," said Gil, haltingly, as if he was trying to say "Please direct me to the nearest restroom" in a foreign language. "And how exactly did you come to get yourself involved with a Native American wonder-worker?"

I swallowed another mouthful of *palinca*. "It was partly by accident, but mostly through the fortune-telling. I don't have any kind of natural ability for it, not like Amelia, but even the dumbest person in the world has *some* psychic sensitivity. Even though I never really believed in it, I guess I dealt out so many Tarot cards and read so many tea leaves, I started to make contact with the spirit world."

"And this Misquamacus? What's his beef?"

"His beef is that he doesn't like America occupied by white people, or any other kind of people for that matter, only Indians. He tried to call down his ancient gods to get rid of us, but that didn't work, so he tried to demolish all of our buildings, but that didn't work. So this time it looks as if he's using one of our own superstitions to get rid of us. It's like spiritual karate—use your enemy's own strength against him. Like al Qaeda used our own airplanes, only this is going to be a million times worse."

"But he went back into the mirror," said Jenica. "He was about to seize me, but then he turned away. If he is a Native American, and not Romanian, why could I send him back with a ritual that was meant for *svarcolaci?*"

"Well, I guess your ritual must have weakened his host," I suggested. "But I'm pretty sure that this bone had a lot to do with it. I waved it at him, and all of these words came out of my mouth and it wasn't even me speaking. And it *buzzed*, you know. I felt like Luke Skywalker with a light saber."

Gil took the bone, and waved it from side to side. "Maybe it's some kind of magic wand."

"Of a kind, yes, it probably is. My guess is that Misqua-macus used it to wake up Vasile Lup, and that he left it in his casket for a reason."

"If you are right," said Jenica, "perhaps we can do to this wonder-worker what he is trying to do to us, and use his own weapon against him."

I took the bone back. "First of all, I think we need to find out exactly what it is, and how to use it."

"And how do you suggest we do that?"

"We ask the expert. My spirit guide, Singing Rock."

Gil stared at me. "You're serious, aren't you?"

I lit three of Jenica's spicy candles and arranged Singing Rock's bracelet around the biggest of them. We had finished almost the whole bottle of *palinca* between us, and although Jenica had opened a tin of Romanian tea cookies, I was feeling slightly unsteady, to say the least, like crossing over to Staten Island on a choppy day.

While I was preparing the table, Gil went around the Dragomir apartment and broke every mirror he could find, although he hesitated when he came to the gilt-framed antiques. Jenica took the baseball bat away from him and smashed them herself. "Better that my father comes home to find a few broken mirrors, rather than a dead daughter."

"That's the spirit," I told her. "How about one more shot of *palinca*, to give us some Romanian courage?"

"I'll grant you one thing, Harry," said Gil. "You can sure put it away."

"I've had a disappointing life, Gil, that's why."

"You know what your trouble is, buddy? You expect too much. Me, I've never expected nothing, so everything that's ever come my way, it's like a bonus, you know?"

"Gil—I've never expected nothing, either, but that's precisely what I got. Nothing."

We sat around the table. I thought that we were all looking exhausted. All of the adrenaline that had charged us up while we were fighting the *strigoi* had drained away now, and none of us had slept well. But I needed to talk to Singing Rock, if only to confirm that it was Misquamacus who was wreaking so much havoc in New York City, and to tell me if this decorated bone was really as powerful a weapon as I thought it was.

I clasped my hands together and said, "Singing Rock, I know that I've been making a whole lot of demands on you lately, but I really need some advice. It looks like it was Misquamacus who brought all of these vampires back to life, and if that's the case, we're in much more serious trouble here than I first imagined, even though I never imagined that we *weren't* in serious trouble, only this is a whole lot more seriouser. You know, given that Misquamacus is just about as powerful as any enemy that you could think of."

Gil frowned at me, but Jenica gave him a little shake of her head. Jenica knew that you didn't need to be too logical when it came to summoning up spirits. It was your concentration that counted, your *belief.*

"Singing Rock, I know that you're probably going to be very reluctant to square up to Misquamacus again. He killed you, after all. But there has to be a way of beating him again, and I'm ready to take him on myself, but I really need some tips about how to do it."

I carried on for over fifteen minutes, begging and cajoling Singing Rock to help me. As time went by, I even began to lose my temper. "All right, *don't* help me! I don't give a rat's ass! I'm a white man, leave me to fight your Indian demon all by myself! I don't need any help from you!"

Jenica reached across the table and held my hand. "He is not coming tonight, is he? Never mind, maybe we should get some sleep and think about what we are going to do."

"Yeah, come on, man," said Gil. "Let's finish the bottle and crash out."

"Okay," I said. "Maybe you're right. He's probably sick of trying to help me."

We drained the last of the plum brandy. Gil told us some long and rambling story about trying to teach the Bosnians to play baseball, and totally lost the thread. I helped him to bed, even though I was so drunk that I nearly fell into bed next to him.

Jenica stayed up a little longer, but she was still recovering from the shock and strangeness of what had happened today, and she didn't say too much.

Before she went to bed, however, she leaned over and kissed me on the forehead. "I think I have to thank you. I think that creature would have killed me today, if not for you."

"You were very brave," I told her. "I think that it would have killed *all* of us, if you hadn't said that ritual. Misquamacus is hiding inside Vasile Lup, and if Vasile Lup has to go back to his casket, then what is Misquamacus going to do?"

"I don't know. I don't know anything at all about Native American magic."

"It's very strong. That's because it takes its power from the elements. From water, and wind, and earth, and fire."

"I am sorry that your spirit guide did not come to you."

"Well, me too. He's probably sulking. But don't worry, we'll think of something."

"Harry?"

I don't quite know what she wanted to say to me, but

when people are stressed or frightened they often say very emotional things that they don't really mean. In my experience they do, anyhow. So all I did was squeeze her hand and say, "Sleep well, okay?"

19

BLOOD PACT

I opened my eyes. It was 3:47 in the morning and the first hallucinatory light of dawn was beginning to lighten up the sky toward the east. I lifted my head from Razvan Dragomir's sandbag of a pillow, and Singing Rock was sitting in a chair in the opposite corner of the room.

"Singing Rock?"

"Of course, little brother. You didn't really think that I would leave you to fight alone against Misquamacus, did you?"

I shuffled on my butt down to the end of the bed, like a kid. "Did you know it was Misquamacus? Right from the beginning?"

"No. He concealed himself very well. I only caught the smell of him when your friend recited her ritual, and the spirit in which he is hiding himself started to weaken."

"Vasile Lup, the Vampire Gatherer."

"A spirit, yes, and the spirit of a very strong man, a warrior. But only a man, and not a wonder-worker, like Misquamacus."

It was so dark in the corner where Singing Rock was sitting that I couldn't see more than his outline—the shine from his glasses, and his combed-back hair, and the buffalo-bone necklace that he always used to wear.

"I thought that I had gotten rid of Misquamacus for good," I told him. "I thought that he was totally dispersed, into the elements."

"You did, and he was. But one element is greater than all of the others, and that is fire. Fire can dry water, and split rock, and fire can swallow the very air that men breathe. It was fire that brought Misquamacus back to life—fire that fused his soul back together again."

"Fire? What fire?"

"A fire that killed many, but which had far greater consequences. A fire that burned at one thousand four hundred degrees Fahrenheit, and was intense enough to draw back together the separated parts of his being."

"You mean—you mean nine-eleven? The World Trade towers?"

"I have spoken to the souls of many who died that day. Each one of them remembers a great light, and a great rush of wind, and a word spoken in a language that they could not understand. Some of them believed that it was a last Islamic prayer, as the terrorists offered themselves to Allah. But the word they heard was '*Ma'iitsoh!*' "

" 'Ma'iitsoh?' What does that mean?"

"It means 'Wolf' in Navajo. It was Misquamacus calling for the spirit of Vasile Lup to rise up, so that he could possess him. After Misquamacus was dispersed to the elements, he no longer would have had any coherent spiritual substance of his own, so he could not have appeared in the world of men without Vasile Lup's spirit to wear . . . like a borrowed suit of clothes."

I climbed off the bed and went to the window. The sky was growing lighter and lighter, and I imagined that all of the *strigoi* who now infested Manhattan were slinking back to their coffins, or their mirrors, or wherever they were hiding during the day.

"You were going to warn me about Vasile Lup," I said. "You warned me about the strigoi, for sure, but you never got round to Lup."

"I did, but once your friend had told you about the *strigoi*, you stopped looking for the signs. Don't you remember walking past the Hudson Street Grill?"

I smacked the back of my head. "You're right. Hudson Street Grill, with only the 'l' still lit up, and 'supper' with only the 'up'. 'L' and 'up'. Lup. Mind you—I probably wouldn't have realized what it meant."

"It is of no consequence now. You have discovered who your enemy really is, and you know that he is far more dangerous than Vasile Lup."

"But if Misquamacus can't appear in the real world without using Vasile Lup—we can seal Lup back in his casket, can't we, and then Misquamacus won't be able to get out?"

"Misquamacus gives Vasile Lup's spirit a far greater resistance to your friend's rituals than he normally would have possessed. Vasile Lup has considerable strength of his own, but Misquamacus has also given him the influence of the Great Old Ones. Your friend's ritual was able to weaken Vasile Lup, yes, to the point where Misquamacus had to reveal himself, but it was not enough to force him to return to his casket."

"So what can we do?"

"You must follow Vasile Lup, and find out where he is hiding during the hours of daylight. Even with your friend's ritual, you won't be able to send him back to his casket because Misquamacus won't allow it. You will have to destroy him, utterly, so that Misquamacus no longer has a spirit in which to hide himself."

"I see. But Vasile Lup hides in mirrors. How am I going to corner him, without smashing every single mirror in the continental United States?"

"I don't have any idea. I know Native American magic, but nothing of *svarcolaci*."

"Well, you're a terrific help. Not."

"I am always willing to give you my advice, little brother, but I cannot tell you what I do not know."

I sat down on the end of the bed again. As the morning brightened, Singing Rock's image grew fainter and fainter, and now I could barely see him at all.

"I'm sorry," I said. "I know there's no easy answer."

"There is one thing I can help you with. I can help you to fight against the *strigoi*, and if the *strigoi* are beaten, Vasile Lup will no longer have an army to protect him."

I looked up. "You can do that? How?"

"Have you ever heard of Changing Woman?"

"No. Except that she sounds like every woman I ever tried to have a relationship with."

"The story of Changing Woman is the Navajo story of creation. In the time before time began, the world was ruled by the Great Old Ones, who were the gods of chaos and destruction. Those were the gods that Misquamacus first called upon to destroy the white man, and which are still giving him strength."

Singing Rock was talking in that deep, portentous voice he always used for telling Native American legends, but I was too tired to rib him—and, besides, if he knew something that could help us to beat the *strigoi*, I wanted to hear it.

"In those times the world was terrorized by monsters that the Navajo used to call *Binaayee'*, and it was a place of darkness and appalling violence. Almost all of the human race had been slaughtered, except for First Man and First Woman, along with their two young children. But First Man and First Woman were too old to bear any more children, and their children were related by blood.

"One day, however, a black cloud came down upon the mountain Ch'ooli'i'i, and there was thunder and lightning around its peak. First Man climbed the mountain and found a turquoise figurine. It was only the size of a small baby, yet it had the body of a fully grown woman. He took the figurine back to First Woman, and at first they were unsure of what to do with it, so First Woman suggested they take it back to the top of the mountain.

"Up on the mountaintop, in a storm, Nilchi the Wind transformed the figurine into two living deities, Changing Woman, and her sister White Shell Woman.

"Changing Woman and White Shell Woman felt very strong attractions toward the elements. So one day Changing Woman lay naked on the mountainside, with her thighs wide apart, and opened the lips of her vagina with her fingers so that the Sun could shine its warmth directly inside her as it made its way across the sky. White Shell Woman did the same in a shallow stream, letting the water flow into her body.

"In four days, both women discovered that they were pregnant, and in four more days they both delivered boys. White Shell Woman's son was named Water Child and Changing Woman's son was named Monster Slayer.

"Four days later, when he was grown up, Changing Woman's son called on his father the Sun to help him to exterminate the *Binaayee'*. Like the *strigoi*, the *Binaayee'* could be fatally burned by sunlight, and when Changing Woman's son had picked up their scent, and dug them out of their dark hiding places under the earth, he would shine his eyes on them and incinerate them into ashes.

"Changing Woman's son killed all of the *Binaayee'* and so the world became a safer place where humans could flourish once more. All his hundreds of children were born to be monster slayers, too, so that the tribes would no longer be threatened by creatures from the time before time began. Monster Slayer's children were called People-With-Sun-Behind-Their-Eyes.

"Monster Slayer had the constancy of his father and the changeability of his mother—both different, yet in harmony, which is the way in which all Navajo men and women were encouraged to live.

"Changing Woman said, 'You are male and I am female. You are of sky and I am of earth. You are constant in your brightness but I must change with the seasons. You move constantly at the edge of heaven while I must be fixed in one place. Remember, as different as we are, you and I, we are of one spirit. Unlike each other as we are, there can be no harmony in the universe as long as there is no harmony between us.'

"Changing Woman rubbed skin from different parts of her body and each time she did so, she created two adult males and two adult females, and these males and females created clans of their own—the *Bit'ahnii*, the Within-His-Cover People; the *T-d'ch''nii*, the Bitter Water Clan; the *Hashtu'ishnii*, the Mud Clan; and many others.

"She took all of these people to the west, where they lived together in prosperity and peace. This was centuries ago, in the time when time had just begun. But Changing Woman is still alive today, because she constantly rejuvenates herself, with every season. As winter approaches, she becomes a grandmother, all curled up. But in spring she hobbles on a cane of white shell and walks into a room to the east, and grows stronger. Then she takes a cane of turquoise, and walks into a room to the west, and comes out a proud young woman. Finally she walks into a north-facing room, and returns as a young girl so beautiful that people bow their heads in wonder.

"She is the cycle of human life. She goes forward, with the seasons, and the turning of the sun, yet she walks in the opposite direction, from old age to youth. Do you understand, little brother?"

"Well," I said, uneasily. It was a fascinating legend—even

more entertaining than Adam and Eve and the Serpent. But I couldn't see how it going to help us to destroy the *strigoi*.

Singing Rock must have read my mind. He opened his left hand and held it out flat, and then his right hand. "On one side, Harry Erskine, you have the demons of darkness and chaos, who are trying to destroy you. On the other, you have the power of human life, and fertility, and light.

"You have to ask Changing Woman to help you. Only she can call on her son the Monster Slayer, the People-With-Sun-Behind-Their-Eyes, and only they can kill the *strigoi* for you."

"Is that it? That's all I have to do? Talk to the mother of all human creation?"

Singing Rock nodded.

"And what do I say—like, always supposing that I can get in touch with her? 'Dear Changing Woman, I'd really appreciate it if you could send your boys around to kick some *strigoi* ass for me?' "

"Why do you always mock?"

"Because I'm confused, that's why, and I'm scared shitless, and I don't think I've got what it takes to call on Changing Women or any other kind of gods. Sure, I believe you believe in all of this earth-mother stuff, and monster slayers, and I believe it all exists, in some reality, someplace. I've seen it, and I'm talking to you, aren't I, and by all the usual criteria *you* don't exist. But it's not my culture, is it? I don't have any affinity with it, I don't have any faith. It's like asking me to talk to Buddah."

"You don't *need* faith, Harry Erskine. Changing Woman is real. You must have noticed that it grows cold in winter, and the earth grows tired. Yet spring always returns, doesn't it, and the corn shoots up? Changing Woman walks in the opposite direction, but you've turned around and seen her, haven't you, even if it was only a glimpse? You've seen her in the fields? You've seen her in the city streets? You know she's there."

For a fraction of a second, I think I understood what he was talking about. You know what it's like, when you see a pretty young woman walking across the street, and the sun momentarily lights up her face, and she looks at you, and for some reason you feel that something important has happened, but you're not sure what. Singing Rock was saying that she really walks among us, the spirit of change, and that we've all seen her, even if we haven't realized it.

"All right," I said. "Maybe she's real. Maybe I've seen her. But I don't have the first idea how to talk to her, do I?"

"Of course you do. Changing Woman is always looking for harmony. She was deeply saddened when her people were driven from their lands, but she recognizes that all things must change, and that there is brutality in the world, as well as compassion. Out of death rises new life. Out of cruelty comes understanding. Changing Woman grieves, yes, but she never seeks revenge—not like Misquamacus. If you are fighting for harmony, she will listen to you, and help you."

"Okay. But *how?* What do I have to do?"

"If you wish to speak to a spirit, where do you go?"

The window suddenly filled up with sunlight, and all I could see of Singing Rock was the glistening of his eyes.

"You don't mean—?" I asked him.

"You have very little time. You must hurry."

"Singing Rock—"

"No, Harry Erskine. I have already given you more guidance than I should. The living cannot always rely on the dead, or else they are as good as dead themselves."

"But what if I need you again?"

There was no answer. Singing Rock was gone.

I wanted to go alone, but Gil said it was going to be far too dangerous out on the streets, even in daylight. The *strigoi* might be hiding away in their coffins and their mirrors, but the looters and the crazies would be out and about, and maybe the military, too, who would probably have orders to shoot first and play *Wheel of Fortune* afterwards.

In case we got held up, and we couldn't make it back before nightfall, Gil double-checked that he had closed and locked all of the windows in the Dragomirs' apartment and broken every single mirror, so the *strigoi* couldn't get inside, and Jenica would stay safe.

Jenica had plenty to keep her occupied. In her father's desk she had discovered a Ruthenian book about dead vampires called *Oper,* and a pamphlet from Transylvania *Tales of Siscoi*—*siscoi* being a more localized name for the undead. She had also found seven volumes of her father's diaries, all bound in maroon leather, and dating right back to 1971.

"I shall be good," she promised, "Don't worry. I have one more bottle of *palinca*, so I shall be happy."

"Happy and unconscious," Gil remarked, as we left the apartment. "I've got myself the Daddy Bear and Mommy Bear of all hangovers. It even hurts to *think* about it."

We stepped out onto the streets, and here we were, back in a 1970s science-fiction movie, walking through a brown, photosynthetic smog, with cars and garbage strewn everywhere, and crows still picking over the corpses. The city was utterly silent. I was pretty sure that there were plenty of people left alive—thousands, probably—but I guessed that they were all cowering in their apartments, just like us. The only difference was that they didn't know that they had to break their mirrors, to stop the *strigoi* from getting them, and we had no way to warn them.

"You should go see your wife and daughter," I told Gil, as we crunched up Hudson Street over a sidewalk covered with broken glass.

"I will. But first let's see if we can contact this Changing Woman broad. At least I'll feel that we've started to hit back."

"Suit yourself."

As we crossed Morton Street, we saw four or five people

in the distance. They were kneeling on the sidewalk, flapping their arms and howling like wolves. Gil squinted at them through his binoculars, and then handed them across to me.

I could make out three men and two women, all naked, or nearly naked. Their skin was covered in huge red blisters, and smoke was pouring out of their hair.

"Pale people," said Gil. "They're all burning up, the same way that Frank was."

"Well, let's get going before they see us. We know what the pale people want, don't we, and that's blood."

We saw nobody else before we reached Christopher Street. Nobody else alive, that is, although we came across a heap of bodies on the corner of Barrow Street and the whole heap was heaving with maggots.

Around the side of Christopher Street Cashmere, I pressed the shiny brass doorbell for Amelia's apartment and then we waited, wiping the perspiration from our faces with the backs of our hands.

"What if she ain't in?" asked Gil. He didn't add "or dead" because he didn't need to. I was just as worried as he was that the *strigoi* might have reached her already.

I pressed the buzzer again, and almost immediately Bertie's voice said, "Who is it?"

"It's me, Bertie. Harry Erskine."

"Harry! What the hell do you want now?"

"I need to talk to Amelia. It's really important."

"You need to go away and leave us alone."

"Bertie, if you don't open this door and let us in, we're going to knock it down and come in anyhow."

There was a very long pause, and then the door opened.

Inside the Carlsson apartment, it was hot and airless and flies were droning around, just like everyplace else. Bertie was wearing a blue and yellow-striped bathrobe, the Swedish national colors, although his face was crimson.

Amelia came out of the bedroom in a floaty white linen cloud with white flowers embroidered on it.

"Harry," she said. "And—Gil, isn't it?"

"You got it, ma'am."

"Did you get to see Razvan?"

"Razvan's in Bucharest right now, but we got to see his daughter, and she knows as much about *strigoi* as he does."

"You said it out loud."

"What? *Strigoi?* Yes . . . according to Jenica, it doesn't matter too much, so long as they're not very close by, like right outside your window, or hiding under your bed, and provided they're not especially thirsty. You just have to be careful about mentioning their individual names."

"Well, this is a great relief," said Bertie. "Especially since I don't know any vampires by name."

"Don't make a joke of it, Bertie. You don't know how relieved I am to see that you're both okay. These *strigoi* characters can get in almost anywhere."

"Not here. Nobody can get in here. My alarm system here is state-of-the-art."

"I think you'd better sit down," I told him. "You too, Amelia."

As briefly as I could I told them how we had discovered the coffins in the vaults under St. Stephen's Church. I also told them how Gil had come across Frank, and brought him back to the Dragomirs' apartment, and what Frank had told us about mirrors. I told her how the *strigoi* had climbed in through the windows, and how Vasile Lup had appeared in the hallway.

"But Vasile Lup's spirit was brought to life by an even stronger spirit. Misquamacus."

Amelia stared at me in disbelief. "Is this some kind of a joke?"

"I wish it was. I saw him with my own eyes, Amelia. Living head dress, trophy-cloak, everything."

Amelia stood up and walked across to the window. On

the sill stood a blue glass vase with five dead lilies in it, surrounded by fallen petals. She looked down at the street below, and there was a look on her face that I had never seen before—the look of a woman who has tried to escape the fate that has always been waiting for her, but failed.

"This is the same Misquamacus that you fought with earlier?" asked Bertie.

"There's only one Misquamacus, I'm afraid."

Amelia turned around. "I suppose you've talked to Singing Rock?"

"First thing I did."

"And Singing Rock said?"

I told her all about Changing Woman, and her son the Monster Slayer, and the People-With-Sun-Behind-Their-Eyes.

Amelia listened patiently, but then she said, "Why can't *he* communicate with her—Singing Rock? He's far better qualified than I am. He's a Native American, after all, and he's a medicine man, too."

"I know, but Singing Rock has two serious problems. One, he's a Sioux, and I don't think that the Navajo and the Sioux are exactly bosom buddies. Two, he's a man, and Changing Woman doesn't answer to men."

"This is making me insane," said Bertie.

"Better insane than exsanguinated," I told him.

"Harry," said Amelia, "I don't think I can do this. I've read quite a lot about Changing Woman, and she isn't like the spirit of somebody's Aunt Mildred. She's a *deity*."

"I know. But from what Singing Rock told me, she's a very sympathetic deity, as deities go. And she's very much in favor of life, as opposed to having your throat cut and bleeding all over the rug."

It was then that Bertie stood up, and went over to Amelia, and took both of her hands in his. "Amelia," he said, "you should do this."

"Bertie?" I said. "I didn't think you believed in any of this mumbo-jumbo."

Bertie spoke with surprising dignity. "Just now, what *I* believe in is not very important. You only have to look out of the window to see that the city is dying, and that the authorities have abandoned us. If nobody is coming to help us we must help ourselves, and if this is the only way that has been suggested to us . . . well, we must try it."

Amelia said, "I don't know, Bertil. I really don't think that my psychic power is strong enough."

"How do you know, Amelia, unless you try? This Misky Marcus, you fought him before, didn't you, and you sent him packing? If you did it once, you could do it again."

Amelia looked across at me, but all I could do was shrug. "It's your choice, sweetheart."

So it was that we sat around the glass dining room table, underneath a Scandinavian chandelier that was made out of dozens of triangles of blue and white frosted glass. It was almost midday, and the humidity was so high that we were all dripping. Bertie started to fan himself with a table mat, so that the chandelier tinkled, but Amelia said, "*No*, darling . . . you mustn't disturb the air."

"So I should melt?" asked Bertie, irritably.

"Think about an ice-cold Coke," I suggested.

Amelia reached out and we all held hands. She closed her eyes for a while, and then she said, "I am calling on any spirit who can help me."

It always made my scalp prickle when she said that. She had an echoey quality in her voice, like she wasn't here at all, but standing in another room. No matter how many times I talked to Singing Rock, or tried to summon up other spirits, I could never make my voice sound like that.

"I am calling on any spirit who can guide me to Changing Woman. I am calling on any spirit who can touch her shoulder and ask her to speak to me."

We waited in silence, with our hands growing sweatier and sweatier. I could feel a drop of perspiration roll off the end of my nose, and fall onto the table, and I could feel another one building up to follow it, but there was nothing I could do to stop it. The link between us couldn't be broken.

"I am asking to be taken to Changing Woman, to pay my respects to her, and to beg her for a favor, in the names of those who gave her life, Sa'ah Naaghaii and Bik'eh H-zh-."

I had to hand it to Amelia, she always knew her stuff. She had said offhandedly that she had "read quite a lot" about Changing Woman, but knowing her, that probably meant that she had graduated *summa cum laude* in Navajo mysticism.

"Changing Woman, I honor you. Changing Woman, I give you my respect. Changing Woman, I implore you to speak to me."

By the expression on his sweaty, deep red face, I could tell that Bertie was beginning to grow increasingly uncomfortable, but it was obvious that he respected Amelia's talents, even though he found it so hard to believe in spirits and vampires. I might have thought he was an asshole when I first met him, but that was only because I was jealous. I could tell that he loved her, damn it.

"Changing Woman, speak to me. I need your life, and your strength, and your wisdom. I need you to bring me the power of the sun, so that darkness is banished from our city. I need you to bring me your son Monster Slayer, and your son's sons, and your son's daughters, too."

God, I felt like sneezing. I wrinkled and distorted my face, but the itch in my nose grew stronger and stronger, until I felt that I had to pull my hand away from Gil's, or I was going to let out a blast that would hit Bertie right in the face.

But then I saw a shudder in the air, right behind Amelia's chair, and the urge to sneeze was completely dispelled. It looked as if the air was actually *wrinkling*, like the heat from a metal rooftop on a very hot day. Right in front of my eyes, an old woman appeared, transparent at first, but then more and more visible. She was tiny, and hunched, with braided white hair and a face so desiccated that she looked like a monkey, rather than a human. She was wearing a pale gray woolen cloak, and in one hand she was holding a thin stick, which was shiny turquoise blue.

Amelia kept her eyes closed, and continued to call on the spirits to help her. I didn't know if I should say something like "look behind you!" but I was pretty sure that she must be aware that Changing Woman had actually appeared. I had learned from previous experience not to break the spell in the middle of a séance. It could ruin everything, and it could be dangerous, too.

"Changing Woman, I need your courage. Changing Woman, I need your warmth. Changing Woman, I need your benevolence."

Now the air behind Bertie's chair began to shimmer, too. Within a few seconds, another woman had appeared, a handsome woman in her mid-forties or thereabouts. She was wearing a headdress of brown leaves, and a coarse brown blanket, and her cheeks were marked with red paint. She was standing right opposite me, staring at me over the top of Bertie's head, and her eyes were dead black, as if the inside of her skull was empty.

Gil had opened his eyes, and he gripped my hand tighter to indicate that he had seen these two women, too.

"*Don't say anything*," I murmured.

At that moment, however, he gripped my hand again, and jerked his head upward.

"*Behind you*," he said, without moving his lips.

"*What?*" I mouthed.

He jerked his head again, and I suddenly realized that another spirit must have manifested itself right behind me. I very slowly turned my head, and out of the corner of my eye I saw a young woman, dressed in fluorescent white, with maroon zig-zag patterns on her clothes. I couldn't turn around far enough to see her face, but if Gil's expression was anything to go by, it was just as hair-raising as the woman who was standing behind Bertie.

"Changing Woman, hear me. Come to me, from all the four corners of the world. From the east, where the sun rises and everything is born. From the south, where everything grows and ripens. From the west, where the sun sinks in fullness and satisfaction. From the north, where everything dies."

Now, behind Gil's chair, there was another tremble of disturbed air. It flowed for a moment like clear water running over rocks, and then it gradually took on the shape of a young woman, completely naked except for red-and-white beads around her wrists and ankles, and for complicated patterns of terracotta paint on her skin. Her silvery-black hair flowed over her shoulders and halfway down her back.

Gil was sitting on the north side of the table, and when this young woman appeared, I knew that Amelia had succeeded in calling up Changing Woman. Hadn't Singing Rock told me that Changing Woman always walks in the opposite direction? From the north, which usually symbolizes coldness and death, the loveliest of young women had appeared, bringing the hope of fertility, and new life.

Amelia slowly opened her eyes. "You're here," she said, and she couldn't stop herself from smiling.

"*You called me,*" said four voices at once. There was so much psychic charge in the room that it crackled with static electricity. When Changing Woman spoke, blue sparks crept around the edge of the dining table, and all of our hair stood up on end. A caterpillar of electricity even crawled around Gil's dog tags, and up the silver chain that hung around his neck.

"We need your help, Changing Woman," said Amelia. "Misquamacus the wonder-worker has returned, in the cloak of a borrowed spirit. He has raised a tribe of undead people from a far-off place beyond the eastern ocean. They have already slaughtered many thousands, and their evil will spread all across the country unless we can destroy them."

"*I know of this thing,*" said Changing Woman. I could hardly tolerate the sound of her voice, because it made my teeth buzz and my skin feel as if fire ants were crawling all over me.

"Then will you help us?" asked Amelia. "We need monster slayers, who can discover where these undead people are hiding, and can burn them with the sunlight that shines from their eyes."

"*You are speaking of my son's clan.*"

"We don't know anybody else who has the power to help us."

The four women slowly walked around the table, until the young woman was standing behind me, and the old woman was facing me, from behind Bertie's back. Gil was staring at me apprehensively but there was nothing I could do to reassure him, except shrug.

"*You know what Misquamacus intends to do?*"

"Yes," said Amelia. "He wants to rid this country of all but Native Americans."

"*Can you think of any reason why I should stand in his way? Tens of thousands of my people died at the hands of the white man, or because of his greed, and strangers of many different beliefs now walk across the sacred places where our hogans once stood.*"

"I know that our people did you some terrible wrongs," said Amelia. "All I can do is appeal to your humanity."

The four women changed positions again. As they did so, I glanced quickly at each of them, trying to judge from their expressions whether Changing Woman was going to help us or not. But each one of them was impassive, and unreadable, especially the old woman, whose wizened face was barely human at all.

"*I am the daughter of Sa'ah Naaghaii and Bik'eh H-zh-,*" said Changing Woman. "*Sa'ah Naaghaii is the way that all living things achieve immortality through reproduction. Bik'eh H-zh- is the peace and harmony which is essential to the perpetuation of life.*

"*Because I am the daughter of Sa'ah Naaghaii and Bik'eh H-zh-, I will help you to be rid of the undead tribe.*"

I had never heard words that bucked up my spirits so much, so to speak. Amelia smiled, and said, "Thank you, Changing Woman, and bless you," and even Bertie couldn't stop grinning. Gil said, "Now we can kick some ass."

The atmosphere in the dining room was now so charged up with static that sparks were jumping between the chairs, and the glass triangles that hung from the chandelier were tinkling and clinking like wind chimes. The young girl walked around the table to the place where the young woman in the shining white cloak was standing. They stood side by side for a moment and then somehow the two of them *overlapped*, and melted together, so that only the young girl was left. She walked around the table again, and this time she melted into the middle-aged woman.

"*It is the law of nature that everything must grow old and die,*" said the old woman and the young girl, speaking in unison. "*Everything must be reborn. There is no place in this world for those who are dead but not dead.*"

With that, the young girl melted into the old woman, so that she was left standing alone, naked, incredibly beautiful, her hair rising from her shoulders as if it were being blown by an unfelt wind.

"*I call on my son, and my son's children. I call on the clan of the People-With-Sun-Behind-Their-Eyes. I call on them to seek out the undead tribe, and annihilate them all.*"

She started to chant, a high-pitched repetitive incantation that went on and on for nearly five minutes. As she did so, she began to fade, the same way that Singing Rock faded, until all I could see were the faint dancing filaments of her wind-blown hair.

Gil let go of my hand and stood up. Amelia immediately shouted, "*No, Gil! Not yet!*"

There was a crack like a giant tree breaking in half, and then a flash of light that almost blinded me. The chandelier exploded, showering us all in glass, and then the glass-topped table shattered, too. Paintings dropped from the walls, and Bertie's spindly sculpture was sent flying across the living room. One after the other, all the windows in the apartment were blown in, and the noise was so deafening that we couldn't hear each other shout.

Underneath all of this cracking and splintering, I heard another noise. It was so deep and vibrant that I *felt* it, rather than heard it. It was like a huge electrical generator; or a thousand voices humming *basso profundo*.

"What's happening?" said Bertie. "I thought they were going to *help* us."

"Please, Bertil, just wait."

He didn't have to wait long. The humming grew louder and louder, and all of the debris in the apartment was drawn toward the middle of the living room—fragments of glass, broken furniture, pieces of sculpture, pebbles and compost from overturned plant pots, magazines, letters and dead flowers.

They rose up, all of these bits and pieces, glittering and tumbling in the air, and behind them I could see a dark figure forming, like a man made out of smoke. He was huge—nearly seven feet tall—and he actually *smelled* like smoke—like grassfires burning on a hot summer day.

He was insubstantial—after all, he was a spirit, rather than a real man—but he was using the debris to define his outline, so that we could see him better.

Out of the turmoil of shattered glass, his head gradually formed. He looked as if he were wearing a headdress made out of buffalo horns, which gave him a very Satanic appearance, but this magic that had nothing to do with Satan—or with God, for that matter. This was Monster Slayer of the Navajo, whose mother was Changing Woman and whose father was the Sun itself.

"*My mother has asked me to help you,*" he rumbled, and his voice sounded like a fire blazing up a chimney. "*She tells me that you wish me to seek out the tribe of the undead, and burn them.*"

"We honor you, Monster Slayer," said Amelia.

Monster Slayer raised both hands, and said, "*That which my mother asks of me, I will always do.*"

"Just be careful, sir," said Gil, with unexpected bravado. "The undead tribe, they're not stupid, and there's hundreds of them, and they can move as quick as a lizard off a hot brick."

Monster Slayer turned his huge, smoky head, and then abruptly opened his eyes. Out of each eye socket burst a dazzling ray of light, so intense that I had to turn my face away. The twin rays of light hit the wall and with a sharp detonation they burned right through the paint, right through the plasterboard, and into the kitchen. The whole apartment was filled with smoke.

Monster Slayer closed his eyes, and it seemed like everything went suddenly dark, except for the lime-green afterimages swimming in front of me. As my sight gradually came back to me, I saw Monster Slayer take a step away from us, and then another. With each step, all of the debris that he had used to form his material shape made a noise like somebody shoveling gravel. *Choosh, choosh, choosh.*

Gil, still rubbing his eyes, looked at the hole in the wall. "Jesus," he said. "This character sure doesn't need any hints on unarmed combat, does he?"

Monster Slayer stepped back, and back, and then the smoke that had made up his body swirled away, and the debris clattered and sifted to the floor.

When he was gone, Amelia raised both arms, and closed

her eyes. "I bless your name, son of Changing Woman," she said, in a high, sing-song voice. "May the Great Manitou lend you all the trickery you need."

"Amen to that," said Gil.

20

BLOOD STREAM

Monster Slayer's appearance had trashed Amelia and Bertie's apartment so comprehensively that we helped them to move to the colonial-style apartment upstairs, whose owners were on vacation on the Turks and Caicos Islands. I was trying to convince myself that Monster Slayer and his clan would succeed in hunting down the *strigoi*, but I still didn't think it was safe for Amelia and Bertie to stay in a place with no glass in the windows.

Before we left, Gil and I went around their temporary new accommodation room by room and smashed every single mirror.

Amelia said, "Nigel's really going to love us, when he sees this."

"Hey," I reassured her. "Nigel won't care about his front door, or his mirrors. He'll just be happy that you've managed to survive."

"Do you want something to eat?" asked Bertie. "Of course we can't give you any hot food, but we have some cans of soup, and some Swedish rye bread."

"That's all right," I told him. "We'd better be getting back to Jenica. I don't like leaving her too long on her own."

Amelia came up to me and held both of my hands. "Another strange adventure," she said. "Why do these things always happen to us, Harry?"

"We're mystics. It's our job. Who else is going to do it, if we don't?"

"Do you think this will work? Calling up Monster Slayer?"

"I don't know. I hope so. But I still have to find Misquamacus, and fix him."

"You'll come back to see me, won't you? I don't want you to disappear and never find out what's happened to you."

I could see Bertie looking fidgety, so I kissed her on the forehead and said, "You know me. Erskine the Indestructible. Come on, Gil, we'd better *frappez le trottoir*."

Gil left me on the corner of Leroy Street so that he could go back to his apartment and check up on his wife and daughter. The city was still silent as I walked back, but just as I climbed the steps of the Dragomirs' house, I was convinced that I heard a man screaming. I stopped, and listened, but it wasn't repeated. I went inside, and made sure that the door was locked behind me.

Upstairs, Jenica was lying on the couch asleep. One of her father's diaries was lying open on the carpet beside her. I shook her shoulder and she opened her eyes and stared at me as if she didn't recognize me.

"Oh. . . . I was having such a strange dream."

"Nothing could be stranger than what we just did."

Jenica sat up and stretched her back. "How did it go? Did your séance work?"

"*Work?* We raised up the meanest vampire-hunting SOB you can possibly imagine. Monster Slayer! Like, *yesss*! He was made up of smoke, and dust, that's all. But you should have seen him. He has these horns like a demon, and this dazzling light that comes out of his eyes. It's like a death ray.

Zap! And then *bam!* And there's a huge great hole in the wall."

"Will he fight the *strigoi* for us?"

"You should have been there, Jenica, I mean it. Changing Woman appeared and she was four different women, only the same woman at four different ages. Then Changing Woman called up Monster Slayer. Amelia's whole apartment was totaled, I mean it was *wrecked*, but the whole thing was unbelievable."

"Harry—this Monster Slayer—will he fight the *strigoi* for us?"

I began to calm down. "Yes, yes. He'll fight the *strigoi*. Well, he said he would. All we can do is wait and see."

"Then that is good, is it not? That was a successful mission?"

"Yes, that was a successful mission. Well, I hope it was. We certainly did our best."

Jenica picked up her father's diary. "I have learned very much, too, while you were gone."

"Oh, yes?"

"Harry—listen to me. I have learned things that before now I never understood. For instance, why my father was always so obsessed with hunting down the *strigoi*."

"I could really use a drink, Jenica."

"I also learned very important information about myself."

I poured myself a glass of *palinca*, and I was about to knock it back when I realized that Jenica was trying to tell me something very serious.

I stared at her. "You're upset, aren't you?"

"It has been a shock. I never knew any of this before."

"Tell me."

"In his diary, my father says that he met my mother in 1969 when he was a student, in university in Romania, and she was working in the café where he used to study. He says they fell in love deeply and wanted to get married, but her father, Nicolai, threw a big rage when they told him about their relationship and forbade them to see each other anymore. After many arguments my father took my mother to United States with him and they were married here in New York, without her father's knowledge."

"Okay," I nodded.

"My father and my mother were very happy and they could never understand why my grandfather had been so angry that they should not marry. But three years later, when my mother was expecting me, my father took her back to Romania, so that they should have a reconciliation with my grandfather. My father is very honorable, and he believed that no man should be estranged from his daughter or his grandchild.

"I'm with you so far," I said. I swallowed *palinca*, and let out a bark like a sheepdog. "What makes me think that this happy family reunion didn't turn out so happy?"

"Because, now that my mother was pregnant, my grandfather was forced to tell my father and my mother why he had opposed so fiercely their relationship. He said that when *she* was pregnant, my grandmother, Ecaterina, had traveled to Horezu in the mountains to visit her cousins. On the way, the bus broke down, and when night was falling, the driver and the seven passengers had been stranded in the forest near Caciulata.

"In the morning, the driver and six of the passengers were found murdered, with their throats cut, but my grandmother had survived, just—although she had been raped many times.

"Only a few days later, my grandmother developed a burning fever, just like Frank. She gave birth to my mother prematurely, and then she died. She had been infected by the *strigoi*, and she had become one of the pale people. My grandfather named my mother Mariana, which means 'bitter grace.' "

Jenica handed me her father's diary, with its floppy leather cover. She pointed to a paragraph at the bottom of the page, and said, "Read." Razvan Dragomir's writing was very neat, and intense, the writing of a man who has a terrible thing to tell, but wants it to be clearly understood.

" 'Nicolai told me that after Ecaterina had died, one of the oldest and most venerable of the gynecologists at the Pitesti Clinic took him into a private room. The gynecologist said that he would explain to Nicolai what had happened to Ecaterina, and what might happen to Mariana as she grew up, but he must never breathe a word to anybody, for fear of attracting the attention of the undead.

" 'Given certain conditions, baby Mariana's health should not be adversely affected by the sickness that had claimed her mother's life. However her bloodstream would always carry the *strigoica* strain, which could never be eliminated, even by complete transfusion. This strain would be passed down through the female side of the family, forever. Unlike a full-blooded *strigoica*, Mariana would not be unduly sensitive to sunlight, and she would not have the same insatiable thirst for human blood. But she would have many of the characteristics of the pale people, such as the ability to contort her body into seemingly impossible positions, and to climb seemingly impossible obstacles. Furthermore, the gyneocologist said that she would also be able to 'pass through the silver doors' whenever she wished, although he did not clearly explain to Mariana's father what he meant by this."

I lowered the diary. "Silver doors," I said. "Could that mean mirrors? Don't tell me your mother could walk through mirrors."

But Jenica said, "Carry on. There's more."

" 'The gynecologist clearly explained to Nicolai that if Mariana were to bear any girl-child, that girl-child would similarly be infected with the *strigoica* strain. Boy-children would not be affected, and neither would any man with whom she had sexual congress, except if she performed the ritual of Samodiva before she did so. The ritual of

Samodiva would make the man's blood vulnerable to the *strigoica* strain, and he would almost certainly become infected, too."

I put the book down again. "So what your dad's saying in his diary—your grandmother passed the *strigoica* strain onto your mother, and your mother passed the strain onto you, and if *you* ever have a daughter, she's going to be the same. Jesus, Jenica, you're half a vampire. And he never *told* you? Jesus."

Jenica's eyes were glistening with tears. "He has always tried to keep me away from boys, all my life."

"Don't tell me you've never—"

"No, no, of course not. How could he stop me? But he has always turned very cold and hostile if he thinks that I am serious about any particular boyfriend, and he never allows me to bring any of them back to this apartment. He always says that the only man a girl really needs is her father. I always used to think that he was being overpossessive. But all he wanted to do was to stop me from having children. Girl-children, anyhow."

"This gets madder by the minute. Did you ever guess your mother could walk through mirrors? Do you think that *she* ever guessed that she could walk through mirrors?"

"I don't think so. From what my father wrote in his diary, I believe that he did not really understand what 'silver doors' were, any more than my grandfather, Nicolai, did. After all, there is very little in any of the legends to say that *strigoi* can hide inside mirrors, is there? So even with all of his research he may not discovered what this meant."

I was finding it almost impossible to get my head around all of this, but I could understand why Jenica was so distressed. It was bad enough finding out that you were blood-related to the undead, without discovering that your father had known about it for years, and kept it quiet.

I poured myself another glass of *palinca*, right to the brim, and I filled up Jenica's glass, too.

Jenica said, "Look." She held up her left hand, and bent her thumb right back until it was touching her wrist. "I could always do things like this. I used to think that it was ordinary."

It was grotesque, but it was fascinating, too. "Pity we don't have any mirrors left," I said. "*You* could try walking through the silver doors, too."

"I don't think I would wish to try that. Who knows what kind of a world there is, on the other side of the mirror? Who knows if I could ever find my way back? And if that is where the *strigoi* are all hiding during the day—what a frightening place it must be."

"Still, it would be interesting to see if you could just maybe poke your pinkie into a mirror."

Jenica was silent for a while. Then she wiped her eyes with her fingers and said, "Are you hungry? You must be hungry. I have some canned pasta, I think." Jenica made us a meal of cold Chef Boy-ar-Dee spaghetti Bolognese and Saltine crackers. We sat in the living room in the gathering gloom and I told her all about Changing Woman and Amelia's séance. I didn't want to ask her any more about her father's diaries. She obviously needed time to think them over.

"So—how do you plan to find this Misquamacus?" she asked me.

"I'm hoping that Monster Slayer is going to track down Vasile Lup, and burn him up. If he does that, Misquamacus won't have a spirit to hide in anymore."

"All the same, he sounds tenacious, this Misquamacus. To revive himself, even when his spirit was scattered. . . ."

"He's not going to rest until he gets his revenge, that's why."

"*You* should take a rest. You look exhausted."

I stood up, and took Jenica's plate for her. "I will, when this is over. Maybe you and I could take a vacation together. You could show me Romania."

"Romania? I never want to go back to Romania. Without

the superstition of Romania, this would never have happened. They are fools and peasants in Romania. How do
you think they tolerated Ceaucescu for so long?"

"Don't ask me. We reelected Bill Clinton."

The sun set, messy and yellow, like a fried egg with the yolk
broken, but still Gil wasn't back. I stood by the open window, keeping a lookout and trying to make the best of a
slack, sultry breeze. By 10:45 P.M. it was almost ridiculously
dark, with two hours to go before moonrise, so I was peering out at total blackness. Now and then I thought I
glimpsed a hunched-up shape scurry from one side of the
street to the other. Could have been the pale people, could
have been *strigoi*, could have been my eyes playing tricks
on me. I heard screaming again, over toward James Walker
Park; and then again, to the south, toward Clarkson Street,
and about twenty minutes later I saw six or seven small
fires burning.

I was sure that I could feel hysteria in the air, although it
may have been nothing but my own exhaustion. I was hoping that the monster slayers were out there tonight, running
down the *strigoi*, but as the hours went by I became less
and less convinced that they would really come to save us.
Did Native American spirits always keep their promises?
They probably did—but did they keep their promises to
white men?

I was about to close the window when I heard shouting
in the street below, and footsteps. I leaned out, but at first I
couldn't see anybody. Then I saw a flashlight dancing from
side to side, as if it was being held by somebody who was
running.

"Harry! Open the door, Harry! The bastards are after me!"

"Hold on!" I shouted back.

I vaulted over the couch, into the hallway, and out of the
apartment door. Jenica said, "Harry? What is it? *Harry!*"

Gil was already beating on the front door, and screaming out, "Harry! For Christ's sake open the door!"

I took the stairs, gripping the handrails and vaulting down them seven at a time. When I reached the second landing I staggered and twisted my ankle, but I managed to do a complicated pirouette and regain my balance. I threw myself down the next flight, hobbled along the hallway and wrenched open the front door.

Gil threw himself at me and we both went sprawling backward onto the floor. I jarred my shoulder blade and there was blood everywhere—all over my hands, all over my face, all over my shirt. I looked over Gil's shoulder and there stood three pale-faced men, caught in the upward beam from Gil's flashlight. One of them was wearing a heavily bloodstained sweatshirt, as if he had been working in an abbatoir. The second was half-naked, and flabby-bellied, and covered in huge blue weals; and the third was dressed in a tattered suit, like a down-and-out mortician. I saw knives glinting, and I heard that thick, thirsty *hurrrrhh-hhhhh, hurrrrhhhhhh, hurrrhhhhhh.*

"Gil!" I yelled at him. "Gil, for Christ's sake get off me!"

Gil opened his eyes and stared at me. He coughed, right in my face, and then he managed to heave himself up onto one knee. I wriggled out from under him, twisted myself to one side, and kicked out at the first of the *strigoi* as he tried to step into the hallway.

Gil climbed to his feet, and pulled me up, too, even though his hands were slippery with blood. We turned to face the *strigoi* but this time I seriously thought we were finished. They advanced on us, holding their knives high. The mortician had a very long boning knife that was rusty-colored with dried blood.

The *strigoi* in the sweatshirt *blinked* into the hallway right next to us. Gil kicked at him, then karate-chopped him on the side of the neck, but the *strigoi* leaned backward at an impossible angle, so that Gil missed him, and then he swung back upright again, and started stabbing at Gil so frenziedly that his knife looked like a blur of twenty different knives. Gil's hands and forearms were smothered in blood, and I could see a gaping slice in the muscle of his right shoulder.

"Goddamned—blood-drinking—bastards!" Gil was gasping.

The mortician ducked his head down, and the next thing I knew he was right behind me, trying to hook his arm around me so that he could cut my throat. I grabbed hold of his wrist and hit it hard against the banister, and then the hall table, and then the banister again, and then I threw myself backward against him with all of my weight. I felt his ribs crunch between me and the wall.

I was about to turn around and give him the old *Three Stooges* poke in the eyes with my stiffened fingers but suddenly he wasn't there any more. He had *blinked* back onto the porch, and he was almost running at me with his knife held up high.

Gil was wrestling with both of the other two *strigoi* and roaring, "*Aaaahhhhhhhhhhh!*" so loud that I could hardly hear anything else.

The mortician swished his knife one way, and then swished it the other. There was nothing in his eyes at all. No rage, no hatred, no madness. Nothing. But I knew that he wouldn't back off and that he was determined to kill me and slit my throat and drink the blood as it pumped straight out of my neck.

And then—he exploded. Right in front of me, only inches away, *he exploded*. There was only the softest of *whoompphs*, but his insides seemed to detonate. His head flew off sideways and his body burst into the fiercest of flames, and in only a few seconds he had dropped onto the floor and he was blazing like a KKK crucifix.

The other two *strigoi* looked around, their faces questioning, but they didn't stay alive long enough to find out the answer. They, too, exploded, and for a few seconds the hallway was filled with burning bits of them—hands, feet, pelvic girdles, lungs, and loops of rapidly shriveling intestine.

Panting, bleeding, Gil and I looked out of the front door in thankful bewilderment. Out in the street, utterly silent, stood six or seven very dark shapes. They were only visible because of the flaming *strigoi* whose dismembered body parts littered our front doorstep. I thought that I could make out horns, and necklaces, and for a split second I thought that I saw two eyes open, as narrow as the slits in a steelworker's mask, and a molten white light too bright to be looked at.

"Monster slayers," I said, and I couldn't hide how awestruck I was. "The People-With-Sun-Behind-Their-Eyes."

Gil said, "First time the Injuns have come riding to the rescue." Then he sneezed, and sprayed me with blood.

"Hold on," I said. I kicked all the blazing body parts onto the sidewalk. The intestines were the worst because they stuck to my shoes and got themselves tangled around my ankles, and all the time I was trying to get them loose they were making a loud frying noise. Soon, however, all that remained was the mortician's fiery skull, which was lying on the doormat, burning the bristles. I hooked my left foot around it and booted it down the steps, and it bounced all the way across the street, still blazing, until it hit the curb on the opposite side.

By the time I closed the front door, the horn-headed figures of the monster slayers were long gone. Hunting for more *strigoi*, I hoped. This was *their* land, after all, the grandsons and granddaughters of Changing Woman, and because it was theirs they could draw on all of its richness and all of its spiritual power. Judging by what had happened on this doorstep, the *strigoi* needed to find themselves some pretty dark places to hide.

* * *

Gil's hands and arms were criss-crossed with cuts, and his shoulder was bleeding badly, but otherwise he didn't seem to be too seriously injured. I helped him up from the floor, and for a moment we stood looking at ourselves in the hallway mirror. We looked like two walking wounded from a full-scale war.

"Forgot to break that one," said Gil, nodding at the mirror. "Don't want them getting into the building through there."

"Let me get you upstairs. Then I'll come back down here and do the honors."

It was a struggle climbing the stairs. Gil had to stop every now and then, and catch his breath.

"You should have come back before nightfall," I said.

He leaned back against the paneled staircase. "I know. But to tell you the truth, I have a confession to make. I tried to get my wife and daughters over to Jersey."

"What?"

"I went back home and they were terrified. The *strigoi* had tried to break into our apartment three or four times. So I got them to pack a bag and we went to the Holland Tunnel. I thought maybe, because I was military, they would let me through. But there was no way. They have barricades, they have razor wire. They have orders to shoot you on sight, if you try to get through. So I had no choice. I had to bring them back home, and barricade them in again."

"You could have stayed with them, Gil. You *should* have stayed with them. I would have understood."

Gil wiped blood across his upper lip. "I'm a soldier, Harry. I know the meaning of duty."

"Well, I appreciate your coming back. At least we know that the monster slayers are out and about, and doing what they promised. Did you see that old guy blow up, right in front of me? That was something, wasn't it?"

"Harry?" called Jenica, her voice echoing down the stairwell. "Are you okay down there?"

"Battered but unbowed," I called back.

I wrapped Gil's arm around my shoulders, and heaved him up the last two flights of stairs to the Dragomirs' apartment. Jenica was waiting for us, and she immediately helped Gil through to the living room, and together we lowered him onto the couch. Almost at once I could see that he was much more badly hurt than I had thought. The front of his T-shirt was wet with blood, and when Jenica dragged it off him, we could see that it wasn't just from the cuts on his arms. He had a puncture-wound just below his ribcage, and it was bubbling.

"I will bring antiseptic, and bandage," said Jenica. "Meantime, Harry, press this tissues against this hole, to stop more blood."

"It's nothing," said Gil, peering down at it. "Minor stab wound, that's all. I had shrapnel in my leg, in Bosnia. Thirty-seven stitches."

"How about a drink?" I asked him. "Nothing like *palinca* to ease any kind of pain, physical or spiritual."

"Why not? I'll tell you something, Harry, when this is all over, I'm going to open a *palinca* bar on Seventh Avenue, and I'm going to call it Amnesia."

Jenica brought in a plastic basin filled with water from the bathtub. She sponged Gil's stomach and his shoulder and dressed his wounds with Band-Aids and clean, folded handkerchiefs. Then we helped him to limp through to the bedroom and eased him down on the bed.

"What you need is sleep," said Jenica, and she leaned over and kissed him on the forehead.

"Frank died in this bed," Gil protested.

"Well, he did and he didn't. Frank isn't exactly dead yet."

"Thanks for the comforting reminder."

Jenica and I went back to the living room. I could have done with some sleep myself, but I knew that I wouldn't be able to close my eyes. Besides, I had to go down to the hallway and break the mirror. I doubted if the *strigoi* would try to come back here, after the monster slayers had been around, but I decided that it was better to be over-cautious than lose my entire blood supply to some dead-eyed wacko with a box cutter.

Jenica picked up the decorated bone that we had found in Vasile Lup's casket. "You know, I have been wondering all day about this. Where it came from, why it seems to have such power."

"I've seen something like it before. Two of them, as a matter of fact. They were bones from a wonder-worker's legs, which you could tap together, as if he was running, and you could follow him into the spirit world. They used to belong to White Bull, who was medicine-man for Crazy Horse."

"Did they work?"

I didn't really want to talk about it, because it had been a bad experience, but I nodded. "Yes, they did. But not in the same way as this." I reached across and took the bone away from her and lifted it up. "White Bull's bones had to be used as part of a sacred ritual . . . but this one—this has some kind of internal energy all of its own, doesn't it?"

"I ask myself, why was it lying in the Vampire Gatherer's casket?"

"Who knows? Maybe there was no special reason. After Misquamacus had roused up the Vampire Gatherer, maybe he just didn't need it any more, and so he left it behind."

"An artifact so powerful as this? I don't think so. I think your wonder-worker left it lying in the Vampire Gatherer's casket for some purpose. And remember that when you shook at it him, he walked away, very quick, as if it possessed a magic that he could not defy."

I examined the bone more closely. There were tiny figures carved all along it, all intertwined. The interesting thing was—unlike the figures you usually saw in Native American carving—they were all fully dressed, like white men.

Jenica said, "What I ask myself is, how did Misquamacus obtain this bone? So, yes, we know from your spirit guide Singing Rock that the very hot fire of nine-eleven forged back together again the separated parts of his *manitou*, so that his spirit was again whole. But his spirit still had no *substance*, did it?—what the nineteenth-century mediums used to call *ectoplasm*. So with no substance, how did he find the bone, and how did he carry it to Vasile Lup's casket, so that he could revive him? It is eggs and chickens."

"You're asking me for answers I don't even know the questions to."

Jenica's eyes were shining in the candlelight. "Something is missing in this equation. I sense that somebody else is behind the scenes of what happened here."

21

BLOODSTREAM

On the marquetry side table, among the jewel boxes and the decorative paperweights, I found a small bronze ornament of a grinning Romanian gnome. He only a little guy, but very heavy, with a pointed hat, and he was perfect for breaking a mirror. Hefting him up in the palm of my hand, I hobbled downstairs as quickly as I could.

There was a stomach-turning stench of scorched carpet and burned intestines still hanging around the stairwell, like the rottenest barbecue you ever smelled in your life, and I couldn't stop my mouth from filling up with undigested spaghetti Bolognese, before I swallowed it again.

When I reached the hallway, I gripped the gnome firmly by the base, and approached myself in the mirror. I pulled a suitably determined face, and lifted up the gnome. But I was just about to smash the mirror to pieces when I saw something reflected in it—a postcard, lying on the hall table. A postcard that certainly wasn't there before, when we were fighting the *strigoi*.

I turned around and picked it up. The picture on the front showed a large white house, under a deep blue sky, with crimson maple trees in front of it, and a small circular lake. *The Kensico Country Inn, Valhalla, N.Y.* I turned it over. There was no stamp on it, and no address, but someone had scrawled *Heref.*

I frowned at it. *Heref?* Maybe somebody was trying to write *Hereford*, but was interrupted halfway through.

I looked around. The question was, who had put it here? The front door was firmly locked and bolted. I had done it myself. And so far as we knew, there was nobody else in the building. All of the other residents were either on vacation or else they had gone out for one reason or another and hadn't returned. Caught by the pale people, probably, or sucked dry by *strigoi.*

I went across and tried the door of the first-floor apartment. It was locked. Then I went to the end of the hallway and tried the door that must have led out to the back yard. That was locked, too, and bolted from the inside. There was only one other way in that I could think of. The mirror.

I slowly approached the mirror until my forehead was pressed against it, and stared right into it. All I could see was me. Only the *strigoi* could have come through this mirror—but if they had, why hadn't they tried to attack us, and why had they left this postcard?

Then it occurred to me. Frank. The postcard had been left here by Frank. Hadn't he promised me that, whatever happened, he would never forget his oath to protect human life? The scrawl said "Here" and then "f." Frank had come here to tell me where Misquamacus was hiding.

I was still staring at the mirror, trying to decide if I ought to break it or not, when I heard a piercing scream from upstairs, and a door slamming, and the sound of chairs crashing to the floor.

"*Harry!*" shouted Jenica. "*Harry, come quick!*"

*   *   *

I might have hobbled down the stairs but I ran back up them like a mountain goat with a firecracker up its ass. The door to the Dragomirs' apartment was wide open, and Jenica was standing outside on the landing, panting with fear, holding up the bone to protect herself. Inside, halfway along the corridor, stood a thin, wild-eyed man in a loose-fitting caftan, which was heavily soaked in blood. He had shoulder-length hair, which was dripping wet, and a scraggly, unkempt beard. He was carrying a machete, which was dripping blood onto the floor.

"I think he's killed Gil," said Jenica.

"Where the hell did *he* come from? You didn't open any windows, did you?"

"Of course not, are you crazy? I don't know where he came from. I went to see if Gil was all right, and he was standing over his bed, and there was so much blood. Gil— I think he's cut his head off."

The wild-eyed man stared at us, but he came no closer. For some reason he looked edgy and undecided, as if he couldn't work out what to do next. He was making that coarse, greedy sound under his breath, but it almost seemed as if he was afraid to attack us.

"It's the bone," I said to Jenica. "He's afraid of the bone."

"What?"

"Give it to me. Let me try something."

Jenica handed me the bone. I lifted it up in my right hand and shook it, and chanted the only Native American language I knew. "*Hau! Wicasa cikala! He 'cu sni yo! Lo wa 'cin!*"

At first, the wild-eyed man stayed right where he was. I took a step toward him, and repeated my chant. I waved the bone from side to side, and then I prodded it toward him.

"*Wakatanka Itakan nitawa!*" I shouted.

The wild-eyed man raised his machete. My heart was

thumping, but I took another step toward him, waving the bone, and then another. He stared at me and slowly drew his lips back, in a horrible parody of a smile. I thought for one moment that he knew what I was chanting, and that he was laughing at me, but then he turned around and rushed toward the bathroom, his caftan catching on the doorhandle.

I rushed after him, but he had managed to tear his caftan free, and before I could grab him he had run across the bathroom and dived headfirst into the tubful of water. He disappeared below the surface, and he was gone. Not a single splash. He hadn't even caused a ripple.

Holding the bone high in front of me, I walked right up to the edge of the bathtub. There was nothing in it but water. Only a thin swirl of blood betrayed the fact that one of the *strigoi* had used it as a means of escape.

I was still standing there when Jenica came in. She looked around, and then she said, "Where is he? Where did he go?"

"Same place he came from, I'll bet."

"What do you mean?"

"We've just learned something new about the *strigoi*. Not only can they hide inside mirrors . . . they can hide inside water, too. It's obvious, when you think about it. All they need is a perfect reflection."

"Empty the tub," said Jenica.

"If we do that, what are we going to drink?"

"I don't know. I don't care. There is still plenty of wine and beer."

"Okay," I said, and pulled out the plug.

Jenica came up close to me, and together we watched the water gurgling down the wastepipe.

"Gil is dead," she said. "If only I had known that the *strigoi* can walk through water."

We went through to the bedroom. Gil was lying on his

side with his head thrown back, so that he was staring blindly at the headboard. His neck had been cut through to the spine, and the sheets were dark with blood. It reminded me horribly of those terrorist videos, where hostages have their heads cut off. I picked up the pale blue bedcover from the floor, and dragged it over the bed to cover him.

"Shit. He was such a great guy. He didn't deserve to die like this."

"You must not feel guilty, Harry. He was a soldier. He knew how dangerous this might be."

I looked down at the bedcover, which already had blood creeping across it. "I'll have to find his wife and daughters somehow, and tell them that they won't be seeing him again."

"We will do that together."

I followed Jenica out of the bedroom and closed the door behind me. And locked it. I was sure that Gil was properly dead, unlike Frank, but you know, why take chances? If wild-eyed men with machetes could rise out of the bathwater, who knows what was possible?

We went into the living room. The *palinca* was all finished so, without being asked, I took a bottle of death-breath red wine and started to open it.

"So we must revenge him," said Jenica. "It seems as if revenge is the only language that your Misquamacus understands. If only we could know where he is."

"I don't know what good it's going to do us . . . but I believe that we might." I stopped twisting the corkscrew and took the postcard out of my pocket.

"The Kensico Country Inn? Where did you get this?"

"I found it downstairs. I think that Frank brought it. See—it says 'here' and then it's signed with an 'f'."

"And this is all?"

"It must have been Frank. Nobody could have gotten into the house, except through the hallway mirror. And who else do we know who's a vampire? Well, present company excepted."

Jenica waited while I opened the wine and poured us each a large glass. It smelled so strong that you could almost get intoxicated just by breathing it in. She took a sip, and then she said, "You didn't yet break the mirror downstairs?"

"Not yet, no. If Frank is using it to bring us inside information . . . I thought it might be better if I left it intact. We can always lock the doors, can't we? And our trusty bone seems to frighten off *strigoi*."

"What did you say to him? Was that Native American language?"

"Lakota Sioux. I said, 'hallo, little man! Don't do that! I'm hungry!' "

Jenica's eyes widened. "Is that all?"

"Well, a couple of words from the Gospel according to St. Luke."

She smiled. "Perhaps the way to fight madness is with more madness."

"Hey—we called in the monster slayers, didn't we? It isn't easy to get much madder than that."

"But this will not be finished until we have destroyed Vasile Lup, or sealed him back in his casket, and your Misquamacus who hides inside him."

"With any luck, the monster slayers will track him down."

"Maybe they will. But remember that Vasile Lup is *svarcolaci*, a dead vampire, and he leaves no scent that any creature can follow, man or beast or monster slayer. And from what you have told me of your Misquamacus, do you think he will allow the monster slayers to disperse his *manitou* back to the elements? He is a Native American wonder-worker, and the monster slayers are Native American spirits."

"I don't know what else we can do."

"Listen to me, Harry. Even if the monster slayers can find

and kill every *strigoi* but one, it is impossible to stop them from spreading. So long as the spirit of Vasile Lup is still living, and the *manitou* of Misquamacus is living inside him, the *strigoi* will multiply all across America, and you can believe me that darkness will fall in every city and every community from New York to San Francisco."

"Yes. Very dramatically put. But Misquamacus isn't going to make it easy for us, I can tell you. And for starters, we can't get even out of Manhattan. Gil tried, with his wife and daughters, but the military wouldn't let him through, and he's a soldier." I paused, and then I added, "*Was* a soldier, poor bastard."

Jenica held up the postcard. "So how do you think that Vasile Lup managed to avoid the roadblocks? How did *he* manage to get out of Manhattan, and all the way up to Valhalla? That is way up past White Plains, isn't it?"

"He went through the mirror, didn't he? He used the good old silver door."

"Yes?"

"What do you mean, 'yes'?"

"I have *strigoica* in my blood, Harry. I can use the good old silver door, too."

"You don't mean—"

"I can go after Vasile Lup. I can follow him to Valhalla, and I can send him back to his casket, and seal him there. I have the disenchantment, after all."

"What about Misquamacus? He's not going to allow you to do that, just like he didn't allow you to do it right here, in this apartment."

"I have the bone, yes? That will protect me. Once I have disenchanted Vasile Lup, Misquamacus will have no spirit to hide in. I will think of some way."

"You're out of your mind. You said yourself that the mirror world is far too dangerous. For Christ's sake, Jenica, once you go through that mirror, even supposing you can, it's going to be wall-to-wall vampires in there. You won't last two minutes. And if you think you can beat Misquamacus on your own, and without any kind of a plan, forget it. He'll have your soul trapped forever inside some flea-ridden prairie dog before you can say Gitche *Manitou.*"

"I will take the risk. What else can I do? I am the only person in this city who has both the knowledge to send the Vampire Gatherer back to his casket, and the ability to find him."

She paused for a moment. Her face was shiny with perspiration and her black hair was stuck to her forehead. "Gil died for us. Gil died for a purpose. I am prepared to do the same, if it is necessary."

I swallowed wine, and for a moment I thought I was going to experience the re-regurgitation of the spaghetti Bolognese. "It's a very noble idea," I said. "But like most very noble ideas, it's incredibly dumb. Supposing you disappear into the mirror and that's the last I see of you? How am I going to know if you managed to send Vasile Lup back to his box? How am I going to know if you destroyed Misquamacus?"

"Your spirit guide will tell you."

"No, no, this is not going to work. It's suicide."

"Then what are we going to do? Stay in this apartment until we die of dehydration?"

Outside, in the street, there was hideous screaming—the screaming of somebody who was suffering unimaginable agony. Jenica and I went to the window and looked down. The moon had risen now, and we could see at least a dozen black figures, strung right across the street from one sidewalk to the other.

They were monster slayers, creatures of smoke and darkness, their outlines glittering with broken glass and other debris that they had attracted from the surface of the street. I could see their horns and their necklaces and their strange stilted legs, which gave them the appearance of heavy-headed buffalo.

Facing them were three *strigoi*, two men, one of them completely naked, and a half-naked women. A fourth *strigoi* was lying in pieces on the asphalt, with thick smoke pouring out of him, and a few small flames still licking his head.

As we watched, two of the monster slayers stepped forward. The *strigoi* turned to run away, but two rays of searing white light leaped out of the monster slayers' eyes and hit the naked man directly in the middle of his back. For a fraction of a second I could see his insides burning, so that his ribcage glowed luminous scarlet, like a lamp. Then he blew apart, and his arms and his legs went flying, and all of his intestines and his internal organs were strewn across the street, blazing ferociously.

The other two *strigoi* had reached a house on the opposite side of the street. They started to climb the front wall, as swiftly as squirrels, but the monster slayers were too quick for them. They were only halfway up the second story when three monster slayers lifted their heads and opened their eyes, and six blinding rays of light hit them in the head and the back. I heard the woman scream before she exploded, and it sounded like somebody who has just had her first experience of hell.

Fiery pieces of *strigoi* fell into the basement in front of the house. The woman's head rolled under a parked car, and it was still burning when the monster slayers had walked down to the end of Leroy Street and turned right into Hudson. I knew that they were on our side, but all the same I found them very scary, especially that bisonlike way they walked.

"There," I said to Jenica. "We're winning."

"You know that we can never win until the Vampire Gatherer is gone, and your Misquamacus with him."

"I wish you'd stop calling him 'my' Misquamacus. That mook has caused me nothing but misery, ever since I first heard his name."

I turned away from the window. But then Jenica said,

"He is 'your' Misquamacus, Harry. I know how to disenchant Vasile Lup, I believe that *you* can think of a way to destroy Misquamacus. You remember that ritual my father mentioned?"

"Ritual?"

"In his diary, he said that the *strigoica* strain could be passed from a woman to a man if he underwent the ritual of Samodiva. That would make his blood susceptible to her infection."

"I don't understand what you're trying to suggest here. Actually, I think I do, but I'm not at all sure that I like it."

"But you do not want me to go into the mirror to face Vasile Lup alone, do you? So what better answer than if you come with me?"

"Now I *know* you've lost it."

Jenica came up to me and took hold of both of my hands, tightly. I just adored the beads of perspiration on her upper lip. "Harry—nobody else can disenchant Vasile Lup but me, and I cannot do it without you. So what choice do we have?"

"I thought dying of dehydration sounded quite attractive, by comparison."

"I am sure that my father has the words of the ritual of Samodiva in one of his books."

"Okay, but who exactly is Samodiva? Sounds like an Irish opera-singer to me."

"Samodiva is different in different mythology. In Bulgaria she is a wood fairy. In Romania it is neither a he or a she, but the recorder of death. It lives deep in the forests and its face is always hidden in darkness. In Samodiva's book the names of the living are written in red ink, and the names of the dead are written in black."

"So you perform the ritual of Samodiva, and my blood is then open to your infection? I can become half a vampire, too? And I can step through the silver door, just like you?"

Jenica nodded. "It means, yes, you can come with me."

"Well, that's exactly what I'm getting at. In order for me to become infected with this *strigoica* strain, we have to—you know, become intimate."

"Yes."

"And that isn't a problem, as far as you're concerned?"

"Why should it be?"

"I don't know. No special reason. If it's okay with you, then it's absolutely fine by me."

She reached up and gently took hold of my earlobe, and rubbed it between finger and thumb. It was the most arousing thing that a woman had ever done for me.

"Harry," she said, "we have no choice, do we? Our destiny says that we must."

I finished another glass of wine while Jenica looked up Samodiva in her father's books of Romanian mythology. I needed something to give me courage, after all. I wasn't scared about being infected with vampiritis, especially the way that Jenica was going to do it, but I was deeply afraid of Misquamacus. I had been hoping that the monster slayers would do the job for me, but now that Misquamacus had escaped from Manhattan, I knew that the chances of that happening were slim to anorexic.

"Here," said Jenica, at last. " 'The ritual of Samodiva, which takes away a man's natural defenses against the strain of *strigoica,* and other infections caused by witches and possessed women. It adds his name to the list of the dead without erasing it from the list of the living, because he does not actually die.' "

"You're sure about that?"

"One day, Harry, we will all die, and *all* of our names will be written in black."

"Go on, then. Tell me what we have to do."

"This is in very old Muntenian dialect, from Wallachia. 'To commence, the woman or witch must purify the man by shaving him.' "

I rubbed my chin, which now had three days' stubble on it. "That's okay, I could use a shave anyway. Better to die looking sharp, don't you think?"

" 'The razor must be stained with the blood of the woman or the witch.' "

"Oh. Well, I guess you could just nick the ball of your thumb, couldn't you? That wouldn't hurt too much."

" 'The man must be completely shaved from head to toe.' "

"Say *what?*"

Jenica ignored me, and carried on translating. " 'His skin is to be used as the parchment on which the names of the dead are to be written. Every person he has known who is now dead shall have their name inscribed in black ink upon his skin. The names of these people will be his passport and his protection in the world of the dead that he will now partly inhabit. When these names are written and the ink is dry, the witch or the woman shall recite these words three times, while sugar and thyme shall be burned together in a bowl. "Accept this man's name in the list of the dead, O Samodiva. Record his entry into the realm of shadows and paint his likeness on the face of the moon. For the names of all people living or dead are yours to record, and in the columns of blood and in the columns of darkness his name shall appear according to your something.' "

"According to your something?"

"It's an old word, borrowed from the Church Slavic. I think it means 'judgment' or 'decision' or 'whim.' "

"You're going to shave me bald on somebody's whim?"

"It says here that this is the authentic ritual of Samodiva, which can be traced back as far as 1189. It was usually used when a man wanted to talk to a dead friend . . . for instance, if his friend had died without telling him where all his money was hidden."

"All right, then, if that's what we have to do. Bring on the shaving cream."

*   *   *

It was well past midnight. The moon was shining high above the blacked-out Empire State building, and the Hudson was gleaming like a sheet of polished steel. Every now and then we saw a bright flicker of intense white light, as if somebody was welding, and we heard men and women screaming, which told us that the monster slayers were still out and about. There was still a feeling of hysteria in the air, but at least we knew that the *strigoi* were on the run.

Because we had emptied the bathtub, Jenica had to fill the washbasin with water bailed out of the toilet cistern. In her father's bedroom bureau she found an old straight razor in a mahogany box. It was clear from the (very detailed) etchings in Jenica's book that a Gillette Mach 3 was not going to be suitably mythological for the ritual of Samodiva.

First of all, Jenica sat me down in the middle of the kitchen. She took a large pair of scissors and cut my hair off as close to the scalp as she could. I was glad there were no mirrors for me to see myself. I felt like a half-plucked turkey.

When she was done chopping, we went through to the bathroom. I pulled off my sweaty shirt and stepped out of my pants and my red-and-white striped shorts. For some reason I felt incredibly shy, and I stood there with my hands protectively cupped between my legs.

Jenica picked up the razor and opened it.

"I hope it's sharp," I said.

Without hesitation, she sliced the ball of her thumb, so that blood welled up. "Yes," she said, "it is extremely sharp." She smeared her blood along the blade, on both sides. Then she sucked her thumb and wrapped a piece of toilet tissue around it to stop it from bleeding any more. "Are you ready?" she asked me.

"I guess so. Shave away."

She wet my prickly scalp and rubbed menthol shaving gel all over it. When she was halfway through, however, she stopped and said, "You're embarrassed."

"Embarrassed? Me? Do I look embarrassed?"

"Yes, you do. You are standing like a small boy."

"I'm just . . . keeping all my bases covered, that's all."

"I know what I will do," said Jenica. She wiped her hands on a towel, crossed her arms, and lifted up her short linen dress. Underneath she was wearing a lacy white bra and a lacy white thong. "Here," she said, turning her back to me. "Undo me."

I was never Harry Houdini when it came to bra hooks, but this time I managed to slide the hooks out of the eyes with one amazingly deft movement. Her enormous breasts came out of the cups like perfectly set *blancmanges*. She turned around again, and laid one hand on my shoulder to balance herself while she tugged off her thong. She had black pubic hair that was trimmed like a pair of butterfly wings.

"Now you have no need to be embarrassed," she said. She was kidding, wasn't she? My cock started to stiffen and by the time she started shaving my scalp I needed at least two more pairs of hands to hide it.

She shaved my scalp quickly and silently, with the tip of her tongue held between her teeth. She was very good at it, very assured, as if she had often used a straight razor before, and she only nicked my ear once. I stayed as still as I possibly could, even when her nipples brushed against my arms.

Next, she smothered my face and my throat with shaving gel, and started to shave my chin. She was so close that I could feel her breath. When she reached my neck, she held her hand against my chin to stretch my skin. I closed my eyes and didn't move a muscle while the blade scraped around my Adam's apple.

I felt the edge of the razor against the left side of my throat and then she suddenly stopped. I opened my eyes and found that she was staring at me from only inches away. There was an expression on her face that I couldn't interpret. I thought to myself: Harry, this woman is half a vampire. She has the *strigoica* strain in her system, and whatever the legends say, that makes her a drinker of human blood. And she is holding a straight razor right across your carotid artery.

"What?" I asked her.

For one very long moment she said nothing. Then she carried on scraping the stubble from my throat. "I was thinking," she said. "What will you do, when all this is finished? You will still have the infection in your blood."

"It doesn't affect *you*, does it? You never even knew you had it."

"But I am a woman. Maybe it affects men differently."

"Maybe it does. But if I start eating steak tartare for breakfast, at least I'll know why."

Once she had turned me into Mr. Clean, she lifted my arms in turn and shaved my armpits. I didn't have a whole lot of hair on my chest, just a sketchy kind of a crucifix, but she shaved that off, too.

She shaved all the hair off my legs, which gave me an extraordinary sensation, especially up the backs of the thighs. By the time she had finished my cock was sticking out like a hard, curved tusk, and steadily beating in time to my heart. Without hesitation, though, she rubbed gel into my pubic hair and all over my balls and deep between the cheeks of my ass. Then she knelt down next to me and slowly began to edge the hair away, a little at a time, wiping the blade on pieces of toilet paper.

She was very careful, but she still managed to cut me two or three times. A drop of blood ran down my right thigh, and she dabbed at it with her finger and sucked it. Another drop ran down, and she leaned forward and licked that with her tongue.

Now she was shaving the last few hairs away from my

cock, and the razor was right across my distended vein. I held my breath in. I couldn't help it. She had tasted my blood now, and here was her chance to have it gushing out of me like a hosepipe.

But "there," she said, and sat back on her heels, and splashed three handfuls of water between my legs, and picked up a towel. "Now you are a parchment, Harry, ready for me to write on you."

I made myself comfortable on Jenica's bed while she rummaged through her father's desk to find a fine brush and a bottle of India ink. All around the bedroom she had lit clusters of red and yellow candles, rose- and vanilla-scented. Naked and completely hairless, I felt strangely new born, and different. *Spiritual*, almost. I could understand why Buddhist holy men shaved their bodies.

Beside the bed stood six or seven silver-framed photographs of Jenica and her father. I recognized some of the places where the pictures had been taken: the Champs Elysées, in Paris; St Mark's Square, in Venice; the Houses of Parliament, in London. I thought that maybe my eyes were tired, but in almost every photograph her father seemed to be slightly out of focus, as if he had moved. From what I could make out, though, he looked quite handsome, in a very Romanian way, and he was wearing a dangly earring in his left ear.

Jenica came back into the room, wearing a man's white dress shirt, with a wing collar, and only one button fastened. She sat down next to me, unscrewed her hexagonal glass bottle of India ink, and dipped her brush into it.

"Tell me the name of somebody you know who is now dead."

"Anybody?"

"Anybody at all, so long as they no longer living."

"Singing Rock," I said. Under the circumstances, I thought that my spirit guide deserved pride of place.

Very carefully, in beautiful italic handwriting, Jenica painted the name *Singing Rock* across my chest.

When she had finished, I said, "David Erskine. That's my father. George Erskine, that's my grandfather. Jimmy Bonasinga—he was in my class at school."

Without a word, Jenica covered my naked body in names. I was amazed and sad at how many dead people I had known. It took her nearly three hours, and by the time she had finished I had more than a hundred names written all over me. There on my left shoulder was Adelaide Bright, God bless her, who had taught me how to read the Tarot and the tea leaves and most of all how to read the future in people's faces. Along my right forearm was my woodworking teacher, Kenneth Bukaski, who had shown me that putting up shelves that stayed up was more than a matter of faith. And here on my thigh was Sandra Lowenstein, pale and fey, who had written incomprehensible poems for me about smoke and flowers, and eventually died of an overdose in some shitty squat in Baltimore.

I couldn't see the names that were written across my back, but their memories were just as dear to me. The only name that was written on my penis was Jane Forward, my very first love. Jane had been stunning, even with braces on her teeth. Green eyes, long blonde hair, and over two inches taller than I was. We all thought that she was going to be a famous actress, but she had married a stock analyst called Roger and moved to Darien, Connecticut, and drowned in a stupid swimming-pool accident. Eventually Jenica put down her brush and screwed the top back onto her bottle of ink. She took off the shirt that she was wearing and lay down next to me. "Do you know what you are now? You are the book of the dead."

"After all this, I just hope that this works."

With her fingertip, she touched the last name that she had written, John Franzini. "I think that John Franzini is dry now. We can start the ritual."

She had brought in a small ceramic dish. It was filled with molasses and dried thyme, mixed together. She lit a taper and laid its flame in the center of the dish so that the sugar and the herbs started to bubble and burn. The smell was very evocative, but I couldn't think what it reminded me of. Something that had happened a long time ago and very far away.

Jenica opened the book of mythology and laid it on the pillow. Then she leaned over me, with her left nipple brushing against my right nipple. She was so close to my face that I couldn't focus on her properly.

"Accept this man's name in the list of the dead, O Samodiva," she recited. "Record his entry into the realm of shadows and paint his likeness on the face of the moon."

She said this three times, as instructed. As she started the third recitation, however, she took hold of my cock in her right hand and started to massage it. I have to admit that the sensation was not entirely unpleasant. By the time she had said, ". . . according your judgment," Jane Forward's name was at least twice as long as it had been before.

Jenica climbed on top of me. I tried to reach up to touch her breasts, but she pushed my hand away. Since she was in charge of this particular ritual, I decided that I should just lie there and follow instructions. After all, we weren't supposed to be doing this for our own gratification.

All the same, as she reached down between my legs, and guided me inside her, she bent her head forward and kissed me on the lips. Her lips were wet and warm and slippery, and she was the same inside. In spite of everything, I couldn't help groaning.

She rode up and down in silence. Each time she lifted up her hips, she almost lost me, but somehow she managed to judge the moment exactly, and slide herself back down again, until my naked cock was buried in her up to the hilt. The only sound was the bed creaking, and Jenica's panting. Her perspiration dripped onto my lips, and it tasted like swimming in the ocean.

As I felt my climax rising up between my legs, I couldn't stop myself from gripping the cheeks of her bottom, and digging my fingers deep into her flesh. Now she was almost galloping, and she started to pant "*Samodiva! Samodiva! Samodiva!*" The smoke from the burning molasses seemed to grow more and more pungent, until I could smell and taste nothing else, and I was sure that the shadows on the ceiling were dancing in time to our fucking, like mad goblins out of the Transylvanian forests.

Without warning, Jenica began to quake with orgasm. I had never heard a woman make a noise like that before. It was like a low, vibrato dirge. "*Ohhhhhhh, ohhhhhh, dragostea, ohhhhhhhhh.*" It was so erotic and so revealing, as if she had opened up her whole personality to me, everything she was, her folk culture and her fantasies, and everything that she had grown up to be, from her Romanian girlhood.

She arched herself right back, until the back of her head was actually touching her bottom, and I was deeper inside her than I had physically thought possible. I had forgotten that she was partly *strigoica*, and that she could bend herself like a contortionist. That did it. I said, "Jesus, Jenica," and ejaculated, and ejaculated again, and then again.

Afterward, we lay together in sweaty silence. The shadows had stopped dancing, too, as if the Transylvanian goblins were taking a breather, or maybe the candles had simply burned low. I heard the clock in the living room whirr and then strike four, and between the bedroom curtains I could see that the sky outside was already growing light.

Jenica lifted her head and stared at me. "There is one more thing, just to make sure."

"Really? I don't mind doing it again, if you don't."

She put her hand down between her thighs, and then lifted it up to my lips.

"What's this?"

"Taste. It is the taste of me, and the taste of you, and the taste of the *strigoica*."

I licked her fingertips. "Now what? Does this mean I'm infected?"

"Now you sleep. Later, I will bring you tea, or wine, whatever you want."

"I don't think I can sleep."

"Then close your eyes and rest."

She climbed off the bed and picked up her shirt. I knew that there was no way that I was going to be able to get to sleep, not after having sex like that, and not when I knew that we were going to go hunting for Misquamacus. But I closed my eyes and tried to relax.

I could hear Jenica in the kitchen. She was singing what sounded like a love song, but for all the Romanian I knew, it could have been the Romanian equivalent of "You're So Vain."

22

BLOOD GROUP

Suddenly, I felt something cool and wet on my stomach. I opened my eyes and Jenica was wiping the writing off my skin with a makeup-removal pad.

"Did you sleep well?" she asked me.

"Give me a chance, I've only been lying here for a couple of minutes."

"You've been sleeping for nine hours. It's ten past one in the afternoon."

I sat up. "*What?* You're kidding me!"

But the clock next to the bed said 1:09 and through the triangular crack in the curtains I could see that the sun was shining. Jenica had changed into a black-and-white check shirt and tight blue Levis, and she had brushed her hair back and tied it with a black scarf.

"Why didn't you wake me up earlier? Come on, Jenica, if we're going to go after Misquamacus we need all the daylight we can get!"

"Ssh," she said. "You slept so long because you were exhausted. Besides, you needed time to absorb the *strigoica* strain into your bloodstream."

"Yeah, I forgot. I'm half a vampire now." I rubbed the back of my head. "I don't *feel* any different. Apart from having a bean like a bowling ball."

"Believe me, Harry, you *are* different. You can do things now that you could never do before. Look."

She took hold of my right hand, and pulled back my index finger. It was incredible. Without any effort at all, it bent right over until it was practically touching the back of my wrist. I tried my middle finger, and I could bend it back just as far.

"That's fantastic. Harry Erskine, the India-Rubber Fortune-Teller. He unravels your future while he ties himself in knots."

I bent back all of my other fingers, and they were just as flexible.

"There's something else," said Jenica. "While you were sleeping I went downstairs. I did what you suggested, and pushed my hand into the mirror."

"Don't tell me it wouldn't go in?"

"At first, no. I had to try three times, but then it happened. But only when I said to myself, Jenica, this is nothing but a doorway. It needs very strong faith, I think, as well as *strigoica* blood."

"Well, thank God. I'd hate to think that what we did last night was a waste of time."

"Why don't you dress now? Try some of my father's clothes. I will make us some coffee."

I got up, drew back the drapes, and stretched myself. To my amazement, I found that I could lean over backward almost as far as Jenica had. Actually, I *did* feel different. Looser, somehow, more active and alive, as if I were ten years younger.

I rummaged through Razvan Dragomir's closet and

found a black silk shirt and a pair of black pants. The pants were a little too snug between the nuts, but Razvan Dragomir probably didn't drink nine cans of Guinness every day. I went into the kitchen where Jenica was making coffee with club soda, which was the only water we had left. There was no milk, of course, so I ate handfuls of corn-flakes out of the box.

"We need to go to the Kensico Country Inn while it's still daylight," I said. "We need to check out how many mirrors they have. And after what happened yesterday, with that guy coming out of the bathtub, I think we should scout around for any kind of reflective water surface, too. Rain barrels, ponds, that kind of thing."

"Then we wait until it gets dark, yes, and Vasile Lup comes out of his mirror?"

"You've got it. While he's away, we break every mirror in the whole place, so that when he comes *back*, at sunrise, he doesn't have any place to hide. That's when you recite the disenchantment. Vasile Lup will be sent back to where he came from, and that leaves Misquamacus without a spirit to hide himself in."

"But you still don't know how you will destroy your Mis-quamacus."

"I'm counting on that bone."

"Is that all?"

"What else can I do? Agreed—I don't have any idea what it does, or how it works, or why. But it seems to keep the *strigoi* at bay, doesn't it, and it can kill rats better than Ramik Green, and Misquamacus didn't seem to be at all happy when I waved it at him."

"And that is all of your plan?"

"I guess so. I can't think of anything else I can do."

"Maybe you should call on your Singing Rock."

I shook my head. "He won't answer me, Jenica. I've al-ready asked him for far too much help, and he's a great be-liever in working things out for yourself. Don't keep looking to dead people for advice, that's his motto, or you might as well be dead yourself."

"Okay," said Jenica. "Then what shall we do? Go?"

I finished my coffee, stood up, and said, "Why not? You only live once."

Jenica said, "I have one question. Once we step into the mirror, how do we find our way to the Kensico Country Inn?"

"In the ordinary way, I guess, except back-to-front."

"You are not making me feel very confident."

"Jenica, the whole world has gone crazy. Nine-eleven was madness but this is even madder. Let's just try to take it as it comes. It's the only way."

She looked at me acutely. "You lost something very special, didn't you, when you lost your wife and your daughter?"

"I never lost them. I mislaid them, that's all."

"You must never think that life is not really worth living. There is somebody waiting for you, somewhere."

"Maybe. Right now, I have a vengeful Native American wonder-worker to deal with."

Jenica packed her woven bag with her crucifix and her holy water and her book of *svarcolaci*. I took nothing except the bone.

We went downstairs to the hallway and stood in front of the mirror. Jenica said to me, "Try it first with your finger. Make sure that you can pass through it."

I looked at my reflection. In my black silk shirt and my tight black pants, I reminded myself of an out-of-work conjuror. And now, for my next astounding trick, I will push my finger into the surface of this absolutely genuine real mirror, and it will penetrate the glass as if by magic. Which it did.

The sensation was extraordinary. I felt as if the glass was clinging to my finger, cold and heavy and liquid, like mercury. But my finger went in, and joined up with the finger in my reflection, and then it came out again, unharmed.

I turned to Jenica and said, "How about that. How *about* that."

"Then, you see, the ritual of Samodiva really works."

"I'm half a vampire. Shit. I can't believe it."

"Now you have *strigoi* in your blood, yes. Now you are the same as me."

Suddenly I felt very serious. I had taken risks before. I had fought against Misquamacus before. But this time I didn't think that either of us had much of a chance of surviving. I lifted Jenica's chin and kissed her. "At least nobody can say that we didn't go out with a bang."

I decided that I would go first. If something went seriously wrong, I told Jenica that she should stay where she was, and not try to follow me. Even with Misquamacus spreading *strigoi* all across the Northeastern states, she would stand some chance of staying alive.

I stood right in front of the mirror. Harry Erskine, this is a very bad idea. You don't know where the hell you're going or what you're going to do when you get there. But I stepped forward, and I knew and I utterly believed that the mirror was a silver doorway, and that it led right through the frame into a world of reflections.

I closed my eyes. I felt a hard, cold, silent collision, like falling from the top diving board into a swimming pool, and rolling around in noisily bubbling water. When I opened my eyes again, I found myself standing in a hallway, but a very different hallway than the one I had just left. It was light, and airy, with a polished wood floor, and double doors that were open onto a white stone porch. A warm wind was blowing in from outside, and I could hear birds singing.

Strangely, Jenica was standing next to me here, while a second Jenica was still staring at us from the hallway that I had just left. I was here, inside the mirror. I was through.

"Come on," I waved at Jenica, mouthing my words as if she were deaf. "I think it's okay."

I wasn't sure that she could hear me, but she slowly approached the mirror and her reflection approached the mirror just as slowly, until they were both standing with their hands pressed against each other, looking into each other's eyes.

"It's okay!" I shouted. "You can do it!"

She hesitated a moment longer, and then she lowered her head and walked through. There was a sound like crushing glass, and a sparkling explosion of colors and shapes. Jenica and her reflection seemed to smash themselves softly together into one person. Then there was just the two of us, side by side, and the hallway we had left behind was empty.

Jenica stared at me. "Where are we? What is this place?"

"I don't know. I thought that if we went through the mirror we'd simply end up in the same hallway, only in reverse. But, well, apparently not."

Jenica walked over to an antique satinwood bureau and stared up at an oil painting of a man in a curly white wig. "I do not understand this," she said. "Maybe it is better if we go back."

I crossed the hallway to the double doors and stepped out onto the porch. I had expected to see Leroy Street. Well, you would, even if it was teertS yoreL. But outside the front door there was a wide, empty courtyard, and an avenue of maple trees with a white fence running beside it. Through the maple trees I could see a circular pond shining, with geese on it, and in the distance lay a range of hills, with low clouds lying on top of them like down comforters. There was no sign of Leroy Street, no sign of Manhattan at all. On the wall there was a sign saying No Parking, and the writing was the right way round, not a mirror image at all. So this wasn't looking glass land. We had simply walked through one mirror in Manhattan and out of another, someplace else altogether. But where?

Jenica came out and stood beside me, shading her eyes against the glare. The sky was filled with thick, white, cumulus clouds, although there were one or two ragged fragments of blue. The air was warm and humid I could actually smell freshly mown grass. Two silver SUVs were parked beside a stable block, but there was no sign of any life.

"Maybe this is a dream, or some kind of hallucination," said Jenica. "It gives me a very bad feeling."

We went back inside. In one corner of the hallway stood an antique desk with a visitor's book lying open on it. I went over and picked the book up. There was blood spattered across the pages and when I looked down there was blood on the floor, too. I closed the book and read the inscription on the green leather cover.

"We don't need to go back. Don't you get it? This isn't a dream. This is the Kensico Country Inn."

"But how? How did we get to be here, exactly where we wanted to be?"

"I don't have any idea. But my guess is that Frank had something to do with this. It was like he came through the mirror and somehow he left the door open, so that we could come back."

"But how did we manage to go through the mirror in my house, and find ourselves here? It is like the two houses are standing side by side, yet we know that they are miles and miles apart!"

"You're right. But when the Vampire Gatherer came out of the mirror in your apartment, and Susan Fireman took Frank away with her—you didn't see your corridor reflected in that mirror, did you? You saw some beach someplace. Whatever goes on in back of mirrors, it seems to me like the usual laws of physics definitely don't apply."

Jenica looked up at me. Then she licked her middle finger and rubbed it against the side of my cheek. "You still have somebody's name there. Teresa."

Two enormous mirrors hung in the lobby of the Kensico Country Inn—one behind the reception desk, and the other in the corridor—the "silver door" through which Jenica and I had stepped to get here. When the time came, these would be the first two for us to smash. We wouldn't be able to go back to the city the same way that we had arrived, but we couldn't leave Misquamacus any escape routes.

We went along the corridor to the Valhalla Restaurant & Bar. There were thirty tables, all set for breakfast, with shining white tablecloths and cleverly folded napkins. On each table stood a vase of dead roses.

"There's a long mirror behind the bar," said Jenica. "Another one over there, beside the kitchen door."

The kitchens were deserted. On the woodblock table in the center lay three whole legs of lamb, on plates. They were crawling with blowflies, and the smell of rancid lamb fat was enough to make Jenica press her hand over her face.

We returned to the reception area and opened up every door, one after the other. A cloakroom, a closet, men's and women's restrooms (plenty of mirrors to be broken there), and a corridor that led along the back of the inn to a large glass conservatory. We were only on the first floor and we had counted over thirty-five mirrors already.

Jenica went up a low flight of three stairs and opened the door at the top. "Harry," she said.

"What's wrong?"

I followed her up the stairs and looked into the room. It was obviously a conference room, with a projection screen at the far end, and an easel with a brightly colored business graph on it. But I wasn't looking at the display. In the center of the room stood a long boardroom table made of pale polished oak, with at least forty matching chairs. The table was heaped high with bodies, arms and legs all tangled together. Men and women, some of them still wearing business suits, some of them naked, but all with their throats cut wide open. There must have been more than thirty of them, although I didn't feel like making an exact count. Maggots were silently dropping off them and squirming across the carpet. The lamb had smelled sickening enough, but this was ten times worse.

I closed the door and exhaled. There was nothing that we could do. Obviously the Vampire Gatherer and some of his *strigoi* had arrived here through the mirrors, the same way that we had, and taken the hotel staff and guests by surprise. They wouldn't have been shown any mercy. As far as Vasile Lup was concerned, human beings were nothing more than a source of sustenance, or recruits for his ever-increasing legion of *strigoi*; and as far as Misquamacus was concerned, this, at long last, was his glorious revenge.

It took us nearly two hours to search the whole of the Kensico Country Inn for mirrors. We even searched the maids' bedrooms in the attic rooms and took the makeup mirrors out of their purses, and collected them together, ready to be smashed.

The power was out. The phones were dead, and all I could hear on my cell phone was a distant crackling. The *strigoi* must have taken over much more of New York State than we knew. All through that afternoon, not a single vehicle passed along the main highway at the end of the drive, and we didn't hear a single airplane or a single helicopter. All we heard was birdsong.

We went back to the kitchens. Although the refrigerators had stopped working, we found some Monterey Jack cheese and some Italian salami that were slightly sweaty but still edible. We took them outside and sat on the grass

overlooking the pond. The sun was beginning to sink toward the distant hills.

"Can you imagine what this country would be like, if
the *strigoi* took over?" I asked Jenica. "Deserted during the
day, just like this. Silent. Nothing would happen, except at
night. Then they'd all come crawling out of their coffins
and creeping out of their mirrors, and it would be hell on
earth. If you were still human, your life wouldn't be worth
living. They'd be hunting for you, every single night."

Jenica said, "Of course, but to some people, that would
not be hell, but a sort of heaven. We would live forever, yes?
And so we would be able to experience everything, every
taste, every sensation, and visit every wonder that the
world had to offer. My father once said that if everybody
lived forever, human learning would blossom beyond our
wildest imagination, because great scholars would never
die, the way they do now. He said, think of Einstein—how
much was lost when Einstein died, and what more he
could have done if he had lived for another three centuries! Think of some of our greatest writers and our greatest musicians! But what can any of us hope to learn in the
space of a human lifetime? Hardly anything at all, and
when we breathe our last breath, even the tiny fraction of
knowledge that we have acquired so painfully is buried
with us, beyond the reach of our sons and daughters, or
anybody else who might benefit from it."

"Sounds like your father is a pretty radical kind of guy."

"He is a very original thinker. He always used to tell me
that we should never be prejudiced against any idea, just
because it was thought of by somebody we despise. Much
brilliant science came from the Nazis, for instance; and
much great art from some of the world's most oppressive
regimes."

"So even if we don't exactly approve of their dietary
habits, we should appreciate the *strigoi* because they've
been around so long, and because they know so much?"

Jenica didn't answer me, but turned toward the pond. The sun was even lower now, a sullen, smoky red, and it was reflected in the water, so that there were two suns.

"The pond," she said. "What are we going to do about that? It is outside, yes, but even if the sun is shining, I think there is a chance that the *strigoi* might be able to reach it, and escape."

I stood up and walked around the edge of the pond. Nearer the house, the bank was higher, and there was a cluster of bulrushes in one corner. On the opposite side, where the ground sloped away, the bank had been artificially built up, and there was a short concrete dam, and a stopcock.

"Look at this," I said. "They must use this to drain the water when they want to clean it."

"Then we can empty it, while Vasile Lup is away."

"We can try. I don't know how long it's going to take."

It was beginning to grow damp and chilly. Jenica took hold of my arm and pulled me closer. "This is a very strange adventure we are having, you and me."

I nodded, and thought of the other woman who had said that to me, not so long ago.

As it grew dark, we climbed into one of the SUVs, a Toyota Landcruiser. We decided that it was probably safer than hiding in the inn, because the *strigoi* would be less likely to pick up the warmth of our blood. Not only that, the owner had left the keys in it, and if the *strigoi* did realize that we were there, we could burn rubber out of there.

We were cautious enough to stop using the words "*strigoi*" and "*strigoica*" and the name "Vasile Lup." Now that night had fallen, the vampires and the Vampire Gatherer would be stirring inside their mirrors, and they would be hungry, and highly sensitive to any disturbance that would indicate the closeness of human blood.

We hunched down in the front seats as low as we could, and we shared three chocolate bars and a small pack of peanuts. I kept thinking about Katz's salt-beef sandwiches, sliced very thin and very rare, and I wondered if that was anything to do with my newly acquired vampirism. But maybe I was just hungry. I doubt if vampires like rye bread and pickles to go with their blood.

Over an hour went by, and Jenica leaned her head against my shoulder and started to breathe deeper and slower, with occasional gasps, as if she were dreaming.

I was almost nodding off myself when I saw a dark, irregular shape coming out of the inn and crossing the porch. It was followed by another, and another, and then a paler shape. *Strigoi*, at least five of them. They came down the steps and walked across the driveway, until they were standing together less than twenty feet away.

I nudged Jenica and she said, "*Fff!* What? What is it?"

"Ssh. Keep down. Look."

The *strigoi* appeared to be waiting for something. The moon hadn't yet risen, but the night sky was gradually beginning to grow lighter, and after a while I could see that the pale shape was a woman with dark hair. She turned and looked toward us, and I realized that it was Susan Fireman. Standing next to her, looking white-faced and very wild, was Frank. I didn't know the other three *strigoi*. One of them was very tall, with slicked-back hair, like Christopher Lee. Even if he hadn't been a real vampire, he could have easily passed for one. The other two looked like construction workers, shaven-headed and heavily built.

At last the moon appeared, shining through the silver birches like a horrified face. As its light brightened, a huge figure emerged from the doorway. It sloped away from the moon, this figure, a complex arrangement of impenetrable shadows, and it kept shifting and changing and disassembling itself with every step. It was the Vampire Gatherer, Vasile Lup, the *svarcolaci*, the one in whose spirit Misquamacus was concealed, like the blackest of moths folded inside a chrysalis.

One second, the Vampire Gatherer was standing on the porch. The next, in the blink of an eye, he was standing among his *strigoi*. I could see his face shifting—benign and human one moment, white and masklike the next. Then, without warning, he turned his head around.

"Oh my God," said Jenica. "Do you think he's seen us?"

It certainly looked as if he had. He was staring directly toward the Landcruiser, and his eyes were shining. For one terrible moment I thought, *oh shit, this little escapade is going to end for us before it's even begun, and end bloodily, too*. The Vampire Gatherer appeared to lurch toward us, and the *strigoi* turned around, too.

But then, jerkily, like characters in a badly chopped art movie, they all vanished, and reappeared halfway down the drive. They vanished again, and the next thing we knew, they were down by the road, more than a hundred yards away. Another blink, and they were utterly gone.

Jenica puffed out her cheeks in relief.

"Where do you think they're going?" I asked her.

"Who knows? Some small town somewhere, I expect. It is the way they always spread, like a stain."

We climbed out of the Landcruiser. The first thing I did was cross the driveway and walk down to the far side of the pond. I knelt down on the concrete dam and tried to turn the stopcock, but it was rusted up and it wouldn't budge.

"I'll have to find some kind of lever," I said. "Listen—you get inside and start breaking mirrors."

Together we walked quickly back toward the inn. Inside the lobby, I went straight to the antique fireplace. There was a large woven basket next to it containing a small hatchet, and fire tongs, and a long iron poker with a heavy brass knob on the end. I gave the hatchet to Jenica and said, "Okay—get smashing! And for God's sake don't miss any. Not one."

She went straight up to the huge gilt-framed mirror behind the reception desk and hit it dead center with the back of the hatchet. With a sharp *crack*, the whole mirror split diagonally from side to side and then dropped onto the floor. Jenica stamped on the larger pieces, to break them up even smaller, and then she bashed up the fragments so that it was impossible for anybody to see a coherent reflection in them.

As I went back outside, I heard her break the mirror in the corridor, and start to pulverize that with her hatchet, too.

I jogged down to the pond. The night air was thick with mosquitoes, and I had to spit one out of my mouth. I knelt down on the dam again, and inserted the end of the poker into the stopcock. Then I stood up and hauled back on it as hard as I could. I made a whole lot of effortful noise, like *nggggggghhhhhh* and *gurrrrrrrrr*, but it still wouldn't move, and I began to think that it was rusted up solid.

Then I thought: you're half *strigoi*. You have the strength. If you can bend yourself backward, you can open this stopcock. Have faith in yourself, Harry. Believe in what you can do.

I repositioned my hands, and then I hauled on the poker again, gritting my teeth with effort. This time I heard a harsh grating noise, and the stopcock actually moved. I hauled again, and it suddenly turned, and water started to trickle out the drainpipe that ran under the dam. Now the stopcock was loose enough for me to turn it by hand, and the trickle turned into a gush. Within a few minutes, water was pouring across the field below the pond, and shining in the moonlight like the Mississipi delta.

I picked up the poker and ran back to the inn. Jenica was in the women's restroom now, smashing all the mirrors over the washbasins.

"Have you done the men's yet?"

"I didn't like to. I left that for you."

"There's nobody *in* there, for Christ's sake."

*   *   *

Hour after hour, room by room, we smashed every single mirror in the Kensico Country Inn. The moon watched us through one window after another, and then finally sank out of sight. Every now and then, we stopped smashing and listened, in case we heard Vasile Lup and his *strigoi* coming back, but even when the sky flushed pink and the birds started to twitter, they still hadn't returned, and we had finished. We made a last, thorough check, going from one end of the inn to the other, opening closets in case we had missed a mirror that was screwed to the back of a door. We even opened up nightstand drawers, in case somebody had left a vanity mirror next to his Gideon Bible.

Broken glass glittered everywhere and not a single piece of it was large enough for anyone to see one eye in. I had even gone outside and smashed the rearview mirrors of the two SUVs parked on the driveway.

During the night, the level of the pond had fallen dramatically, revealing heaps of soggy green chickweed, and slime-covered rocks, and a child's rusted scooter. There was still an oval-shaped pool of water remaining, about two feet deep and twenty feet across, but it continued to pour steadily out of the drainpipe, and I reckoned that it wouldn't take longer than twenty minutes before it was totally drained.

I looked toward the east. The rim of the sun was just beginning to nibble at the trees.

"They must be back soon," said Jenica. "I pray that they didn't find themselves another place to hide."

"I pray, too."

We went into the inn, and hid in the corner of the lobby, between the heavy blue drapes and a longcase clock. Jenica took out her crucifix and her holy water and laid them on the windowsill. Then she took out the book of *svarcolaci* and turned to the page where Vasile Lup's disenchantment was printed.

"You're ready?" I asked her.

She looked at me with that unreadable expression again.

I was just about to say something else when there was a deafening bang like a bomb going off. The Vampire Gatherer came storming into the lobby, accompanied by his five *strigoi*. He seemed even bigger and darker than he had before, and this time the whole band of them were trailing clouds of smoke. They must have been caught by the sunlight just as they arrived back outside.

They circled around the lobby, beating at their burning coats. All five of the *strigoi* had bloody chins, and the fronts of their clothes were drenched in blood, like slaughterhouse workers. At first, they were too preoccupied with extinguishing their smoldering clothes to notice that anything was different. It was only when the smoke was beginning to clear that the Vampire Gatherer screamed in bewilderment and rage. He stalked up to the broken mirrors, and then twisted around, his shadows slanting away from the windows. His face was contorted with anger, and it seemed as if his shadows were actually *bristling*.

Susan Fireman ran across to the mirror in the corridor—the one that Jenica and I had used to get here. When she saw that this mirror was broken, too, she let out a moan of dread. She must have realized what had happened, and she could guess what the outcome was going to be. The tall *strigoi* opened the doors to the restrooms. The other two hurried up the stairs to the conference room. But yes, Jenica and I had even been back in there, where the bodies were all heaped up. We had broken the three floor-to-ceiling mirrors that stood between the windows, and we had search the pockets of the dead.

Of all the *strigoi*, Frank alone stayed where he was, in the center of the lobby. His head was bowed and smoke was creeping out from under his coat. Susan Fireman came up to him with her pale eyes staring. "It was *you!* This is *your* doing, isn't it? I trusted you, Frank! I trusted you! I could have cut your throat and drunk your blood, but I gave you immortality! Where are they, Frank? Where are they? You brought them here, didn't you? You went to see them and you left the mirrors back-to-back!"

The Vampire Gatherer came up behind Susan Fireman and stared at Frank with such hatred that I felt my skin on my bare scalp shrinking. Frank lifted his head and looked up at him. A thin bar of sunlight was shining across the polished wood floor, and Frank's shoes were starting to smolder.

"You forgot one thing," said Frank, and he sounded infinitely tired. "When some people make promises, they make them because they intend to keep them, even after death. I promised to value human life, and not even you could force me to go back on that."

Susan Fireman took two quick steps toward him. She was so quick that I didn't see the knife in her hand. All I saw was a semicircular spray of blood, like a bright red fan, and then Frank pitched backward, with his head falling sideways from his neck as if it was attached by a hinge.

The Vampire Gatherer let out another scream, and this time it sounded like a whole choir, thousands of tortured souls screaming in unison. He took one ungainly lurch toward Frank's body, and then another.

"*Now!*" I told Jenica, and pushed her out from the curtain.

23

MANITOU BLOOD

The Vampire Gatherer and his *strigoi* turned to stare at Jenica in astonishment and anger. The *strigoi* were probably the scariest bunch that you could ever meet, with their wild eyes and their blood-soaked coats and smoke pouring out of their collars. But Vasile Lup was a nightmare—the way he kept slanting from one side to the other, and his face shifted and altered from blandness to fury, all in nothing but a few seconds.

What was even more frightening about him was that Misquamacus was hiding inside him, giving him an overwhelming vengefulness far greater than he had ever possessed before, even as a *svarcolaci*.

But Jenica, God bless her, she walked toward them as if they didn't frighten her at all. She held up her jewel-studded crucifix and she sprayed her holy water from side to side and she recited the words of the disenchantment in a high, precise voice.

"I dismiss you, Vasile Lup! I disperse your spirit! Let the earth take back the flesh it has given you, and the wind take back the breath it has given you, and the rivers take back their blood! Let the ashes of your soul be scattered like the ashes of your body!"

The Vampire Gatherer tilted forward and roared at her. But Jenica lashed him again with holy water and shouted, "I dismiss you, Vasile Lup! May your memory vanish with the dying day; and your name be washed from the lips of all who ever spoke it. May the stars forget that they ever guided your destiny; and the moon deny that you ever walked beneath her!"

Now the Vampire Gatherer took one staggering step toward her. He opened his mouth, and then another mouth appeared, and yet another, and his screaming made the whole building reverberate, as if a jet bomber were flying right over us.

Jenica turned the page in her book, and she was just about to recite the final dismissal when Susan Fireman rushed toward her and grabbed the book in both hands. Jenica tried to pull it away from her, but Susan Fireman twisted it free.

"*Harry!*" shouted Jenica.

Susan Fireman was heading for the open doors, with the book held close to her chest. I dodged out from behind the curtains and tried to cut her off, but she was too quick for me. She ran down the steps and across the driveway, straight into the rays of the rising sun.

She hadn't run more than twenty feet before smoke began to billow out of her coat. As I ran after her, it blew thicker and thicker, and she began to slow down. Suddenly her hair caught fire, and she screamed in agony.

"Harry! The book!" shouted Jenica. "Don't let her burn the book!"

But it was too late. Susan Fireman had only just reached the grassy slope that led down to the pond when she exploded into flame. She fell sideways and rolled over and over, blazing fiercely. I caught up with her, and tried to snatch the book, but she was clutching it too close to her, and the heat that rippled up from her was so intense that I couldn't get within three feet of her without burning my hands.

She had stopped screaming now, and she was simply lying in a fetal position on the grass, staring up at me, as the sun cremated her. The skin on her face blistered and blackened, her lips swelled up and cracked. I could see her finger bones appearing through the charred flesh of her hands. The smell of scorched wool and barbecued meat was so strong that I couldn't stop retching.

I swear to God that she smiled at me. I don't know why. Maybe she had always suspected that it would come to this. Even though she was one of the *strigoica*, maybe she still felt some remorse for the people she had murdered.

"Harry!" called Jenica.

I was about to turn around when Susan Fireman blew up, in a pick-a-stick scattering of blackened bones. The book lay among the wreckage of her burned body, its ashy pages curling up one by one, and I could see that it was beyond saving.

"Harry, they're getting away!"

Now I looked back to see the Vampire Gatherer and the three remaining *strigoi* running across the driveway, toward the pond. The oval of water had shrunk even more, but there was still enough reflective surface for Vasile Lup to escape. I drew the decorated bone out of my belt and started to run toward the pond, too. I was sweating and panting and cursing the name of Guinness Breweries with every step.

Smoke was pouring from the Vampire Gatherer's shadows, and by the time they reached the grass, the three *strigoi* were actually alight, with flames flapping behind them like orange flags.

"Harry, you have to stop him!"

I don't know how I managed to run down to that pond

so fast. Maybe Singing Rock had summoned up the Spirit of Wind, to get behind my back and blow me there. Maybe Adelaide Bright caught hold of one hand, and Frank Winter caught hold of the other, and they pulled me along, because they didn't want to have died for nothing.

Whatever it was, I came hurtling down that slope with my arms rotating like windmills, and I splashed knee-deep into the water while the Vampire Gatherer was still thirty feet away from me. The three *strigoi* didn't stand a chance. They were still only halfway down the slope before they exploded, and their fiery remains were strewn across the grass.

I stood in the water, facing the Vampire Gatherer, and I held up the bone.

"That's it, Lup! Don't come any further!"

The Vampire Gatherer's shadows were slanting at almost forty-five degrees away from the sun, and so much black smoke was pouring out of him that I could hardly see his face. He was burning, he was seething with anger, but he stopped where he was. Whatever power that bone contained, it held much more power than the sun.

I saw flames, amid the smoke, and the Vampire Gatherer screamed at me with a thousand voices, like a congregation trapped in a burning cathedral.

"You stay there!" I shouted at him. "You and Misquamacus both!"

I was still standing there with the bone upraised when I saw a black SUV speeding up the driveway, between the maple trees. Jenica was hurrying down toward me, but she must have seen it, too, because she stopped, and stared at it, and shaded her eyes.

Without slowing down, the SUV left the driveway and drove between the trees. It came directly toward us, over the grass, and only twenty yards away, it stopped. A man in a gray shirt and gray pants climbed out of it, and came hurrying toward me.

"Get the hell out of here!" I yelled at him. "Do you want to get yourself killed?"

But the man ignored me and came splashing into the water to stand beside me. He was fiftyish, with greased-back hair, and a hooked nose. A complicated earring dangled from his left ear, silver and feathery, like a miniature dreamcatcher.

"I am Razvan Dragomir," he said. Then, as if I hadn't heard him, "I—am Razvan Dragomir."

"What the hell? You're supposed to be in Bucharest, aren't you?"

"I have always been here. It is too long to explain. Quick—you must let the *svarcolaci* into the water, before he burns."

"Excuse me? I don't think so. Don't you know what this sucker has done to New York City? He's killed thousands!"

The Vampire Gatherer roared again. More flames were lapping through his shadows, and smoke was trailing all the way across the grassy slope and through the trees. Jenica was skirting around him, one hand lifted to protect her face from the heat, and she was looking totally baffled.

"Father?"

"Jenica, there is no time for me to tell you what has happened. But this man must allow Vasile Lup to escape, *now*, or everything I have ever worked for is finished!"

He took two splashing steps toward me, and tried to grab the bone, but I changed it the other hand and pushed him away.

"There is no time!" he shouted at me. "There is no time! You must let him escape, or he will be lost forever!"

"You must be out of your freaking mind," I screamed back at him. "Do you know how many people have died?

Do you know how many people have been turned into vampires?"

"Of course I know! Of course! This was how it was always meant to be! Now please allow the Vampire Gatherer to escape from the sunlight! I am begging you! Please!"

He lunged at me again, but I took two steps back and he fell to his knees in the dwindling oval of water. He looked up at me in utter desperation, but it was too late. At that moment, the Vampire Gatherer let out one last multi-throated scream and burst into flame.

The fire crackled and spat, and it was blinding, like burning magnesium. I couldn't look at it directly, but I could see that, bit by bit, it was erasing Vasile Lup's shadows, like a child rubbing out a drawing.

Razvan Dragomir stayed where he was, on his knees, his gray pants soaked black, watching Vasile Lup with his mouth open in stupefaction, like an artist who sees his life's work destroyed right in front of his eyes. Jenica came cautiously down to the edge of the water and stood close to him, but none of us spoke while the Vampire Gatherer was still on fire.

As the last shreds of smoke fled away between the trees, however, there was a sound like the wind rushing, and the surface of the water actually *shuddered*. Something huge and invisible slammed between us, really close, like a truck that speeds past you on the highway, and almost sucks you along with it. I turned around and looked at Jenica in bewilderment, and Jenica looked at me, but I could tell that she didn't know what it was, either.

Razvan Dragomir slowly stood up. At first, he appeared exactly like himself, the Razvan Dragomir I had seen in all of those blurry photographs in the Dragomirs' apartment. Urbane, swarthy, with a very Romanian face. But as he rose to his full height, he grew taller and taller. His face began to distort and his shoulders hunched over.

I looked up at him and although he still resembled Raz-van Dragomir, he had changed into somebody else, too. His eyes were deep-set, his slab-like cheeks were scarred with magical cicatrices, and he was wearing a living head-dress made of cockroaches and beetles and wriggling lar-vae.

"*Misquamacus*," I said.

"You think that you are my nemesis, white man?" he said. I could feel his voice vibrating through the bones in my skull, rather than my ears. "You think that you have de-feated me?"

I was breathless, and my heart was beating like a tom-tom. "Looks that way, from where I'm standing."

"You are a fool. You are a man of grass. Have I not shown you now that even in death I can never be defeated? I will remain your implacable enemy, forever, until the lands that were once ours are restored to us, and your cities have van-ished beneath the earth."

"Misquamacus—you just don't get it, do you? We've lived in this country for four hundred years now and there's mil-lions of us and what do you think you're going to do, kill every single one of us? You count for absolutely nothing! You don't even have your own *spirit* for Christ's sake! Look at you—hiding inside some white man's soul!"

"Without me, this man is powerless," said Misquamacus. "Without me, he could never have raised up the Vampire Gatherer, and without the Vampire Gatherer he could never have done what he so desired to do, and raise up the blood-drinkers."

"What are you saying?" Jenica demanded. She was al-most hysterical. "What are you *saying?*"

Misquamacus turned toward her, and his face went through an eerie transformation, like morphing, so that he looked much more like Jenica's father. When he spoke, his voice was soft and rich and heavily accented.

"My darling—didn't I always tell you how wonderful the world could be, if men and women were immortal? A world of learning, and culture. A world in which genius was no longer buried, generation after generation. Yes, we would have to live by moonlight, and conceal ourselves by day. But what a small price to pay!"

"*You* raised Vasile Lup?" said Jenica.

"I always dreamed of it, but I could never do it until I found the sacred bone."

I looked at him narrowly. "The sacred bone? You mean, *this* bone?"

"It is the leg bone of Father Juan de Palos who came to Florida in September of 1542, with the Spanish fleet of Alvar Nuñez Cabeza de Vaca."

Jenica shook her head as if she had water in her ears. "I don't understand, father. I don't understand."

"It isn't difficult, my darling. Father Juan was a *vampiro*, which is what the Spanish call the *strigoi*. Cabeza de Vaca had brought him on his expedition so that he could exterminate the Apelachan Indians, because they were so hostile to the Spanish explorers. But one night, off the coast of Florida, five of Cabeza de Vaca's ships were wrecked in a storm, and Father Juan was swept ashore, and captured. When the sun rose, it burned him alive, as it does all *strigoi*. But a great Apelachan wonder-worker kept his leg bone, and carved it with magical symbols, and invested it with the power of Dachilin. In Apelachan legend, Dachilin is the *manitou* who can call the dead from limbo to serve the living—or, if he so wishes, dismiss them back to limbo.

"The wonder-worker did this so that the Apelachan would have a weapon that they could use against any more *strigoi* that the Spaniard conquistadores brought with them—although, as it turned out, they never did."

"But why did *you* need it?" I asked him.

"Because I wanted to rouse the *strigoi*, and the *strigoi*

can only be roused from their coffins by one of the *svarco-laci*, and I discovered that, in his turn, a *svarcolaci* can only be roused from his coffin by the spirits of the land in which he finds himself. There are no Romanian spirits here in America, thousands of miles away from the Carpathian mountains. Gheorghe Vlad's plan to wipe out the Sioux would never have succeeded, because he would never have been able to wake up Vasile Lup, not without the sacred bone, and the power of Dachilin."

Jenica said, "You never told me about this. You never even told me that you had found the *strigoi's* coffins."

"My darling, I found them many years ago. But what was the point of telling you that I had found them, if I had no way of bringing them back to life?"

"What was the *point?* I am your daughter! I am your flesh and blood! I am half-*strigoica* myself!"

"Well, I am sorry if you think that I have deceived you. I wasn't sure that you would approve of what I wanted to do. You are so much like your dearest mother."

"How did you find the bone?" Jenica demanded. She was so angry that she couldn't speak straight.

"It was very difficult, my darling. It took me more than a quarter of a century. Sometimes I despaired, but I never gave up, because I knew it was the key to my great design. I discovered it at last in a private collection in Pascagoula. It was owned by an old woman, a retired anthropologist who had no idea what it was, or what it could do.

"Only this sacred bone could revive Vasile Lup . . . and only a Native American medicine man would understand the ritual to make it work.

He gave a harsh, humorless laugh. "After all of my years of searching, though, my great design almost came to nothing. Do you think I could find a Native American wonder-worker who understood how the bone worked, or knew the rituals of Dachilin? I read all the books and articles I could find on Apelachan magic, but there was nothing about raising the dead.

"Then—like an act of God—came nine-eleven. Of course I understood nothing of what had happened. How could I know that the fire in the World Trade Center towers had literally welded back together the spirit of Misquamacus? I only discovered this much later, when I was able to gain access once more to the vaults under St. Stephen's church. As soon as I entered, I felt immediately as if I was blown by a hurricane. Misquamacus entered me like a great wind, and spoke to me. He gave me the power and the knowledge to use the bone, so that I could bring Vasile Lup back to life."

"Talk about a deal with the devil," I said.

"Yes, if you wish to call it that, we made a deal. Misquamacus would revive Vasile Lup, and once he was revived, Misquamacus could live within him. Vasile Lup did not wish to be woken from his sleep, but he had no choice, and I left the bone in his casket so that he could never return to it."

"So you gave Misquamacus a war party of vampires?"

"If you like. The *strigoi* would feed on the blood of white men, and anyone else whom Misquamacus counted as an enemy—but not, of course, on Native Americans. Within a few years, the Native Americans would have their lands returned to them by day, and the *strigoi* would rule the country by night."

"Nice scenario," I told him.

But Razvan Dragomir turned to Jenica. "It is a tragedy that you had to interfere, my darling . . . you and this man, whoever he is. This could have been a golden age for two great peoples . . . the Native Americans and the *strigoi*."

I approached him, and prodded him with the end of the bone. He stepped back, almost as if it had shocked him, like a cattle prod.

"So this bone can call spirits out of limbo, can it? And it can send them back, too?"

"Not without the Apelachan ritual."

"Oh, I don't think I need an Apelachan ritual. I just think I need to shove this sacred bone right where it hurts the most. Maybe I could do a bit of Draculea-style impaling, if you know what I mean."

I prodded him again, and this time he literally jumped, and his eyes rolled up, like an epileptic. "I do not know who you are, but there is nothing you can do to stop the *strigoi* now. They are everywhere, and every night there will be more of them, and more."

"Oh, yes? That's what you think. The monster slayers are after them, Changing Woman's grandchildren, and they're going to hunt them all down, every single one of them, and frazzle them. And even if some of them manage to stay alive, or undead, or whatever it is—what do you think Misquamacus is going to do, once all his enemies have been wiped out?"

"We have a pact. We have an agreement. Native Americans by day, *strigoi* by night."

"You might have Misquamacus hiding inside of your soul, sir, but you don't know him at all, do you? Do you seriously think that he's going to let a bunch of blood-sucking white folks roam around his precious prairies all night? He's using you, pal. He's using you to get his revenge, and once he's gotten his revenge, you and your vampires are going to be screwed back into your coffins where you all belong."

"*Silence!*" shouted Razvan Dragomir, and his face changed dramatically to the face of Misquamacus. He snatched at the bone, but he missed it, and I jabbed him with it again, and again, and each time he convulsed.

"*Strigoi!*" he roared. "I need you! *Strigoi*, rise up and take this man! His blood is yours, take it!"

I took a step back into the water. It was almost drained away now, but there were still three or four inches left. As I stepped back, though, a hand reached out of the reflection and seized my ankle. Another hand followed it, holding a triangular-bladed kitchen knife, and it stabbed straight through my shoe and into the side of my foot. It hurt. I can't even describe how much it fucking hurt.

I shouted, "Get the hell off of me!" and whacked at the hands with the bone, but another hand appeared, and then another, and another, until twenty or thirty of them had risen from the water to snatch at my feet and legs. They blistered and smoked, because the sun was shining on them, but they started to drag me downward. I suddenly thought: shit, I'm half-*strigoi* myself, which means that I can be pulled into reflections, too. I kept on struggling and hitting them with the bone, but the hands clung on harder and harder and they wouldn't let go. Even though the water was only inches deep, it wasn't long before I had sunk into that morning-sky reflection as far as my hips.

"Jenica!" I shouted, but when I looked around I saw her running away, toward the inn. "*Jenica!*"

Misquamacus came closer. "I am going to let these blood-drinkers take you wherever they wish, and slaughter you like a buffalo, and empty your veins. Then I shall feed your carcass to the crows."

I was frantic now, but the hands were too many and they were much too strong for me. It took them less than a minute to pull me down into the reflection up to my chest, and soon I couldn't even swing my arm wide enough to knock them away. I saw six or seven knives shining, and they started to stab at my buttocks and my thighs and my back. I shouted out with pain, but Misquamacus did nothing but stare at me, his headdress alive with insects.

"Jenica!" I yelled, but now I couldn't see her at all, and already the *strigoi's* fingers were clawing at the back of my shirt collar.

"You have fought me many times, my friend," said Misquamacus. "But you cannot fight your destiny. Your destiny lies here, in this piece of sky."

It was then that I realized where Jenica had gone. She must have run across to Susan Fireman's body and picked up her knife, and now she was standing right behind Misquamacus where I couldn't see her. Without any warning at all, she reached around with one hand and cut his throat, just like that. One slice, left to right. Then she stepped away from him. Her face was a picture of horror and alarm, like a character from a children's nursery book.

Misquamacus was still staring at me, but his expression had changed entirely. Instead of triumphant, he looked disbelieving. He raised one hand toward his neck, but only halfway. As blood began to spout down his shirt, his face started to collapse and alter, and right in front of my eyes he shrank back into the features of Razvan Dragomir. By the time he was falling to the ground, he was no longer the vengeful Native American wonder-worker, but the Romanian academic, Jenica's father, and he was plastered down to his knees in blood.

At the same time, the *strigoi* in the pond began to release me. The last of the water drained away, and they disappeared, as if they had been sucked into a swamp. I found myself on my hands and knees, my pants soaked in blood, wet and coughing and cursing.

Razvan Dragomir lay amid the heaps of pondweed, his blood squirting out of his neck, his eyes glazing over.

As he lay there, I saw a glassy, liquid figure rise out of him—a figure that rippled in the morning sunlight. It was huge, and it was so cold and malevolent that ice began to crackle on the pondweed, and my breath steamed. Misquamacus, almost invisible now, because his spirit had no ectoplasm.

I held up the sacred bone of Dachilin. "By all the power invested me by a free America, in the name of common humanity, in the memory of Singing Rock, in the name of Changing Woman and the spirit of forgiveness, get the hell out of here."

I saw things then that still give me nightmares. As the fluid figure of Misquamacus grew larger and larger, I saw a living kaleidoscope of suffering and cruelty. I saw demons and gods. I saw crows gathering, to turn the sky black, and herds of buffalo falling like landslides. I saw history, like a huge river of screaming people, carrying us all away.

I swept the sacred bone from side to side, and advanced on these visions as if I were going into battle. As I did so, I heard a hollow sucking sound, as if all the oxygen was being dragged out of the air. There was a split second of intense compression, and then there was a massive thunderclap. I was thrown backward across the pond and up against the concrete dam, jarring my shoulder. Stunned, I looked up. Misquamacus had gone, and the air had rushed in to fill the vacuum that he had left behind.

Awkwardly, I stood up, and limped out of the pond and up the slope. Jenica was sitting on the grass with her head bowed, still holding the bloody knife with which she had cut her father's throat. I stood beside her for a while and then she looked up at me with tear-blotted eyes.

"You're hurt," she said. "You're bleeding."

The sun had risen high above the trees now, and the last scattered remains of the *strigoi* were smoldering into dead-white ashes. The birds began to twitter again, and I saw cows moving in a distant field.

I helped Jenica onto her feet and then the two of us

walked up toward the inn, saying nothing. As I climbed the steps, I stopped, and turned around, and looked up at the sky.

Jenica said, "What is it?"

"I don't know," I told her. "I think I was trying to see God."